ANTALE

An Allegory of a World Reborn

*To Vancouver Unitarians
Best wishes for good reading
Desmond Berghofer
24/10/09*

Desmond E. Berghofer

• Canada • UK • Ireland • USA •

© Copyright 2006 Desmond E. Berghofer.
All rights reserved. No part of this publication may be reproduced, stored in a retrieval system, or transmitted, in any form or by any means, electronic, mechanical, photocopying, recording, or otherwise, without the written prior permission of the author.

Note for Librarians: a cataloguing record for this book that includes Dewey Decimal Classification and US Library of Congress numbers is available from the Library and Archives of Canada. The complete cataloguing record can be obtained from their online database at:
www.collectionscanada.ca/amicus/index-e.html
ISBN 1-4120-6504-6
Printed in Victoria, BC, Canada

Printed on paper with minimum 30% recycled fibre. Trafford's print shop runs on "green energy" from solar, wind and other environmentally-friendly power sources.

TRAFFORD
PUBLISHING

Offices in Canada, USA, Ireland and UK

This book was published *on-demand* in cooperation with Trafford Publishing. On-demand publishing is a unique process and service of making a book available for retail sale to the public taking advantage of on-demand manufacturing and Internet marketing. On-demand publishing includes promotions, retail sales, manufacturing, order fulfilment, accounting and collecting royalties on behalf of the author.

Book sales for North America and international:
Trafford Publishing, 6E–2333 Government St.,
Victoria, BC v8t 4p4 CANADA
phone 250 383 6864 (toll-free 1 888 232 4444)
fax 250 383 6804; email to orders@trafford.com

Book sales in Europe:
Trafford Publishing (UK) Ltd., Enterprise House, Wistaston Road Business Centre,
Wistaston Road, Crewe, Cheshire cw2 7rp UNITED KINGDOM
phone 01270 251 396 (local rate 0845 230 9601)
facsimile 01270 254 983; orders.uk@trafford.com

Order online at:
trafford.com/05-1415

10 9 8 7 6 5 4 3 2

TO GERRI

WHO NEVER CEASES TO BELIEVE AND SUPPORT

NOTE TO READERS
"ANTALE" IS A COMBINATION OF TWO WORDS: "Ant allegory."
THE CORRECT PRONUNCIATION IS AN-TAL-EE.

CONTENTS

Foreword · i
Parade of Characters · iii

YEAR 1: DARKNESS ACROSS THE LAND

CHAPTER 1
    The Expedition · 1
CHAPTER 2
    Diplomacy and Disappointment · 14
CHAPTER 3
    Worthless Words of Honor · 30
CHAPTER 4
    War · 43
CHAPTER 5
    Victory at a Price · 59
CHAPTER 6
    The End and the Beginning · 71
CHAPTER 7
    Union Without Vision · 86

YEAR 2: SHAKY DREAMS

CHAPTER 8
    Happy New Year · 99
CHAPTER 9
    New Hope · 109
CHAPTER 10
    Potential Builds · 121
CHAPTER 11
    Out of Control · 132
CHAPTER 12
    Adrift with Delusions · 143

YEAR 3: RENEWAL

CHAPTER 13
    Famine   155
CHAPTER 14
    The Return   168
CHAPTER 15
    The Message   180
CHAPTER 16
    Fire   187
CHAPTER 17
    Rescue   193
CHAPTER 18
    A Grim Discovery   200
CHAPTER 19
    A Shift of Energy   208
CHAPTER 20
    Resolution   219

FOREWORD

AT SOME ANCIENT TIME AND PLACE BEYOND the history we know or can even imagine, a human ancestor began to tell a story. Surely the purpose was to teach, to entertain, to excite and above all to transmit the lessons learned by one generation to the next.

As time moved forward to known history, the images of these stories were painted on the walls of caves and in tombs dedicated to preserving the prerogatives of dead leaders in their imagined world after death. Eventually these stories carried the moral ethos of culture, first told orally, then written in ancient script in the Biblical texts and in the early dramas of our humanity.

These stories took many forms: poems and plays, letters, short stories and eventually full length novels. Each new form, realistic or symbolic, straightforward or satiric, created the legacy and the heritage on which the storytellers of the new generations built.

Antale: An Allegory of a World Reborn is a new form of storytelling for our time, but imbued with the same purpose as the stories of antiquity: to teach the lessons learned in a twentieth century both brutal and full of outstanding possibility, as well as to excite and especially to entertain.

Using the allegorical format frees the author to describe the history of the twentieth century, including its violent wars and the consciousness that perpetrated physical and soul destroying atrocities, as well as the new ideas and structures that could create a better future.

Readers will recognize our human history as the ant characters of the story struggle to dominate each other, to achieve advantage and eventually to become the sources of each other's salvation. Highly original in form, *Antale* provides an entertaining and page-turning read while it instructs the mind, engages the heart and inspires the spirit. If anyone had told me that the fortunes of an ant world would cause an experienced, inveterate reader of all kinds of fiction and non-fiction like me to weep and eventually cheer, I would not have believed it.

Beyond the allegorical story of war, struggle for power and search for peace, this story is grounded in the most important and profound truths of our time. Its lessons deeply affect the psyche of a twenty-first century consciousness. It is one of the new stories that can and should become central in influencing the way humanity can live on this blessed planet together and in peace.

Antale is a warning that old ways must give way to new thinking, and its novel and original solution contains the hope that this generation can leave a legacy of great promise. Above all, *Antale* continues the tradition of the storytellers of all time in an original style building on the allegorical traditions of Swift's *Gulliver's Travels* and Orwell's *Animal Farm* to speak in a voice for both the young and seasoned reader. Funny, moving, profound and sensitive, *Antale* is a jolly good read.

Geraldine Schwartz

PARADE OF CHARACTERS

(In order of appearance)

YEAR 1

Wiseria	Prime Minister of the Black Ant Colony and Deputy Chief of the Antale Federation of Ants
Roanda	Personal Aide to Appesia
Appesia	Leader of the White Ant Colony and President of the Antale Federation of Ants
Antonia	Leader of the Yellow Ant Colony
Serenta	Leader of the Sugar Ant Colony
Bravada	Leader of the Salt Ant Colony
Barbaria	Leader of the Green Ant Colony
Narcissa	Leader of the Brown Ant Colony
Intrepida	Leader of the Acid Ant Colony
Aggressa	Supreme Commander of the Red Ant Colony
Explora	Leader of the Antale Expeditionary Force for Enlightenment through Discovery
Observa	Head of Mission Control on Mount Opportunity (a Sugar ant)
Pacifica	Intern at Mission Control (a White ant)
Inebria	A drug addicted Sugar ant
Sota	Deputy Head of the Acid Ant Colony
Bluffasta	A Pepper ant
Wacka Wacka	A Digger ant
Aristica	Chief of Staff to Appesia
Wiseria	Becomes President of the Antale Federation of Ants
Monta	Commander of the Black Ants First Division
Alena	Commander of the Black Ants Second Division
Matilda	Leader of the Digger Ants
Electra	Head of Research in the Red Ant Colony (a Jedda ant)
Agrippa	Commandant of the Prison Camp in the Red Ant Colony
Alexa	Commandant of the Portal Nest in the Sugar Ant Colony
Domina	Chief of the Sugar Ant Military Forces
Stanza	Leader of the White Ant Resistance Fighters
Roda	A daredevil Black ant
Jocula	Leader of the Rocky Mountain Ant Colony
Alexander	Leader of the Male Winged Ants in the Black Ant Colony

Roma	Chief of the Red Ant Military Forces
Pacifica	Becomes Conductor of Unicol
Bluffasta	Becomes Captain of the Guard for Unicol
Monta	Becomes Prime Minister of the Black Ant Colony

YEAR 2

Roanda	Becomes Assistant Conductor of Unicol
Ventura	Leader of the Visionants (a White ant)
Gromelia	A Salt ant scientist and Senior Officer in the Salt Intelligence Service (SIS)
Ivana	Head of a Military Police Unit in the SIS
Natasha	An old White ant
Wanda and Nada	Two young White ants
Observa	Becomes leader of the second expedition beyond the Rim
Sora	An old Red ant soldier
Bravura	Another old Red ant soldier
Regina III	Old Queen of the White ants in Centrasia
Anastasia I	New young Queen of the White ants in Centrasia
Cassandra	An eccentric priestess-prophet ant
Democrika	A rebel ant from the Barb Clan
Rocha	A rebel leader (a Pebble ant)
Mona	Commander of the Unicol Peace Keeping Force
Alexa	Now Leader of Mission Demolition
Serba	Commander of the remnant Salt forces in Freedom Pass
Helena	Chief of Social Stability in the Sugar Ant Colony
Esoterica	Self-styled Queen of the Paradise Colony
Rotunda	Head of Research in Paradise Colony

YEAR 3

Alexa	Becomes Leader of the Sugar Ant Colony
Cota and Runta	Two Sugar ant soldiers
Futura	Leader of the Peace Team (a young Red ant)
Oora	A Dragon ant
Supreema	Leader of the Dragon Ant Colony
Constella	Head of Mission Control on Mount Opportunity (a Sugar ant)
Hedra	Medical Officer from the Black Ant Colony
Centura	A Sugar ant Captain
Provaska	A Pepper ant
Valencia	Leader of the Yellow Ant Colony

YEAR 1

DARKNESS ACROSS THE LAND

CHAPTER 1

The Expedition

THE FIRST RAYS OF EARLY SPRING SUNSHINE stirred new life into the ant colonies of Antale. Dozing lightly in an upper chamber of her mound, Wiseria stretched lazily, then began to move slowly through the darkness towards the surface. She passed the large central chamber where the great mass of her ant colony was still moving in a rhythmic dance to generate warmth against the chill air. A few initiator ants, who knew that it was time for the year's activity to begin, had detached themselves from the mass and were also making their way toward the surface. They sensed the presence of Wiseria, greeted her, and respectfully made way for her to pass. Ahead she could see the small round hole of the blue sky.

At the surface a few sentinels were sunning themselves as they assisted one another in their morning washing and grooming. On seeing Wiseria they paused and nodded a friendly greeting.

"Good morning, Ma'am," said one. "You are off for an early start. Good speed on your mission. Would you care for some company on your journey?"

"Thank you, yes," replied Wiseria, "that would be pleasant. Just as far as Crag Rock. I shall be meeting an escort party there."

Before setting off, Wiseria carefully attended to her own cleansing. Because an ant has so many appendages—six legs, two antennae, and two maxillary palps in the mouth—cleaning is both complicated and ritualistic. Wiseria was no longer young, already in her fourth year, and knew much of life. She appreciated the importance of keeping her sensitive antennae clean and her supple body free from clinging dirt and sticky residue. She had been involved in many campaigns in her three-and-a-half years of life, as an initiator, worker, warrior, attendant to the Queen, and now as the democratically elected leader of the Black Ant Colony. She always set a strong positive example for her companions and followers. It was no less so this morning as she was about to set out on one of the most important missions of her life.

The Black sentinel ants gathered around as Wiseria cleaned herself. She first passed her left antenna through the strigil and under the foreleg, then repeated the process with the right one. Twisting her head around, she passed both antennae, together, through first one hook, then the other. Now that her antennae were clean she felt much better, because they were so important to her for gathering information and communicating. She paused a moment, then, to the mild amusement of the watching sentinels, she waved her antennae in the air. They all waved back to assure her that everything around was quiet and safe.

Satisfied, Wiseria continued with the complicated process of cleaning. She stroked her head with her forelegs, then the abdomen and thorax with her hind legs, almost rolling herself into a ball to wash the gaster at the bottom of her abdomen with her mouth. After that she wrapped the first two legs on each side around each other, like the tangled branches of a berry bush, and in this way scraped off all the dust clinging there. To clean her back legs she flipped herself forward and waved the two legs high in the air, like a flag, brushing them against each other. Then came the *piece de resistance*! Balancing herself like a tripod on the tip of her gaster and on one middle and hind leg, she passed all of the other legs through her mouth. Without pausing for a moment, she repeated this feat the other way round to clean the remaining legs. Now thoroughly clean, though with a mouth full of dirt, Wiseria shook herself all over. The sentinels waved and applauded. Wiseria nodded in acknowledgment, discreetly discharged a few pellets of dirt from her mouth, then set off down the side of the mound toward Bramble Path. Two of the sentinels fell in behind her.

It was very pleasant ambling along the well-worn path early in the morning. They passed alternatively through patches of sunlight and shade. Overhead the odd leaf and blades of grass were fresh with dew, and the party could refresh themselves with the cool moisture whenever they chose. They had only a short distance of about ten yards to go to reach Crag Rock. In a week's time this path would be humming with the activity of worker ants, but this morning they had it almost to themselves. Only a few initiators and scouts were up and about. They all greeted Wiseria cheerfully and respectfully, wishing her good speed on her journey.

At Crag Rock three scouts from the White Ant Colony were waiting to escort Wiseria on the next part of the trip. They had enjoyed a piece of good luck while they were waiting. Foraging in the short grass off to the side, one of them had found the remains of a black beetle that had become entangled and died there. She immediately summoned her companions and together they carved the booty up. Word was sent back to the colony for a party of workers to transport the food to the nest, but in the meantime the scouts were enjoying a hearty breakfast. They greeted Wiseria and her companions in great good spirits.

"Good morning, Madame Wiseria," said one of them. "I am Roanda, personal aide to President Appesia. We have come to escort you. But first please join us for a meal. The day has greeted us with good fortune."

"Thank you, Roanda, "said Wiseria. "Yes, I will have a little. This old body must keep up its strength."

Because ants have two parts to their abdomen, they are both able to nourish themselves and store food in their social stomachs for sharing with others. There was more than enough to go around from the lucky discovery of the beetle, so that all of the ants, including Wiseria, were well provisioned for the next part of the journey.

They had about fifty yards to go to reach the White Ant Colony. It was on the other side of Copper Creek, the quietly meandering stream that drained south from the Rim into Lake Miasma. The ants crossed the creek by a narrow land bridge about three feet wide. Once across the bridge they were beyond the normal ranging ground of Wiseria's Black ant nest. The colonies of Antale observed no fixed territorial boundaries, but custom dictated that the ants would have exclusive ranging rights within ten to twenty yards of their nest. Beyond that they would share the commons. At least that was the general understanding. However, every year it seemed the colonies and population were expanding, and though no one knew the carrying capacity of the land, there was growing concern and tension that things were getting out of hand.

Wiseria was visibly reminded of the problem a few yards further along the path. She had just crossed the land bridge over Copper Creek and topped a rise in the path. Looking over to her left she could see in the distance half a dozen low mounds of the Red ants. She could remember when there were only three. And that was just in this sector. All over the three hundred acres of Antale the Red ants, more than any other group, were pushing the limits of territorial and population expansion.

"Ho there, Black ant! Where are you going with your silky White bodyguards?"

Wiseria stopped in her tracks, antennae waving. The challenge had more of an impudent ring to it than a threat. When the ants of Antale speak, it is not in words of sound, but rather electrical impulses. Well tuned antennae can pick up and transmit the most subtle fluctuations in tone and cadence. Wiseria recognized this intervention as a typical Red ant provocation.

She looked around, following the direction of the electrical impulse. At first she saw nothing, then in a jumble of twigs just a few inches off to the left of the path, and a little above her, three large red ant heads appeared over a dead leaf. Six cheeky antennae waved at Wiseria. Seeing that they were detected, the three Red ant sentinels came into full view, flexing their lithe blood-red bodies in a posture of defiance.

It was Roanda who replied to them, not Wiseria.

"You should show some respect, Red ant buffoons," she said. "Don't you know that this is Prime Minister Wiseria, Deputy Chief of the Antale Federation of Ants?"

"Well, pardon me," replied the middle Red ant. "Anyone who wanders along in such a casual way can't expect to be given much consideration."

"We are not all like you Red ants, full of pomp and wind," Roanda shot back.

"Wait a moment, Roanda, please," Wiseria intervened. "We don't need to insult one another here." She turned to the Red ant who had spoken. "I'm sorry, I don't know your name."

"Sentinel 3103," replied the other.

"Ah, yes," said Wiseria. "That's Supreme Commander Aggressa's new way of designating the Red ant troops. Well, my good ant Sentinel 3103, may I ask that you convey my regards to your supreme commander. I am expecting to see her later today at the official ceremony in Centrasia."

With that Wiseria continued on her way. Roanda tossed her head at the Red ants and followed. The sentinels on the leaf hurriedly withdrew.

A short while later, the small party topped the last rise on the path and looked down at the shining white dome of Centrasia. It was a breathtaking sight. Perfectly symmetrical, and built of the finest white clay packed hard, the dome of this great underground city rose to an unusual three feet in height with a diameter of ten feet at the base. Traces of dew still clung to its surface in irregular patches which sparkled merrily in the sunlight. But what added to the city's grandeur was the bare wide sweep of hard packed white earth that surrounded it in a perfect circle, reaching ten feet outwards. Dome and courtyard were molded of a piece, as if sculpted out of the earth with the careful hands and fine eye of a nature artist.

The chief occupation of the ants who lived in Centrasia was harvesting. They foraged wide and far for grass seeds of all varieties. A few of the sentinels and scouts like Roanda also had a taste for other things, like the beetle they had found for breakfast, but for the thousands of workers who built and maintained the city, harvesting and storing a granary of earth's produce was their sole reason for being. The spotless courtyard around the dome was part of the grand design, for it served as a drying area for grass seeds dampened by rain, and as a break against any flash fires that might sweep across the surrounding area. This morning, however, the work-a-day world of the city was transformed by its jewel-like splendor.

"Now we'll see how a reception should be handled," said Roanda. Standing proudly beside Wiseria, she transmitted a signal down to the city. Instantly everything came alive. Pouring out of a dozen entrances on the portion of the dome facing the visitors, solid columns of White ants marched down the mound then onto the courtyard. Here they fanned out into a mesmerizing pattern of parading columns. All of this was accompanied by the trilling of ten thousand ant voices singing:

"Ho! Ho! Ho! We go!
Workers of the earth, you know.
Lift your voices high and low.
Masters of the land, you know.
Ho! Ho! Ho! We go!"

and so on, over and over, until the very air trembled with the singing. One might wonder that the ants would leave themselves so exposed to scavengers from the sky, but it would be a very brave or foolish intruder, indeed, who would attempt to attack a column of ten thousand parading ants when their spirits are soaring with pride of who they are.

"Come, Madame Wiseria," said Roanda, "President Appesia welcomes you to Centrasia."

The path sloped straight down in front of them, joining the courtyard where two stones had been carefully placed by the ants as a main gateway to the city. By the time they reached this entrance, the marching ants had lined up in two columns facing each other about six inches apart. They provided an honor guard for Wiseria as she crossed the courtyard. Each soldier ant raised its right antenna in salute as she went by. Halfway across, she was met by a large White ant who greeted her warmly.

"My dear Wiseria," she said, "you are most punctual as usual. You are the first to arrive. It has been too long since you last visited us. Come let us walk together to the city."

"Thank you, Appesia," replied Wiseria. "You look well. This promises to be a most eventful day."

The two ants, Black and White, fell into step beside each other. Wiseria nodded to the troops on either side and to the other worker ants who were coming out of the nest to see what was going on. Appesia observed it all with a benevolent air, obviously well pleased with everything.

They entered the nest, with Appesia leading the way, by a slightly larger than normal entrance toward the base of the mound. Inside, the cool darkness was a sharp contrast with the warm bright sunshine outside. Ants are equally at home in darkness as in light because of their acute sensing abilities. Wiseria immediately noticed that the smell of Centrasia was quite different from her own Black ants' nest. She knew that she would be equally detectable by all White ants as someone different. But there was no cause for concern on that score. She was in friendly quarters here, and rightly so, because of her own staunch efforts last year to forge strong ties among all the ants of the federated colonies of Antale.

Appesia led them into a relatively large chamber a short way into the mound. Wiseria had been there several times before. It was the main conference centre for the Federation, and could hold upwards of a hundred ants quite comfortably. But for the moment there was just the two of them, with a small number of attendants hovering discreetly in the background.

"Where is Explora and her party?" asked Wiseria.

"Quite nearby," replied Appesia. "They spent all day yesterday preparing for the expedition. They are resting now. They will join us at the official departure ceremony once the other Heads of Colonies arrive."

"Is everyone coming?"

"I believe so."

"Including Aggressa?"

"She sent word to say she would be here."

"That's good. We met three of her Red guards along the way. They are quite impudent ants. I don't like their military antics. Somehow we must get Aggressa to bring her Red ant colonies into the federation, otherwise there could be trouble."

"Yes, yes, Wiseria. I know your views on this point." Appesia's tone was just a little impatient. "I am confident that this spring we'll see a fully formed federation. Beginning today with Explora's expedition will be a great bonding."

Wiseria did not reply. She certainly hoped that Appesia's confidence would be justified, but she had some well-founded nagging reservations.

Not long afterwards word was brought that all of the other Heads of Colonies who were participating in the Explora expedition were arriving with their delegations. They were assembling at the crest of the hill where Wiseria had looked down to the city a while earlier.

"Roanda," Appesia summoned her assistant, "tell Explora to be ready to bring her party to Federation Square within thirty minutes. Come, Wiseria. Let's greet the delegations together."

President and Deputy emerged from the city of Centrasia by the same way as they had entered. Outside, the sweep of clear white earth had become a great parade ground.

The White ant troops were marching up and down with their "Ho! Ho! Ho-ing!" going at full tempo in a seemingly hopeless melee of swinging bodies and legs. Then, miraculously, all at once, the ranks opened into a large square. The White soldiers came to attention, and all singing ceased.

Looking across to the high ground on the other side of the square of troops, Appesia and Wiseria could see a marvelous mélange of multicolored splendor. The ant Heads of Colonies were assembling. Even at this distance Wiseria could pick out the friendly Yellow ants from the north, the great ambling golden Sugar ants from the far side of Lake Miasma, and the grey, blackheaded Salt ants from the very farthest reaches of Antale at the steepest part of the Rim. Standing off a little apart from that group were the hard-shelled Green ants from Carpentaria and the strong-jawed Browns from Woodsonia. Further back, a cluster of Acid ants stood out in bright vermilion. Straining her eyes to the utmost, and tuning in all signals on her antennae, Wiseria was unable to pick up any trace of the Red ants.

Appesia had the whole ceremony well orchestrated. She was obviously a little nonplussed at the absence of the Red ants, but she nevertheless gave the signal to commence right on cue, and the delegations came down to Federation Square formed by the White troops. All over the dome of Centrasia, and out onto the cleared earth around, the White worker ants poured in their thousands in gay holiday mood to witness the ceremony.

Each delegation of five or six ants marched to its own rhythm and beat as they came down into Federation Square. They assembled in colored blocks facing Appesia as she, followed by Wiseria, moved out into the Square. Standing side by side in the centre, President and Deputy then waited as one by one the Heads of Delegation came forward to be officially welcomed. First came Antonia of the Yellow ants, who greeted Appesia and Wiseria as old friends. Serenta of the Sugars likewise embraced them energetically. Bravada, Head of the Salts, was also friendly, though more reserved. However, when it came the turn of Barbaria of the Green ants and Narcissa of the Browns, a clear breath of coolness prevailed. Finally, General Intrepida of the bright vermilion colored Acids came forward, twitching and clicking her antennae and legs in military precision. When they were all lined up facing her, Appesia spoke so that everyone could hear.

"Welcome to you all, Heads of the ant colonies of Antale who have joined in federation for the peace of our land. It is a tribute to our accomplishment and progress that we can assemble here today as friends to mark the first of our great initiatives as a Federation. Sending a joint expeditionary force, representative of our ant colonies, across the vast and unknown expanses of the Rim, is a bold step forward into our common future. We don't know what our brave explorers will find out there. We do know of the perils they face, for all other efforts to penetrate into those unknown regions have failed. However, it is in the expectation that we are not alone in the universe, and in our common need as adventurers of the future, that we must find the great civilizations that surely lie beyond the Rim. From them we can learn new secrets of science that will lift our own progress even higher and further than we have been able to take it in our own great strides of recent years. I welcome you all here, my fellow leaders and servants of our colonies. It is time now for us to greet our expeditionary force."

The conclusion of Appesia's speech was greeted with applause from all delegations and enthusiastic cheering and antennae waving from the thousands of White worker ants. Appesia turned to face the dome of her city, but hardly had she done so when a commotion broke out on the far side from which the delegations had come. Everyone turned to see what it was.

The Red ant delegation had arrived. Wiseria suspected that they had been hiding in the bushes all this time waiting for the right moment to make a grand entrance. There were at least twenty in the party: big-headed, tough-skinned soldier ants formed into a square. In the middle, riding on a leaf platform supported by some workers, was a large Red ant, sitting on her back legs and abdomen, with front legs crossed and her sharp, saw-toothed mandibles rhythmically opening and closing, as if she were chewing her way forward. This was Aggressa, supreme commander, as she liked to be called, of the Red ants in the fourth quadrant of Antale.

Wiseria winced, not only at the spectacle of such absurd pomposity, but at the sight of the workers bearing Aggressa's platform. They were the progeny of Black, White and Yellow slave ants whom the Reds had captured in marauding raids in the past. Though the practice was now officially outlawed in most ant colonies in Antale, everyone knew that the Reds had a substantial slave population in their nests whom they treated as inferior creatures. The irony was that many of these lower caste ants were the best scientists and teachers in the Red ant colonies. To see several of them subjected to the indignity of platform bearers for Aggressa's red posterior was a little too much for Wiseria to stomach.

By now everyone was watching the Red ant entourage. The soldiers were marching in a strange, slow-motion, stiff-legged fashion, which must have been quite difficult to master with six legs to coordinate. The worker slaves didn't dare do it for fear of toppling their cargo of supreme commander. The soldiers intoned a rhythmic chant as they came that sounded like the amplified grinding of a hundred thousand sets of teeth. They came right on down into Federation Square, the other delegations moving to each side to let them pass. Barbaria and Narcissa, heads respectively of the Green and the Brown ants, seemed pleased with the performance, and saluted Aggressa as she went by. The other leaders maintained airs of nonchalance or inscrutability. Appesia with Wiseria by her side stood quite still facing the approaching line of Red soldiers.

The troops slow-stepped their way straight up to the President and Deputy, until it seemed they would march right over them. At the very last moment, however, the line halted, then opened so that Appesia and Wiseria directly faced Aggressa. The latter sat silently for a full minute on her elevated platform so that everyone had to look up to her. Then the workers lowered the platform and Aggressa stepped forward. Appesia extended no greeting, just waited. Complete silence hung over Federation Square. Finally, Aggressa spoke.

"We have come to show our support for the Explora enterprise," she said. "Where is the expedition?"

"You are welcome here, Supreme Commander," Appesia said civilly. "I had arranged a welcoming ceremony for the Heads of Colonies. I am sorry you were too late to participate."

'Never say you're sorry to the likes of Aggressa,' Wiseria thought to herself.

"No matter," said Aggressa. "I believe everyone has noticed our arrival. You may proceed with the ceremony."

Appesia nodded. She and Wiseria turned to face the dome of Centrasia. A bugle-like fanfare sounded. Out through the main entrance came a large Black ant, powerful and strong, her big-framed body shining in the sunlight. Behind her a troop of a dozen other ants of all colors emerged from the mound. On their backs they carried another smaller ant who faced toward the rear and held, tightly clenched in its jaws, a line attached to a large wagon-like leaf container that rolled along on small round nuts. The wagons were filled with grass seeds, and riding on the top of each was another ant with a very large distended abdomen. These were honey ants, filled to bursting with the honeydew from last year's harvests that would be so valuable as nutritional support for the expedition as it crossed the empty barren desolation of the Rim.

The lead ant was, of course, Explora. Walking on either side of her was a Yellow and a White ant. The Yellow had strapped to her thorax, just behind her head, a small container that carried the very latest electronic communication technology. This allowed her to expand her own transmitting and receiving capabilities to very great distances. The White ant carried a similar device as back-up, plus some sensing equipment for detecting organic life that could be potential food sources.

The arrival of Explora and her party was greeted by wild cheering from the White worker ants who now crowded in by countless thousands to get the best view. Explora came up to Appesia, halted and saluted.

"The Antale Expeditionary Force for Enlightenment through Discovery is ready to depart, Madame President," she said. "With respect and honor to all member colonies, we declare our allegiance to the Federation, and commit ourselves to spare no effort in the furtherance of its communal objectives."

"You are a brave and most worthy band of true ant adventurers," declared Appesia. "I can have no greater honor as President of the Federation than to wish you good and safe speed on your journey. Your reports of progress throughout the summer months that lie ahead will enrich our work here in

Antale with a new, higher-order purpose. In recognition of the great esteem in which the Federation holds your enterprise, Deputy Wiseria will accompany you on the first part of your journey through Antale and onto the Rim."

Before Wiseria could speak, Aggressa intervened.

"Where are the troops?" she asked.

"Excuse me, Commander?" queried Appesia.

"The troops," repeated Aggressa. "You can't send an expedition out onto the Rim without protection."

"Each member of the party is a fully-trained warrior ant," said Appesia. "Explora, perhaps you could explain to the Commander."

"With pleasure," said Explora. "We understand the need for protection, but have balanced that against the need to carry our own provisions. Each member of the team is trained in all aspects necessary for our survival against unknown difficulties."

"I see you have two of our Red ants pulling wagons while a White and a Yellow here strut along with joy packs on their backs. That offends me." Aggressa was gnashing her mandibles menacingly at Explora.

Wiseria could stand it no longer.

"Supreme Commander," she said. "The first rule for sending out a force like this where everyone's life is at risk is to put full control in the hands of the leader. We have done that. Explora has our every confidence. With respect, this is not the time for leaders like ourselves to be expressing differences. This is a public ceremony of honor. It is time to send our party forward with the strongest possible endorsement. Come, Explora, I will walk beside you."

"Pair of Black ant toadies," hissed Aggressa, just strong enough for the official party to hear.

But Wiseria and Explora paid no further attention to Aggressa. They saluted Appesia, then stepped forward at a brisk pace through the lines of White ant troops forming the square. The White ants snapped to attention and began stamping their feet and singing:

"Ho! Ho! Ho! They go!
Seekers of the truth, you know.
Raise your voices high and low.
Let them know we love them so.
Ho! Ho! Ho! They go!"

Thousands of White ant workers picked up the beat and sang out the song until the electrical energy of their transmissions made the air above Centrasia crackle and dance. Two wheeling black birds high above the mound who had come in to see what the commotion was all about were hit by the electrical waves, and they banked sharply to get out of the way. The ants of Centrasia were giving their party of explorers a resounding send off.

It was hardly any less exuberant anywhere they went. For the next eight hours as they crossed Antale heading towards the Rim, colony after colony of ants came out to greet them and wish them well. Through the copse of Avalon the leaf-cutting Tree ants poured a shower of leafy confetti on them. Along the shores of Lake Miasma, Sand ants went running along in front, dropping a shiny white sand carpet for them to cross. To help them through the marshes of Windermere, the Water ants built a flotilla of leaves and twigs to ferry them across the wet spaces. And finally, as they reached the foot of Escarpment Slope, ready to begin the long and arduous ascent to the top of the Rim, the short, stout Rocky Mountain ants came out in droves, and insisted on pulling the heavily loaded wagons so that the team could still be fresh at the top. This last gesture was particularly appreciated by Explora, who knew that they must continue all night to get as far as they could across the bare, open rock of the Rim under cover of darkness.

It was a long, hard climb up the escarpment. On either side the walls of the cliff face were so sheer and smooth that they could never have made it to the top by that route with the loaded wagons. Indeed, all around Antale, except for Escarpment Slope, the rock walls of the Rim were just like glass, and towered straight up for two hundred feet. It was a major struggle for any ant to climb those walls, and dangerous, too, because of exposure to attack by birds, who were always swooping around looking for insects. Besides, there was no incentive to make the effort, because at the top the rock of the Rim was just as smooth and bare as the cliff face, and stretched away in all directions for unimaginable distances. No ant from Antale had ever ventured out onto the Rim with success. The few who had returned after days, and sometimes weeks of absence, had nothing to report but endless barren emptiness with little food and moisture. There was almost no cover to escape the marauding eyes of enemies from the sky, and only the shield of darkness offered any respite from the constant threat of danger. In effect, the Rim was the end of the ant world. It was an unknown and unknowable emptiness. The possibility of life "out there" was no more than the fantasy and speculation of dreamers and storytellers.

But still, the desire to know, to go further, burned in ant consciousness. Surely Antale could not be alone in the universe. Did not the existence of the Rim prove that there must be something beyond it? Perhaps other Antales, more wonderful and developed than their own land. Moreover, their science of the last few years was changing belief, from possibility to probability. Intercolonial initiatives by scientists from across the Federation had developed technology that could transmit and receive electrical signals from great distances. They had set up a receiving station on the top of Mount Opportunity, just a short distance out on the Rim from the top of Escarpment Slope, which the Explora party was now ascending. From this observation post, scientists had received weak but clear signals coming across the Rim. They could make no sense of them, and had no idea how far away their source might be. But they were definitely there, and that was enough to justify the mounting of a major journey of exploration.

Explora had been chosen to lead it because of her long and distinguished career as a scientist and explorer into the farthest reaches of Antale. She had completely circumnavigated the Rim, and charted its features for up to a mile outwards from Antale. It was to be expected that when a decision was made to send an intercolonial probe across the Rim that Explora would be chosen to lead it.

From the start, Wiseria had taken a particular interest in the probe. While not a scientist herself, she had a keen appreciation for how scientific enquiry could benefit the colonies of Antale. The fact that Explora was a Black ant from Wiseria's own nest, and that they had known each other for over two years, provided an added source of interest. Wiseria was sure that if any ant could lead a successful expedition across the Rim, Explora was the one to do it.

These thoughts ran through Wiseria's mind as she labored beside Explora on the last few yards of the climb up Escarpment Slope. Roanda, personal aide to Appesia, had also accompanied the party. Wiseria noted with some satisfaction that despite her age, she was handling the climb much better than Roanda, who, though much younger, was panting along behind her, taking every opportunity to rest. The sun was already setting, so their timing for reaching the top was good. After a brief rest, Explora's party could set off under cover of darkness on the first leg of their journey. They would be guided on their route by the observation post on the top of Mount Opportunity. This large outcrop of rock, which towered fifty feet above the Rim, was already visible to the party, its huge bulk bulging against the darkening sky. Wiseria and Roanda would accompany the party to the foot of the mountain, then leave them there and climb up to the observation post where they would spend the night.

At the top of the slope, the expedition bade an emotional farewell to the Rocky Mountain ants, who had helped them on the climb. They were lively, jolly workers and fighters who didn't know much about science or politics, but respected bravery when they saw it.

"When you bump into a Rim monster out there," one of them said to Explora, "don't give it a chance."

"Distract it from the front," said another.

"Then attack it from the back," added a third.

"And sting! sting! sting!" all of them chortled together.

There was much embracing, back slapping, and antennae waving. Then the Rocky Mountain ants scuttled off down the slope shouting: "Sting, sting,

sting the thing. That's the way we sing, sing, sing!"—and so on until they were gone.

The party hitched up its wagons and continued. A half hour later they arrived at the foot of Mount Opportunity. Wiseria and Explora embraced in the darkness.

"So it's time, old friend," said Wiseria.

"Yes, and there'll be more time again for us soon, when I get back," replied Explora.

"That will be a great day for Antale."

"In the meantime, don't think you've gotten rid of me. We'll be sending back reports every day. And we'll want to hear the news from your end."

"We will try to make it good," said Wiseria.

"Don't take any guff from Aggressa and her thugs," said Explora.

"Just so," replied Wiseria. "But that's our concern. You'll have more than challenges enough where you're going. Goodbye, my dear."

Wiseria embraced all members of the party, as did Roanda. Then they both stood quietly to one side as the expedition left. When the explorers had disappeared into the darkness, Wiseria acknowledged to herself and Roanda that the expedition was now well and truly underway. They turned and began the slow climb to the top of Mount Opportunity.

CHAPTER 2

Diplomacy and Disappointment

IT TOOK WISERIA AND ROANDA ALMOST TWO hours to get to the top of Mount Opportunity. Not being familiar with the path, they had to pick their way carefully among clumps of loose rock and short, sharp blades of grass. It grew much cooler as they climbed higher into the night air, and their bodies became more sluggish with the drop in temperature. All around, the vast empty immensity of the Rim enveloped them like the darkness of a tomb.

But at last they came to the observation post. It was built into a bluff right at the top, on the edge of the mountain looking away from Antale. They would never have found it except that Wiseria knew the frequency of the homing signal the post was using to guide visitors in. Roanda was more than a little amazed at how confidently her companion came up to an almost invisible crack in the rock and slipped inside. They went down a rather long passage at the end of which they were challenged by a sentinel. Wiseria gave her security clearance and the guard then cheerfully led them along another series of passages until they came into a large open chamber. Everything was, of course, in total darkness, so the ants were using their extraordinary sensing capabilities to know what was going on. Wiseria immediately detected the scent of several different kinds of ants. Unmistakably stronger than the rest was the sweet smell of a Sugar.

"Well, well, Madame Deputy, you do us great honor to visit the Federation's Mission Control." This was a very friendly greeting, full of energy and good humor. "I am Colonel Observa. I'm supposed to be in charge around here, but you'd never know it from the respect I get."

There was a murmur of jocular signals from the other ants.

"See what I mean? No respect at all," Observa continued in mock complaint.

"However, for a ragtag bunch of scientists and technicians from several colonies we don't do so badly."

"The efficiency of your work is well known, Colonel," said Wiseria. "We know that the success of the Explora expedition is very much in your hands."

"Team work, that's the ticket," said Observa. "Our job is to guide and support those brave ants on the ground. They're the ones putting their lives on the line. We're monitoring them closely. Would you like to see?"

Observa led Wiseria across the room, then along a short passage where the cool air from outside could be felt. They came out onto a rock platform. Up above, the stars of the night sky were visible.

"This is our observation deck," Observa explained. "These instruments here allow us to boost our own normal transmission and receiving signals enormously. If you hook up to these antennae, you'll find you can tune in on the expedition party quite easily."

Wiseria twined her antennae around two others protruding from a panel on the edge of the platform. She immediately picked up signals from members of the expedition party. She could detect Explora's signal quite clearly.

"Hello, Explora," she said. "This is Wiseria. Roanda and I are at Mission Control. It's wonderful to be able to contact you like this. How's it going?"

"Just fine," replied Explora. "You had a much harder climb than anything we've done so far."

"I'll speak to you again before we go back to Antale," said Wiseria. "Goodbye for now." To Observa she added: "That's wonderful, Colonel. Will the transmission always be as clear as that as they get further away?"

"So far as we know, Ma'am. We're just guiding them along those other strange signals that are coming in from out there. If they get to the source of them, then we'll know what we know."

"Any speculations?"

"No more than to say that they seem like ant transmissions to me. Rather jumbled and confused, but they have ant frequencies and modulation."

Wiseria and Observa went back inside. Roanda had already made friends with the other ants at Mission Control. They were enjoying a good meal of portions of an earth worm that they had caught during the day. Wiseria joined them for a while, then feeling tired from the long day's journey, she asked for a place to rest.

"Pacifica will show you to your quarters, Ma'am," said Observa. "Have a good night's sleep. We'll see you in the morning."

Wiseria followed a young ant who showed her into one of several sleeping chambers opening off a larger room. The ant paused uncertainly, and Wiseria sensed that she wanted to speak, but did not want to impose.

"Your name's Pacifica?" asked Wiseria. "That's a portent for the future. Antale will need its young peacemakers if it is to prosper. You are a White, aren't you? From Centrasia?"

"No, Ma'am, further east. My home is Buranda."

"Ah yes, I know it. There's a good academy there. Is that where you studied? You seem rather young to be at Mission Control."

"I'm just interning here for the experience," said Pacifica. "I have to return to Buranda soon to complete my studies. I, I, wondered…"

"Yes, my dear, what is it?"

"I wondered if I might travel back with you when you leave."

"I'm sure that can be arranged," said Wiseria. "Let's talk about it in the morning. Good night, Pacifica."

"Good night, Ma'am."

When Wiseria emerged the next morning, she quickly made her way outside the observation post. She was surprised to find the sun well up. She had slept late. She cleaned herself, then thought about something to eat. She looked around to see Observa and Pacifica coming towards her.

In the daylight Wiseria could now see that Observa was a very good looking golden colored Sugar ant, well-built and athletic. Beside her, the young white Pacifica looked more fragile, but carried herself with grace and assurance.

"Good morning, Ma'am," greeted Observa. "I was told I'd find you here. I trust you slept well."

"Yes, thank you, Colonel. What's the news of the mission?"

"They had a good first night. Traveled about two miles across some very rough terrain. They're bedded down for the day now under some cover and the camouflage of their own wagons. Now, I have a treat for you for breakfast. Show her, Pacifica."

Pacifica disappeared for a moment behind a small rock, then came back carrying a large lump of sugar beet in her jaws. It was almost as big as she was. She placed it in front of Observa, who deftly carved it up into three pieces.

"There you are. Fresh from the sugar plantations in Torida. One of the benefits of the job. You get some of your special cravings provided for when provisions are brought in."

Wiseria enjoyed the sweet tasting root, which she ate slowly and felt its nutritional strength energizing her body. She rather doubted, however, that she would care for it as a constant diet. Observa seemed pleased that her guest was enjoying the treat.

"It's very good," said Wiseria. "We don't often get sugar beet in the north. I would like to see how you grow it."

"You should visit our plantations," said Observa. "One of the most amazing sights in the world."

"Actually, Colonel, I was going to raise that with you. I've been thinking that on my return I would like to visit your colony, along with the Salts and the Acids. Since you are all on the south side of Lake Miasma, I could go the long way round and visit all three. I am hoping I might convince the leaders to have your colonies formally join a Federation that would eventually encompass all Antale."

"Well, that's a noble objective, Ma'am," Observa was waving her antennae thoughtfully, "but likely a bit ambitious. Mind you, I'm no politician. Just a whiz-bang merchant, that's me. But if you want my view—which you probably don't…" Observa paused and looked at Wiseria, quizzically.

"Please continue," said Wiseria.

"Well, I think the chances of those three colonies coming together are not very good. I mean, the names say it all. We Sugars are very affable ants, but we sure don't need any help from anyone to be successful. And the Acids, stuck there on those islands at the edge of the lake, well, it's made them a very sour bunch. You just can't trust them. And the Salts, well, who knows? They're a pretty ruthless lot. No one really knows what's going on with them. But you hear rumors, and I just wouldn't want to be their neighbors. But there, I've probably spoken out of turn. I know we need ants of vision like you, Ma'am, who will try to pull us together. If there's anything I can do to help, just say the word."

"Thank you, Colonel. I would like you to send messages to the Heads of the three colonies to arrange the visit. You can work with Roanda on the details."

"There's some dangerous territory between here and our colony. You have to pass through the Dark Country. Who'll be traveling with you?"

"Well, Roanda, of course, and Pacifica has asked if she could return with me. If that's all right with you, Colonel."

"Why sure," replied Observa, looking mockingly at Pacifica. "Our top student here could use some worldly experience. When do you want to leave?"

"I would like to rest today and leave before sunrise tomorrow morning, to get down Escarpment Slope before daylight. Now, if I could borrow Pacifica for a while, I would like to cross to the other side of the mountain to see the view of Antale."

Observa returned to her duties inside the observation post, and Pacifica led Wiseria along a winding, sheltered path around the edge of the summit. A short while later they emerged on a rocky outcrop. Down below, shimmering in light mist and brilliant sunlight was the jewel of Antale. Wiseria had never seen it before from this perspective. Her heart leapt at first with joy, before a strange sadness enveloped her. She must have caught her breath, for Pacifica looked at her inquiringly.

"Oh, Pacifica," Wiseria exclaimed, then continued slowly, haltingly. "It's so beautiful. That's our world we're looking at. Excuse me, I don't know how to say this, but it seems, just so full of everything. We are so blessed to live there. I never quite understood before, but now I know why I feel so called to work for cooperation and peace. You can't take a priceless treasure and squander it. We are meant to nurture and preserve what we have been given. Somehow, ants like you and I have to find the words and the ways that will bring that message to everyone. They can't all come up here to Mount Opportunity and know what we know as we look down into that great ocean of magnificence, but somehow, somehow, we have to get them to understand."

Pacifica, despite her youth, or possibly because of it, was profoundly moved at how the sight of the blue-green jewel of Antale set in the darkness of the Rim, had affected her companion.

"We will find the way, Ma'am. If it's in our hearts, we will find the way," she said.

"Yes, I know." Wiseria seemed to have recovered her composure. "Now, help me, Pacifica. Your eyes are much better than mine. Help me to see the features."

The scene that Pacifica described was a large round depression of green vegetation about a mile in diameter. At its widest point, cutting almost all the way across in an east-west direction, was a long blue lake. This was Lake Miasma. It was fed by two creeks, Copper Creek running in from the north about half way across the depression, and Cruel Creek running in from the south much closer to where they were standing. The latter creek was so named because it drained through the mysterious, heavily wooded Dark Country that they could see clearly below. The two creeks and the lake roughly divided Antale into four sectors. In the northeast, known as the fourth quadrant, Centrasia stood, capital of the White Ant Colony, which shared that sector with the colonies of the Reds, the Greens and the Browns. All of this was too far away to be seen clearly from Mount Opportunity. On the western side of Copper Creek, still to the north of Lake Miasma, was Wiseria's Black Ant Colony. Further north and across the creek, where it took a bend, was the Yellow Ant Colony. All this was quadrant one. Its western margin was marked by Escarpment Slope up which the expedition had climbed yesterday.

The other two quadrants lay to the south of Lake Miasma. Quadrant two was the Dark Country. Not much was known about this sector, which was very wild country, at the back of which a large colony of ants was believed to exist. They were known as the Dragons and their land was located entirely in the shadow of the Rim where they chose to remain in almost total isolation. Across Cruel Creek was the largest sector, quadrant three, shared by the Sugars, the Acids and the Salts. There were almost two hundred smaller colonies spread throughout Antale, and some of them were still relatively unknown to ants living in the larger more developed colonies. All this Pacifica described to a carefully attentive Wiseria.

"You know, Pacifica," her older companion said, "we ants are really blessed by our biology."

"What do you mean?" asked Pacifica.

"Well, all of us workers and soldiers and scouts—all of us responsible for caring for things—all of us are female. Now, we're not like the Queens who've got the special role of laying the eggs to produce future generations, but we've got the same instinct to preserve the species. The males don't have much of a role. Just a brief life to fertilize future Queens and then they're gone. But the rest of us worker females are left to carry on. And we do it magnificently. We just have to take one more step in our evolution. We have to learn that we are part of one great family and that the nurturing of life is the nurturing of all of us together, not just our own nest or colony, but the whole of the one ant world of Antale. That world lying down there. We have the potential for that in our genes. We just have to realize it in our thoughts and behavior. That is why I get so upset with the posturing and aggression of groups like the Red ants. We have to call that life-threatening behavior for what it is and stand up against it. That is why I work so hard for the Federation. I see it as our one great hope. World union probably won't happen in my lifetime, but I will spend all my energy in bringing it closer.

"I'm sorry, my dear. I don't mean to lecture. It's just that I feel so strongly on this point."

"I understand, Ma'am," said Pacifica. "I am deeply honored that you would share your thoughts with me."

"All right, then," Wiseria was more business-like now. "There's one last thing I want to say and then we must get back to the others. Do you see those red and black smudges rising over the land? I can even see them with my old eyes. They mark the beginning of a new threat. We ants have lived for millions of years and built very successful civilizations. It's only in recent years that we've learnt how to build industries. Those red and black smudges mark the beginning of danger unless we learn how to build our industry without poisoning our land and our air. Along with preserving peace, that is the major issue your generation will face. Now we must go back. I'll follow you. Please lead the way."

The remainder of Wiseria's visit to Mission Control passed swiftly. She spoke once more to Explora, just before leaving early next morning with Roanda and Pacifica. Explora's group was making good progress. They had already covered another two miles on the second night of their journey. Wiseria wished them well, then set off with her two companions on her own journey. Four hours later, just as the sun was rising in the east over the Rim, they were safely at the bottom of Escarpment Slope and preparing to turn south into the Dark Country. Their friends, the little red Rocky Mountain ants, who had helped Explora's party climb the slope two days ago, shook their heads worriedly when told of the trio's plans to go that way.

"Beware of the great grey gonzonga," one of them warned.

"The what?" asked Roanda.

"Look out for the Tigers, too," said another.

"Sting! Sting! Sting!" they all chortled and scurried away to continue their work.

A short while later, Wiseria and her companions knew why this was called the Dark Country. Though the sun was well up, they were making their way along a path almost hidden under thick vegetation. Only occasional shafts of sunlight reached the ground. Mostly they were moving through dark, dense, eerie stillness. This was not the friendly darkness of the inside of a nest, but the cold wet dark emptiness of a place where fear was the only dweller. They were traveling in single file with Roanda leading, Wiseria in the middle, and Pacifica bringing up the rear.

Suddenly, all three felt a belch of hot air and recoiled from the dreadful smell of rotten stomach gas. A great spiked claw attached to a long hairy leg crashed onto the path beside Roanda. She leapt back in fear and bumped into Wiseria. Before any of them could act, another clawed leg thumped down beside Pacifica. Then another to the side, and another, and another, until they were surrounded by eight great hairy legs like the bars of a cage. The gloom of before became total darkness as they felt the hot body heat of some dreadful beast settling upon them. The rancid smell of the stomach gas was overpowering. It was then that Wiseria looked up into the baleful gleam of a wicked green eye. She sensed rather than saw the great gaping jaws moving to swallow Roanda. All the fighting instincts of three years on the front line of survival welled up inside her.

"Roanda, look out!" she screamed. "Attack! Go for the legs!"

Without waiting for the others, Wiseria sank her jaws deep into the nearest hairy leg. She felt the crunch of bone under her powerful grip. Roanda and Pacifica moved just as swiftly on two other legs. All three ants gripped their attacker and hung on for dear life. The effect was immediate. The huge grey trapdoor spider, for that's what it was that had attacked them, convulsed like a recoiling spring and tried to shake the ants off. They held their grips like leaches. The spider relaxed for a moment, and each ant let go and grabbed another leg. With six of its eight legs now crippled, the spider rolled into a ball and tried to smother the ants against its body and bring its jaws into play. Wiseria found herself crushed up against the nauseous hairy bulk of this ugly beast. She let go the leg and sank her jaws into the soft under belly. A flood of thick green slime rushed out and covered the ants. The spider went into violent spasms. The ants, still hanging on to whatever part they could grab, were beaten and bashed against each other, the ground, and the body of the spider. What with the pounding and the nauseating smell and the stinging slime, they were almost senseless. Wiseria felt herself slipping into unconsciousness.

"Yoddle-loddle-loddle-loddle-loo!"

It was a war cry coming from somewhere above.

"Chukka-ducka-ducka-doo!" came another one.

"Tigers one! Tigers two!"

The spider gave one more great convulsion then collapsed. The three badly beaten ants crawled out from under the body.

"Ho there, you warriors! Yuk, you smell awful!"

The three stunned ants turned and looked around. Sitting on the carcass of the spider were two large black ants with white stripes.

"It's lucky for you three that we were around," said one of them.

"We killed the beast as dead as a stone," said the other.

"Tigers to the rescue!" they both shouted together.

Sensing diplomacy as the best course of action, Wiseria spoke up before either of her younger companions could protest that they had more than a little to do with the death of the spider.

"Thank you. We are most grateful," said Wiseria. "Might I know to whom I am speaking?"

"We are Tiger One and Tiger Two of the Tigers Ant Platoon," replied one of the others. "Who are you?"

"I am Wiseria, Deputy Head of the Federation of Antale. These are my companions. We are on our way to the Sugar Ant Colony. May I ask that you give us safe escort through the Dark Country?"

"Nothing for nothing," rejoined Tiger One. "What can you pay?"

"Would you accept our small contribution in distracting the spider while you killed it? We would be glad for your colony to keep all of it for food."

"Deal is done," said Tiger One. "I'll take you. Tiger Two, you stay with our victim until the transport troop arrives. Come on, you three, follow me, but not too close. You don't smell too good."

Tiger One moved off down the path.

"Buffoon in a waist coat," whispered Roanda. "We killed that thing, not her."

"But she knows the way to the Sugar Ant Colony and we don't," said Wiseria. "Diplomacy is the art of getting what matters most to you. She can have the spider and the glory. We'll just get out of here. Come, Pacifica, are you all right? That was a dreadful experience."

"Yes, I'm fine now," said Pacifica, but she kept very close to Wiseria as they hurried off after Tiger One.

They still had quite some distance to travel through the Dark Country, so they were glad of the escort, as eccentric as it was. Tiger One paraded along ahead of them talking to herself, and making mock skirmishing attacks, first to one side of the path, then the other. Soon they met up with another Tiger ant. There was an elaborate explanation of how Tigers One and Two had killed the great grey gonzonga, and saved this miserable hapless trio from certain death. Then Tiger One handed Wiseria and her companions over to the newcomer and said that she, Tiger Three, would now be their escort. This procedure was repeated at least a dozen times during the day, and with each hand over the story of the Tigers' conquest of the spider was embellished. Eventually, night fell, and the three travelers spent the dark hours under a rock with Tiger Fifteen supposedly standing guard, but mostly snoring lustily through the night.

Late next morning they reached the dark waters of Cruel Creek. The Tigers had found a tree fallen across the stream and had mounted a guard at either end to ensure they would maintain control of the bridge. The three travelers were escorted across the log by three Tigers who sang heartily about the conquest of a dozen spiders by their brave comrades. On the other side, Wiseria and company took advantage of the creek water, as much as ants have an aversion to water, to remove the last traces of the green slime of the spider. A short while later they came to the far edge of the Dark Country, and the last Tiger escort bade them farewell. Wiseria looked back and realized that they had seen nothing throughout their journey through the Dark Country of the mysterious Dragon ants. One day she must mount an expedition to visit them.

They were now in an open grass field quite close to the lake. The moist leaf-strewn path of the forest had given way to a sandy track. Keeping a wary eye cocked against possible attack in this open space, they climbed to the top of a small hill and looked down on an incredible sight. They were only a few yards from the water of the lake, and just below was a patch of sand about six feet long and four feet wide. It was packed with thousands of golden Sugar ants lying around baking in the sun. The three visitors from the north could not believe their eyes. Worker ants are of course entitled to snatch a few moments of relaxation from time to time, but to see a whole mass doing nothing but sunbathing was unbelievable. As they looked more closely, they noticed several large black beetles spread around the sand patch. The ants had built a leafy canopy over each beetle to protect it from the sun. The beetles seemed to be the focus of much attention, for the Sugar ants were coming up to each in a continuous stream. Every ant would stroke the beetle's head, kiss it on the mouth, then stagger away and quite contentedly flop down on the beach.

Even more astonishing and terrifying, several birds were strutting around unmolested in the midst of all this activity, contentedly eating the fattest, juiciest ants they could find.

"Waal, howdy, doody, doo. We don't see a lot of tourists around these parts. Come and join the beach party."

All three northern ants turned as one to find themselves face to face with a large overweight Sugar ant, who was waving her antennae at them in very friendly fashion.

"Ah, thank you," replied Wiseria, "but we're on our way to meet the President. Could you perhaps show us the path? We are expected."

"Waal, waal, waal! Quite the big time visit, is it? Going to meet the Prez, are you? Waal, you just sashay along down the road a piece and you'll come to the Gold House. That's where she hangs out. Tell her Inebria sent you. You'll be given a grand welcome. Bye now."

The Sugar ant turned to head toward the beach. Roanda couldn't stand it. She called after her: "Inebria, be careful! There are birds eating ants on the beach."

Inebria turned. "Birds?" she asked. "What are birds, honey? Just messengers from Nirvana. When you gotta go, you gotta go." She continued her unsteady path towards the beach. Wiseria and her friends got out of there as fast as they could.

Ten minutes later they came on a most different scene. Just in front of them they could see a low golden dome of an ants nest. The path opened out into a small square in front of the dome. The square was lined with Sugar soldiers standing stiffly to attention. Wiseria went up to the captain of the guard.

"Good morning, Captain," she said. "I am Deputy Wiseria of the Antale Federation. You received word through Colonel Observa from Mission Control on Mount Opportunity that we would be coming."

"Why certainly, Ma'am, I recognize you," said the captain, saluting. "I was with the President a few days ago at Centrasia for the send-off for the Explora party. We've been expecting you. Come along, please."

The captain led them across the square, past the stiff, immobile guards, who moved not a muscle as they went by. They entered the mound at ground level, and went upwards along a broad passage, which opened into a large oval office lit by skylights. There they were greeted warmly by President Serenta.

"My dear Wiseria," she said. "How wonderful for you to visit our Sugar Colony. We are most pleased to see you here."

"Thank you, Serenta." replied Wiseria. "Allow me to introduce Roanda, personal aide to President Appesia, and Pacifica, who has been studying under your Colonel Observa at Mission Control."

"Excellent, excellent," Serenta greeted them. "You are all most welcome to the Gold House. How is the Explora mission going, Pacifica?"

"Most successful so far, Ma'am," replied Pacifica. "They made good initial progress. We have been on the road ourselves for the past two days, so I expect your office has more up to date information."

"Yes, yes, I expect so," said the President. "Now tell me, how long can you stay and what would you like to see?"

"We can stay just one day," said Wiseria. "I hope that you and I might have some time to discuss the future of the Federation."

"But of course. We can do that over dinner this evening. Let me show you around the colony, then you can rest before dinner."

Serenta had a map of the colony etched into a leafy parchment on the wall of her office. It was really quite enormous. It consisted of fifty nests spread over an area of five acres. All nests were connected by long underground passages. One nest in particular stood apart from the rest. It was down by the lake, facing the land bridge that gave the Acid ants access to the shore from their islands on the lake. Wiseria mentally noted that she would like to see that nest more closely when they left tomorrow to visit the Acid Ant Colony. For now, however, Serenta had other things to show them.

Most notable were the sugar plantations. These were in the heart of the colony around a nest called Torida. The set-up was ingenious. The worker ants nourished the sugar beet plants on the surface with compost they ground up with their teeth. Underground they had created large storage caverns and elaborate passage ways that allowed them to snip off the succulent sugar beet, which was about half the size of an ant, when it was ready for harvest. The beets were then stored in the caverns until needed. This was their staple diet, but in addition they had a wide range of other vegetable and meat products. There was no shortage of food in the Sugar Ant Colony.

Serenta also proudly showed them through some of their industrial and research facilities in nests toward the back of the colony near the Rim. They had an active chemical industry focused on food supplements and somehow connected with research going on in another nest that was heavily guarded and that Serenta chose not to show them. The facilities for caring for and raising the young through egg, larva, and pupal stage were clean and very efficient. The learning chambers where the young ants were taken after birth for instruction and socialization were well-lighted, cheerful spaces always near the top of the mound. Occasionally the visitors thought they sensed the presence of something like the black beetles they saw on the beach, but they were quickly whisked away from such encounters. When Roanda asked about the beach party, the subject was immediately dismissed. This was something the Sugar ant establishment did not want to talk about.

They dined that evening with Serenta and some of her officials in one end of the oval office on sugar beet, fresh grass shoots and caterpillar. It was very friendly and hospitable. When Wiseria raised the topic of the Federation, Serenta expressed her support in principle, but pointed out that there seemed little advantage to the Sugars for a more formal association, seeing that they were so far away from the more complicated intercolonial issues of the fourth quadrant. Concerning relations with the Acids and the Salts in their own quadrant, she expressed similar isolationist views as Observa had outlined to Wiseria on Mount Opportunity. The Sugars obviously considered that they were a world unto themselves where they were doing very nicely.

Wiseria and her companions left the Sugar Ant Colony the next morning. At Wiseria's request they went by way of the nest at the lake. It was called Portal and was connected to the main colony by a broad tunnel wide enough for three ants to move abreast. It was fundamentally a military establishment, built in a strategic position to remind the Acid ants that their powerful neighbors were on guard. In actuality, though the nest was well-equipped, Wiseria thought it lacked somewhat in discipline and the officers were over confident.

From Portal it was about fifty yards to the land bridge leading out to the islands of the Acids. Their reception at the entrance was as rigid as it had been casual with the Sugars. Ten vermilion-colored Acid guards slow-stepped their way in front of them, and another ten slow-stepped behind. The bridge was only about a foot wide. It was a natural land mass, but had been heavily reinforced by the ants over the years. It ran fifteen yards out to the main island of Omaka. There was very little to see as they arrived, for the Acids had built their cities mainly underground and used the excavated material to build up the land bridge. The visitors were taken directly to the deep underground quarters of the leader of the Acids, General Intrepida.

The chamber was pitch black, so the conversation was carried on through sensing without sight. The visitors knew immediately they were in a strict military presence.

"Your request to visit our colony has been granted, Madame Deputy," said Intrepida. "What is it you wish to know and see?"

"I am carrying the greetings of President Appesia, and the express hopes of all of us who are formally joined in federation that the Acid Ant Colony would consent to participate more fully." Wiseria chose her words very carefully.

"We see no advantage to that at the moment," replied Intrepida. "What else?"

"We believe there is great opportunity for expanded trade among the colonies," Wiseria tried again. "Surely that would be an advantage to you as an island colony."

"Don't presume to judge our limitations, Madame. When we decide we need expanded capability, we shall act accordingly. I suggest you avail yourself of the opportunity while you are here to see how extraordinarily well developed we are on our island colony, as you put it."

There was more, but none of it any better, and Wiseria resigned herself to at least getting a better understanding of the Acids. They did not meet Intrepida again. They were shown around the colony by her deputy, Colonel Sota, and when they were leaving the next day Sota delivered a perfunctory farewell message from her commander.

What they saw in the colony was a hard-working, determined, well-organized operation. There was no down time. Activity seemed to be going on all day and all night with shifts of workers replacing one another on regular schedules. It was a bare-bones, no frills community. Soldier ants were everywhere on hand to keep the workers moving. There was no playing, no amusement, no relaxation—only work.

The colony consisted of five large islands, all approximately twenty square yards in area and connected by natural and constructed bridges. There was a sixth smaller island, about half the size of the others. They were not shown on to it, but at the nearest point Pacifica suddenly felt uncomfortable. She whispered to Wiseria.

"Ma'am, there's something strange going on over there," she said. "I don't know what it is, but I'm picking up unusual vibrations. Can you feel them?"

"No, not really," replied Wiseria. She called to Sota. "Colonel, I notice a smaller island over there. Can you tell us about it?"

"Uninhabited," replied Sota. "There's nothing to see there."

"That's a damned lie," Pacifica said to herself.

They spent the night in sparse quarters on the main island of Omaka. Their dinner consisted of something resembling squashed seaweed. Next morning they declined breakfast and left early for the territory of the Salts.

They were now making their way into the south east corner of Antale. The territory here was open and grassy. It was well populated with ants' nests, but they all seemed rather independent and socially isolated from one another. There was plenty of activity along the path, ants going about their business of foraging, having occasional disputes, but mostly keeping out of each other's way. No one paid much attention to the travelers, other than to look at them curiously, then hurry past. From time to time Wiseria would ask directions, but when the local ants heard that they were going to the colony of the Salts, all they got was a hasty waving of forelegs and antennae in a south-easterly direction, and the ant would hurry on.

"They seem to be afraid of something," Roanda observed after several episodes like this. "I wonder what it is."

A short way further on they began to find out.

They were coming in close towards the Rim and the open grass country had given way to rocky terrain. They topped a rise, went down into a narrow gorge, then suddenly found themselves face to face with a platoon of fierce looking ants. They were all of a kind, not large, but tough featured with big heads and a mottled grey and brown body. One of them, obviously the leader, stepped out in front, planted her six legs firmly to the ground and shouted, "Halt!"

Everyone stopped: the platoon behind her, and the three travelers facing her. "You three ants. Who are you and where are you going?" she demanded.

"I am Wiseria, Deputy Head of the Federation of Antale, and these are my companions. We are traveling to meet President Bravada of the Salt Ant Colony."

"And I'm the mother of the Queen on the way to my summer palace," retorted the platoon leader, sarcastically. "You are under arrest!"

"For what reason?" demanded Wiseria.

"I don't need a reason," replied the other.

"Are you a Salt? Will you take us to the President?"

"No, I'm a Pepper, and I'm taking you to prison."

"You can't do that," said Wiseria, forcefully. "I told you who I am. I expect and demand safe conduct through your country."

"No one demands anything of Bluffasta," shouted the big-headed ant. "You want to leg wrestle?"

"What did you say?"

"I said, do you want to leg wrestle? You beat me at leg wrestling and I'll take you to the President."

This sudden turn of events obviously pleased the platoon of mottled ants, who all began to cheer. Wiseria was at her wits end. She had never encountered anything like this before.

"I'll wrestle you," said Pacifica.

"Pacifica, don't. You can't," Wiseria protested.

"Stand aside, old mother," shouted Bluffasta. "I'll tie your little white friend up in knots."

With that Bluffasta reared up on her two back legs and waved the other four menacingly at Pacifica. The latter stepped forward and deftly whipped one of her opponent's back legs out from under her. Bluffasta crashed to the ground.

"Fall one to us!" shouted Roanda. "Good work, Pacifica. You've got her measure."

Wiseria looked on, not knowing what to make of this new side she was seeing of her two companions.

Bluffasta came roaring back to the attack. This time she put her big head down and charged. Pacifica skipped nimbly aside and tripped the other up. Bluffasta was down again.

"Fall two!" cried Roanda.

The ant platoon howled in despair. Bluffasta got up, gnashing her mandibles, and began to circle Pacifica. They kept this up for almost a minute, then Pacifica tripped over a stone and Bluffasta, seeing her chance, rushed in, grabbed her smaller opponent around the waist, and dumped her heavily on the ground.

"Fall one!" shouted the ant platoon, uproariously.

Pacifica got groggily up, but before she had a chance to set herself, Bluffasta rushed in, leapt onto her back and rolled her over.

"Fall two!" The platoon was delirious. Roanda groaned.

Pacifica got up again, more carefully this time. She reared up leg to leg with her opponent and they locked in combat. Twelve legs and two twisting abdomens wrestled in the dust. They tumbled over and over, neither one giving the other an inch. The platoon broke rank and cheered their leader on. Roanda danced around shouting encouragement to Pacifica. And the battle raged furiously.

"Enough!" This was a fierce shout of authority. Wiseria had stepped in and with all her strength wrapped her forelegs around the heads of the other two, pulling them together, until all three ant heads pressed against one another.

"You've fought well, both of you," Wiseria panted. "Now declare a truce."

Pacifica and Bluffasta looked each other in the eye, then both let go. Wiseria stepped back. Bluffasta dusted herself off.

"By the force, you fight good, little white ant," she exclaimed. "You've earned your passage. Come on then, all of you. You, too, old black mother. We'll take you to the Salts."

Bluffasta insisted that Pacifica walk beside her at the head of the platoon as they set off down the path.

"I wonder where she learned to fight like that," Wiseria whispered to Roanda.

"In school," Roanda replied. "She was a wrestling champion. She told me about it. It's a good thing Bluffasta didn't know."

They reached the entrance to the Salt Ant Colony about thirty minutes later. Bluffasta and her troop handed them over to the Salt guards. It turned out that the Peppers, which was just a small colony of a few nests, worked as a kind of independent police force for the Salts. They were a rather swashbuckling race of daredevils with no particular allegiance to anyone other than themselves. Pacifica had made a good friend in Bluffasta, which would later prove most fortuitous.

The visit to the Salt colony was both revealing and perplexing. President Bravada was friendly, but stern. Everything in the colony seemed much like that, too. There was something mysterious about the place. Whereas the Sugars were open and flamboyant, and the Acids hard-working and secretive, the Salts had an air of ruthless determination about them. They were a powerful force of forty or more nests spread along the foot of the Rim. The visitors were shown only a few of the mounds at the front. Wiseria had a sense that there were things going on at the back of the colony that Bravada didn't want her to know about.

But the Salts were good hosts for all of that. They kept a good table, so to speak, though ants, of course, don't dine at a table. The evening meal of red meat, vegetable roots, and mash was eaten outdoors, with much singing and circle dancing lasting well into the night.

Bravada asked Wiseria probing questions about what she had found in the colonies of the Sugars and the Acids, but she was not very forthcoming about her own colony. She was obviously proud of the discipline and endurance of her soldiers and her workers. The Salts were themselves a small federation of many different nests that Bravada had brought under central control. The ants around her enjoyed considerable power and privileges from their positions. Wiseria was less confident that as much could be said for the rest of the population. Bravada was content to be involved with Wiseria's Federation in a token way, but had no interest in more formal association.

When Wiseria and her party left the next day to make their way north back to their own quadrant, the old, experienced diplomat could not help feeling disappointed at the outcome of her mission to the southern shores of Lake Miasma. While there was no obvious aggression here, such as they had experienced with the Red ants in the north, there was no desire either for friendship or cooperation. Remembering her emotional view of Antale from the top of Mount Opportunity, Wiseria wondered what more would have to happen before the ant colonies would begin to see themselves as one world.

CHAPTER 3

Worthless Words of Honor

Wiseria was now anxious to get back to her own colony. She had been away for almost a week. When she left, the nest was just emerging from hibernation. With the good weather, everything would now be in full swing, so there were many administrative details for an ant leader to attend to. It was time to return home.

The path took them north along the shores of Lake Miasma. Away to the north-east were the colonies of the Greens and the Browns. Both of them had joined the Federation last year, but of late they were coming under the influence of the more militant Reds. Wiseria knew that she should pay them a visit, too, but there would not be time on this journey. Perhaps in a week or two she could arrange it.

Pacifica and Roanda were in good spirits this morning, anticipating the return to their nests, where they would have more than enough stories to tell of their adventures. All three ants were stepping along briskly, aiming to be home by nightfall. It was then that they heard a curious song.

"Once a jolly doodong sat on a dilly dang
Down by the shores of old Duranlea.
And she sang as she sat and waited for her grilly groll,
'You'll come a digging, my darling, with me.
Digging, my darling, digging, my darling,
You'll come a digging, my darling, with me.'
And she sang as she sat and waited for her grilly groll,
'You'll come a digging, my darling, with me!'"

The song went round and round in a lusty chorus of ant trills, the singers obviously in good spirits and enjoying themselves. Wiseria and her companions stopped still in their tracks, looked at one another, then went over to the side of the path by the lake to see who the singers were. They looked down from an embankment about three feet high and some ten yards from the shore of the lake. Below, they saw a single, large, flat-topped mound filling most of the space between the path and the lake. That was strange enough, because ants don't normally build their mounds with flat tops. Even more strange, however, was the water-filled ditch surrounding the mound, which had been dug in such a way that the water from the lake drained into it, creating a moat. The mound was a veritable red-earth castle, its sheer sides rising straight up to a height of about two feet above the water in the moat.

The singing was coming from a party of dusky brown worker ants, carrying out repair work to the side of the mound. There must have been more than a hundred of them, all working in unison, digging lustily in the red earth as they sang.

"And she sang as she sat and waited for her grilly groll,
'You'll come a digging, my darling, with me!'"

"Hello there, down under," called Wiseria. "You're all in fine voice this morning."

The singing stopped. All ants turned as one and looked up at the three travelers on the path above. One of them, apparently the foreant, replied.

"Well, good day, mates," she shouted. "What's the news?"

"About what?" asked Wiseria.

"About the world," said the other. "We don't hear much down here."

"The world could be better. I am Wiseria, Deputy Head of the Federation of Antale. We need all ant colonies to join together in cooperation."

"Yeah, well I don't know about that, matey. We're all diggers here, and we've dug ourselves a moat for protection. Seems to be the best bet with the kind of neighbors we've got."

"But that's no solution. We can't all live behind moats. We have to learn to work together. There's so much to share and trade."

"You should talk to our guv'nor about that. She likes to gad about and gab. The rest of us diggers just keep our heads down and do our jobs."

"You seem to enjoy doing it."

"That's the truth, matey. What's the point of moochin' around like some half dead dodo?"

"You know," Wiseria laughed, "I don't understand half of what you say."

"That's all right, mate. You're a pretty strange looking crew yourself."

"What's that song you were singing?" asked Roanda.

"That's the 'Diggers Song.' We made it up."

"What's a grilly groll?" asked Pacifica, laughing.

"It's a grilly groll. A good mate."

"Well, I think all you diggers are a bunch of grilly grolls." Wiseria joined the fun.

"Good on yer, mate!" all the diggers shouted.

"I tell you what," the foreant said, "if you ever need help straightening out the world, just call on us diggers. We'll fix it for you."

"I'll remember that," said Wiseria. "Who should I ask for?"

"Wacka Wacka," replied the other.

"Goodbye, Wacka Wacka," said Wiseria.

"Ta, ta, mates. And don't step in any dilly dangs."

The diggers went back to digging and singing, and the travelers continued on their way. The good cheer of the Digger ants stayed with them throughout the day as they trudged homeward.

It was just an hour before sundown when everything changed. They were now very close to the White Ant Colony where Pacifica would leave them and head off to her own nest, called Buranda. There was a strange stillness all around. The worker ants who should have been on the path were nowhere to be seen. Almost as one the three companions sensed an agonized trembling in the air. Pacifica climbed up on a rock and looked east towards her home.

"Oh, no!" she cried. "Something's happened."

"What is it?" asked Wiseria.

Roanda had climbed up beside Pacifica. "Good grief!" she exclaimed. "They must have been attacked."

"Roanda! Pacifica!" Wiseria cried out. "What is it? What can you see?"

"There are thousands of ants on the move," replied Roanda. "They've been routed out of their nests. They're carrying cocoons and pupae with them. We've got to go over there and help. Come on, Pacifica."

Without waiting for Wiseria the two young ants scuttled away down the other side of the rock. Wiseria climbed up to look. What she saw filled her with rage and despair. White ants by the thousands were pouring along a broad trail that connected the many nests of the White Ant Colony. All of them were carrying something: eggs, larvae, cocoons, pupae, food, other ants, whatever. The largest stream was heading towards the big mound of Centrasia, about fifty yards away. Other streams were peeling off and heading towards some smaller mounds. All were seeking refuge for their precious burdens. Wiseria had seen all this before—too many times! Something had routed the ants out of their nests. It had to be a vicious attack for them to abandon their homes and take their young. Wiseria knew she could do nothing to help down amidst all the confusion. She decided to head for Centrasia to find President Appesia.

Meanwhile, down among the ant throng, Pacifica and Roanda soon became separated. It was absolute pandemonium. All of the fleeing ants were trembling with fear and terror. Pacifica could find no one coherent enough to tell her what had happened. She tried to make her way towards her home nest, but found herself going against the flood and getting bumped and pushed aside.

She stumbled into an ant carrying a large grass seed. The ant dropped her burden in the collision.

"Look out! Be careful! Get out of the way!" the ant screamed at her.

"What's going on?" asked Pacifica. "I've been away. I don't know what's happened."

"The Red devils! The Red devils!" cried the other ant. "They've attacked our nests."

"How many nests?" asked Pacifica.

"I don't know. At least three."

"My home is Buranda. I've got to go there."

"It's gone! It's gone! You can't go there. The Red devils are swarming all over it. You better help here. That's more useful. I must go on."

Pacifica stood dumbfounded for a moment, not believing what she had just heard. Then she turned off the path and began scrambling across country towards Buranda.

Fifty yards away Wiseria came onto the courtyard of Centrasia just as the first wave of fleeing ants was reaching it. Workers were rushing out of the mound to help. Soon everything would be mass confusion on the courtyard. To make matters worse scavenging birds were swooping in on the helpless ants and taking a heavy toll. Wiseria fought her way over to the main entrance, hoping to find Appesia inside. At the opening she recognized the captain of the guard.

"Captain," said Wiseria, "where's the President?"

"In the transmission room, Ma'am," replied the captain.

"Take me to her, please."

The captain seemed uncertain.

"At once," commanded Wiseria. "I must speak to her."

The captain came to a decision. "Follow, me, Ma'am," she said.

They entered the mound and climbed up a steep passage to the top. They came out into a small chamber. It was dark, but Wiseria sensed Appesia's presence with a few others.

"Deputy Wiseria is here to see you, Ma'am," announced the captain.

Appesia turned. Wiseria embraced her and immediately sensed her anguish and despair.

"Wiseria, I'm glad you're back," said the President.

"Tell me what's happened," said Wiseria. "Was it Aggressa?"

"How did you know? Yes, the Red ants attacked three of our outside nests just over an hour ago. I've already protested and spoken to Aggressa directly by transmission. She claims that our ants provoked it. I know that's a lie. But she seems ready to negotiate a settlement. I've decided to go over to see her first thing in the morning and work out the terms of a binding peace treaty."

"What!" exclaimed Wiseria. "You're the victim, Appesia. She's the aggressor. You can't negotiate with her from a position of weakness."

"It's my decision, Wiseria. We don't want this to escalate. I've also spoken to the Heads of all the other federated colonies. I've called an emergency meeting of the Federation for tomorrow afternoon. I'll be back from the Red Ant Colony by then. I plan to have an agreement with the Reds for ratification by the Federation. That will put a stop to this kind of thing forever."

"How much do you plan to give away to try to buy peace with a bully?" Wiseria's tone was harsh. Then she softened a little. "I'm sorry, Appesia. I know this is a terrible time for you. But you have to think this through. Aggressa won't stop here. We know her style."

"Yes, and I know your style for fighting, too, Wiseria." Appesia was distraught, almost hysterical. "The fighting has to stop," she continued. "I am resolved. You'll have your chance to speak in council tomorrow afternoon. By then you'll see what diplomacy can bring."

"All right," said Wiseria, "But Appesia, please be careful. Take a good guard with you. You're not just dealing with an adversary, but a ruthless, blood-lusting butcher. I'm going back to my own colony now. I will be back tomorrow afternoon for the meeting. Goodbye and take care, old friend."

Wiseria turned and left. At the entrance she met Roanda, who was just arriving.

"Roanda," said Wiseria. "Thank goodness you're all right. Where's Pacifica?"

"I don't know. We got separated. It's just terrible out there. But everyone's doing the best they can. It will be dark soon, so we'll have cover to get the young ones safely settled in their nests."

"You should be with the President, Roanda. She needs you. She's planning to go to Aggressa's head-quarters tomorrow morning. Stay with her and keep her safe. I'm returning to Blackhall now."

Wiseria hurried off, taking a few White guards with her as an escort. As she left the confusion of the courtyard, she thought of the contrast with the scene of celebration when Explora's expedition had set off just over a week ago. Explora? How was she doing out there on the Rim? Wiseria had been out of touch for a few days. And now this had happened. She had hoped to send Explora good news from home. How soon everything could change!

It was dark when Wiseria arrived home. Her nest was called Blackhall, capital of the prosperous Black Ant Colony. She went immediately to her quarters where her assistants were delighted and relieved to see her. They were used to her independence of movement, but worried about her safety all the same. News of the attack on the White ants had preceded her, and though everything was peaceful in the colony, apprehension had mounted.

"I want an immediate meeting of the governing council," Wiseria announced. "Please get word to all members to meet me in the House of Ants within the hour."

The governing chamber was an old and venerated hall in the middle of the mound. It was large enough to accommodate four hundred delegates, ten from each of the forty nests that made up the colony. As she waited for the members to arrive, Wiseria chatted with the first comers. None of them could remember an emergency so pressing that all members were called out for an evening session of the assembly.

When all of the councilors had taken their places, and the air in the hall was heavy with the close press of the bodies and the seriousness of the moment, Wiseria spoke solemnly to them:

"My dear colleagues, thank you for responding so promptly to my call. As dark as is the night through which you have traveled to be here, it is no less dark than the situation which faces us. At approximately 1800 hours this afternoon, the brigands of the Red Ant Colony struck without provocation or warning against our sister Whites, and savagely attacked and occupied three of their nests on their eastern perimeter. As we meet, many thousands of our sisters are struggling to save their young ones without knowing how many thousands more were slaughtered in the brutal attack. But for location, it may well have been our nests and our sisters who suffered such a pernicious onslaught. The red aggressor knows no bounds to her appetite. She is embarked, I fear, on a terrible adventure that can bring no comfort to any of us. I have spoken to President Appesia, who is persuaded in her mind to seek accommodation with the tyrant. I understand the principles behind such thinking, but I disagree with the strategy, and have told her so. I fear that unless we in the free colonies prepare ourselves against aggression from a hostile neighbor, before the summer is out we shall find her incursions crossing the water of Copper Creek into our territory."

Murmurs of "Shame!" and "Never!" ran through the assembly. Wiseria continued:

"No one has fought harder than I to create the Federated Colonies of Antale. Such progress as we have made is now in peril. I believe that the Greens and Browns are ready to slip the traces and join with the Reds in a hostile alliance, if they perceive for a moment that it is to their advantage to do so. That would leave only ourselves, the Whites and the Yellows in formal association. I have just returned from visiting the Sugars and the Acids and the Salts in quadrant three, and find no desire there to join our coalition. If we are to maintain a Federation worthy of the name, we must stand boldly now against the Red aggression. I go tomorrow to a meeting of the Federation and I seek your endorsement of this stand."

Wiseria paused. As one, the Black assembly cried out, "Agreed!" Wiseria waited for silence.

"Thank you, dear friends. Your support gives me the strength I need. Now I ask one thing more. At first light tomorrow, call on your generals in each of your nests to put their troops on alert. In particular, form a strong line of defense along our side of Copper Creek, so that the Red devil might see our preparations, and know that to provoke us will mean a terrible retaliation. We stand steadfast for peace, but if we must fight to preserve it, no one will ever say we were not prepared to do so. Go in courage, my sisters. We will prevail."

The assembly adjourned; the council members returned to their nests; and Wiseria retired to her chambers. Was she right, she asked herself, in taking such a war-like stance when her greatest desire was to bring peace to the land? She knew she was. It was the times in which she lived. By standing up to aggression now she might create the opportunity for Pacifica's generation to forge the peace. The thought reminded her of the precious moment the two had shared on the top of Mount Opportunity. That already seemed so long ago. And where was her young friend now? With all her heart, Wiseria wished for Pacifica's safety.

It was well she did not know. As Wiseria fell into a troubled sleep in her room, Pacifica was hiding in the grass on the outskirts of her own nest, keeping an all night vigil, waiting for the dawn. She had arrived there after a hard struggle across difficult terrain, just as darkness was settling over Buranda. On the surface the nest seemed undisturbed, but it was strangely quiet. Neither friend nor foe was to be seen. Pacifica decided to stay concealed for the night on a grassy knoll, just to the south of the nest. Tomorrow she might have a clearer idea of what was to be done.

The night passed slowly. She had become cold and sluggish in the first light of early morning, when, through her stupor, she became aware of a commotion down at the nest. She forced herself awake. The low symmetrical mound looked peaceful enough, but at its base she saw something that made her heart leap. A White ant had emerged from the nest, running hard across the open courtyard surrounding the mound. She was carrying a cocoon, fleeing for safety with her precious burden. Close behind a Red ant soldier was in hot pursuit. Weighed down with her load, the White had no chance to outstrip the Red. Pacifica did not hesitate. She scampered along the knoll until she was immediately above the running pair as they reached the edge of the grass. The Red ant was lunging for its victim's hind quarters when Pacifica launched herself into the air and crashed down on top of the soldier.

"Run, sister, run!" shouted Pacifica to the White ant as she tumbled in the dust with the other. Pacifica never saw the White ant again. Her own safety was now the problem.

The Red soldier came to her feet and lunged in for the attack. Pacifica stepped nimbly aside, then made to run in the opposite direction, to lead the soldier away from the fleeing White. This took Pacifica toward the nest. Knowing the danger, she swerved to run for the grass, but before covering a hundred paces came face to face with a party of six Red soldiers. She stopped, and moments later felt the pain in her back, as she was seized from behind in the jaws of the first soldier. Paralyzed, she waited for the next blow that would end her life.

"Hold off!" This was a command from one of the group of soldiers. "Bring her into the nest and put her to work with the rest of the slaves." Limping painfully, Pacifica was half pushed, half dragged by her captors, a prisoner in her own home.

At the same time, only twenty yards away on a different path, Appesia and her party were making their way toward the Red Ant Colony. Appesia had not slept well as she wrestled in her mind with the agonizing choices facing her. She was seeking peace with honor, but was mindful of Wiseria's warnings that to Aggressa such ideas had no meaning. But she must try. The alternative could be a blood bath that would envelop all Antale.

Aggressa's home nest was deep inside Red ant territory. As they came closer, they were met by a Red platoon. No pleasantries were exchanged between the two sides. The Reds positioned a troop in front and behind the White party, and escorted them down the path. Soon they were in sight of the nest, a nondescript collection of earth and twigs rising about eighteen inches above the ground. The Red ants were not great architects or artisans. Functionality was their credo. Appesia shuddered to think of what might happen to her magnificent city of Centrasia if it ever fell into the hands of such functionaries.

Just then she noted some activity on the path ahead. She spoke to Roanda who was at her side.

"Roanda, look there," said Appesia. "Is that a party of Green ants coming out of the nest?"

"I believe you're right, Ma'am," replied Roanda, "they seem to be in rather a hurry."

"Now, look, there's a party of Browns," exclaimed Appesia. "What's going on here?"

The captain of the Red guard at the head of Appesia's group suddenly realized she had blundered by arriving too soon. She called a halt and tried to use her troop to obscure the White's view of the path ahead.

"Captain," demanded Appesia, "why are we stopping?"

"A technicality," replied the captain. "We must pause a moment." Appesia argued with the captain and tried to move ahead. The Red troop would not budge, until suddenly the captain relented and said they could continue. By then Appesia and Roanda could see that the Green and the Brown parties had disappeared. At the entrance to the mound Appesia called a halt of her own.

"Captain," she said, "would you please take word to your Supreme Commander that I will meet with her out here."

"Those are not my orders," replied the captain. "I am to take you inside."

"I don't care what your orders are," Appesia retorted testily. "I want you to take my message to your Commander."

The captain was obviously confused. Appesia turned her back on the other and walked to the rear of her party to rest in the shade of a rock. Finally, the captain made up her mind and went inside the mound.

A full ten minutes passed. Appesia remained immobile and silent, her White guards gathered around her, returning scowl for scowl with their Red counterparts. Finally, some activity appeared at the entrance to the mound. Aggressa's personal guard came slow-stepping out, intoning the same grinding chant as when Aggressa had made her dramatic entry at the Explora celebrations at Centrasia. The guard halted, formed two ranks and saluted stiffly as a swaggering Aggressa emerged. Appesia's party similarly created an honor guard for their leader, and the two Heads of Colonies met face to face.

Aggressa did away with any pleasantries.

"You offend me, Appesia, by not coming to meet me in my quarters."

"You are not one to complain of offence, Aggressa, when your troops occupy three of my nests."

"They provoked our anger by continually straying into our territory."

"That is not true, but I have not come to argue the issue." Appesia sought to gain a vantage point. "Our White troops are now on full alert and I have an emergency meeting of the Federation this afternoon. I expect all members' unqualified condemnation of your actions and their full support in resisting further aggression. I demand your withdrawal from the nests you have occupied and the release of all White ant hostages you are holding inside. If you agree to that, I will undertake to convince the Federation not to take any retaliatory measures against you."

Aggressa burst out laughing.

"My dear President," she said, contemptuously, "I wonder what retaliation you think the Federation might have the stomach to mount against us. You would find it inconvenient to the life of grace and ease you seem to prefer on your rich lands. However, we do not intend to be unreasonable about this. As I said, we acted only out of provocation. If we can have your assurances that there will be no retaliation and no further provocation, then you have my word of honor that we will be peaceful neighbors."

"And you will withdraw from the occupied nests?"

"Now that requires some further consideration."

"It is an unconditional requirement on our part."

"Oh, I see. Unconditional, is it?" Aggressa minced her mandibles. "All right, I tell you what. You have your meeting of the Federation, and if you can bring us assurances of a process for meeting our needs for better shared access to common territory, then we will withdraw from your nests."

"Do I have your word of honor on that?" asked Appesia.

"Absolutely," replied Aggressa.

"Very well then, Aggressa. I believe this meeting has achieved its purpose. I shall take your assurances to the Federation. I am sure you can expect a favorable response."

Without further ceremony, Appesia and her party withdrew. Four hours later she was greeting the Heads of the federated colonies in the large conference chamber of Centrasia. President Antonia from the Yellow Ant Colony was the first to arrive with her delegation. They had the farthest to travel from the sweeping curve of Copper Creek where it came down from the Rim. Their path had taken them close to Red ant territory. Antonia remarked that she had seen no evidence of Red soldiers along the path, which was unusual and possibly a good sign. Wiseria was next to arrive. She was relieved to see Appesia safely returned from her meeting with Aggressa. The three leaders waited for Barbaria and Narcissa, Heads respectively of the Green and the Brown Colonies. A full two hours passed before these two finally came into the room together.

"We are sorry to be late," apologized Barbaria.

"Difficult affairs of state in these troubled times, you know," said Narcissa.

"You are all welcome," Appesia formally greeted everyone. "I now declare this emergency meeting of the Federation in session.

"You are all aware of the brutal and unprovoked attack on three of our White ant nests by soldiers of the Red Ant Colony. This has caused grievous death and suffering to thousands of my sisters. I immediately protested to Supreme Commander Aggressa. Rather than retaliating in like fashion, I chose this morning to meet with Aggressa to find another solution to this crime. Understanding that none of the rest of you has been in touch with her on this matter, I am ready to report to the Federation."

Appesia paused. Roanda, who was nearby, understood what her leader was doing. She was providing an opportunity for Narcissa and Barbaria to explain the presence of their delegations at the Red Ant Colony this morning. Neither of them said a word. Appesia continued:

"I informed Aggressa of our resolute condemnation of her action and demanded withdrawal of her troops from White nests. She has given me her word of honor to do this. She seeks only some mechanism to allow her colony more access to common territory. I am sure we can readily work this out and therefore believe we have a bloodless and speedy resolution to this matter."

"Well done, Appesia," declared Barbaria.

"You have acted with dignity and honor and preserved peace," announced Narcissa.

"Well, I am greatly relieved to know we have a workable solution," said Antonia. "My colony certainly did not want to go to war."

Wiseria alone remained silent.

"If we are agreed that there is no need for us to mount a retaliatory attack against the Reds," Appesia continued, "I would like to make an announcement to my sisters. There is great fear throughout the colony which I would like to put at ease."

"You had best be sure the ant will not sting again before you lower your guard." Wiseria had finally spoken.

"We have her word of honor," said Appesia.

"And you still have her troops in your nests," replied Wiseria.

"Damn it!" Appesia exploded. "Do you think I don't know that? Someone needs to take the high ground here. How can we expect her to move if we don't show some moral leadership of our own? I would like to make an announcement to my sisters. Do I have the Federation's agreement to do so?"

Wiseria did not object further, and the others all agreed. Appesia sent word for all ants who could be spared from their duties to assemble on the courtyard outside the mound. As the leaders waited, Wiseria had a word to Antonia.

"My troops are on full alert. I received word from our observation points before I came here, that there was some movement of Red troops in the vicinity of your colony. Do you know of that?"

"No, just the opposite," replied Antonia. "Everything seemed to be remarkably quiet."

"They may have moved into position overnight and be lying low. Now let me ask you another thing. Why do you think Barbaria and Narcissa were late for the meeting?"

"You heard their explanation. It could happen to any of us."

"Yes, and it could have been intentional to delay the meeting."

Roanda, who had been listening, joined the conversation.

"I don't know that the President told you," she said, "but when we got to the Red Ant Colony this morning, we saw Green and Brown delegations leaving."

"No, I didn't know," exclaimed Wiseria. "Now I am concerned."

At that moment Appesia called all of them to join her on the courtyard. It was late afternoon. The sun's rays cast long shadows across the broad expanse of open ground as thousands of ants were pouring out of Centrasia. Thousands more arrived continuously from other nests until the whole space was a seething mass of expectancy, looking up towards President Appesia and the other Heads of Colonies. Appesia spoke to them from a small platform one third of the way up the mound.

"My dear sisters," she shouted. "There is always but a short space between the worst of times and the best of times. It was only yesterday at this very hour that a cruel assault was made against our peace, and thousands of our number perished in the treachery. We have acted swiftly to reply; not in like manner to the wickedness wrought against us, but with the dignity and determination that befits our nature. I now can tell you, with all the assurance of my office, that I have this day received commitments from Commander Aggressa of the Red Ant Colony on her personal word of honor, that she will promptly and unconditionally withdraw from our occupied nests."

A first wave of cheering broke out from the multitude, but Appesia waved it down.

"Moreover," she continued, "I and the other leaders of our federated colonies have met in special session, and can now announce to you our firm and unswerving resolve to stand together, to determine an accord that will ensure continuing peace in our time."

A second wave of cheering rolled out. Appesia shouted above it:

"You may now return to your nests secure in the knowledge that your homes and lives are safe, and that a prosperous and wonderful summer lies ahead. Good health and happiness to all of you!"

With that the crowds of ants broke into uncontrollable cheering. A few began their Song of the Nests, then others picked it up, and the air and the bodies danced with the magic of hope in their hearts:

"Ho! Ho! Ho! We go!
Workers of the earth, you know.
Lift your voices high and low.
Happiness and peace to know.
Ho! Ho! Ho! We go!"

Appesia stood proudly waving to the crowds as they marched away. She turned beaming to her companions, and looked directly at Wiseria.

"Now we see the true power of diplomacy and appeasement," she said. "Let us return to our work of high purpose."

At that moment, Roanda, who was standing behind the leaders felt a tug on her shoulder. She turned to see an excited technician from Transmission Central.

"What is it?" asked Roanda.

"Terrible news!" gasped the other. "We've just received a distress transmission from the Yellow Ant Colony. They are under heavy attack by Reds. Every nest is being overrun. They're facing total annihilation."

Roanda's heart sank. She looked at the beaming Appesia and couldn't bring herself to break the news. She turned to Wiseria and told her instead. Wiseria immediately spoke to the other leaders on the platform. Roanda saw Appesia visibly crumble. Antonia, too, staggered at the news. Wiseria ushered them all inside. When they reached the conference chamber, the five leaders all knew that a state of war now existed between the Federation and the Red Ant Colony.

CHAPTER 4

War

THE LEADERS HUDDLED WITH THEIR OFFICIALS IN the conference chamber. Appesia's energy was ebbing away.

"What have I done?" she cried. "I sought to build for peace and all I did was give Aggressa time to strike again. Oh, Antonia, can you forgive me?"

Antonia was still too distraught to answer. Appesia continued: "And my own sisters! I have sent them off cheering for peace when the Reds are probably preparing to strike again."

"That's where we have a window of opportunity." Wiseria had now spoken out. "There are limits on Aggressa's strength. She must have sent a major force west to attack Antonia's colony. If we can cut them off and hold them there, while we mount a counter attack ourselves against her home nests, we may bring her quickly to her knees."

"What are you proposing?" asked Antonia.

"All my Black troops are on alert," said Wiseria. "My colony is safe enough for now across Copper Creek. I propose we send one Black division up to assist your troops, Antonia, then another to combine with the Whites to push directly against the Reds." Wiseria now turned to face the leaders of the Green and Brown colonies. "Barbaria and Narcissa," she said, "If you bring your forces to join with Appesia's to push from the south, then Aggressa will be bottled up, and this will be over in a few days. Will you do that?"

"Well, I don't know that we're prepared for war," said Barbaria.

"Aggressa has not attacked us," added Narcissa.

"The Federation either stands together or we'll fail," Wiseria asserted.

"You can't bully us into this kind of decision," protested Narcissa.

"We have to consult our councils," said Barbaria.

"My colony is being hacked to pieces right now," Antonia shouted. "What is there to consult about?"

"Precisely," said Wiseria. "Look, we all have to get the approval of our councils, but that must not delay our response. I know I can get my council's approval within the hour and our troops will be on the way."

"We can't move that quickly," said Barbaria.

"Then move as quickly as you can," returned Wiseria. "I propose we now adjourn this meeting to return to our colonies. Do you agree, Appesia?"

Throughout the discussion Appesia had sat motionless, head bowed. "Yes, yes," she said in answer to Wiseria's question, then fell silent again.

"All right, then," said Wiseria. "Barbaria and Narcissa, I'll be in touch with you by dawn to know your answer."

The leaders of the Green and Brown colonies hastily withdrew with their delegations.

"I don't think those two are on side," Wiseria said to Antonia and Appesia. "We'll probably have to move without them. Are we three agreed on that?"

"What choice do I have?" asked Antonia. "I need your help right now."

"And you shall have it," said Wiseria. "Appesia, can you get your forces ready to move at dawn? Appesia? Appesia, are you all right?"

"It's no use, Wiseria," Appesia could hardly be heard. "I've got no stomach for this now. Too many ants have already died because of me. I'm handing over to you. The Federation and my colony are in your hands. I would like to leave now. Antonia, I'm so sorry. Goodnight."

Appesia turned and moved slowly out of the chamber. Wiseria spoke to Roanda.

"Stay with her tonight," she said. "We'll discuss this further when she is more herself." Wiseria turned to another White ant, Aristica, Appesia's Chief of Staff. "Aristica, summon all your council members and generals to an immediate meeting here. I am going to Transmission Central to contact my own council. Antonia, why don't you come with me. There may be further word from your colony."

So war had begun in Antale. For Wiseria it was bitter irony. Two years ago she had foreseen the possibility of this and began to work with Appesia, to forge the Federation. Ant attacks on neighbors had always been part of life in Antale, but with growing populations in the colonies and more powerful technology, the potential for something worse was building. Now it was upon them. The Federation that was supposed to prevent it was collapsing, and her old friend had stumbled and fallen as its leader. Wiseria felt strangely alone, but at the same time exhilarated by the work she knew she had to do. This was her hour, as if all her life before had been preparation for this moment.

Events now moved very quickly. From the transmission room in Centrasia Wiseria spoke in coded messages to her governing council in Blackhall. Within the hour the Blacks First Division of ten thousand troops under the command of General Monta was moving out. They had a long way to go, across the land bridge, then a mile north and west along the banks of Copper Creek to the besieged Yellow Ant Colony. In the meantime, the Second Division was forming under General Alena to meet up with the White troops to attack the Red Ant Colony at dawn. Wiseria spent many hours with the White ant governing council and military command. Buoyed up by Appesia's hopes for peace, they had not been ready for war. Many hours of confused activity occupied the night as the generals slowly got their troops into position, and the workers in the nests began to accept that the peace Appesia had promised them had evaporated.

By dawn, however, the Blacks' and Whites' combined divisions were in place. Wiseria was also in constant touch with General Monta and the First Division. They had marched unmolested throughout the night and were now close to the Yellow Ant Colony. Wiseria had, with difficulty, prevailed upon Antonia to stay at Centrasia away from the fighting for now. Her task would be to instill new hope in the colony when it was liberated. Still unknown was the position the Greens and Browns would take. At dawn Wiseria's several messages to Narcissa and Barbaria remained unanswered. This did not look good and prompted Wiseria to dispatch her personal emissary to seek an answer. Whatever the response, the White and Black force must strike against the Reds within the hour. Wiseria was counting on Aggressa's complacency that the Whites would never attack a Red nest because of the sheer ferocity of the Reds as fighters.

After a night of feverish activity, waiting was not easy. It was out of Wiseria's control now. The commanders in the field would give the orders to attack. All Wiseria could do was wait to see if the strategy would work. In Transmission Central with only a few technicians standing by, she had time to think. To think about Appesia, whose condition throughout the night had deteriorated, so that Wiseria now feared her old friend would not recover from the shock of Aggressa's treachery. Time to think of Pacifica and wonder what had happened to the brave young ant. Time to think of Explora and wonder where she was out in the vastness of the Rim. Well, the last, at least, was a question that could be answered. Wiseria instructed the technicians to connect her to Mission Control and within a few minutes she was in touch with Colonel Observa.

"You know about our situation here, Colonel," said Wiseria. "We are now in the darkness before the dawn, militarily as well as physically. I am wondering if you might have some good news for me from Explora."

"I can do better than that, Ma'am." Observa's friendly drawl was itself a comfort to Wiseria. "I am connected to the Commander right now. Let's see if I can patch you through."

There were a few moments of silence, then Wiseria picked up Explora's signal. She could sense the excitement coming from her old friend so far away. Apparently Explora knew nothing of the critical situation facing Wiseria in Centrasia.

"Hello, Wiseria. How wonderful to speak to you tonight of all nights! We've just made a halt from struggling to the top of a mountain range. You'll never believe what we can see in the distance as the sun is coming up behind us. Way out there, probably still three or four night's travel from here, we can see a blue-green haze on the horizon. There's something out there, I'm sure of it. The Rim doesn't just go on forever. The transmission signals are stronger, too. We still don't know what they are, but I'm absolutely sure we're on the edge of a great discovery."

"That's wonderful news, Explora." said Wiseria. "We'll be waiting every day for your reports."

"How is it with you in Antale?"

"We have our challenges as always. But yours is the greater mission. Take care, old friend."

Wiseria spoke again to Observa before she ended the transmission. "Colonel, depending on what happens here in the next twenty-four hours, use your judgment on how much to tell Explora. She doesn't need to be burdened with our problems."

"I understand, Ma'am. Good luck to you."

During the next four hours the Federation troops were engaged in bitter fighting on two fronts. In the north, General Monta's forces had a bitter time of it. The Red soldiers now occupied the Yellow nests and were lurking inside. When the Black troops entered, they were met with fierce snapping jaws that lunged at them from every twist and turn. They stumbled over thousands of Yellow bodies that had met a similar fate as they had tried to defend their nests. After several hours of this, and suffering heavy casualties, General Monta decided to withdraw and put her troops into siege formation around the nests. While they waited, their numbers were swelled by struggling Yellow ants who had survived the first attack of the Reds and were hiding in the rocks and grass surrounding. They were a badly beaten and sorry lot, but were eager to rejoin the fray with the Black reinforcements.

Meanwhile, in the south, things went better for the Federation forces. Wiseria had guessed correctly that Aggressa had sent a large force north, not expecting retaliation from the Whites and Blacks. Consequently, General Alena's troops supported by two White divisions swept over the Red's front line of defense and struck swiftly for Aggressa's central headquarters. If they could take the Red Commander in the first attack, the war would be over before it had hardly begun. Thousands of Black and White soldiers swarmed over Aggressa's nest. The elite Red guards came out to meet them. The full savagery and ferocity of ants at war erupted in spasms of torn and mangled bodies, as wave after wave of attackers stormed forward, were repulsed, then came again, each time pushing further and deeper towards their objective. There is little doubt that they would have been successful then in crushing the Red aggressor, had not another act of treachery struck the Federation.

The word came through to Wiseria in Transmission Central shortly after midday. Roanda was with her and neither could at first believe it. A garbled transmission from a terrified White observer in one of the southern nests far removed from the fighting suddenly came in.

"Emergency! Emergency! Help! Oh, help! Can you hear me?"

"Transmission Central here," replied a technician, "Who are you and what is the emergency?"

Wiseria and Roanda both tuned in to the frequency.

"This is Operator 25. We are under attack! There are thousands of them just pouring in! We can't survive this. We need help. Please send help!"

"This is Deputy Wiseria," shouted Wiseria. "Who's attacking you? Is it Reds?"

"No! No! It's the Greens and Browns! There's no end to them! They're like fiends. We can't stop them. We've got no soldiers. They're just running all over us. Please send help! You've got to stop them!"

Wiseria looked at Roanda dumbfounded. She had doubted that Barbaria and Narcissa would support them in attacking Aggressa, but at no time had she anticipated treachery such as this. The leaders of the Greens and Browns knew the Whites would concentrate their forces in the north against Aggressa, so they had struck against the defenseless southern nests. This was a calculated and desperate move. With sickened heart, Wiseria knew they must intend to push through to Centrasia. Reluctantly she called General Alena at the front.

"Alena, you've got to divert your troops to the south. The Greens and Browns have attacked and are running unhindered through the colony. At this rate they'll be at Centrasia within the hour."

"Zit!" Alena exploded. "We've almost cracked Aggressa's nest. We can't pull back now."

"You must," Wiseria replied; "otherwise we'll lose everything here and you'll be cut off."

"If we get Aggressa, we'll have one helluva hostage."

"Yes, but we'll lose thousands of white workers and children."

"We'll probably lose them anyway. Let me at least get Aggressa."

"No, Alena. It's too big a risk. We could lose everything including you and your troops. I'm ordering you to fall back and defend Centrasia."

The next two days were the worst in Wiseria's life. She brought in reinforcements from her own colony, but even so, the combined White and Black troops could not stem the flood. Once they pulled back from attacking the Reds, Aggressa got momentum, and soon Wiseria's troops found themselves fighting a retreating action. The ground was swarming with White ant refugees, desperately fleeing the battle zone and trying to save their cocoons and pupae. Everything was wild confusion. It was impossible to accommodate all the refugees in Centrasia, so Wiseria sent them in a steady stream across the land bridge into her own colony. The combined Red, Green and Brown forces were closing in on Centrasia. Two White divisions were cut off and trapped, then ten thousand of them were slaughtered in skirmishes that raged both day and night. Wiseria could see that Centrasia, too, was lost. It was the hardest decision she ever made when she gave orders to evacuate the great white city.

Her first thought then was for Appesia. Wiseria had not seen her old friend since the fateful first night of Aggressa's attack on the Yellow Ant Colony. She pushed through the confusion of the nest to Appesia's chamber. But she was not there. Instinctively, Wiseria went to the old Federation conference hall. It now doubled as a nursery and was stacked full of cocoons which workers were struggling to remove. Wiseria found Appesia alone in the place she had so long occupied as President. She now seemed little more than a ghost in the dark.

"Hello Appesia," said Wiseria. "How are you?"

"It's lost, isn't it?" said Appesia faintly. "Centrasia's gone."

"Only for now. We'll be back when all this wickedness is punished. You must come with me to Blackhall."

"No. I will never leave Centrasia. When Aggressa comes strutting in here, she'll find this old White ant's jaws around her throat."

"Her guards will kill you first. You can't stay here."

"But I don't intend to leave. So I'm an ant without a place. I'll just pass into nothingness. Go, Wiseria. Save the Federation and leave this old carcass to its just rewards."

Wiseria embraced her friend one last time and left.

From the courtyard to the land bridge a living river of ants poured out of Centrasia toward Blackhall. Wiseria spent the last hours in Transmission Central trying to enlist aid for her desperate situation. Her first call was to Serenta, leader of the Sugars to the south in quadrant three.

"It makes me sick to hear what's happened," said Serenta; "but look, that's why I turned down your offer to join the Federation. I knew it wouldn't hold. I'm sorry, but you'll have to make the best peace you can. We can't get mixed up in it from here."

Bravada of the Salts was no more helpful. "We've lived with those Green and Brown bandits on our doorstep, but they never dared come this way. They knew what would happen if they did. Appesia was weak. She brought this on herself."

Wiseria did not speak to Intrepida of the Acids. She knew there was no help there, likely more treachery. Of all the rest, the smaller colonies in quadrant three, only Matilda of the Diggers showed any sympathy, but there was nothing they could do to help for now. Wiseria turned her attention to some friends she knew she would have need of to the west in quadrant one. But first she spoke to General Monta, commander of her troops trying to liberate the Yellow Ant Colony in the north.

"It's all over for us here for now, Monta. I'm afraid you're on your own up there. We can stop these savages from crossing the land bridge into our territory, but there's no way for us to get a relief force up to you. How much help can you get from the Yellows?"

"Not enough to make a difference. We've got the Reds pinned down inside the nests, but it's going to be a long siege to get them out. I need some rotten gas to pump in to drive them up."

Monta's remarks reminded Wiseria of her encounter with the great grey gonzonga in the Dark Country. That at least had been an enemy you could sink you're teeth into.

"Hold on for now, Monta," Wiseria said. "We won't leave you stranded."

Wiseria then sent a transmission west to the Wood ants and the Water ants who had cheered the Explora party so enthusiastically when it went through. She recalled how they had helped the party across the marshes. She anticipated she would need their help again soon on a much larger scale.

Finally, the evacuation of Centrasia was complete. The communication systems in Transmission Central were taken out and the technicians packed them up for transportation to Blackhall. The hostilities outside were now on the eastern edge of the courtyard. The Black and White defenders retreated, fighting every inch of the way in a tight circle right up to the mound. Wiseria stayed almost to the end, then finally departed surrounded by her own personal guard.

As she left, Roanda brought her a message. "Several of the technicians have run off with the communications equipment," she said. "They plan to hide out in the woods and set up a resistance centre."

"Poor brave souls," said Wiseria. "It's well they didn't tell me. I would never have allowed it."

At the top of the rise near the land bridge she looked back sadly on Centrasia. The retreating defenders had now given up the mound, and hordes of Red, Green and Brown invaders were triumphantly swarming all over it. A loathing against such wickedness welled up so strong in Wiseria's heart that she trembled visibly for several minutes while her troops pulled back across the courtyard.

"I will not rest," she cried into the breeze carrying down towards Centrasia, "until every last villainous intruder has been driven out, and the vile odor of this aggression expunged forever from Antale." Those around who heard her cry could not help but feel, even in this darkest hour, that somehow she would make good her words. For the moment, though, it seemed that all was lost. Centrasia was gone; Appesia had perished with it; and thousands of other brave young ants like Pacifica had been sacrificed in its defense.

What Wiseria could not know, however, was that Pacifica was still alive. After being captured and taken under guard into her own nest, she had been put to work with other White prisoners on clearing the bodies of dead White ants out of passage ways. The remains were stored deep in cool dark caverns as future food supplies for the hungry Red troops. It was loathsome work. Pacifica's protected early life had in no way prepared her for barbarity such as this. When word filtered down to the White prisoners through leering Red guards that the whole of their colony, including Centrasia, was overrun, it seemed that the end of the world had come.

Not long after that, Pacifica and many of her fellow prisoners were roughly herded out of the nest and driven with still more White survivors in long lines of living misery towards the Red Ant Colony. They were dispatched as slaves to work in different nests. Pacifica's intelligence and education were recognized and she found herself assigned to a small nest in the middle of the colony where special research was going on. It was obviously a closely guarded secret, and Pacifica as a laborer had no idea what it was. She soon learned, however, through the rumors running around among the workers, that the research was under the control of a scientist called Electra. The surprising thing about this was that Electra was not a Red ant, but belonged to a caste called the Jeddas.

Pacifica knew a little about the Jeddas. They had no colony of their own, but were dispersed throughout many of the colonies of Antale where they usually distinguished themselves as industrious, intelligent workers. Pacifica had known several as fellow students in Buranda. They were among the brightest in the group, and though they kept one part of their lives to themselves, they had participated enthusiastically in all the student affairs. Never had they seemed to her to be aggressive, and she wondered how one of them could rise to such prominence among the Reds. She hoped that she might one day meet the mysterious Electra.

Meanwhile, at the land bridge across Copper Creek, Wiseria's Black and White troops had formed into a solid block packing the narrow path that crossed ten feet above the water, which ran in this part of its course between steep high banks. The bridge was the only way across. It was an arch of rock bound up with earth and shrubs that had accumulated over ages. Less than three feet wide, it provided a good line of defense, and the Black and White troops felt they could hold it indefinitely. Over the next few days their confidence was to be supported. Though the Red, Green, Brown coalition threw wave after wave of attackers at the bridge, they were beaten back each time with heavy casualties. Finally, they withdrew to a respectable distance from the defenders, where they set up a leering, taunting line as the conquering invaders of the White Colony.

The retreat from Centrasia was a very dark time for Wiseria. She would have found it darker still had she been aware of the distress call received by Colonel Observa at Mission Control just when the fighting was at its fiercest. A few hours earlier Mission Control had been the scene of wild celebration, for Explora had called in to say that at dawn they had reached the far edge of the Rim, and were looking down into a long lush ravine, heavily forested and stretching away for as far as they could see into a whole new world. It was the moment that everyone associated with the expedition had dreamed of. Antale was not alone in the universe! For the first time an expedition had definitive proof of habitable land and the possibility of another civilization.

Observa had immediately tried to reach Wiseria, but communication with Centrasia had already been broken. She had called Blackhall and asked them to relay a message, but Wiseria, in the midst of the battle zone, had not received it. Caught in a desperate struggle to preserve freedom in her own world, she was not aware of the momentous discovery that could lead to achievements beyond the wildest imagination.

That was four hours ago. Explora, elated with the discovery, had not paused at the end of their night's travel, but had pushed on down into the ravine. Mission Control tried to maintain contact, but communications became distorted and heavily impacted by the other transmissions that had now strangely increased in intensity. Then they lost contact with Explora altogether. Try as they might, they could not raise her. All that Mission Control could do was wait.

Then suddenly Explora's signal had burst through the static: "Mission Control! Mission Control! Observa! Are you receiving?"

"Yes! Yes!" shouted Observa. "Go ahead, Explora."

"There's something strange here. I'm not sure what. Can't tell. We're in tall grass. Something's rolling in around us. Like a fog. Those other transmissions, very strong. Something's here! Something's here. Can't tell…"

The transmission had ended. Mission Control struggled for hours to regain contact, but without success. A disheartened Observa tried again to reach Wiseria. By now the Black leader had arrived at Blackhall.

"Hello, Observa," she said. "I've just received your earlier message. It's wonderful news. Is there anything further?"

"Yes, Ma'am, and it's not good. We lost contact for a while, then got one last message, then lost them again. They seemed to be in trouble. We don't know what. That was three hours ago."

"Tell me exactly what Explora said."

Observa repeated the message for Wiseria.

"All right, Colonel. Thank you. Keep trying to reach them. It's all we can do."

So, this on top of everything else, Wiseria thought. It seems that everything the Federation has tried to do is lost. Could her old friend and all the hopes of Antale that went with her, have perished? She refused to believe it. There had to be an end to misfortune.

But if there was to be an end, it was not then. Caught in the maelstrom, Wiseria could only keep dealing with each emergency as it came.

Working with her council, her most pressing concern was to accommodate the enormous influx of White ant refugees. Days grew into weeks as new nests were constructed, Queens were settled in, workers foraged far and wide for increased food supplies, and life settled into a strained but workable routine. There was no further news from Explora. There was no change on the battle front.

Then the next crisis struck.

Wiseria had been expecting it. She kept in close contact with General Monta and her First Division of Black troops who were trying to liberate the Yellow Ant Colony on the other side of Copper Creek to the north and west. The liberators had made little progress in freeing the nests, though they were successful in keeping the Red invaders pinned down inside. Using this strategy, they would have eventually starved them out, but Wiseria and Monta knew that long before this would happen, Aggressa would send an invading force up from the south. Monta tried to prepare for this by rounding up as many Yellow survivors as she could to complement her own troops in a solid defense of the path the Red army must take.

Finally the attack came. Monta's troops held fast for several days, but as casualties mounted and she had to draw more troops away from the siege of the nests, she opened up her flank to a new peril. The original Red invaders poured out of the Yellow nests and released their pent up fury in vicious attacks on the Black and Yellow forces. Outnumbered and squeezed between two attacking Red armies, Monta ordered her troops to retreat towards Copper Creek. The conflict would have ended there in a terrible massacre of Blacks and Yellows had not Wiseria's preparations proved effective. Even so, it was a brush with death never to be forgotten by all involved.

At this part of its course Copper Creek ran wide, but not too fast. For many days feverish activity had been underway some distance upstream on the Black ant side. A contingent of Wood and Water ant workers had responded to Wiseria's call for help. They instructed Black ant workers on how to build a flotilla of flimsy water craft that might be floated across Copper Creek to pick up retreating Black and Yellow troops and ferry them to safety on the Black Colony side.

The call for help came from Monta early in the morning just before sunrise. It was relayed from Blackhall up to the work site, and the most amazing rescue in the history of Antale got underway. Several thousand small craft large enough to carry ten to twenty ants pushed out into the dark water. They were a rough and ready conglomeration of leaves and twigs, each one steered by two worker ants—Black, Wood, Water, White; it didn't matter. They floated out perilously into the gentle current, while their navigators worked hard to steer them to where they hoped the Black and Yellow troops would be waiting on the other side.

Everything was carried out with amazing calm, not to alert the Red troops to what was going on. When the first wave of water craft pushed in under the overhanging branches on the edge of the creek, Black and Yellow soldiers leaped aboard. As each craft received its full complement, the workers who had steered it in struggled to get it back out again into the current and paddle it to the other side. They now of course had many passengers who, though by no means skilful, could nevertheless help to paddle. All things considered, the whole thing worked amazingly well. There were many collisions, upsets, ants thrown into the water to be pulled spluttering to safety, others holding back out of fear being pushed forcefully from behind until they made their fateful leap. At the height of the maneuver, just as the rising sun touched the water, more than a thousand of these ridiculous, brave craft were spread out over two hundred yards of Copper Creek. By the time the marauding Red ant troops realized what was happening and came pouring down to the banks of the creek in a red, angry sizzle of energy, the last of the Black and Yellow soldiers were safely away. In their fury at being denied their brutal conquest, the first ranks of the Red army leapt into the water in pursuit. Black and Yellow soldiers beat them off and more than a thousand of them perished in the water. Two hours later it was all over. The evacuation by water was complete. More than ten thousand Black and Yellow troops had been saved by their worker comrades.

The tired soldiers rested for a day, then marched bravely back to Blackhall where they were welcomed as returning heroes. News of the rescue had spread like wildfire through the colony. Thousands of workers took time off from their labors to cheer their returning troops. General Monta marched proudly at the head, side by side with the Yellow commander. When they reached the square outside Blackhall, Wiseria and Antonia were there to meet them. It was a bitter-sweet moment for the leaders of the two colonies. There had been little enough to cheer about in the past weeks, and both felt the irony that today the cheers were not for victory over the enemy, but for achieving a miraculous retreat. It was a fitting summation of the situation facing them in early summer.

The once proud White and Yellow colonies were in the hands of a hostile foe and former treacherous friends. Many of their sisters were being held as prisoners or had scattered for refuge in the woods. Thousands more had perished in the attacks. The remainder were crowded as refugees into the Black Ant Colony, whose only claim to safe haven was its position across the formidable Copper Creek. If that barrier could be breached by the attackers, the destruction of the free ant Federation would be complete. It was well that neither Antonia nor Wiseria, as they welcomed home their troops, knew how close they now were to that final moment of annihilation.

The one who had stumbled on the truth was Pacifica. Poor White prisoner in a Red slave camp, she seemed least able to do anything with the information. She had been imprisoned now for several weeks and was learning how to get some privileges from her Red captors. The commandant of the prison was Agrippa, a small, brutal ant driven by fierce ambition. Ignorant but cunning, the commandant saw certain advancement with Aggressa if she could swiftly bring the research to aid the war effort. Pacifica's intelligence and resourcefulness had come to Agrippa's attention; so she moved the young White ant to work more directly on the research. That was how Pacifica met Electra.

"So, Electra," Agrippa had one day sneered when she visited the scientist in her laboratory, "you make haste far too slowly. I've brought you some new research assistants. Now perhaps we'll see some results."

Pacifica was one of the assistants. In Electra she saw a distinguished, older version of the Jeddas she had known as a student. Electra was small, but her head was large, and she went about her work with swift and certain precision. Like Pacifica she was white in color, but her Jedda heritage showed in black markings on her body.

Electra paid little attention to Pacifica or to anyone else. No one seemed to know much about the true nature of the research being carried out. Pacifica served as little more than a skilled laborer, sorting out different materials and carrying them to and fro between storehouse and laboratory. But one day, not long afterwards, she learned the truth. She was working in a side passage when she overheard a conversation between Electra and Agrippa,

"So the stuff is ready for testing at last," said Agrippa. "Good. I'll round up some prisoners and you can give it to them."

"What do you mean? That's murder," replied Electra. "That's not what my research is about."

"Oh, well what do you think you've been doing here all these months?" asked Agrippa.

"I've been trying to identify what causes the epidemics of convulsions of the nervous system that have killed thousands of ants throughout the colony. Now I believe I've found it in this mould that gets on our food when it is stored too long."

"Exactly. Now I want you to test it on some prisoners to make sure you've got it right."

"I won't do that. I'm trying to save lives, not destroy them."

"If you don't do it, someone else will. Stubborn Jedda!" Agrippa made no effort to conceal her anger. "We are fighting a war here, you know. I have no patience for insubordination. I'll give you until tomorrow to think about it."

Agrippa left and Pacifica came out.

"Who's there?" Electra demanded.

"It's Pacifica. I overheard." Pacifica decided to risk everything by plunging right in. "You know what's going on here, don't you?"

"What do you mean?"

"The Red ants are looking for some way to efficiently wipe out their enemies. Your research is giving it to them."

"They never told me that."

"Why should they? You're a scientist, not a general. But now you know."

"Who are you that you're telling me this?"

"I'm just a prisoner; a good candidate as a test for your mould. But I can tell you before I was taken prisoner I was a confidante of Prime Minister Wiseria from the Black Ant Colony. I'm not sure what is happening on the outside now, but the rumors are that only the Blacks are holding out against the Reds. You can be sure your discovery is to be used against them."

"That's intolerable. I want no part of it."

"It's probably too late to stop it, but maybe you can slow things down. Are there others here who can replicate your work?"

"In time, yes."

"How much time?"

"I don't know, Maybe several weeks."

"Good. That gives us a chance. Look, I know you don't know anything about me, Electra, but if you believe that what I'm telling you is true, then you should destroy as much of your work here as you can, and use your security clearance to help both of us escape. Perhaps we can make it through to Black troops wherever they are and warn them. Will you do it?"

Had Pacifica known more about the true state of the war outside, she would perhaps have been less confident she could make a difference. Had Wiseria known about the Red plans for biological warfare, she would have felt her situation to be more desperate. However, beyond what either of them could know, an event was about to happen in the south that would plunge Antale further into the darkness of escalating war.

It was just after daybreak on a beautiful morning in midsummer. Colonel Alexa, commanding officer of the Portal nest in the Sugar Ant Colony, stretched herself luxuriously as she looked around from the top of her mound. To the south she could see the humps of other nests in the colony, the sun just starting to light them up like golden domes. Away to the west the usual early morning mist hung a shimmering white curtain over the Dark Country. Across the wide vista to the north, Lake Miasma stretched away blue and calm, with the islands of the Acid Ant Colony in the foreground. In the east everything was dark, still lying in the shadow of the Rim. Another beautiful day was shaping up for the pleasant life in the world of the Sugars.

Alexa, of course, knew about the war raging across the lake in quadrants four and one. She received daily briefings from headquarters in the Gold House and, as a military officer, she privately regretted what had happened to the once strong White and Black forces. It underlined the need for vigilance and strength, a far more effective strategy than the conciliatory approaches used by President Appesia. That was what her command was about, keeping Portal on alert for any signs of unusual troop movement by their neighbors. Using that strategy they enjoyed peace and the comfortable life of the dominant colony in their sector.

Alexa was joined by two of her junior officers in charge of the early morning watch. She nodded to them, and turned to leave for breakfast. Suddenly, one of the officers stiffened a little, looking attentively to the north.

"That's strange," she said.

"What's strange?" asked Alexa, turning back.

"There, over the Acid islands. There's something stirring. What is it?"

All three officers strained to see.

"Looks like they're swarming," said Alexa. "Nothing strange about that. The Acids have to do their mating dance, same as the rest of us. Just so long as they keep it over their own territory, there's nothing to worry about."

"I guess you're right, Ma'am," said the officer, "but I don't know, there's something different about this. Look, see, they're all coming out of that one small island. We've never seen activity there before."

"Yes, that's true," said Alexa.

"You know," the second officer now interjected, excitedly, "I don't think they're winged ants at all. Look, there's thousands of them now, rising and flying in circles. Have you ever seen ants behave like that?"

"They're getting into formation," cried the first officer. "What is this?"

The activity the three Sugar officers were watching was taking place about a hundred yards away. It was over the island where Pacifica had thought she detected some strange energy when she had visited the Acid colony with Wiseria and Roanda several weeks ago. Even as the observers on Portal watched, the sky above the small island darkened in a funnel shape as countless thousands of winged insects flew upwards in a spiral.

"Zit! They're coming this way. Sound the alarm!" shouted Alexa.

The two junior officers scurried away while the colonel continued to watch the approaching swarm. What were the Acids up to? It couldn't be an attack. Winged ants are useless as fighters. But were these creatures ants? As they came closer, Alexa grew more certain that they weren't. But what were they? Had the Acids been breeding something in the nest on that island? What was it?

The swarm had come into a V formation and the leaders were now only about twenty yards away, flying low about thirty feet above the ground. Alexa strained every faculty she had to try to make them out. At the same time, she was aware of her own nest coming alive as soldiers poured out of entrances all over the mound and looked skyward. Now the flying mass was directly overhead and came swooping down on Portal. In those few moments before the deluge was upon her, Alexa saw something that froze her blood with fear. The winged creatures were not ants, but much larger and more like wasps. More amazing still, an Acid ant was clinging to the underbelly of each flying insect, and the ant was carrying a small white object in her jaws that looked like a cocoon.

More than that Alexa had no time to tell before a shower of Acid ants was falling all around her. The ants were letting go as their winged carriers came low in over the mound. Without ant passenger and pilot, the flying insect then veered off into the sky and drifted aimlessly away. But there was nothing aimless about the Acid ants. They had a clear and terrible intent. Alexa understood when one of the cocoon-like objects exploded nearby and a stinging pungent smell filled the air. Alexa gasped and felt her limbs stiffen. The devils were using some kind of poison gas! If it got into the nest, every ant inside would be killed.

The Sugar soldiers quickly realized what was going on and attacked the invaders ferociously, trying to roll the cocoons down and off the mound. But thousands of ants and cocoons kept pouring from the sky. As quickly as the Sugars dispatched one invader, ten more filled her place. Cocoons were breaking, and defenders and attackers alike were overcome by the fumes. The Acid plan was to force an entry by the sheer pressure of numbers, not caring how many of their own side perished in the attack. It was a suicide mission of staggering proportions, and the nest soon gave way under the attack.

Alexa still had enough strength and consciousness to see the danger. She crawled back inside the mound and found her strength returning as she got away from the poisonous fumes. She had to get the nest evacuated back through the passage linking it to the Gold House. The Acids would not have counted on that. In the jumble of confusion she managed to eventually get her orders understood, and a stream of workers began to move eggs, larvae, cocoons and pupae out through the labyrinth of passages leading to the main tunnel.

Meanwhile the Acids were penetrating at the surface. Soon the gas fumes were seeping through the mound. Sugar soldiers by the thousands fought bravely before succumbing. But still the hordes of invaders poured in. Alexa, acting more out of instinct than any good information, kept the evacuation going. She sent word to the Gold House for reinforcements, but when they came pouring up the tunnel, they only created confusion among the evacuees. Finally, Alexa got the message through for troops to stay out of the tunnel and engage the enemy on the outside. By now Portal was lost. The nest was filled with poisonous gas, which was beginning to seep back along the tunnel towards the Gold House. Alexa gave the terrible order to seal the passage blocking any further retreat for ants still alive in the nest. Hundreds of workers bent to the task, tearing at the walls, piling up debris along with dead bodies to seal the passage. It was a terrible, terrible time, but finally the job was done. The once glorious Portal, military bastion and pride of the colony, was sealed off as a tomb.

Outside the raid was over. Thousands of dead Sugar and Acid soldiers lay everywhere. Sugar reinforcements were now pouring in and the last of the suicide invaders were dispatched. Hundreds of lethal unbroken cocoons littered the ground. The Sugar soldiers milled around, staring in disbelief at the carnage. The Sugar Ant Colony had now had a first and brutal taste of war.

CHAPTER 5

Victory at a Price

THE ATTACK ON PORTAL WAS A BRUTAL, premeditated and daring gamble by the Acids to take advantage of the war launched by Aggressa in the north. It had been planned at a secret meeting held a few weeks earlier between Intrepida, President of the Acid Ant Colony, and the leaders of the Red, Green, and Brown colonies. With the White and Black forces pinned down on the other side of Copper Creek, the northern aggressors were now looking to the south. If they moved immediately, they could have a third of Antale under their control by the end of summer. In Intrepida they found a hungry and ambitious ally, ready to risk much to gain territory on the mainland to support her island colony. The prize was all the land occupied by the unorganized nests west of Lake Miasma.

There was no intent to engage the Sugars or the Salts in all out war. They could keep for next year, after the Blacks and Whites were crushed and all the other territory was under the control of the aggressive new alliance. But first Intrepida wanted to display her power. The sight of the fortified Portal on her doorstep was a continuing affront to her ambitions. She had been developing the wasp breeding program since last summer, and though it was not quite ready, she decided to use it. As a price for assistance from the northern alliance, she also shared the technology with them, and Aggressa quickly got a breeding program underway to use against the Blacks. Time was of the essence for these cruel invaders to consolidate their gains this summer.

Intrepida's strike against Portal was intended to show the Sugars the terrible power of her new weapon. While the carnage was still on the ground around the poisoned nest, she sent a transmission to President Serenta in the Gold House. It came in as Colonel Alexa was reporting the details of the attack to her visibly shaken leader. An aide relayed the message to the President.

"President Intrepida wishes to inform you," said the aide, "that the attack on

Portal was in retaliation for the hostile act of building a fortification so close to Acid territory. No more attacks are planned, but if there are any reprisals against Acid nests, swift and terrible punishment can be expected."

"That murderous lump of excrement!" Serenta exploded. "Reprisals! She talks of reprisals! She hasn't begun to know what reprisals are!"

"One thing I'd like to say, Ma'am," put in Alexa. "I don't think they've got control of those wasps or whatever they are. They can't get them back once they're released. That means there's a limit to what damage they can do."

"But we don't know what the limit is," said the President. "We have to shore up other nests against attack." She turned to General Domina, the chief of the Sugar military forces. "What percentage of our troops was lost in the Portal attack, Domina?"

"Almost fifty percent, Ma'am," replied Domina, "and they were our best soldiers."

"Good grief! So many? If Intrepida knew that, she'd probably strike again. Let's hope you're right about her limits, colonel. So many dead?" Serenta choked, then continued: "All right. Now we start to rebuild. Every available worker must be trained! See to it, Domina. And spread them out around the colony. No more Portals as sitting targets. Secure all the nests, and put Project S on full production. Intrepida will soon find out more than she wants to know about secret weapons. Now I want to talk to our allies in the north. Get me President Wiseria."

Within the hour, the Sugars were in the war. For the hard pressed Wiseria, this was welcome news, though it was by no means clear what an ally so far away could do. Even to plan strategy seemed impossible. Open transmission with all their enemies listening was out. They would have to find a way to meet. In the meantime, Wiseria was expecting some new offensive from Aggressa. What would it be, and when would it come?

Unknown to Wiseria, the answer lay partly with Pacifica. Following her conversation with Electra, the young White prisoner spent several anxious days wondering what Electra would do. Would she accept her lot as unwilling scientist to support Red atrocities, or would she cut free and join Pacifica in a bid to escape?

Finally, Electra took Pacifica aside and spoke to her in the laboratory. "There's been a new development," she said. "The Acids have attacked the Sugars with trained wasps and poison gas. Aggressa has set up a similar program here. It's total madness. The whole world will soon be at war. I've stalled Agrippa for as long as I can. We have to escape and do what we can to help your friends. We will leave tonight."

Electra made an excuse to the guards for Pacifica to stay and work after the other prisoners had been returned to their cells. When all was quiet, scientist and assistant then ruthlessly destroyed all the experimental specimens in the laboratory. Now they were ready to leave. Three guards stationed sequentially in a narrow passage lay between them and freedom. Electra, followed by Pacifica, approached the first.

"The prisoner is ready to leave now," Electra said to the guard. "You may escort her out."

Electra squeezed aside to let Pacifica past. The guard did likewise, intending to follow behind the prisoner.

"Oh, just one moment," Electra spoke again, distracting the guard. In that instant Pacifica acted. In the tight confines of the passage she used one of the wrestling tricks she had learned in school. She thrust herself hard against the guard, twisted her abdomen forward between her hind legs, and grasped the guard's head with her forelegs. Electra grabbed the guard from behind while Pacifica inserted a drop of formic acid from the end of her gaster into the guard's mouth. The guard was immediately knocked unconscious.

"One down, two to go," said Pacifica.

The next one was not so easy. As they approached, Electra following Pacifica, the guard challenged them.

"Who goes?" asked the guard.

"Otta and prisoner," replied Electra, trying to imitate the first guard.

"What? Otta, is that you?" The second guard was suspicious.

"Of course it is," said Electra, doing a good job of mimicking. "Who did you expect, Agrippa, the gripe?"

The second guard chuckled and moved to lead them out. Pacifica leapt on her from behind, clamped her jaws around the guard's neck and paralyzed her. Another drop of formic acid left her unconscious like the first.

"My word, you're good at that," said Electra.

"Come on," replied Pacifica. "It's your turn to lead. You have to play the guard one more time."

The third guard was dozing at her post at the entrance to the nest.

"Come on! Wake up!" Electra barked. "Prisoner coming out." The guard moved sleepily aside to let them pass, then realized something was wrong.

"Hey, who are you?" she shouted. Pacifica charged from behind and crashed the Red guard against the side of the passage. The deadly sting swung round to attack, but before the guard could use it, Electra grabbed her head and twisted her mouth up towards Pacifica who sprayed her with formic acid. The guard collapsed unconscious.

"We're a great team," said Pacifica, but Electra was already heading out of the passage into the night air. Both of them looked around trying to get their bearings. Electra recognized a landmark in the moonlight.

"That nest is to the north," she said.

"Then this way is west to Copper Creek," said Pacifica. "Let's loop around so that we try to avoid any Red patrols. I don't know what we'll do when we get there, but we'll worry about that when the time comes."

Two hundred yards away on the bank above Copper Creek, a small band of White resistance fighters had tunneled out a small nest. Their leader was Stanza, one of the technicians who had worked in Transmission Central in Centrasia. She with a few others had made off with transmitting equipment when the nest was being evacuated. Ever since, over the long hot weeks of summer, they had been constantly on the move, sending brief messages to Blackhall and managing to avoid being captured by Red patrols. There wasn't much that they could do. Their main objective was to stay free so that when the opportunity to help arose, they would be there. The opportunity came quite suddenly for them that night.

Stanza was keeping watch from a vantage point on a rock above the nest. The night was almost over and the moon sat low in the western sky. She could almost see the mounds of the Black Ant Colony on the other side of the creek. A hundred yards to the south the land bridge stood as the only crossing over the swiftly running waters. The staunch line of Black defenders held the bridge. The Red army periodically pressed its attack from this side. That had been the status for many weeks. Stanza and her friends sought to keep the Blacks informed of any unusual troop movements by the Reds.

Suddenly, a few feet away across some open ground, Stanza sensed a commotion. As she watched, she dimly saw two ants come scuttling out into the open. She could tell that one of them was white. They were running in her direction. A moment later half a dozen Red soldiers came rushing out in pursuit of the other two.

"Halt, you two!" shouted one of the Reds. "Halt, damn you, or you're dead."

Stanza could see that the fleeing pair had little hope without some help. She scampered down the rock and ran out to meet them. When they saw her, they veered to get by. Stanza waved frantically.

"Get over behind the rock!" she shouted. Without waiting to see what they did, she rushed past them directly towards the Red soldiers. They were only about a foot away.

"Now we've got you, Red dungheads!" Stanza screamed. "Get them from behind!"

The soldiers slithered to a stop. It was only for a moment, but it was enough. Stanza turned and flew over the ground towards the rock. On the other side she rushed by Pacifica and Electra, panting and confused. Without pausing, Stanza shouted, "Follow me!" and darted inside a hole under the rock. Immediately inside she twisted around and waited for the other two. They came tumbling in.

"Keep going down," Stanza said, then she grabbed desperately for some leaves and twigs and covered the entrance to the hole. A few moments later the Red soldiers were at the hole, sniffing and scrabbling around it, looking for the entrance.

By now Pacifica and Electra were down inside a small chamber facing three surprised White resistance fighters. Stanza rushed in.

"Come on! We're out of here!" she cried, grabbing up some transmitting equipment and heading out the other side of the chamber. None of the others paused to ask questions. The White fighters pushed Pacifica and Electra after Stanza, then followed, the last one pulling down a pile of pebbles behind her to block the entrance. The passage ran for only a short distance before it came out into the open. They all knew the Red soldiers were not far away. With Stanza leading they kept running. She took them over the bank, then slithering and sliding for several feet down among large rocks by the water's edge. Finally, Stanza decided it was safe to stop.

"Now," she said, turning to Pacifica and Electra, "who are you, and why were those soldiers chasing you? This had better be good. We just gave up our best hideout."

"My name's Pacifica. I was a prisoner. This is Electra, one of Antale's leading scientists."

"Whew," Stanza whistled. "I've heard of both of you. Pacifica, weren't you at Mission Control and came back with President Wiseria?"

"Yes. Is Wiseria President now? What happened to President Appesia?"

"Too long a story. I'll tell you later. Now, Electra—you worked for the Reds, didn't you?"

"Yes, I'm afraid that's true. But that goes back before the time of Aggressa. They weren't as warlike then."

Pacifica intervened: "They were using Electra to develop a means for biological warfare. We've wrecked the labs and set them back a bit. We're trying to get the information to our side. Can you help? By the way," she continued, "thank you for saving us. That patrol almost caught us."

"That's all right," said Stanza. "It looks like it was worth losing our post to save you two. What do you want to do now?"

"Get to Blackhall," replied Pacifica. "How do we do that?"

"There's only one way. Over the creek."

Pacifica looked at the black water rushing by only inches away.

"That's impossible," she said.

"Yes," replied Stanza, "most everything in this damned war is. But do you want to try anyway?"

It turned out that Stanza had a contact on the other side of the creek; a Black ant called Roda. She was a daredevil who had already risked her life fifty times in ferrying escaping refugees across the creek. A dozen or more had been drowned in the process. Roda had learned the trick from the Water ants when they lifted the Black and Yellow troops from under the jaws of the Red forces several weeks earlier. Since then she had been doing it in the much faster current just above the land bridge.

"If you go now, you can be in Blackhall by the time the sun is up," Stanza said. Pacifica looked at Electra. Electra looked at the rushing water.

"Maybe this Roda is a good scientist and knows how to replicate her work," she said. "Let's try it."

Roda was anything but a scientist. Stanza called her by transmission using code. An hour later, with streaks of dawn lightening the sky, the small group of ants clustered on a rock by the creek heard her coming.

"Yo ho, there, you six-legged land grubbers. Make way for Roda's raft!"

"Hsst, Roda, you idiot!" hissed Stanza. "There's Redbacks all around here. Do you want to have them down on us?"

"Then step lively and pull me in. Where's the booty? Who are Roda's renegades today?"

What had arrived was a collection of sticks strapped together with coarse grass. Two upright sticks crossed at the back served as a guide for a long wooden oar. Bouncing up and down on the end of it where it came over the cross sticks was the largest ant Pacifica or Electra had ever seen. This was Roda. Fully an inch and a half long, she held on to the oar with strong forelegs, and, rearing upright, gripped the deck of the raft with the other four. The raft slithered in over the rock, Stanza and her companions grabbed hold of it, Pacifica and Electra tumbled on board, and the resistance fighters pushed the raft away.

"Good luck," shouted Stanza.

"Takes more than luck," chortled Roda. "Takes a bloody miracle! Welcome aboard, sailors. Hang on with everything. Here we go!"

Indeed, it took a miracle to cross the creek like that. It was less than ten yards wide, but the current was running fast and the creek was full of sticks, leaves, weeds, and other debris. Roda fought with everything, heaving on the oar, maneuvering them out into the current, keeping up a stream of invective against the water and the weeds and everything else. Pacifica and Electra watched the shoreline rushing by. At this rate they would be under the land bridge before they reached the other side, and Pacifica remembered seeing rapids in the creek below the bridge. Still, they were getting there. The halfway mark was passed. Only three yards to go.

Suddenly they were dive bombed by a dragon fly. With a stick-like body of three inches, it was about as long as the raft. It came droning in at terrible speed and tried to land on the deck. The wind of its wings tore at the ants like a hurricane.

"Freeloader!" roared Roda. "Drive the bugger off or she'll sink us!"

Pacifica wondered how you drove away a tornado, but she tried sinking her jaws into one of the dragon fly's legs. Instantly the beast took off and Pacifica would have gone with it, had not Electra lunged for her companion's abdomen and pulled her back.

The dragon fly was gone, but the other perils of the creek weren't. Before Roda could do anything to avoid it, they careened into a jungle of water grass. The raft lifted out of the water and hung almost vertical like a squashed leaf among the sharp stems. The ants clung desperately to their perch as the raft turned and twisted with the grass.

"Abandon ship!" shouted Roda.

"For what?" cried Pacifica.

"For better or for worse," replied Roda. "Come on, follow me."

The big Black ant leapt off the raft onto a blade of grass. Reluctantly, the others followed. Timing her leaps carefully with the swinging stems, Roda led them, springing from blade to blade, for fifteen minutes, until they reached the shore. Pacifica looked around and saw that they were under the land bridge. Six feet downstream she could sense the roaring of the rapids.

"I'm sorry about your raft," Pacifica said to Roda.

"Not to worry, little ant," Roda replied. "Saves me hauling it back upstream. Look, here's you're welcoming party."

Pacifica looked up and thought she had never seen anything more wonderful. Coming towards them was a shore patrol of Black and White soldiers. She and Electra were safe.

Wiseria's reunion with Pacifica was the first really good moment for the Black leader since the war began. One she had presumed lost had returned. It was a good omen and a wonderful surprise. That she had brought Electra with her was more than Wiseria's war office could have hoped for. With her knowledge of the Red's technical capabilities and the contribution she could now make to the Black and White joint effort, Electra would play a major role in the weeks ahead.

For the moment, however, it seemed that the winds of war were blowing a gale for the aggressors. Flush with her stunning annihilation of the Sugar's main military post, Intrepida sent the Acid ground forces out on searing raids against the neighboring unorganized nests. She used the winged-wasp offence in a scatter-gun effect to strike terror into the inhabitants, then her fierce vermilion warriors came driving in like a fiery holocaust. Within days they had overrun all the territory east to the edge of the Salt Colony and were driving north with the speed of a brush fire. At the same time, Green and Brown forces were pushing south with equal ferocity. The Red troops kept pressing the attack on the White and Black troops at the land bridge so that once the conquest to the south was complete, a final massive offensive could be launched by the full aggressive alliance against the Black Colony across Copper Creek.

It was then that part of the alliance made a serious mistake. The Brown Ant Colony had long been in dispute with the Salts over certain marginal nests where their territories met. Tasting the blood of her successful raids, first against the Whites, and now against the unorganized nests, Narcissa, leader of the Browns, ordered her troops to drive right into the disputed territory of the Salts. They first enjoyed spectacular success, and, lusting for more, the Brown generals continued pushing south into undisputed Salt territory. Bravada, leader of the Salts, responded immediately by sending several of her divisions into action against the Browns. The Salts were now in the war.

When word reached Wiseria of these developments, she knew she had a brief span of opportunity to forge a new alliance with the Sugars and the Salts. Because communication by transmission was both unreliable and insecure, she decided to send an emissary to Serenta and Bravada, to try to convince the two leaders to meet with her somewhere midway between the three colonies. Who better to lead the delegation than Pacifica, who was already known to Serenta and Bravada? Wiseria sent Roanda as well; so the two young White ants were together again on a long journey across Antale. To avoid the zone of hostility they would have to go west around Lake Miasma, then south through the Dark Country to the Sugar Colony. Wiseria decided to ask the friendly Rocky Mountain ants to host the meeting by the lake at the foot of Escarpment Slope. Pacifica's and Roanda's job was to bring Bravada and Serenta back with them to the rendezvous. Wiseria would meet them there.

It would be a long and difficult journey for the two White emissaries, taking at least three days for them to reach the Sugar Colony and as long again to meet with and convince Serenta and then Bravada to attend a summit with Wiseria. So the Black leader set the meeting for a week's time and sent Pacifica and Roanda off.

A week was a long time in this crucial stage of the war. Wiseria worried that Aggressa would strike with new weapons of her own before Wiseria could do anything to mount an offensive from her side. She spoke to Electra about it in her war office at Blackhall.

"What do you think Aggressa will do?" Wiseria asked. "I mean, what are her technical options?"

"It's as well you ask me that," replied Electra. "I don't know what she can do militarily, but technically, I think she can have the biological program I was working on ready in four weeks. It will take about the same amount of time for her to breed those wasp eggs that the Acids gave her. Allow another week for testing and I think she'll be ready."

"Ready for what, exactly?" asked Wiseria.

"You're the war leader, Wiseria," Electra replied. "What do you think she'll do?"

"You mean we can expect those infernal flying hordes to come over here carrying those germs? The Reds aren't suicide fanatics like the Acids. They won't want to drop down on us themselves with this stuff. How will they deliver it?"

"Probably as a fine powder. They can drop it from the sky. It will form a coating over everything. Any ant that comes in contact with it will get infected, and it will spread throughout the nest. Your colony could be wiped out in a week. It's a horrible weapon."

"And those fiends are capable of using it. How can we stop them?"

"There's only one way. You have to destroy their ability to deliver it."

"You mean the wasps?"

"Yes."

"But how?"

"They're using only one nest for breeding purposes. I know where it is. It's Number 37 at the back of the colony."

"We could never get there."

"Not by conventional means, no. But I have an idea."

"Go on." Wiseria looked at Electra attentively.

"We could train your male ants to fly in carrying some of the powder on them, which I would prepare. The males, of course, will die, but they are born to do that anyway. We would use them for a different purpose than the one their biology prepared them to do."

"My gosh, Electra. Is that possible?"

"I don't know, but we can try. I think it's your only hope."

A week later Wiseria and her delegation arrived at Escarpment Slope. The Rocky Mountain ants were waiting for them. This time she met Jocula, their leader.

"Hello. Hello. Welcome. Welcome. Yes. Yes," she gushed.

Wiseria wondered if she always said everything twice. "Thank you for hosting us," she said. "Is this where we meet?"

"No. No," replied Jocula. "Down by the lake. Down by the lake. Come. Come."

Jocula had selected a lovely location for the meeting. It was an opening in the cliff face overlooking the water, a kind of cave with private chambers leading off from it—a perfect place for a summit. The one problem was that Wiseria was the only one there. She waited all that day, through the night, and well into the following afternoon. She had received word by code two days ago that they were on their way, but since then it had been a total communications blackout. Wiseria could not understand it.

Jocula posted lookouts at strategic points among the rocks and kept Wiseria company. Now that she had overcome her nervousness, she spoke more easily. Wiseria knew she had a friend here whom she could count on in the future. Suddenly Jocula looked up, antennae's twitching.

"The relay says they're coming," she exclaimed. "Must look lively! Look lively!" She scuttled off up the rock face.

Wiseria took the longer way round and came out on top of the cliff. Ten yards away, coming towards her was a small procession of ants. At the head she recognized the striking golden figure of Serenta, with Pacifica beside her, and a collection of Sugar ants behind. Further back was another group, a huddle of Salts. Wiseria could not see Bravada. Right at the back, bringing up the rear, Roanda strode along. Around the whole procession a bevy of Rocky Mountain guides were scuttling back and forth, in and out, like so many ants at a picnic. Jocula had run down to meet them. She came back up, leading Serenta and Pacifica.

"Hi there, Wiseria," said Serenta, pleasantly. "Gad, you pick the damnedest places to meet. Say," she added in a whisper, indicating Jocula, "does she always say everything twice?"

"Only when she's excited," laughed Wiseria.

"Come. Come," exclaimed Jocula. "Follow me. Follow me."

Wiseria embraced Pacifica. "Well done, Pacifica. I was getting a little worried. Where's Bravada?"

Pacifica shrugged a little. "Back there," she said.

Serenta intervened: "Our esteemed partner has got her abdomen tied in a knot. In other words, she's a pain in the gut."

Wiseria didn't wait for an explanation, but hurried down to meet the other group. The Salt bodyguards looked at her suspiciously, then parted to reveal a flustered looking Bravada.

"Hello, Bravada," Wiseria greeted her. "It's good to see you again."

"You will never, never put me through this again!" Bravada snorted. "We Salts don't need this aggravation."

Wiseria decided not to enquire further, but let the group pass. Then Roanda came up, whom she greeted warmly.

"What's wrong with Bravada?" Wiseria asked.

"She never wanted to come in the first place," said Roanda as they walked side by side following the others. "Pacifica was at her wits' end to convince her. Then word came of a crushing defeat of her army. So she decided to come. She thought she might get some help from the Sugars. But she and Serenta didn't hit it off. Then halfway here she wanted to turn back. She would have, too, if it hadn't been for the Tigers."

"The Tigers!" exclaimed Wiseria. "What did they do? No more gonzongas, I hope."

"No, but they blocked the bridge over Cruel Creek after we got across. Bravada insulted them, so they demanded ransom to let her back. Her Salt guards tried to push them around. Then we had hundreds of them swarming all around us. I thought it was all over for the lot of us. That's when we lost our communications gear in the scuffle. It was Pacifica who got us out of it. She's a whiz at negotiation. But Bravada hasn't been on speaking terms with anyone since."

It makes for an interesting start to our meeting, thought Wiseria.

The Rocky Mountain hosts put on a wonderful meal of snail, butterfly, grass shoots, and a special sweet berry dessert, just for the Sugars. Rested and replete the leaders then settled down for their meeting. Jocula discreetly withdrew, and all other members of the delegations moved to the back of the chamber, leaving Wiseria, Serenta and Bravada in relaxed discussion at the front. The long rays of the setting sun lit up the calm waters of Lake Miasma in brilliant technicolor as Wiseria opened the session.

"We meet in mythic times," she said. "The old Antale that all of us have known has been swept away. We stand at the crossroads of a potential future of cooperation and peace, or a darkness more horrible than any of us can imagine. I believe, my friends, the outcome for good or ill depends upon what we decide to do."

"Good opening, Wiseria," said Serenta. "Yes, I like that. Mythic times. Very good."

"Words are words," said Bravada. "Only actions count. I didn't come all this way for words."

"Very well, Bravada," Wiseria continued. "I have proposals for more action over the next three weeks than most would expect to see in a lifetime. We are hard pressed on all fronts. But we have not yet begun to work together. There lies the key to our success in destroying the enemy."

"Let's hear your proposals, Wiseria," said Serenta. Bravada remained sullenly silent.

"I am expecting a final assault by the Reds on my colony within the next three weeks using deadly biological warfare. I have a plan, which I will detail later, to prevent that and attack the enemy in her base. As that happens, we must be ready with a ground assault to liberate Centrasia and the rest of the White Ant Colony. That is where I need help from you, Serenta. At least fifty thousand troops."

"Gad, we just lost that many at Portal. That's a tall order for us."

"I know," replied Wiseria. "But we need them anyway. We will throw as many of our own into the fray. My military advisers tell me we can cross Copper

Creek at a point where the enemy will not expect it by diverting the flow of the water. I will ask someone to explain that more fully shortly. At the same time we will launch an offensive across the land bridge and catch the enemy in a pincers."

"All that is at your end," Bravada intervened. "We've got Acids, Greens and Browns snapping at us on all sides. Where's the help for us?"

Wiseria looked hard into Bravada's cold eyes. "My dear, Bravada," she said slowly, "I have visited your colony and what I saw there convinced me that if once the mighty Salt passion and anger is engaged, there is no force in all Antale that can stand against your warriors. The moment to engage that passion is now, and push those clamoring hordes of disgusting insects back where they belong. As you do that in the south, and we attack in the north, we all will win the day. The benefits of that you can well imagine."

Wiseria had struck a chord. Bravada's eyes lit up and her head moved up and down.

"And we've got a score of our own to settle with that dunghead, Intrepida," Serenta now put in. "You spoke of biological weapons, Wiseria. Well, we've got a surprise to plant on Intrepida's doorstep pretty soon. It'll take her and her whole damn colony out of the war so fast that she'll never know what happened."

A deep, heavy silence settled over the group of three. Finally, Wiseria spoke.

"These are terrible things we speak of here, my friends. My heart is heavy with our words. But we are not the agents of this misfortune, simply the poor fools who must correct it. May the spirit that guides our hearts and minds ensure that as we act, we do not invoke greater evil for the future."

"Victory has a price. Same as everything else," said Serenta.

"Yes, but we must not make it too high," replied Wiseria. "Now, we have many details to discuss. With your agreement, I would like to bring our advisers into the circle."

The discussions continued long into the night and half the next day. When the delegations separated after that, the Blacks to return to the north of the lake and the Sugars and Salts to the south, the plans for an allied reprisal to the aggression were in place.

CHAPTER 6

The End and the Beginning

A KEY PART OF THE ALLIES' PLAN was to make a crossing for troops over Copper Creek. Wiseria remembered well the construction work of the Digger ants that she had seen on her previous journey. She wanted their help now. Pacifica volunteered to try to bring them, but this meant going right into the war zone. Wiseria was reluctant to risk her young friend's life again, but Pacifica was adamant; so she returned south with the Sugars and the Acids. Serenta gave her two soldiers for company and protection, and the three continued east with Bravada's party into Salt territory. It was there that Pacifica renewed a former acquaintance.

They were passing through a gorge that somehow seemed familiar to Pacifica when one of Bravada's guards called out, "Ho there, Bluffasta and you Peppers! Show some respect for the President."

Pacifica looked off to the side and saw the same platoon of mottled gray and brown Pepper soldiers she had encountered when last she came this way. The burly Bluffasta stood at their head and raised her right foreleg in mock salute as Bravada's party passed.

"Ho there, Bluffasta," Pacifica shouted. "You want to leg wrestle?"

"By the force!" exclaimed Bluffasta. "The little White ant!" She rushed over and embraced Pacifica with a fierce hug. Pacifica's Sugar guards looked on amazed.

"What brings you back in these bad times?" asked Bluffasta.

Suddenly Pacifica had an idea.

"I have to go north to the Digger nest," she said. "Do you know it?"

"Yes, but it's bad news out there. The whole country is crawling with those fire-tailed Acids."

"Could you take me and my companions to the Diggers?" asked Pacifica.

"Only if I lost my mind."

"Better your mind than your honor."

"By the force! What do you mean by that?" Bluffasta waved legs and antennae furiously. The Sugars stepped back.

"I mean, I need your help. We're working to put the Acids and all the rest of their like back in their nests."

"You say that while you travel with Salts?" Bluffasta waved contemptuously at Bravada's party now some distance ahead. "They can be the worst of the lot."

"That's why I need your help. We've got to get things into balance. I need the Diggers' help, too. Will you take me there?"

Bluffasta munched her mandibles for a moment, then said, "All right, White ant, I'll do it. But remember, when they make you President one day, I want to be Captain of the Guard."

"You've got it," replied Pacifica.

They did a little wrestler's dance with each other, then Bluffasta selected two of her platoon to accompany them, and they all chased off after the party of Salts. Pacifica told Bravada she was leaving with the Peppers. Bravada said nothing, just looked contemptuously at Bluffasta, then continued on her way.

"Bad news Bravada," Bluffasta snorted, but not strong enough to be detected.

Bluffasta was right about the presence of Acid ants everywhere. They spent the next day and a half dodging patrols and could easily have been caught several times. But the Peppers knew the territory and could melt out of sight in the twinkling of an eye or the twitching of an antennae. Finally, they came out on the spot where Pacifica had first seen the Diggers' nest. It looked just the same, a solid, flat-topped castle surrounded by its moat. Pacifica saw a lone Digger ant patrolling the ramparts.

"Hello, Digger," she called. "Do you know an ant name of Wacka Wacka?"

"Who wants to know?" the guard called back, suspiciously.

"The name's Pacifica. I was here a few weeks ago with President Wiseria. Wacka will remember us."

"Don't bet on it, mate. She's got a memory like a cobweb. Misses more than it catches. Hang on a minute, I'll get her for you."

A few minutes later she returned with another ant.

"Who's looking for Wacka Wacka?" asked the other.

"Hello, grilly groll," called Pacifica. "Have you stepped in any dilly dangs lately?"

"Well, strike me!" said Wacka Wacka. "It's one of the White ants. Who's the rum looking crew with you this time?"

"Hey, did she insult me?" demanded Bluffasta.

"No, they just talk like that," said Pacifica. "These are my escorts," she called to the Diggers. "They're Sugars and Peppers—friends. Can we come over? It's dangerous out here."

"Yeah, red bums everywhere. We've kicked more than a few lately."

"Well, can we come in?"

"No one comes in here. We come and get you."

"How do you do that? The moat looks impassable."

"Hang on. Stay where you are."

Five minutes went by. Other Digger ants had sauntered up onto the ramparts, casually looking at the strangers. Pacifica and company were getting nervous, expecting an Acid patrol to come by any time. Suddenly a small rock beside Bluffasta popped up followed by Wacka Wacka's head. Bluffasta leapt three inches into the air.

"Ha, almost gotcha," chuckled Wacka Wacka. "Come on, don't stand around gawking. Follow me. Last one in pull the rock back."

Pacifica followed her Digger friend down the hole. It was long and narrow and at one point very damp. She guessed they were passing under the moat. Finally, they came out into a large chamber.

"I expect you want to see the guv'nor," said Wacka Wacka. "So I brought you right to her."

Pacifica sensed the presence of several other ants. One of them spoke.

"Hello, I'm Matilda. Would you like a bit of something? You must be tired and hungry from your journey."

Everyone, even Bluffasta relaxed with the Digger hospitality. They were given a salty tasting paste to nibble on. They found it strange but very refreshing. Pacifica quickly explained why they had come. She wanted a party of five hundred Diggers to help divert the waters of Copper Creek for an allied crossing. Without hesitating, Wacka Wacka volunteered to lead them. Matilda agreed.

"We need to start right away," said Pacifica. "It will take at least three days to get around the lake."

"Why would we go that way?" asked Wacka Wacka. "We'd wear our legs down to the knees before we got there."

"Do you know another way?" asked Pacifica.

"Too right, mate," said Wacka Wacka. "You better get some shuteye while I get the crew together. We'll leave in a couple of hours."

After a short rest, Pacifica found herself two hours later saying goodbye to her Sugar and Pepper companions, who were enjoying exploring the mystery of the Digger nest.

"Don't forget, little White ant," said Bluffasta, giving her another fierce Pepper hug, "Captain of the Guard."

"No, I won't forget. Thank you for helping me."

The other way that Wacka Wacka took them was north along the shore of the lake so that they were barely out of the water most of the time. Finally, they came to the obstacle that Pacifica had been waiting for—the rapidly running Copper Creek, more than ten yards wide where it entered the lake.

"Come on. Alley oop. Stay close to me, Whitey," said Wacka Wacka, and started climbing a large tree. Five hundred dark brown Digger ants strung out behind her like a trickle of sap running over the bark. Pacifica stayed close to the leader. They went up the trunk, then out along a thick branch, then a thinner one, then another, each one thinner than the last, until they were in amongst the leaves on the outermost branch, swaying in the breeze thirty feet above the rushing water of Copper Creek. Pacifica was terrified. But the worst was still to come.

Their tree was connected to a similar one on the other side by a slender vine, about a half inch in diameter, that whipped and danced in the breeze. Without pausing for a moment Wacka Wacka set off along the vine. Pacifica followed, not daring to pause or think, for fear her nerve would escape her. As the infernal branch dipped and swung and twisted, they were sometimes right side up looking down, but more often wrong side round looking up. Pacifica hung on for dear life, following step by step behind Wacka Wacka. Five hundred Diggers followed, not one losing her grip.

Finally, they were down the other side. After such a crossing, nothing could be difficult. They struck north along Copper Creek and soon came up under the land bridge. There they were picked up by a Black patrol who led them on another two hundred yards where they were to build the crossing for the troops.

The creek was quite shallow here, but ran fast through a narrow channel in an otherwise broad and dry creek bed. The idea was to cut a diversionary channel, about eighteen inches wide so that they could drop a bridge of some sort across it. At the right moment, they would open up the channel, the water would be diverted into it, and they would have a crossing over the prebuilt bridge.

Wacka Wacka took one look at the project and muttered, "Bloody impossible! But let's get on with it anyway, mates."

Back in Blackhall the days were passing quickly for Wiseria as she plotted the strategy for the allied offensive. Only one week remained of the original four that Electra had told her Aggressa would need before she would launch her deadly attack with winged wasps. Wiseria must strike first or all would be lost.

Electra had worked day and night to prepare enough of the poisonous mould for an attack on Aggressa's wasp-breeding nest. This work had to be coordinated with the breeding of the male ants who must carry the poison to the enemy before the wasps could get out of the nests. A great scare went through the Black Ant Colony a few days later when a wave of wasps came over. Their flight was uncoordinated and erratic and caused no damage.

"That was a trial run," Electra warned Wiseria. "They're programming the wasps to land on your nests. We can expect at least one more of these before the real thing."

Two days later another wave of wasps came over. This time they divebombed the nests without landing. Terrified Black ants scurried around in futile panic.

"I think they're ready," said Electra. "We're out of time. We have to go tomorrow."

One Black nest had been selected for developing the male ants who would carry the future of the entire Black colony on their wings. Electra had carefully managed their emergence from pupation so that they would be ready to go at the right time. They were fed a chemical secretion to dampen their natural sex drives so that they could focus on the work they had to do. In the last few days of preparation Pacifica worked closely with Electra in overseeing the operation.

A single male ant named Alexander had been selected to lead the raid. Pacifica spent the last few hours with him before they left.

"Biology is not kind to us males," Alexander said sadly. "A brief moment is all we have. I haven't even seen the outside world. What's it like, Pacifica?"

"Come, I'll show you," she said. Pacifica led the way from the large breeding chamber where the rest of the males were milling around. They went up along one of the tunnels that the workers had enlarged to accommodate the bulky wings of the males. They emerged on the top of the mound under a bright star-filled sky in the darkness of early morning just before dawn. Alexander sighed in wonder.

"What's it all mean, Pacifica?" he asked. "It feels wonderful, but I don't understand."

"I wish I could tell you," she replied. "But I don't know either. All I can say is that there's a spirit coursing through everything. At its best it runs very sweet. At its worst, it's cruel and bitter. When you leave, the day will be cool and sunny. And you'll be up there in the sky with the breeze at your back, and you'll see the lush green of Antale spread out below you with the blue water of Lake Miasma away to the south just coming alive in the dancing sunlight. In that moment, Alexander, you'll know the sweetness more fully than I can ever know it. Because you will be in free flight with the energy of life and light in your wings, and you will know then the answer to your question. Oh, how I wish I could be up there with you at that moment!"

"You will be, Pacifica. At least, I will feel you're with me."

"Then, I'll give you my energy, too," she replied, coming close to him and feeling the strength of his wings touching her. "For now comes the bitter spirit," she continued. "You must travel east on the course that Electra has given you until you find that nest of evil, and lead the attack to destroy all the wickedness inside. In that moment you will know more of life than the rest of us learn in a lifetime."

She fell silent. Nor did Alexander speak again. They stayed close together on the top of the mound watching the stars fade and the first streaks of dawn light up the sky. Finally, Pacifica spoke.

"I must go now," she said, "to bring the others. Good speed to you, Alexander. I will never forget you."

Pacifica went back down inside the mound to supervise the workers who were beginning to bring the winged males out. Specially trained officers were stationed at the entrance of each passage to give every male a tiny cocoon containing the deadly mould Electra had prepared. Great care had to be taken against accidental perforation of any cocoon on the ground for fear of contaminating the nest. After about an hour a thousand winged males, each clutching his deadly cargo, were assembled on top of the mound. A thousand more Black and White soldiers were on hand to cheer them on. Wiseria came out to speak to them. She stood beside Alexander.

"Words cannot begin to say how much the hopes of our entire colony go with you this morning," she said. "We stand fixed in a terrible moment. If you are successful in your mission, the free colonies of Antale will be given the time they need to turn back the aggression that is upon us. Even as we assemble here, fifty thousand troops from our sister Sugar colony are but a day's march away. The preparations for their invasion supported by your sisters, now gathered around you here, are almost complete. Your mission this morning strikes the first blow for freedom and the new world. Go with the power and glory of your cause!"

A resounding cheer broke out from all the soldiers looking on. The winged warriors picked it up and tossed it back. Alexander waved for silence.

"Squadron leaders, prepare your sections!" he shouted. "In formation, follow me!"

Alexander saluted Wiseria, then lifted into the air. He rose straight up, hovering alone for a moment, until squadron after squadron took to flight, and the sky turned black under the cloud of their beating wings. With Alexander leading, the swarm turned eastward over Copper Creek, driving into the heart of the Red Ant Colony.

Alexander led them unerringly to their target. He had a complete map of the territory in his mind. He saw the great dome of Centrasia to the south, then swung north east, over the outer ring of Red ant nests until he fixed on Number 37 at the back. As the swarm closed in, the Red guards at the tunnel entrances leapt in terror and moved to raise the alarm. Before anything could be done, a thousand Black ant warriors dove down into the large, wide open tunnels. Inside, they were soon among the buzzing fury of several thousand wasps and Red worker and soldier ants. The Blacks exploded their deadly cocoons into the thrashing frenzy. Others stationed on the surface crushed their contents among the seething Red soldiers coming to the attack. As the agony of realization spread throughout the nest, the full panic of the terror they had sought to unleash on others—now turned upon themselves—gripped every Red ant and the hordes of wasps. They fought to escape from the mound, but the entrances were blocked by the Black forces crowding in and by the accumulating bodies of dead and dying victims. The dreadful surprise of the Black ant invasion was complete.

Word of the success was brought back by a small communication corps of winged males who had been selected beforehand for that purpose. Jubilation spread throughout the whole Black Colony as the message passed from mound to mound. For the first time in almost two months, the hard pressed Blacks and Whites had something to cheer about.

The energy carried down to the excavation work the Digger ants were doing to divert the flow of Copper Creek.

"Bloody good show, mate," Wacka Wacka exclaimed when Pacifica brought her the news. "You Blacks have gone up a notch or two with that. Now just you wait until we pull the plug on this here creek, and you'll see another bloody miracle."

The Diggers had been joined by a contingent of Wood ants, whom the Diggers called Chompers, whose job it was to cut and position branches across the channel the Diggers had dug for the creek water. All of this activity was well camouflaged from observation by any Red patrols on the other side of the creek by heavy bushes growing in the creek bed. It took a few more days, but finally Wacka Wacka declared they were ready for the test.

"Hey, you Chompers," she said, "I hope you've got that bridge well anchored. When this water comes through, look out for a gusher!"

The Diggers had constructed the holding dam with an elaborate system of vines and rocks and earth so that when they pulled the vines away, the whole thing would come tumbling down. The force of the creek water would do the rest, and if the plan worked, a new channel would be cut. The Chompers' bridge was already in place so that the invading troops could cross over the new channel, and once the old one had dried up they could get to the other side of the creek. At least that was the theory. No one had ever put such an audacious scheme to the test.

The fifty thousand invading forces of Sugar troops had now arrived and were camped in temporary quarters not far away. An equal contingent of Black,

White and Yellow troops were waiting in their locations near at hand. Wiseria, Pacifica, Antonia and all of the generals were there to watch the Diggers "pull the plug," as Wacka Wacka described it.

"Here we go, mates," she shouted. "Give her the old heave ho!"

The five hundred Diggers supported by hundreds more Black workers began to tug at the vines. Nothing happened at first, but with every ant putting her back into it, slowly the dam began to move. Then some water came, first a trickle, then a small stream, then a jet through a narrow opening, and finally a torrent, as the whole thing came crashing down.

"Thar she blows!" screamed Wacka Wacka, dancing up and down. "What a bloody beauty!"

All the Diggers and other workers cheered, but the excitement was short-lived as the flood waters rose up and began to tug at the bridge.

"Get onto the bridge! Get onto the bridge!" Wacka Wacka bellowed. "Hold the bugger down before we lose her!"

A feverish torrent of more than a thousand ants poured onto whatever footing they could find among the branches of the bridge, and formed chains of ant bodies to hold on to the quivering structure. For ten agonizing minutes it seemed the bridge would be swept away as the waters tugged at it, but finally the flood subsided into the new channel and the bridge held firm above the rushing water. The Chompers dashed up onto their creation and did a crazy war dance.

"Not bad, eh?" their foreant shouted at Wacka Wacka. "You Diggers didn't steal the whole show!"

"Good on yer, mates," Wacka Wacka called back. "There's hope for you Chompers yet."

Wiseria came over to congratulate them. "Well, Wacka Wacka, you certainly made good on your promise to help straighten out the world. Thank you."

"Don't think we're going to stop here, mate," said Wacka Wacka. "Me and the Diggers intend to be first over the bridge to kick some red bums. We're good at that, too, you know."

"I'm sure you are," laughed Wiseria. "All right, we'll be honored to have you—Diggers, Chompers, everyone. But now take the rest of the day off. You've earned it."

Though this was a moment of celebration, Wiseria knew there was no time to lose before launching the invasion. She anticipated the fury of Aggressa at being thwarted in her planned wasp attack, and expected some other form of retaliation at any time. Indeed, Aggressa's anger at her first real setback knew no bounds. Everyone responsible for planning the wasp sortie who was not killed in the Black raid was executed for incompetence. The furious Red leader demanded that the scientists train their own Red males to perform as the Blacks had done. When told this would take several weeks to prepare, she howled in rage for two days, thereby giving the Black and Sugar forces the valuable time they needed to prepare for their invasion.

Aggressa's next move also played into Wiseria's strategy. Determined to show some form of retaliation, Aggressa pulled her troops back from the southern offensive to leave that effort to the Greens and Browns. The full Red fury was then turned on the land bridge to try to force the crossing that had for weeks been denied them. Wave after wave of Red soldiers hurled themselves against the barricades the Black troops had built across the bridge. The fighting was the fiercest of the war. The Black forces held, but when the Reds lobbed cocoons of poisonous gas, obtained from the Acids over the barricades, the Black defense began to crumble. It was then that the Black and Sugar joint command gave the order to launch the invasion over Copper Creek.

Code-named Liberation, the operation moved off in early evening. Throughout the night, a hundred thousand Sugar, Black, White and Yellow troops scrambled over the crossing built by the Diggers and the Chompers, and slowly worked their way south under the shelter of the high creek banks, towards the fighting at the land bridge. The Sugar forces commanded by General Domina were to come up on the enemy right at the bridge. The other allied forces commanded by General Monta would circle inwards toward Centrasia and strike the massed Red army from behind. General Alena was in charge of the defending Black forces at the bridge.

Just after daybreak, Domina sent a transmission to Alena that they were ready. Alena pressed the attack from the Black side. The Reds retaliated and the Blacks fell back. Sensing a breakthrough, the Reds threw everything they had at the defenders. The Blacks slowly retreated. Red soldiers, massed in thousands, crowded onto the bridge, pushing the defending Blacks slowly back. When almost the entire bridge was packed with Red soldiers, General Domina gave the order for the Sugars to attack.

They caught the Red forces entirely by surprise. The strong Sugar soldiers poured up the creek bank from both north and south of the bridge and threw themselves into the attack. They cut through the Red line, trapping thousands of Red troops on the bridge while they pushed the remainder back, away from the bridge. Just as the Reds were struggling to recover from this onslaught, General Monta's forces hit them from behind.

The Red army was now cut in two, one part caught on the bridge between Black and Sugar troops, the other part trapped on the approach to the bridge between Sugar and other allied forces. Terror, surprise and confusion weakened the normal Red ferocity. General Alena now attacked hard from the Black side, pushing the Red soldiers back against the Sugars. Those who were not killed in the fighting jumped off the side of the bridge, plunging to their death in the swift waters below. Soon the bridge was clear of Red invaders and General Alena's Black troops poured across to support Domina's Sugars.

Not that they needed much support. The Red army was now in complete disarray. Caught between the fierce pincers of troops fighting for liberation, they lost control of the field. Splintering into disorganized units, Aggressa's once mighty fighting machine began to fall back, then run, scattering in all directions with allied soldiers in hot pursuit. In less than four hours of the fiercest fighting Antale had ever seen, Operation Liberation had achieved a spectacular triumph. The Red army was routed. The victorious allied forces regrouped and began the march to liberate Centrasia.

In the south, in the other theatre of war opened by the Acids' brutal surprise attack on the Sugars' military post at Portal, events were building towards another climax. When President Serenta received a cryptic message from Wiseria saying, "Liberation is launched," she moved on her own initiative against the Acids. So far the Sugars had made no attempt to engage the enemy, and the Acids had established a strong grip on territory to the east and north. The Salts were beginning to come out of their slumber, but so far they were pressing mainly against the Browns in the north. The Acids had undisputed control over the territory they had invaded. The Sugars were now ready to take that away from them.

Serenta's strategic centerpiece was the Showdown Project, otherwise known as Project S. For several years Sugar scientists had been experimenting with technology unique in Antale for creating an explosive force. They had stumbled on this somewhat by chance and had learned how to make small explosive charges by mixing certain chemicals together. The Showdown Project had taken this a step further by formulating a delayed action component, thereby allowing the experimenters to plant a device then move to safety before it exploded. They had carried out successful tests in underground sites at the back of their colony near the Rim, slowly increasing the size of the charge each time. Since the day of the attack by the Acids on Portal several weeks ago, they had stepped up their research to the point where they now believed they had a device that could destroy an entire ant nest. Though the scientists felt they needed more time to perfect the instrument, President Serenta and her joint chiefs of staff were pressing to use it against the Acids. When they received word that the troops were going into action in the north in Operation Liberation, they decided to activate Project S in the south.

The main problem was how to get the bomb into an Acid nest. It had to be inside to be effective. Various schemes were considered, based on floating it over to the islands and using a task force to try to get past Acid sentries. Other possibilities were to try to drop it from the sky. But all of these were rejected as unworkable. Finally, one of the team hit on the idea of using a delusory beetle.

This beetle was the very same creature that Wiseria, Pacifica and Roanda had seen on the beach when they had visited the Sugar Colony in early summer. There they had been appalled at the intoxicating effect it seemed to be having on the dissolute Sugar ants around it. Now the Sugar generals were proposing to use this same effect to induce the Acid ants to take the beetle into their nests.

They began with a test to see if the Acids could be deceived. A small task force of Sugar soldiers herded a beetle up close to the enemy lines. When an Acid patrol appeared, the Sugars fled in mock fear, leaving the beetle behind. The Acid soldiers milled around it and before long tasted its secretions, which they obviously found desirable, for they quickly took the prize away. Next day the Sugars allowed another beetle to be captured the same way with similar results. They decided it was time for the real thing.

They had prepared the bomb as a small cylinder, which they strapped in place under the beetle's stomach. Though this caused the creature to waddle a bit, it could nevertheless move along quite well, and the bomb could not be seen behind its hairy legs. When the beetle stopped, which was as often as it could, it squatted down, completely covering the bomb. The Sugars used a group of ordinary workers as a decoy, who took the walking weapon out close to Acid lines and pretended to make quite a fuss when a waiting Acid patrol pounced on them and seized their charge. The last thing the Sugars saw of their prize beetle, it was waddling along under a cooperative Acid guard, across the causeway to the main Acid nest of Omaka.

Though the Sugars could not know it, the Acid leader, Intrepida, had taken a particular interest in the first two delusory beetles. Though she detested the effect its secretions had on her own troops—and anyone who succumbed was severely punished—she saw the possibility of preparing the secretions in quantity to be used to weaken an enemy's will to resist attack. She could see the irony of turning a Sugar weakness against themselves. When she heard that a third and even larger beetle had been captured, she ordered it brought into her own quarters, where she asked a team of scientists and military officers to attend with her in inspecting it. That was what they were doing when the bomb exploded.

Colonel Alexa, the Sugar officer who had been on duty on the top of Portal on the day of the infamous Acid attack, was standing in the same place again. Portal was partly recommissioned, but nowhere near its original strength. It served mainly as an observation post of Acid activity. That is what Alexa was doing that day. With two other officers, she had been tracking the progress of the walking beetle bomb toward Omaka. When she saw the Acids take it inside, she informed President Serenta by transmission, then looked meaningfully at her companions and waited.

It took another hour for the chemicals inside the bomb to complete their deadly integration. It was high noon of a hot, cloudless summer day. Into that benign atmosphere erupted the birth of explosive warfare on Antale.

As Alexa watched, the whole top of Omaka blew up into the air, particles of dirt and sand cascading into the water twenty feet away. She saw a small tongue of flame licking at the rim of a crater that had once been the pride of the Acid Colony. The nest, which had been built low to the ground, was now just a gaping hole, from which billows of smoke and dust were rolling out. Alexa's message to her President was succinct: "Showdown! Mission accomplished!"

Meanwhile, up on the northern front, Aggressa had just learned of her army's defeat at the land bridge. Since the conquest of the Whites, the Red leader had operated from Centrasia out of the quarters formerly used by Appesia. That was where her head of military command, General Roma, found her to bring word that an allied invasion force was heading for Centrasia. For the first time, fear clutched at Aggressa's heart. She rushed to the top of the mound and looked out. Down on the courtyard she saw a tide of fleeing Red soldiers. Up on the rise, less than fifty yards away, a broad line of enemy invaders was coming towards her.

"Why are those ants running?" she screamed at General Roma. "They must turn and fight."

"We're bringing up reinforcements now, Commander," said Roma. "We'll form a line at the edge of the courtyard. But we may not be able to hold the city."

"Then destroy it!" ordered Aggressa.

"Excuse me, Ma'am?" Roma looked quizzically at her Commander.

"Destroy Centrasia!" Aggressa shouted. "Set every worker ant to tear it apart. Kill all the White slaves! Wipe every trace of this place out of existence!"

Roma was dumbfounded. To make her point, Aggressa tore at the earth around her, scattering small pebbles and shards in all directions.

"You understand me, General?" Aggressa was now raging. "Destroy everything! Those Whites will never come back here. And after this place, every last White nest. We will fight on from our own colony, but the Whites will have nothing. Gone! All gone! Do you hear?"

"Commander, I must go to the front," said Roma.

Aggressa seemed to regain some composure. "Yes, General," she said, "take the battle to them. But if you must fall back, destroy everything. I will return to the homeland and rouse the mighty spirit of our workers. Hold the enemy, General. We will strike again."

Aggressa turned and rushed away into the mound. Within the hour she was heading rapidly with her guard back to her own nest in the Red Colony. Behind her the Red army had already engaged the advancing allied line in bitter fighting.

In the south, President Serenta lost no time in following through on the destruction of Omaka. The Acid troops who had witnessed the devastation were paralyzed with fear. Workers from the adjoining islands poured out of their nests in mass confusion. Troops on the causeway abandoned their posts and mingled helplessly with the workers. When they turned and saw a solid line of ten thousand Sugar soldiers advancing over the causeway, they offered no resistance. By the end of the day, a Sugar occupying force had secured the entire colony.

At the same time, Serenta sent two more divisions north along the shore of Lake Miasma. Word spread ahead of them of the destruction of Omaka. Acid troops, who only a day earlier had terrorized the chain of unorganized nests, now themselves looked in terror at the advancing Sugar line. The fight had gone out of the once marauding Acids. In broken and disorganized units they fled from the nests they had occupied, and struggled to get around the Sugars to return to their colony. The Sugars advanced unresisted and triumphant right up to the edge of the Green forces pushing south. This now formed the southern front, only a few hundred yards from the fighting around Centrasia.

To the east, the Salts had also gained momentum and were now driving Brown troops back into their own territory. Bravada seemed to be able to call up unlimited resources, as tough and wiry workers from the back of her colony were pressed into service. Though not skilled soldiers, these ants fought fiercely under the direction of regular Salt commanding officers. It almost seemed that death on the battlefield was preferable to these recruits than whatever life they had back in their nests. Under such a fierce onslaught, the Brown troops were soon in full retreat.

As Narcissa and Barbaria continued to receive continuing reports of reverses on the battlefield, they began to realize the folly of their first treacherous attack against the Whites at the beginning of the war. Their former Federation partners were again at Centrasia, driving the Red invaders out. Aggressa was holed up in her own nest and no longer seemed interested in the Greens and Browns. Word had reached them of the weapon the Sugars had used to devastate the Acids. Now these same Sugars were at their own doorstep, flanked by the unstoppable fighting fury of the Salts. Realizing their ambitions were lost, Narcissa and Barbaria looked for a way to escape.

They had several choices to solicit for peace. Unfortunately for them they made the wrong decision. They assumed their former Federation partners would show them little sympathy. Likewise the Sugars, who were now close allies of the Blacks and Whites. That left the Salts. Bravada, they reasoned, was one after their own heart. If they could do a deal with her and avoid further fighting, there might still be a future for them.

The two fearful dictators arranged a secret meeting with Bravada on the edge of the battle zone in neutral territory. Bravada arrived with a heavily armed escort. She listened to their proposals for an hour, then invited them to dine with her. At the end of the meal, Bravada nodded to her guards who moved in and executed Narcissa and Barbaria on the spot. Their soldiers offered no resistance. The next day Salt troops marched unopposed into the Green and Brown colonies and Bravada laid claim to them as her conquest of war.

At Centrasia, General Roma knew she could not hold the city. The allied forces were far too strong. Her best strategy was to withdraw from the whole White Ant Colony and try to keep the allies from invading Red territory. She transmitted her decision to Aggressa. The Red Supreme Commander had only one question.

"Is Centrasia destroyed?" she asked.

"Yes, Commander, Centrasia is destroyed," replied Roma.

"And all the rest of the White ant nests? Are they all destroyed?"

"Yes, Commander, they are all destroyed."

"Then come home, General. You have done well."

After Roma had issued the orders to withdraw, she went one last time to the top of Centrasia. Despite some scars of battle, the great white city stood as proud and beautiful as ever. The other White nests all around looked similarly at ease. General Roma knew that if she had achieved nothing else in this long and bitter war, she had at least preserved a core part of Antale heritage from mindless destruction.

Wiseria had not waited for the fighting to cease before she went to the front to be present at the liberation of Centrasia. Accompanied by Pacifica, she walked across the courtyard as her troops were entering the mound. Within minutes a flood of freed White workers rushed out of the nest and leaped and danced with joy around their liberators. No one recognized Wiseria or Pacifica. The two could mingle anonymously with the jubilant crowd, rejoicing that at last the nightmare of Red occupation was at an end. Pacifica and Wiseria climbed to the top of the mound. It was late afternoon, and long shadows were beginning to fall across the nests of the colony.

"It was an evening like this," Wiseria said, "when we returned from our journey to the Rim. Do you remember, Pacifica? We stepped then into the first quagmire of treachery, and I thought I lost you. Now, here we are together, again. The war is ending, and, perhaps, just perhaps, tomorrow we can start a new beginning."

Two hundred yards away in her nest Aggressa received the last of several grim transmissions. She turned to Agrippa, the only officer attending her.

"Narcissa and Barbaria are dead," said Aggressa. "Bravada has executed them and taken their colonies. Intrepida perished in a hellish explosion triggered by the Sugars. Our own troops have fallen back to our lines. What do you say, Agrippa? Did you think it would come to this? We almost had them. Just a few more days. It's a pity you let that scientist escape with our bacterial secrets. Did you know that caused us to lose the war, Agrippa?"

"No, Commander, I hardly think... ."

"Hush, Agrippa. Don't think. It doesn't suit you. They'll sell me out, you know."

"Who, Commander? What do you mean?"

"The generals and you, Agrippa. All of you will sell me out. Just to save your skins. You see these cocoons, Agrippa? Presents from Intrepida. We used them on the Blacks. Very effective. At least you and I will die with honor."

"No, Commander, don't!"

Agrippa tried to scuttle from the room. Aggressa blocked her path and crushed one of the poison gas cocoons. Within moments, both ants were writhing in death agony.

"At least Centrasia was destroyed, Agrippa," gasped the dying Supreme Commander. "No one can deny me that."

CHAPTER 7

Union Without Vision

THE GREAT WAR IN ANTALE WAS OVER. The longest, hardest summer in the history of the ants was also coming to an end. Little time remained to put new structures in place before winter would be upon them. Wiseria knew that she must move quickly to bring the hope of a new beginning while memories were still fresh, and while her own strength lasted. She doubted she would see another summer.

The Red army, now under the control of General Roma, capitulated quickly. Orders were given to withdraw all Red troops from the Yellow Ant Colony, which they had occupied for most of the summer. As bitter as were the feelings of the Yellow survivors against their Red aggressors, their joy at the return of their leader, Antonia, with her small band of troops was unbounded. The same sweet breeze of liberation blew across all of the White mounds and on down among the unorganized nests along the eastern shore of Lake Miasma, where the Acids had not so long ago swept in. Likewise in the Black colony, which, though never occupied, had stood so close to the brink for so long, both workers and soldiers celebrated the joy of victory. In the colonies of the Sugars and the Salts, though each had its own particular bitter memories of the war, the same breath of relief filled expectations of a new and better time ahead. The question facing the leaders was how to manage the aftermath of war. What would define the last few weeks of this year ending in preparation for the new?

Wiseria, acting in her capacity as President of the Federated Colonies, invited the leaders of the victorious coalition to Centrasia. They met in the great conference hall of the Federation. Here the memory of Appesia was still fresh, particularly for Wiseria. Whatever might have been her failings, the old White ant, and former President of the Federation, had always sought to serve with honor. Her place as leader of the White Colony was now temporarily held by

Aristica until a new leader could be elected. Wiseria opened the session by paying tribute to Appesia, then turned to the matters at hand.

The first question was how to treat the conquered aggressors. An allied military command had been placed in the Red Colony. The Sugars still maintained an occupying force on the Acid islands. The Salts were firmly in control of the Greens and Browns. Wiseria made her proposal.

"In times of upheaval it is all too common to look to the past and remember old grievances, rather than look to the future and imagine new agreements. I would hope that we do not make that mistake today. The wounds inflicted against all of our colonies in these past weeks are still raw and deep. It would be all too easy for us to seek the healing through persecution of the colonies that inflicted them. However, the leaders who launched those attacks against our freedom have all perished in the carnage of their creation. There is no need for we who survived with dignity and honor to visit the crimes of those monsters on the ones who follow them. That is the pathway to eternal torment. We have, instead, the unique and historic opportunity today to create a new association of all the colonies of Antale, an assembly of former foes along with old and new friends, meeting in a forum where our thoughts are focused on creative cooperation for mutual improvement. That, I believe, must be the spirit of our common future. If we can embrace that in full sincerity, we surely can fashion the structures we need to achieve the outcome."

That was Wiseria's opening statement. Through hours that became days, that became more than a week of heated discussion, of proposal and counter proposal, she held fast to those principles of creative cooperation. Finally, what emerged was a new structure to be named Unicol, of which the five victorious colonies of Blacks, Whites, Yellows, Sugars and Salts became the first members and invited every other colony, even those as small as a single nest, to participate as equal members. The existing Federation was dissolved and its conference chamber in Centrasia declared to be the new House of Assembly for Unicol. Invitations were sent by messenger to every colony and the day of the first meeting set for one week's time.

One part of the structure, of which Wiseria disapproved, but on which all other founding leaders insisted, was the creation of a second governing group to be called the Protectorate. The function of the Protectorate was to act to protect member colonies from aggression by others. Its membership was restricted to the five powerful colonies of Blacks, Whites, Yellows, Sugars and Salts. Each had the power to veto a proposal made by one of the others. Wiseria anticipated problems with this arrangement, but nevertheless cast her approving vote for its creation. A new office of Conductor of Community was established as the chief administrative position to serve both the House of Assembly and the Protectorate.

The Day of Inauguration of Unicol dawned clear and warm over Centrasia. An intercolonial day of celebration had been declared throughout Antale and every worker who wished to attend the festivities was given leave to come, no matter how far she had to travel. The visitors had been arriving over the past two days, filling all the available space around the nest. Ants of every color, shape and size were there, eager to witness the historic ceremony. As the morning wore on, they sought for vantage points from which to watch, packing every square inch of mound facing the assembly area, clinging to bushes and blades of grass, even building living pyramids, where they continually changed places at the top so all could have a turn at watching. Any birds, flies or other marauders who tried to take advantage of the seething mass of ants were promptly beaten off by the enthusiastic spectators.

The object of all this interest was the courtyard immediately in front of the main entrance to Centrasia. This was the same area from which Explora's expedition had departed in early spring. Since then it had been for too many times a main stage in the theater of war. But now those scars were healed, and all Antale seemed to be here to celebrate a new time.

An intercolonial guard had cordoned off an area three feet square on the courtyard. The soldiers stood three deep, shoulder to shoulder, around the perimeter, holding back the masses pressing forward. As the sun reached the high point of noon, and as a gentle breeze stirred the ant-laden bushes, the signal was given to begin.

Roanda was serving as Mistress of Ceremonies. She stood on the official platform on the mound about six inches above the square below. On her signal a grand procession began on the far side of the courtyard, coming down the ant path from the land bridge. Antale had never before seen anything like this. It was a dream of delight for all who put their hearts and hopes in the future of cooperation and enterprise. Two hundred colonies had responded to the invitation to attend, and they now came marching in, ten to a delegation, weaving their way into a multicolonial tapestry of living anthood.

In five blocks they entered, each behind the leader of a major colony. Wiseria was at the front, first into the square, coming down the centre, in front of her Black delegation, stepping out proudly, nodding and waving to the thunderous acclaim from more than a million ants who recognized her contribution. This was the old warrior who had held fast to the cords of freedom when they seemed for certain to be torn from her grasp. Though today was for the inauguration of Unicol, there was no one watching who did not also know that it was the day of honor for Wiseria.

Following the block of colonies led by the Blacks, the next group came in with Serenta of the Sugars at the front, gold, athletic, a delight to see, striding down to the foreground to stand to the left of Wiseria. Next came Bravada, stern and disciplined, her sober delegation of Salts leading another block of forty colonies to line up to the right of the first. The pattern was completed by Aristica of the Whites and Antonia of the Yellows leading their blocks in to stand on either side of the square. The united colonies of Antale were assembled. Large and small stood side by side; friends and former enemies: Blacks, Whites, Yellows, Sugars and Salts; Reds, Greens, Browns and Acids; the former colonies who had never before formed in coalition: the Wood, Water, Marsh and Rocky Mountain ants; the Tigers, the Peppers, the Diggers and the Chompers—all were there, and almost two hundred others from near and far across Antale. Of all the prominent colonies, only the Dragons from the far side of the Dark Country were missing. They remained aloof and mysterious, but their absence here today could not daunt the significance of the achievement displayed on the courtyard. It was a first for Antale—the harbinger of a new united world.

Roanda from her platform looked down on the assembled multitude. "In the name of all the free colonies of Antale here assembled," she proclaimed, "I bid all delegations welcome to this Day of Inauguration of our United Colonies. As the first official act of our new organization, I place you in the charge of the first Conductor of Community, duly elected by unanimous approval of all members. Delegates of Unicol, I give you Conductor Pacifica."

Pacifica, who had been standing at the back of the platform, came forward. Delegates and spectators cheered and waved. Looking up at her protégé, no one was more satisfied at that moment than Wiseria. She had lobbied hard among the delegations over the past week to secure Pacifica's appointment, throwing the whole weight of her considerable prestige behind the effort. Though still young, Pacifica had proved her mettle, and Wiseria had convinced the other leaders to give this key appointment to her. Pacifica now spoke to the assembly:

"My dear sisters—delegates and citizens alike—to all of you I offer the greatest gift in life. I give you the gift of hope, symbolized here in the birth of our new assembly. For the first time in the history of Antale, we stand together, representatives of almost every colony in our world. In this place, all too recently the scene of bitter conflict, we can now stand side by side with hope in our hearts for a future we can forge together. As you have placed your confidence in me to be the Conductor of your Community, so I give my assurance to you, that I will with every last ounce of my energy strive in your service to keep Antale free from war and want. To the leaders of all colonies gathered here today for this occasion I say, let us commit to this one great cause. I ask you to instruct your ambassadors to work as one. There is no freedom unless all are free. There is no hope unless we all have hope. And there is no peace unless all of us have peace in our hearts. We, the ants of all Antale, stand together today determined not to repeat the mistakes of the past, and to learn together what we must know to create the future we all would wish to live in. Let us go now to the House of Assembly to begin our work."

That was how Unicol began. Would that it had lived up to its promise. Pacifica worked tirelessly to get things done, and much, indeed, was achieved in the first two weeks of operation: agreements of cooperation, offers of assistance, the development of trade, the sharing of expertise—as much and often more than could have been expected. This was in the House of Assembly. It was in the Protectorate that trouble first began.

At the end of the war there had been general agreement that occupying forces should be withdrawn from defeated colonies. The Sugars complied and brought their soldiers home from Acid territory. The Blacks and Whites likewise withdrew from the Red Colony. The Salts, however, refused to leave the Browns and Greens to independent rule, claiming Salt rights to protect their borders. The Sugars moved a motion of censure; the Salts vetoed it; and a new line of division was drawn. The Blacks tried to get agreement on reducing the size of armies; the Whites and Yellows supported the move; but the Sugars and the Salts rejected it. Thus the pattern was set for the buildup of armaments in the two largest colonies in Antale. That was where things stood when the first session of Unicol adjourned and delegates returned to their colonies for winter.

Pacifica traveled to Blackhall to discuss the outcome with Wiseria. She found the aging Black leader looking a little more frail, but still strong and powerful in her mind.

"You must understand, Pacifica," said Wiseria, "that we ants can change our nests, but we do not easily change our habits. We have a grand new House of Assembly, but we've still got some old ants, myself included, behind the scenes giving the orders. The Protectorate was a mistake. It perpetuates old power blocks. You must work to change that."

"I know, but how?" asked Pacifica.

"If I knew the answer to that, I would have proposed it," said Wiseria. She paused a moment, thinking. "You know," she continued, "it was to find such an answer that we sent Explora out onto the Rim. We hoped that she might discover a civilization that had solved the problem. But it seems that Explora is lost and we are left stumbling on our own."

Wiseria fell silent again, reflecting, thinking about the last communication they had received from Explora so many weeks ago. She had found something beyond the Rim, but what? Her last message was cut off. Something had happened to Explora out there. The Federation should have tried to send a rescue mission, but Antale had been so embroiled in war that no thought for anything else could be considered.

"You know, Pacifica," Wiseria spoke again, "I am at the end of my days, but there is one last thing I would like to do before I go. I would like to go again to Mount Opportunity. We were there together, you and I. That's where I met you. Perhaps if we went again together, you might find an answer to your question."

"It's a long way. Do you think you should?"

"Old bones do not make old hearts, Pacifica. I am at the limits of my strength, but nowhere near the margins of my mind. What I have done in war I did because others pushed me to it. But now I can do in peace what I alone may choose. There is little call for me now at Blackhall. Monta can take up the challenge here. I will go to Mount Opportunity. Will you come, my friend?"

"With all my heart," Pacifica replied.

Before they set off there was one thing Pacifica had to do. She sent an urgent message to the Pepper Colony: "They didn't make me President, Bluffasta, but if Conductor will do, then I have need for a Captain of the Guard." Two days later Bluffasta and two other Peppers were at Centrasia.

"By the force, little White ant," said Bluffasta, "I must be crazy to leave home with winter coming on. Do you have warm cellars here for my cold feet?"

"Where we have to go," laughed Pacifica, "they say you can forget your feet. It's so cold you don't know you have them. I want you to come with me and Prime Minister Wiseria to Mount Opportunity."

"Aiyee! You don't want a Captain of the Guard. You need a doctor for your mind."

Despite her protestations, however, no one was more enthusiastic about the journey than Bluffasta. Along the way she and her Pepper guards were a constant source of merriment, telling stories, singing songs, challenging all passersby, and unstintingly seeing to the welfare and comfort of Pacifica and Wiseria.

When they reached the foot of Escarpment Slope, the old Black leader looked apprehensively at the long climb ahead. They had been greeted by Jocula and her friendly Rocky Mountain ants.

"It's good to see you again, Jocula," said Wiseria, "but I wish it might be at the top of this climb rather than at the bottom."

"By the force!" exclaimed Bluffasta, looking at the Rocky Mountain ants running around. "All this ant power. We should put it to some good use."

"Too true! Too True!" said Jocula. "How do? How do?"

Bluffasta looked at her strangely, then went into a huddle with her ants. Minutes later a large green leaf mysteriously appeared, moving along the path led by Bluffasta. Underneath the leaf a bevy of energetic workers were carrying it along.

"A chariot for your esteemed Prime Ministership," announced Bluffasta.

"Oh me! Oh my!" said Jocula.

"Up, up, up you go, go, go," said Bluffasta.

"Oh, no, no, no!" protested Wiseria. Then everyone burst out laughing, and Wiseria gratefully accepted the ride. They began the climb up Escarpment Slope, Bluffasta merrily leading the way, and keeping an ever expanding audience of Rocky Mountain ants entertained with her jokes.

When they reached the top, Wiseria insisted on getting down and walking with the others. Jocula said goodbye, but Pacifica asked if the Rocky Mountain ants carrying the leaf might continue with them. She was thinking of the hard climb still ahead up Mount Opportunity. Jocula readily agreed and the party set off under the cover of darkness now descending over the Rim.

When they reached the foot of the mountain and began to climb, Wiseria again gratefully accepted the offer to ride on her leaf carriage. The air was cool and a steady breeze blew across the open country. Wiseria felt her body growing sluggish, and heavy, too, in a way she had never before experienced. Finally, they were at the top. The stars were out, cradling a crescent moon that hung before them over Antale. The starlight lit the pathway over the top of the mountain to Mission Control.

Colonel Observa and her party were waiting for them. It was a joyful reunion for Pacifica with the team who had been an important part of her life until she had returned to Antale with Wiseria last spring. Wiseria, too, was pleased to be back with the easy going but dedicated scientists at the observation post. Bluffasta and her guards strode around checking, touching, probing everything in genuine amazement. The Rocky Mountain ants huddled together near the entrance, feeling uneasily constrained from their normal activity of running about in endless motion. The closeness of the small scientific establishment was no place for them for any length of time.

Wiseria's party had picked an auspicious day on which to arrive. It was Thanksgiving. Colonel Observa, as a Sugar, knew how to celebrate it. She had put together a sumptuous meal from the produce of the granaries and new day's foraging. Protein dishes of butterfly, earthworms and snail were garnished with grass seeds, fluffy fungus and, of course, the all important sweet sugar beet from Observa's home colony. All this was spread around in great abundance so that travelers and residents alike could sample, chat and generally enjoy themselves. Despite the lateness of the hour, no one seemed inclined to want to end the festivities. It was, indeed, a time for all to be thankful for the outcome of the summer that had once seemed so dark and hopeless.

The only cloud that hung in the memories of the key participants was the unknown fate of Explora. On the observation balcony, after the meal, Wiseria, Pacifica and Observa stood together looking out over the starlit expanse of the Rim.

"Tell me, Colonel," Wiseria said, "have you had any indications at all in these past weeks of what might have happened to Explora and her party? Is there any possibility they could still be alive?"

"Well, Ma'am," replied Observa, "if those ghostly transmissions we receive were facts, I might have news enough. They multiplied enormously for weeks after the Commander's disappearance. Sometimes I thought I almost heard her coming through amongst them. But we could never be sure. We need to get to the bottom of this mystery. We're just too far away. If we could get a listening post out there, along the route the expedition took, then I'm sure we'd learn something. I mean, we know now there's something out there beyond the emptiness. Explora discovered that much. We can't just leave it at that."

Pacifica put into words a thought that came to her as she listened to what the colonel had to say. "Would you like to lead such a party, Observa, to go out there next spring and retrace Explora's path to see what you can learn?"

Observa's enthusiasm was immediate. "I've been twitching at these control panels for weeks, hoping someone would ask me that. Yes, Pacifica, I would go in a minute. I'd make it more scientific, cautious, no heroics—step by step stuff to get to the bottom of this mystery."

"Then I think you should spend the winter putting your ideas together," said Pacifica. "Unicol needs to get a scientific program underway next year. Your mission could launch it. What do you think, Wiseria?"

The old leader spoke slowly in reply. "I think Antale could be well served by the two of you and what I hear you say. Yes, we must go again. Would that we could have done it sooner." She turned to look up at the stars. Pacifica noticed her tremble a little, crouching down somewhat, as if her legs would not support her.

"There's a truth out there," Wiseria continued. "We stumble and strain to put what little we know of it to good effect. I'd like to think we've made some progress on that, but the danger is we can't see the way ahead. Everything around us, the woods, the streams, the life of which we are a part, everything, even those stars and this great empty Rim, everything is unfolding. If we are to be a creative part of that, and not just a consequence, a mindless landmark along the way—if we are to be more than that, we must learn to look ahead. We need your listening posts, Observa, we need the scientific probes, but most of all we need to tap the energy of those stars and see in our hearts and minds what they must surely see." She turned to face her companions. "Well, those are the words of an old ant on this Thanksgiving night. I'm cold now. I must go in and get some rest. Goodnight to both of you. I'm glad to know Antale has the likes of you to care for its future."

Wiseria retired to the same chamber she had used when last at Mission Control. Pacifica and Observa rejoined the others. Their conversations and merrymaking continued into the early hours of the morning.

When Pacifica stirred the next day, the sun was well up. She recalled the journey she and Wiseria had made once before to the other side of the mountain and wondered if her old friend would like to go again. As Wiseria had not yet stirred, Pacifica went to wake her. When she entered the chamber, she knew immediately that something had happened. There was no life force in the dark room. She approached her sleeping friend and felt her carefully with her antennae. No energy flowed. Wiseria was dead.

Slowly, carefully, with soft and gentle reverence, Pacifica eased the body out, then carried it, as a nurse might lovingly carry a newborn pupae, to the large room which had been the scene of last night's Thanksgiving celebrations. She placed her friend in the midst of the abundance that still lay all around. The Rocky Mountain ants were sleeping together in a huddle, close to the entrance. Bluffasta and her Peppers also slept nearby. The scientists of the post were all either in their rooms or at their stations. Pacifica folded Wiseria's legs and antennae together in the manner that they form in a pupae just before birth. As Wiseria had come to life so might she leave it. Pacifica crouched beside her friend and mentor, mourning.

That was how Observa and the others found them not long afterwards when they entered the room. A new day had replaced the old. A good life had also passed away. Winter was coming and the travelers were a long way from home. They must make haste to start their solemn journey back.

Observa sent word from Mission Control to every colony about what had happened. A state funeral was set for two days hence in Blackhall, giving time for all those who would wish to attend to come. Outside the entrance to Mission Control, the Rocky Mountain ants steadied the leaf that had carried Wiseria in as a chariot, and must now serve to carry her away at the centre of a funeral procession. Pacifica, alone, wanting no assistance, lifted Wiseria's body and carried it outside. She placed it on the leaf, then moved to the front to lead the cortege out. Observa joined her, desiring also to pay full respect to one who had been such a friend to scientific exploration. Despite the danger of daytime travel across the Rim, the sad party set off with Bluffasta and her Peppers keeping a vigilant guard.

They crossed the Rim unhindered and proceeded on down Escarpment Slope. Halfway down they were met by Jocula and thousands of Rocky Mountain ants who had come out to pay their respects. The energetic spring had left the little ants' movements as they stood quietly while the procession passed. Jocula walked with Pacifica and Observa and continued with them to attend the funeral at Blackhall.

And so the pattern was established for all the distance home. Word was out ahead of them, and every colony suspended their winter preparations to line the route the procession had to take. The Wood ants and the Chompers came down bearing branches that they bowed in salute as the party passed. The Water ants built their sturdiest craft to be a safe funeral barge across the marshes. The Leaf ants spread a carpet of leaves and flower petals as they passed through the woods of Avalon.

They traveled slowly throughout the day and most of the night, resting only long enough to renew their strength for the final march into Blackhall. An autumn mist hung over the morning as they covered the last few hundred yards. Along this winding part of the trail the numbers coming out to mourn soon swelled to thousands. The Black ants poured out of their colony, spreading like a shining sea of ebony to welcome their honored leader home, as much triumphant in death as she had been in the last weeks of her life. Most of the mourners could not even see the cortege, but that did not quell their desire to be there in respect. General Monta and the whole four hundred strong Black governing council met the procession and led it into Blackhall.

The leaders of the other colonies were already there, two hundred of them, all returning again so soon after the inaugural celebrations of Unicol at Centrasia. Antonia of the Yellow Colony, who had spent most of the war as a displaced leader and guest at Blackhall, was particularly grief stricken. Serenta of the Sugars had been asked as the senior leader present to give the eulogy. Bravada of the Salts did not attend, but sent her representative.

The procession wound its way to the land bridge over Copper Creek which stood as a symbol to Wiseria's intransigence to hold the enemy at bay throughout the weeks of war. A small cairn of rocks had been erected as a monument on the Black Colony side. Wiseria's body was carefully placed into a cavity at the base. Serenta said only a few words of the many thousands that could have been spoken, but would mean no more.

"As she was in life, we remember her now. Brave, determined and above all wise. Of all of us, she was the only one who would never say her peace alone was sufficient. With all her great heart she wanted peace for all Antale, and would not flinch from what she had to do to secure it. Those of us who knew her well can best honor her life by now committing our own to secure the lasting peace that she so longed to know."

Pacifica with Antonia and Serenta rolled the final stone in place to seal Wiseria in her monument by the bridge. She would rest there now, a forever memory for all who passed that way: one great life that strived throughout to serve them all. The year of greatest danger for Antale was at an end, and winter's cool breath slowly settled in.

YEAR 2

SHAKY DREAMS

CHAPTER 8

Happy New Year

IT IS HARD FOR ANTS TO BE active during the winter. Their biology calls for hibernation and restoration of their bodies for next year's work. Long before cold frosts freeze the surface of the nests, the ants have filtered down the passageways, moving to higher temperatures in the lower galleries where they huddle together for added warmth. Any newly-hatched larvae are taken with them to be carried through the winter for transformation to pupae in the warmth of early spring.

Pacifica followed this winter pattern with her sisters in Centrasia, where she now lived to be close to her work at Unicol. She moved with the other ants deep inside the mound and felt the comfort of a secure and healthy community. But though her body was heavy and torpid with the change of season, her mind remained actively engaged in thinking about her responsibilities. The great achievement of Unicol was in place, but if it was to be successful in the coming year, she must develop a plan to guide her in conducting its affairs. It was one thing to be named Conductor, but quite another to be good at it. She thought about the two most important models in her life, Appesia and Wiseria. Both had been strong and capable leaders, but the one had been too gentle in the face of evil, leaving the other to carry the enormous responsibility of fighting back. Whatever else it did, Unicol must ensure that war never again engulfed Antale as it had last summer.

But the sores of future conflict were already festering. The creation and spread of weapons could be the crucible in which the next conflagration was mixed. The major colonies all had powerful new means of destruction, nurtured and used on the last grim battleground. If the leaders chose next summer to build that kind of strength, then it would breed fear across the land, thwarting all the best efforts of Unicol to work for cooperation and peace. How to avoid this direction was the question that Pacifica turned over and over in her mind.

She recalled two things Wiseria had said in her last days: old habits die hard, and the greatest failure of her generation was its inability to look ahead. If Wiseria was right, it was all too likely that the current leaders would see only the security of might and not be stirred by any new whisperings of a different future world. What could Pacifica do in her new found role as the Conductor of Unicol to lead toward the second kind of future?

One thing she knew was certain: effort moves to what the mind sees most clearly. The most likely reason why a future of cooperation and peace would elude the ants of Antale was that they could not imagine it. Old habits die hard and crowd out the fragile images of foresight. That was the essence of what Wiseria had said, and it suggested to Pacifica a strategy she should follow. She would use this winter time of dormant physical activity to stir the imaginings of what could be achieved next summer. She could at least try to do that in Centrasia. Communication between the nests would not be possible until spring. But if she could engage the ants around her here in creating a vision so powerful it would capture the imagination of others, then that might prove to be the catalyst she needed to make Unicol really work.

She looked for an ally and found a ready one in Roanda. The latter now served as Assistant Conductor at Unicol, so the two were working close together. Pacifica took Roanda a little way apart from the press of other ants so she could speak with her. She shared her thoughts about a winter strategy of visioning, then said, "I don't want to do anything formal on this. It mustn't have any connection with Unicol. That will only constrict it later on to what ambassadors feel they can agree with. It needs to be a grass roots movement among worker ants who see its value in their lives. Can you think of anyone who might get a group together for us to talk to?"

"Ventura comes to mind," Roanda replied. "She's one of the younger ones, born in early summer as a refugee. She was carried out of here as a pupae just ahead of the attacking Reds. She was literally bumped and tumbled into life as we fled over the land bridge. It had a profound effect on her outlook. She's articulate and has good credibility, even with the older workers."

"Speak to her about this, Roanda, and let me know if some interest builds up."

It was in this way over the next few weeks that discussion developed among a small circle of ants about an initiative which could be launched next spring and which could eventually spread across Antale. The young Ventura, as Roanda had anticipated, became a natural leader among the group. She was energetic and enthusiastic, bringing a fresh perspective that most of the older ants found strange and even a little disquieting. She would use the natural rhythm of the slowly circulating ant mass in the heart of the nest to spread her ideas.

"Is it so strange to think," she would say to a group of semi-dormant listeners, " that ants don't have to stay in their own nests, or even their own colonies, but can move around Antale, working in other communities, learning about the richness of the whole of life instead of just our small piece of it? We saw what could be done during the Great War. Do you remember the heroic co-operation of soldiers from different nests? But why does it take a war to find that out? Why couldn't we do it as part of a normal life of peace? Is that so strange?"

Some of her listeners would nod wisely and drift away into the ant mass. Others would show no indication that they had even heard. But a few would listen attentively, asking questions, making suggestions of their own. Over the weeks, this group grew to be several hundred, and one day in mid-winter, Roanda brought a message from them to Pacifica.

"Ventura has a group who would like to meet with you," she said. "Will you come?"

"Of course, lead the way," replied Pacifica.

The group had gathered in a chamber just large enough for them all to squeeze in and keep one another warm. When Pacifica entered, Ventura greeted her.

"It's good of you to come," she said. "We thought you might like to hear our ideas on how we could help you in your work with Unicol next summer."

"Why certainly," replied Pacifica. "I'd like to know what you think."

"Well, we know we're just ordinary workers, and some of us are very young, but we saw a lot of things during the war that make us think that we have to look at the future differently. We've been trying to imagine what it would be like if we could move around more freely, ants in different colonies helping one another. It seems to us that there's more than enough of everything in Antale for everyone to live well. We shouldn't have to be afraid of attacks from our neighbors. If we showed that we cared, then we wouldn't need these big armies to protect us. Do you think this is so foolish?"

"Not at all," replied Pacifica. "I've visited many places in Antale and I think the workers I've spoken to in most colonies would agree with you. The trouble is, even among well-meaning ants, old ways are slow to change. We've got new technology now that's moving faster than our ideas about how to use it. That's where the greatest danger is. We'll try to put some agreements in place through Unicol that will help, but the real future lies in fresh thinking like yours. Do you have a name for your group?"

"We were just talking about that before you came," said Ventura. "Seeing that we're ants talking about vision, we though we might call ourselves Vision-ants."

"Sounds good to me," said Pacifica. "What do you think, Roanda?"

"Yes, it has a good ring," said Roanda. "One thing about a new word, it has no baggage to it. You can make Visionants become whatever you want it to be."

"Yes, and I think you should," added Pacifica. "Thank you for inviting us, Ventura. I look forward to hearing a lot more about the Visionants."

With that, Pacifica left, allowing herself to think that by encouraging Ventura she might have done more for the long term future of Antale than she could hope to achieve at Unicol. Had she known the details of what a different kind of thinking was even then preparing elsewhere in another colony, she would have been a lot more anxious about the future.

Bravada had gone into the winter feeling uneasy about the growing dominance of the Sugars in Antale. It was an outcome from the war which she would like to redress. The Salts had participated in an alliance with the Sugars and the other members of the former Federation, but for Bravada, this was no more than an arrangement of convenience. With a similar sentiment, she had agreed after the war to join Unicol once the Salts had secured a seat on the Protectorate, because in that way, she saw she could exert control over what happened in other colonies. The Salts had already used their veto to maintain their domination of the former Green and Brown colonies, and they had refused to consider any proposal on the reduction of armed forces that would affect their own capability to maintain a strong military presence. The problem was that the Sugars were doing the same thing, and they had a weapon the Salts did not. The S Bomb, as the Sugars called it, that had knocked the Acids out of the war, could just as easily be used against the Salts. Bravada was anxious to close that gap as soon as possible.

Salt scientists were close to the development of explosive technology and could catch up quickly if they could get access to some of the Sugar secrets. This was, of course, very difficult to do, but Bravada had moved swiftly last autumn on a strategy to achieve her objective. In the early days of Unicol, the Salts had proposed a program of scientific exchange among members of the Protectorate. It involved sending top scientists from each colony to spend time with their counterparts in other colonies. The Salts were very generous and cooperative in hosting Sugar scientists, then in late autumn, it was their turn to send Salt scientists to the Sugar Colony. They sent three, and one of them, Gromelia, was something more than a scientist. She was a senior officer in the SIS, Salt Intelligence Service. Her orders were to obtain whatever information she could about Project S.

The Sugars, of course, did not include Project S on the list of things they were prepared to share, but Gromelia was very affable and good at what she did, and soon made friends with members across the Sugar scientific community, including some involved with Project S. However, for all her efforts, she learned no useful military secrets. When it came time for the Salt scientists to return to their own colony for the winter, Gromelia made an excuse to stay a few days longer, seeking for more time. She kept delaying her departure until she finally was trapped by the first frost. This meant she must stay in the Sugar Colony for the whole of the winter. This was all part of her original plan, for it gave more opportunity to penetrate the Sugar's security system.

The difficulty for the Salts was that they had no way of keeping in touch with Gromelia during the winter hibernation. The best they could arrange was that they would send a contact group to a specified location just outside Sugar territory to be there after the last frost of winter. Gromelia was to make contact with them as soon as she could. The reason for choosing that time was to try to catch the Sugars off guard, while their slower metabolism left them sluggish in the cool weather.

That was where matters stood in the middle of winter. While Pacifica was meeting with Ventura to hear about her ideas for a spring initiative, Bravada was waiting impatiently for the end of winter to see if she would be able to launch a very different initiative. By the time spring arrived, the stage was set for the Salts to make their move and for the Visionants to go out on their first appearance.

Now, it is very hard to know when the last frost of winter has gone. The Salt contact group came out too early. They were caught by two very cold days and freezing nights and almost perished. Their leader was Ivana, a crusty commander, veteran of some of the heaviest fighting in the war and now head of an elite military police unit attached to the SIS. She was feeling very irritable on this still, cold spring morning as she huffed and stamped around, trying to get warm while she kept a lookout from their camp toward the Sugar Colony. Her two companions felt even worse as they huddled together in a patch of weak sunlight.

Suddenly, Ivana saw a lone ant coming toward them. She kept out of sight until she could see more clearly. Then she recognized Gromelia. Ivana stepped out and greeted the other roughly.

"At last, you come," she said. "We damn near died of cold out here. What have you got for us?"

"Not as much as we wanted, but it could be enough," said Gromelia. "It's impossible to get any information out of the Sugars. They're too careful for that. But I had one piece of luck. I found out where they're storing some early prototypes of the bomb they used last year on the Acids. If we could get one of them out and back home, we could probably analyze its contents."

"Carry a bomb?" Ivana was not enthusiastic. "Can the thing go off?"

"No, there has to be an activating agent. The real problem will be getting it. They're stored deep inside the nest. There are guards everywhere, but things are still very lax because of the cold. If we move right away, we might pull it off."

Ivana stirred her companions. "Come on," she said. "We're going bomb hunting."

Gromelia led them on a circuitous route that finally came out at the mound where Project S was housed. They had encountered no guards or workers. Everything still seemed dormant.

"How do we get in?" asked Ivana.

"There's one main entrance, but we can't go that way," replied Gromelia. "There'll be guards everywhere. Even if they're still groggy, we'd never get through. But there's at least one side entrance on the north side of the mound, near the base. They've sealed if off, so it can't be seen from the outside, but I know it's there."

"If we can't see it, how do we find it?" Ivana asked.

"I've got a good sense of direction," said Gromelia.

"I'm glad you've been here before."

"Oh, I haven't been here, but I've seen a map."

"Good grief! She's seen a map!" Ivana muttered.

They searched the base of the mound for half an hour, fearing all the time that a Sugar patrol would come by. But their luck held and finally, Gromelia found what she was looking for. The five of them dug around until one broke through into a passage.

"That's it," said Gromelia. "Come on! I'll lead the way."

The passage was narrow, just large enough for one at a time. Ivana followed Gromelia. They had traveled about twelve inches when Gromelia stopped and cursed.

"Damn!" she said. "That wasn't on the map."

"What's up?" asked Ivana.

"The passage is blocked. They've closed it off from both ends. We'll have to dig our way in."

Working in cramped space in the cold and dark was not easy. They took it in turns to dig at the blockage and spread the loose dirt out along the tunnel. They worked for at least an hour with no sign of a breakthrough and Gromelia began to fear that they were off course. Then suddenly, the wall she was digging at gave way.

By now, all of the ants were covered in dirt and their sensing ability was greatly impaired. They had broken through into what was a large chamber, but beyond that, they couldn't tell much. They did their best to clean their antennae and began to grope their way forward. It was Ivana who first sensed the presence of other ants, just before she stumbled into them.

"Whassat? Who's there?" said a groggy Sugar voice.

None of the raiding party moved. The Sugar ant relaxed. Ivana veered off toward the centre of the chamber, where she bumped into a pile of smooth objects about as big as herself. Gromelia was right behind her and Ivana felt a reassuring touch to indicate they had found what they were looking for. Ivana felt her way forward, trying to get hold of one of the objects. She tugged a little and then the whole pile came rolling loose.

That was the start of a scene of wild confusion. Ivana had left one of her team in the entrance to the passage to mark the way out, but the other one and Gromelia were now lost in the jumble of loose bombs and stirring Sugar guards. Ivana grabbed one of the bombs and headed back to the entrance. She found her guard and shoved the bomb at her.

"Here, take this and get out," she said.

The Salt soldier scuttled away with the bomb. Ivana turned back into the chamber, looking for the others. Unknown to Ivana, the second Salt soldier had also grabbed a bomb, but became disoriented and headed out a wrong passage. Gromelia knew what had happened and tried to pull the other back, but she was tackled herself by a Sugar guard. When Ivana reached them, Gromelia was getting the worst of it. Ivana grabbed the Sugar by the head, twisted around and brought her sting down hard on the other's spine. The Sugar fell away paralyzed and Ivana pulled Gromelia free.

"Come on, we've got to get out of here," Ivana hissed, and pushed a limping Gromelia over to the entrance where they had come in. The Sugar guards missed them in the confusion, not expecting anyone to enter through the sealed tunnel. They were concentrating their efforts on the remaining Salt intruder, whom they had now caught and overcome. Reluctantly, Ivana realized she would have to leave her companion behind. She hurried out after Gromelia.

Outside, Gromelia and Ivana were hailed by the other Salt soldier and the three of them hurried away, carrying the bomb. They were well clear of Sugar territory before any patrols were sent out after them. Two days later, they delivered their prize to Bravada, along with a diplomatic incident that would set the tone for Antale's new year.

Back in Centrasia, Pacifica was working to call an early meeting of Unicol's House of Assembly. However, before she even got the invitations out, she received an urgent demand from the Sugars for an emergency meeting of the Protectorate. The session had hardly begun before an angry Sugar ambassador was storming at her Salt counterpart.

"This is the most blatant act of espionage anyone could ever expect to find," she raged. "We demand an immediate apology from the President of the Salt Colony and restoration of our stolen property."

"To restore something, we would have to have it," replied the Salt ambassador. "You say you have captured one of our soldiers as an intruder. If that is so, return her to us and we will see she is punished. She was not acting on our instructions."

"Are you saying, Madame, that you are not in possession of one of our S prototype weapons?" demanded the Sugar ambassador.

"That is exactly what I'm saying," replied the other.

"Then, Madame, you are a damned liar!"

"Come, come," the Yellow ambassador intervened. "We need to deal with this on the basis of evidence, not accusations."

"Evidence!" the Sugar ambassador exclaimed. "How much evidence did you have last summer of Red intentions before their army stormed into your nests? How much evidence did we have of Acid plans before they let loose a swarm of wasps against our Portal? Do we have to wait for the next atrocity before we act? This Protectorate was set up as a means to deal with this kind of thing before it escalates."

"With respect," Pacifica intervened, "we had a chance to do that last year with the resolution to restrict the development of military expansion. The Protectorate could not agree on that. Would you like to reconsider the matter?"

Both the Sugar and the Salt delegations looked at Pacifica in stony silence. The Black ambassador spoke quietly: "Before we can act reasonably and responsibly with each other, we have to have trust. Regrettably, that is still missing from our discussions." Pacifica knew, as did the others, that the Black ambassador was right. Absence of mutual trust precludes the possibility of true collaboration. This was the issue that now threatened to place Antale in a climate of troubled peace. Fortunately, another movement was beginning outside their conference chambers with Ventura and the Visionants that would begin to raise the consciousness of what it would mean to live in peace in Antale.

At first, Ventura had no clear strategy of how to get her visioning program underway. She, along with her fellow Visionants, had been greatly encouraged by Pacifica's good wishes during the winter, but they knew she was far too preoccupied at Unicol to give them any direct help. So they decided to simply go out and talk to others.

Once spring activities got underway, they all had their individual responsibilities as workers or attendants to the Queen or nurse maids for the larvae. They used this time to talk about peaceful cooperation among colonies. No one disagreed with these ideas, but neither could the workers in the nest see how anything they could do would make a difference. This was a matter for their governing councils and for Unicol. Wasn't that what they had fought the war for? Now they just wanted to get on with their lives. It was all a little discouraging to Ventura, who wanted to move on some specific peace initiatives.

Her opportunity to do so happened quite suddenly and unexpectedly on the way to Buranda.

It was a pleasant sunny day. The year was still in early spring and everywhere, the signs of new growth spilled out along the ant paths. Fresh blades of grass with small insects clinging to them provided good hunting for the foragers. Tender petals from the early wildflowers bulged rich with juice and nutrients. Drops of dew still hanging in the thicker clumps of grass made a pleasant oasis where workers could rest a moment from their labors. It was a good time for the ants of Centrasia after their bitter memories of the year just past. Ventura and her three companions made their way easily through this spring setting on the path to Buranda.

As one of the first nests that Red invaders had attacked at the outbreak of the war, Buranda had acquired the dubious distinction of a place with brutal associations. It had been used by the Reds as a prison where thousands of White ants were held and forced to work to feed the hungry Red troops on the way to war against their kin. Even at the time when Pacifica was briefly held there as a prisoner, it was developing its reputation as a mound of despair. Now, months after liberation, its unhappy memories still clung to it like a dank mist that refused to lift.

Because of these hard times in the recent past, Ventura wanted to test Buranda as a birthplace for new and liberal thinking. If something fresh could bloom there, it would be a good signal to all nests everywhere, at least in the White Ant Colony. That was why she and her three companions were on the path to go there on this beautiful spring morning.

They were just coming up to the courtyard surrounding the nest, at a point where the path branched, one way going west to Centrasia and the other northeast toward the Red Ant Colony. They noticed a cluster of ants off to the side and went over to take a look. At the center of the group was an old White ant, moving around in a circle as she talked to the others. Ventura noticed immediately from the ant's strange gait that she had lost a leg.

"So what do you say, then?" the ant was asking. "Who'll come with me? This is not for the faint hearted, but I warrant if you come, you'll be the better for it."

"What's going on?" Ventura asked a bystander.

"That's crazy Natasha," replied the other. "She's a bit touched from the war. She's trying to get anyone she can to join her to go over to the Red Colony."

"What for?" asked Ventura.

"To tell them she forgives them. Can you imagine that? She, with her leg chewed off by a Red soldier, wants to go and say that that's all right. Have you ever heard anything so crazy?"

"Sounds just the opposite to me," replied Ventura. She called out to the ant in the center: "Hello, there, Natasha. I'll come with you."

"Why, bless you, dear," said Natasha. "Come on over here on the side of decency." Ventura went over to stand beside her. "Anyone else?" Natasha called out to the crowd. Ventura's three companions came over. "Look, it's becoming a crowd," Natasha chuckled happily. "Plenty of room still, though. Anyone else?"

It was then that Ventura noticed two small ants nodding gratefully at her. "Hello," she said. "Who are you?"

"We're Wanda and Nada," said one of them. "I'm Wanda. That's Nada. We're with Natasha. She saved us from the war."

"And you're going to forgive the Reds?" asked Ventura.

"Yes," said Wanda. "At least, I think that's what it is. We're not really sure, but we're with Natasha. If she says it's right, it must be."

By now, the crowd around Natasha was drifting away. No one else had joined her. She turned and spoke warmly to Ventura and her companions.

"I'm glad you came by, dears," she said. "I was beginning to feel a little lonely."

"That's all right," said Ventura. "I think we were coming to meet you, anyway."

"Oh, that's nice," replied Natasha. "I see you've met Wanda and Nada. They're wonderful children. I looked after them as pupae in the nest. Mona and Sona aren't here. They died, you know. But they would be here, if they could."

"I'm sure," said Ventura. "So you want to forgive the Reds for what they did to you? Why do you want to do that?"

"Well, I don't know what else to do. The Red workers didn't do anything bad. And even the soldiers who did won't ever know anything different if someone doesn't show them another way. It seems to me that's the most useful thing I can do—not so much for me, but for Wanda and Nada, and Mona and Sona, too, in their own way. Do you know what I mean, dear?"

"Yes, I do. I'm glad to meet you, Natasha. My name's Ventura. These are my friends. We are Visionants. That's a new word for ants who are trying to invent a better future."

"Oh, I'm one of those," said Natasha.

"Yes, I can see that. We were on our way to Buranda, but I think we might spend our time more usefully in going with you to the Red Colony. Are you leaving now?"

"Yes, right away. Come along, Wanda and Nada. We've got wonderful new friends to keep us company."

So Ventura, instead of taking the right fork in the path to Buranda, turned left with Natasha toward the Red Ant Colony.

CHAPTER 9

New Hope

AFTER THE TURBULENT SESSION OF THE PROTECTORATE, Pacifica was anxious to get something more positive going at Unicol. She organized teams of workers at Centrasia to renovate a large portion of the mound to accommodate the permanent delegation of the two hundred member colonies. It was a bright and colorful time as the delegates arrived, bringing with them a new and fresh spirit of cooperation. Clouds of distrust might be gathering at higher levels between members of the Protectorate, but here at the beginning of the year, in the House of Assembly, hopes were high for what the ants of Antale might do together.

One of the first initiatives that Pacifica introduced was an expedition across the Rim to search for Explora and follow up on her discoveries from last year. Colonel Observa came to propose a mission that could be carried out under the direction of Mission Control as part of Unicol's general scientific program. As the colonel described the dramatic moments of the last transmission from Explora, and the potential first contact with civilizations beyond Antale, the imagination of every delegate in the House was stirred. This would be a landmark project for Unicol to support, an opportunity to extend knowledge beyond all bounds, to reach deep into the fascination of the unknown. Observa's proposal was given ready approval, and Pacifica was asked to establish a special scientific directorate to look after it. Before Observa left to begin preparations, Pacifica had a quick word of encouragement.

"Go with our great good wishes, Observa," she said. "You are not doing this just for Antale, but for the memory of Wiseria and for the hope we have that you will find Explora. We will need good news at Unicol this summer. With all my heart, I hope yours might be the best."

Approval of the Observa expedition marked the real beginning of Unicol's work. Pacifica now found herself fully engaged with building the necessary administrative structures to carry out the programs approved by the House. At this stage, little was known in the far flung nests in member colonies about the work of Unicol, but for those involved at its headquarters in Centrasia, a whole new industry of intercolonial cooperation developed. The challenge would be to make all this activity meaningful for improved life and security across Antale. It was a challenge that Pacifica wholeheartedly embraced, while her recent experience of tension and distrust in the Protectorate left her ever alert to warning signs of danger.

If Pacifica's life was being consumed by high order administration, Ventura and her Visionants were operating at the other end of the spectrum. Their arrival in the Red Colony with Natasha and her "children" was the beginning of a journey that would take them close to the hearts of ants all across Antale in ways that they could never have anticipated.

The start was unpromising enough. As they came upon the first Red nest, they sensed immediately an atmosphere of gloom and dejection. The Red workers were going about their business without the joyous spring in their step that should have been there at this time of year. The sight of a group of happy White ants seemed to make them feel worse, rather than better. They did not return any of Natasha's cheery greetings and typically would hurry past on the other side of the path.

"Seems like everyone's going to someone else's funeral," said Ventura. "I guess that's what comes from losing a war."

"No one loses a war," replied Natasha. "And no one wins it, either. Everybody suffers to get to a place that they'd rather not be."

"That's one way to put it. I wonder how we can get to talk to these ants."

Just then, they received a friendly greeting.

"Hello, folks. What are you doing so far from home?"

They looked around to see a striking young White soldier with a platoon of ants of mixed colors coming down from the mound.

"Good morning, officer," Natasha responded. "We've come to visit our neighbors."

"Oh? I'm not sure you'll find anyone too neighborly around this place," said the soldier.

"What's your role here?" asked Ventura. "I understood all occupying forces had been withdrawn."

"We're not an occupying force. We're a Unicol unit. Just trying to help out and keep order while the new administration gets set up in each nest."

"What's happened to the former Red soldiers?" Ventura queried further.

"That's one of the problems. All the old units have been disbanded. Some of the soldiers have become workers, but a lot are just hanging around. There's a group over there."

"That's who I want to talk to," said Natasha, and she hurried over in her limping gait to the group of Red ants the officer had indicated. There were about a dozen of them, clustered together on a patch of bare earth in the sunlight, idly stirring the dust with their forelegs. They looked up, surprised, when Natasha hobbled into their midst.

"Hello, I'm Natasha. Is this a private game or can anyone play? What's the trick? Make a circle in the dust and step into it? Let's see if I can do it." Natasha tried to imitate the Red ants, but every time she lifted one of her forelegs, she lost balance and tumbled over.

"Guess I'm not much good at this," she laughed. "Let's try it this way." This time, she squatted down and propelled herself around in a circle, tracing out a mark in the dust with the tip of her abdomen. "There," she chuckled, "I've made my circle and sat in it."

Some of the Red ants laughed a little in spite of themselves. "What happened to your leg?" one of them asked.

"Oh, I lost it," said Natasha. "Pretty careless of me, wasn't it? But, look, I'd like you to meet someone. Come on over here, Wanda and Nada. These are my children, at least I call them that."

Wanda and Nada joined Natasha in the middle of the circle of Red ants. "Hello," said Wanda. "I'm Wanda. That's Nada. Natasha saved us from the war. That's how she lost her leg."

The Red ants shuffled uncomfortably.

"Hush, Wanda," said Natasha. "Don't mind her. She does go on a bit. We're from Buranda. We thought we'd like to come over and visit, then perhaps you might come and visit us."

"Buranda, you say," one of the Reds spoke up. "I was there. We —-." Then she stopped abruptly.

"Oh, well, you must come again," said Natasha. "It's different now. It will soon be the way it used to be."

"Nothing can ever be the way it used to be," another Red said sullenly.

"Well, maybe not exactly," responded Natasha. "I used to have six legs. I guess the other one isn't going to grow back, but I'm not going to let that stop me from enjoying life."

"Yes, and that's the point." Ventura had stepped into the circle. "Hello. My name's Ventura. I was hatched in Centrasia last spring just before the invasion. I think I actually came to life as someone was carrying me away. I got a rather strange introduction to the world. I thought everything was a rush of scurrying, frightened bodies. But now I know better. I'm grateful to have lived and learned the difference."

"And what do you think you've learned?" asked one of the Reds.

"I've learned that everything moves forward. Nothing stays the way it is and you can never go back to the same place twice. The important thing is to make where you're going where you really want to be."

"And for ants, that has to be a together thing," added Natasha. "We're nothing on our own. Our whole life is in our nests. But we have to be secure. Living in fear is not living at all. That's why we all have to learn to be good neighbors."

"Quite the pair of philosophers, aren't you?" said one of the Reds cynically.

"Hold it, Sora." This came form the Red who said she had been to Buranda. "They make a lot of sense. Say, Natasha, my name's Bravura. I was a soldier. I came to your nest as an invader. I brought war and destruction into your life. What can you say to me about being a neighbor?"

"I've already answered that by coming here," replied Natasha. "The more important point now is what we can say to each other and then, together, to everyone else."

"Exactly," added Ventura, "the old soldier who carried the war and the nurse who suffered its consequences. That was then. It's gone. Now what about tomorrow? Bravura, why don't you and your friends come back with us to Buranda, so we can start to heal the wounds? Who better to do that than soldiers and victims together?"

"And don't forget us," Wanda put in. "Nada and I don't want to lose our legs or our lives."

"You won't, dear, you won't," said Natasha. Then she did something that changed the whole energy of the moment. She went up to Bravura and embraced her affectionately, leaning on her, just for an instant, for support. She then turned to the ant beside Bravura and embraced her also. She continued around the circle. Several backed away, signaling they did not want this, and Natasha let them be.

Everyone stood in silence. Ventura noticed that the White platoon leader they had met earlier and several of her soldiers had gathered round, watching. Then Bravura spoke:

"All right. I'll come with you. And maybe some of the rest of these old war warts will come, too. Who knows? Perhaps there is something we can all do together."

That was how Natasha, Ventura and the other Visionants took their first full step into the future and found some unlikely companions to accompany them. In the weeks that followed, their activities would make an important counterplay to events unfolding elsewhere.

The first real signs of trouble were brought to Pacifica's attention in late spring by Bluffasta. The problems arose in Salt territory, where the pugnacious Pepper was not without her own intelligence sources close to the Salts. She spoke to Pacifica one day as they were taking a break from the Unicol routine by strolling around the courtyard at Centrasia.

"Seems like the Salts have invented a new game," said Bluffasta.

"Oh?" replied Pacifica, sensing something strange was about to be revealed.

"Yes, by the force. It's called 'eruption,' or 'how to blow your nest over the Rim.'"

"What are you talking about?"

"You'll hear soon enough, I expect, but not from the Salts. The Sugars are keeping so close that they almost went up with the bang."

"Bluffasta, will you speak plainly for once."

"It's plain enough. Has been for weeks. First a little puff here. Then a bigger one there. Now, all at once, the whole top of a mound goes off. It started raining rocks and dirt all over the Peppers. Things are building up for another hot summer."

Bluffasta essentially had the details right, but not all of the facts. Later that day, the Sugars requested a meeting of the Protectorate and Pacifica once more found herself trying to manage a Sugar-Salt confrontation.

"The pattern is now entirely clear," said the Sugar ambassador. "We've got a member colony not only dangerously experimenting with powerful weapons, but using them to intimidate free and independent members of Unicol. I am referring, in particular, to the deliberate expansion of Salt influence throughout Quadrant Three."

"It is both tiresome and inappropriate, Madam Conductor," replied the Salt ambassador, "for us to have to listen to these kinds of innuendos. If we are invited by our neighbors to assist them with their development, we are not going to turn away."

"You're using the technology you stole from us to threaten the nests and put your own lackey leaders in charge," the Sugar ambassador retorted.

Her Salt counterpart turned to Pacifica. "Madam Conductor," he said, "could we ask our distinguished colleague if she has a specific resolution to bring forward so we can vote on the matter?"

The Sugars did not pursue the issue, realizing that the Salts would use their veto against any resolution condemning them. The meeting ended in an uneasy stalemate. A few weeks later, Pacifica knew things were deteriorating when another meeting of the Protectorate was requested, this time by the Salts.

"We have been accused in this assembly in the past," said the Salt ambassador, "of stealing technology and improperly interfering in the affairs of our neighboring colonies. Both charges were, of course, proved to be false. Today, we wish to express our own concern on a matter that does indeed have substance and which is a palpable threat to peace in Antale. What makes the situation most serious is that it arises from actions taken by other members of this council. We very much regret that four colonies represented here have chosen to collaborate on the sharing of military and other technology, leaving us out of the discussions. We refer specifically to agreements establishing the Quadrant Four Alliance with a military headquarters right here in the White Ant Colony. Such agreements run counter to the principles on which this Protectorate was founded."

Pacifica, of course, knew what was happening, but she was powerless to prevent it. Distrust among former wartime allies had now led to a schism in the Protectorate. The Sugars, alarmed at the growing power of the Salts, had convinced the Blacks, Whites and Yellows to form a new alliance in Quadrant Four in northeast Antale, but with full participation by the Sugars from Quadrant Three. This sent a clear message to the Salts, who were also in Quadrant Three. The new alliance included provisions to share the military technologies which all colonies had continued to develop since the war. Tests in biological warfare, airborne delivery and explosive technology were now going on in secret sites in all colonies. If this pattern were to continue, the potential for a much more destructive war than the one that had ravaged the land last summer was very high. The other colonies rejected the Salt complaint as groundless. Pacifica met privately with the heads of all colonies, but got nowhere. In desperation, she turned to an old friend for advice and assistance.

Electra had continued to maintain a busy research program following the end of the war in which her contribution to destroying the Reds' biological offensive was widely acknowledged. But she was not, and never had been, supportive of research for military purposes. She saw this as an escalating problem that could only get worse, unless parallel initiatives directed toward the development of peaceful relationships were also pursued. She very much regretted that the products of her work were now part of the technical package being exchanged among members of the new Quadrant Four Alliance, allegedly as a deterrent, but potentially for actual use. She could see the day not far ahead when such hideous destructive power would once again get into the hands of unscrupulous political leaders. In her own work, she was therefore putting all of her energy into achieving a very different outcome.

Pacifica knew where Electra's real passions lay. They had been prisoners together, then fugitives and war heroes, all the time sharing a deep commitment for peace. It was not unusual, therefore, that Pacifica would seek her old friend's advice about the problems troubling Unicol. She called on Electra in her research laboratories in Blackhall.

"When we talked in the past," Pacifica said, "you told me that our communities are a product of our consciousness. What I see coming is ever more violence, because that is what we are thinking about. Even worse, we seem to be fascinated, instead of horrified, by our increasing ability to inflict violence more effectively."

"Yes," replied Electra. "Our dilemma is that our ideas are getting ahead of our biology. This is a breaking point in evolution. Up to the present, our biology has made us a very stable species. We are losing that now, and last year's war showed us how rapid the decline will be unless we turn to using our ideas, our science, to raise our biology at a rate equal to our expanding consciousness."

"What do you mean?"

"I mean that, for the first time in our evolution, we are dramatically out of balance. In the past, our biology kept us balanced between aggression and nurturing. Now, we have intervened with our intelligence to tip the scales toward aggression. We can even argue rationally in support of it. Exterminate unwanted populations to preserve the best. That's the nightmare story we are starting to tell ourselves as truth. To redress the balance, we must turn our science to enhance the nurturing side of our biology."

"That's very interesting in theory, but do you have something specific to propose?"

"Yes, I do."

"What?"

Electra moved about, flexing her limbs, twitching her antennae, as if seeking to focus her thought energy fully on Pacifica. Finally, she spoke.

"We have to look to our Queens," she said.

Pacifica had not expected this. In ant communities, the Queen was the long-lived great broodmother. Kept out of harm's way by the workers, fiercely protected to the point of virtual imprisonment in her own regal chambers, her one function was to lay the eggs that would be the future offspring in her nest. All other matters affecting the life of the community—its food, safety, social development—occurred around her, not through her. What did Electra mean by "look to our Queens"?

"The imprinting of who we are is in the eggs laid by our Queens," Electra continued. "True, who we become is influenced by what happens to us after birth, but there is a basic genetic foundation on which all of that behavior is laid. If we want to dramatically improve the nurturing, cooperative side of our nature, we have to affect it at birth, and even before, in the biology of our Queens."

"My gosh, Electra," Pacifica said slowly, "you're really pushing the margins on this one. Are you suggesting we deliberately interfere with the biology of the Queens in every nest in the whole of Antale?"

"That's no more radical than using biological and explosive weapons to exterminate living ants in those same nests. We've already shown our readiness to do that in war. My proposal is an intervention for peace before the war starts."

"But, heck, Electra—the Queens!" Pacifica was still struggling with the enormity of the implications.

"Let me be precise. Then you'll see what must be done. Come with me." Electra led Pacifica into an adjoining chamber, which was filled with row upon row of tiny cocoon-like containers. "As you know," Electra continued, "in the birth and breeding process in our nests, interaction between Queen, attendants, larvae and pupae is influenced by the secretions being exchanged among them. The Queen influences the attendants, the attendants influence the Queen and larvae, the larvae influence the attendants, and so on. Then attendants go out and become workers and the pupae become new attendants; so the cycle continues, all with the intent to preserve the nurturing of the species."

"Yes, I understand all that," said Pacifica.

"Well, then, the question is: Can these secretions—and we have samples in the containers you see here—can they be enhanced in some way so that the nurturing instinct is strengthened before birth and during the breeding cycle? Our research suggests that it can. In fact, by analyzing the secretions and combining them with various natural foods, we have prepared a new substance which I have called the Royal Elixir." Electra held up a small container and showed it to Pacifica. It contained a heavy, dark liquid.

"The Royal Elixir!" Pacifica exclaimed. "Now, come on, Electra, if you are suggesting what I think you are —."

"You question whether we should feed our Queens a substance that will trigger a favorable biological shift in the species?" Electra fixed all of the intensity of her powerful consciousness on Pacifica. "I tell you that is exactly what would happen in nature, if there were time to do it. But there isn't time. We have already shortened time by intervening scientifically on the other side of the scale. Now we must do so on this side, or we are lost."

Pacifica stared at Electra. The Conductor of Unicol looked hard at the great scientist. The one with great influence over the course of social development in Antale stood, weighing the words of the most powerful scientific mind in the land. Finally, Pacifica replied.

"You are proposing something as fundamental as life itself," she said slowly. "You must take me through this in fine detail, then I need other advice. Tell me exactly what this Royal Elixir is and how it would be used."

A few hours later, Pacifica was making another visit, this time to a place she had never been before. As she entered the royal chambers deep in the heart of Centrasia, she thought how strange it was that her society had relegated the role of the Queen to breeding, with no sense of its relationship to governance. Perhaps that was now about to change, but its consequence to date was that Pacifica, despite her important responsibilities as the Conductor of Unicol, had made no contact with any of the Queens in any of the nests throughout all of the colonies of Antale. This was why she felt so strange in approaching the quarters of the great dowager Queen of Centrasia, Regina III.

She had sent word ahead, requesting an audience, so the attendants were expecting her when she arrived. They took her immediately to the Queen. In the dark coolness of the royal brood chamber, Pacifica found herself in the presence of the enormous White mother of all the ants of Centrasia. More than three times Pacifica's size, Regina's huge body seemed to occupy the whole chamber. In fact, she was the chamber, filling the space around her with a comfortable feeling of absolute serenity. Pacifica found herself slipping immediately under the spell of this great quietude, embracing its peace and tranquility as she bowed her head respectfully to the Queen.

"Come closer, dear," said Regina. "I've been expecting you."

'What did she mean by that?' Pacifica wondered. 'How could she have been expecting me? Unless she was merely referring to the audience I had requested. But something in her tone suggested more than that.'

"I'm not as young as I once was," the Queen continued. "My faculties are a little dull of late, so you need to be near for me to sense you. Yes, that's better. Ah, you are young and strong. That's good for someone with such important work. You must tell me all about Unicol. I try to stay well informed, but it is very difficult when one is so isolated."

"I am pleased to find you well, Ma'am," replied Pacifica. "I apologize for not coming to see you sooner. I will do better in the future."

"Ah, not so well, now, my dear. I am a great age, you know. I have lost count myself, but these fusspots around me say it's almost fifteen years since I moved into the chambers. Of course, we had that terrible disruption last summer. I'm sure I aged many years, what with the evacuation and return. I have been waiting since then for you to come. Now tell me your important news."

'There she goes again,' thought Pacifica. 'She almost seems to know why I'm here.' Aloud, she said "You are very perceptive, Ma'am. But I have come more for your advice than to bring you news. It concerns the future of Antale." With that, Pacifica plunged right in, explaining in detail her fears about the growing violence throughout the colonies, and her discussion of this with Electra. When it came to describing the latter's proposal about the Royal Elixir, Pacifica found herself stumbling over her words. But the Queen was not surprised. She responded immediately.

"So, the time has come," she said softly. "You should know, my dear, that though we Queens seem to live a life apart, we are all connected because we are the life force of the species. When it is in danger, we respond. So I understand what your great scientist wishes to do. And I understand, too, the responsibilities of your office. These are new and different times. The two of you have come together to offer new life to Antale. Your friend is right to propose to bring the change through the lineage in the nests. But you need a royal advocate. It cannot be me. My time is closing. My role is to tell you of one who is coming who can be the champion of this cause. Seek her out from the top of the mound at the end of the coming nuptial flights and you will have your Queen and your champion. Go in peace, now, my dear one. Your work is truly blessed."

Regina had graciously signaled the end of the audience. Pacifica bowed low and withdrew, immediately going to the transmission room to report the conversation to Electra in Blackhall.

"So, she knew," Electra mused. "That's very interesting—and encouraging. I'll come right away to Centrasia. The nuptial flights will be in a day or two. It seems you and I have a rendezvous on the top of the mound."

Two days later, in the soft air of mid-morning after a light rain shower, the winged sexuals, male and female, emerged from their tunnels in Centrasia. The males took off in a cloud and hung, hovering a little down wind, waiting for the females. When the latter rose, the two swarms came together and the miracle of mating proceeded throughout the day, after which the males fell to die and the females, now carrying the life sperm of future generations in their bodies, sought a place to establish themselves as Queens. Such great numbers provided their guarantee for the future, for before the day was out, more than ninety percent of them had been lost to birds and other predators. It was one of the survivors for whom Pacifica and Electra were waiting.

They stood together in early evening on the top of Centrasia, watching. A breathless, quiet hush hung across the colony. All activity on the courtyard below was at an end. The workers had come in from the paths, and the nest was settling down for the night.

Neither Pacifica nor Electra paid attention to the passing minutes. This was a timeless moment in which the future was waiting on the birth of a new and different present. As actors in the drama, Pacifica and Electra quietly waited for their cue.

Pacifica was the first to sense someone coming. Ever so quietly, she drifted in, hovering just for a moment before she landed at the tunnel entrance only an inch from where the two friends were standing. She folded her wings and looked around.

"There she is," Pacifica whispered to Electra. "Come on, let's go and meet her." Pacifica led the way over to the winged ant, who suddenly realized she was not alone and stepped back in alarm. This was a little incongruous, for as a sexual, she was much larger than either of the other two.

"Don't be afraid," said Pacifica. "We've been waiting for you. My name is Pacifica and this is Electra. Queen Regina told us you were coming."

The winged ant was still confused. "I didn't know," she said, "I mean, I didn't expect anyone to be waiting for me. I wasn't even sure I should come back to Centrasia. I drifted away at first, with a lot of others. Everything was really quite confused and terrifying. Then, somehow, I was alone on air currents carrying me here. What do you mean that Queen Regina told you I was coming?"

"Just that," replied Pacifica. "None of us knows the whole story. In fact, we seem to be writing it. Now it's our turn to work together. What is your name?"

"Name? I have no name."

"Quite so," Electra spoke for the first time. "The one destined to be Queen will receive her royal name when the time has come. The present monarch has foreseen her successor. This is very propitious for what we must do. Can we go in, Pacifica, and find a place to talk?"

The outcome of the conversations that took place that night set a new course, not just for Centrasia, but for all Antale. The three companions went first to Pacifica's quarters, but had barely settled down when one of the royal attendants arrived, saying that the Queen had sent for them. When they reached the regal chamber, it seemed somehow darker to Pacifica than before and the atmosphere heavier. The great Queen was lying on her side, her attendants clustered anxiously around. Also present were the Governor of the city and the Grand Keeper of the Royal Traditions. Pacifica knew both of these officials quite well, and understood immediately from their presence that something of great importance was anticipated.

"Let me see the young one," the Queen said when their arrival was announced. The young female sexual came forward, her large wings rustling gently as she moved.

"Ah, yes," the Queen continued, and she reached out to embrace the other. "You have come to take my place, my dear. It is a great responsibility and soon you must shed your wings for the task. Help me up a little, so that I can see everyone more clearly." The old Queen, leaning heavily on her new protégé, addressed the group. "My dear friends, I have lived a long and blessed life as your Queen, but now my course is run. It is time for Centrasia to move into a new and different future under the nurturance of one who will be a great mother to the generations that follow us. Will you please welcome now your new Queen, Anastasia I. Grand Keeper, you must see to her coronation. It will be the grandest ever seen in Centrasia."

So it was that a number of key pieces for the future fell into place. Regina, for the moment, was the leader. Despite her failing strength, she engaged all the officials present in a vigorous discussion of Electra's proposals for enhancing the nurturing biology of future generations. The old Queen saw immediately what must be done. It was as if her ending life gave her the energy to focus on the new. The coronation of Anastasia must be the stimulus, the epicenter of a spreading wave of awareness, rippling out to eventually engulf all Antale.

The Grand Keeper would use her connections to invite her counterparts from royal households everywhere. Pacifica would activate the political community through Unicol. What under normal circumstances would be a local celebration in a single nest suddenly assumed intercolonial significance: a new Queen was coming to Centrasia and with her, a new hope for the larger future of Antale.

So the invitations went out. So the plans were laid. The coronation would be held in one week's time. The only cloud dampening the excitement was the failing health of the old Queen herself. Having set the machinery in motion, she began to fade away to give place to the one who could bring the energy of youth to the work that must be done. When word went out again summoning the officials to her chamber, all knew they had come to say goodbye.

Anastasia had never left her side. She supported Regina's head as the old Queen sought once more to speak.

"It is good to go knowing that one's life work will carry on." Her words gathered strength from the thoughts that comforted her. "When the howls of war raged all around, it was hard to see a purpose for giving birth to life that faced such awful death. But now, all that has changed. I see a future coming in which all of you as players will show the world a way out of its present dangers. And to you most of all, my dearest daughter and Queen, falls the task of creating the life to be the light of the new way. My dear friends, will you join me in tribute: Long live the Queen!"

Though their hearts were aching, all those gathered around repeated the words, as much in memory for one whose work was done as for the one whose new life was just beginning: "Long live the Queen!"

That day, Regina died. She was buried deep in the nest with the Queens who had preceded her. The next day came the coronation of Anastasia I.

CHAPTER 10

Potential Builds

WHEN EPOCHAL EVENTS OCCUR, THEY SWEEP UP on the participants, cresting like a wave, carrying everyone along with the energy of the moment to another place in time. While everything is happening, it is hard to get perspective, but afterward, one can look back and say 'that was the moment when everything changed.' So it was with the coronation of Anastasia.

It was played in two acts. The first, staged on the courtyard, rivaled anything ever seen there in pomp and ceremony. All of the Unicol delegations turned out, filling one half of a large semicircle of spectators. The second half was crowded with royal attendants from hundreds of other nests and colonies across Antale. Behind these official guests, filling the courtyard and clinging to vantage points on rocks and bushes around, was the great mass of White ants of Centrasia, turning out to see their new Queen crowned.

To the great delight of this last group of spectators, Anastasia came out in royal procession from the top of the mound, proceeded down the far side, and came around the courtyard in a winding path lined with guards to control the crowds. The new Queen was preceded by the Grand Keeper of Royal Traditions, who stepped along with all the dignity of her high office. Behind her, Anastasia moved gracefully. Folded across her back, she still carried her large wings that gave a super-being appearance to her stature. The wings were only lightly attached now, for during the ceremony, they would be shed as Anastasia ceremoniously assumed her new status.

As the royal procession came round to the back of the semicircle of official guests, the excitement of the massed crowds of White ants reached fever point. The air crackled with the energy of their shouted transmissions of good will, several hundred thousand antennae waved their best wishes, and a chorus of singing broke out spontaneously:

"Ho! Ho! Ho! She goes.

Queen of all our life, you know.
Sing her praises high and low.
Ho! Ho! Ho! She goes."

The ceremony itself was short. The climax came when the Grand Keeper, standing just behind the new Queen on a platform about one third up the mound, so everyone could see, disengaged the wings, then held them aloft and spoke these simple words:

"With the shedding of these wings, do you, Anastasia I of Centrasia, now ascend to your ordained status as our most loved and honored Queen, mother and life sustainer of our generations to come. In the presence of this, your loyal and loving family of all Centrasia, I ask if you are today willing to assume your new responsibility."

"With all my heart, I so declare." With these words, Anastasia became Queen of Centrasia and the courtyard rocked again in wild enthusiasm. So ended Act One of the coronation.

Act Two took place inside the mound in the large chamber, which had first been the conference centre for the old Federation, and which had since been renovated and expanded to become the Assembly Hall for Unicol. Today, however, it was the setting for all the royal households of Antale to meet in special session under the sponsorship of the young new Queen Anastasia I of Centrasia. Because Queens do not travel, Anastasia was the only royal present. Her audience was the grand Keepers of Royal Traditions and the senior attendants of Queens throughout two thousand nests in Antale. In all, there were more than four thousand ants pressed into the Assembly Hall.

Anastasia glided in like a feather floating on the massed energy of the multitude. Her path as she came made a ripple through the throng as the gentle wake of a skiff moves across calm water. She stopped in the center of the hall on the Conductor's mound, where Pacifica would normally take her place to conduct the affairs of Unicol. Today, Pacifica was taking a much lower profile. At her own request she, accompanied by Electra, was at the back of the hall. They were the only ants present who were not part of a royal household. They were there as special guests to witness how Anastasia would handle the charge of introducing Electra's Royal Elixir into the lineage of ant colonies throughout Antale.

Centrasia's Grand Keeper of Traditions hushed the assembly and presented the Queen. "My dear colleagues," she said, "our assembly here today is without precedent. It is also without parallel in importance. I give you Queen Anastasia."

"Dearest friends and family," said the young Queen, "I address you thus, because it is so. We may have many nests and colonies throughout our world. We may go by many names. We may be distinguished by many colors, sizes and physical appearances. But at the core, at the deep, still center of everything, there is a universal life force from which we come and to which we are always inseparably connected. As a new Queen, I now embrace my role and work as a sustainer of and provider to that life force. With great humility, I accept the honor of this calling and commit my being and energy to its continuous fulfillment throughout all the days and seasons of my time.

"My predecessor at Centrasia was the great Queen Regina, who served as the life mother of this colony over many years. None of those years was more eventful than the one just past. I did not know it. I am newly born into the life that has followed the Great War. In that, most of you have in one sense the advantage over me. You lived through that time and served Queens who brought life forward into the jaws of the great monster death that stormed the land because of how colonies had chosen to deal with one another. The Queens were not part of those political decisions. We do not and never will have such responsibilities. Our calling is much deeper, for we are the mothers, and it is from that sacred place that we derive the greatest responsibility of all. For without us, there is no life to the ant world. Without us, our species would cease even to be a memory within a few short years. My great Queen Mother Regina understood this, but knew further the threatening chasm to our life-sustaining function that had opened in her last days, and which threatens now to swallow all of us who follow."

Anastasia paused in her delivery. Pacifica had been present in many assemblies where messages of great import were delivered, but never had she known a moment such as this. The young Queen had stepped beyond all time and place into an eternity of the spirit, and now she proceeded to bring every last ant present with her.

"My dear sisters," Anastasia continued, "you must now listen closely and hear the truth of the time to come. These are not my words. This is not my truth. It was given to me by Queen Regina. But they were not her words or her truth either. They came from much deeper and farther—from the core of the universal source of all our life. The new truth of our time is that the broodmothers of all our nests, the Queens who carry the life force in their bodies, must bring forward generations for all time to come who will embrace life and peace as the only reason for being. We are already very close to that, but even a breath away can be sufficient to destroy everything, as was seen in the uncontrollable chain of destruction unleashed in the Great War. We must not allow such a time to come again, but it is already almost upon us. So it is up to us to act.

"Our political and military sisters with whom we were gathered a short time ago will do their best to steer a course of intercolonial cooperation, but without a shift in the deep consciousness of our species, their best efforts will collapse under the magnitude of complexity and growing populations. To the

Queens and their households must fall the task of preserving future life by enhancing the consciousness of our species. It has fallen upon me to find the words to convince you this day of the urgency and truth of what I say, and to announce to you the means by which it can be accomplished."

"Here it comes," Electra whispered to Pacifica. "With these next few words, she can pull Antale back from the precipice."

Anastasia continued: "Our biology, our consciousness, and our spirituality are woven together in the eggs that we Queens lay. Those eggs come from our bodies which, in their turn, are nurtured by the food we eat and by the chemical secretions passed from mouth to mouth within the royal chambers. This chain of connections continues further among the larvae when they are born and the nurses who attend and feed them. Within our spheres of influence, we lay the foundations for the ant societies that can build a strong or divided future world. All of this is true and has been so from the beginning. That is the old truth. The new truth that I can declare to you today is that we now have available, through my royal household in Centrasia, a new source of sustenance, a Royal Elixir, that can greatly enhance the foundational strength of that future life in all the nests of our world. It is freely and openly available to all of you as the Grand Keepers and senior attendants to your Queens and your households. It is yours to choose for a more abundant life. It is my most deep and fervent wish that you will now so choose."

That was it. Anastasia had delivered her message. She stepped down from the platform and glided out through the throng with the same effortless motion as when she entered. A deep hush hung over the assembly. The Grand Keeper of the Royal Traditions in Centrasia mounted the Conductor's platform and spoke:

"You have heard my Queen," she said. "Now your responsibility is to take her words to your own Queens. They will know what to do. As you leave, you will be given a small quantity of the Royal Elixir. When your Queen decides to participate, you may then return here and we will make arrangements for a continuous supply for your royal household. Before you go, you will all be given individual briefings on the nature and use of the Elixir. As you leave this chamber, speak with our attendants and they will set it up. Go now, my sisters, in the peace and sacredness of your task."

At the back of the hall, Pacifica and Electra shared a long moment of silence. Then Pacifica spoke softly: "So, your grand strategy is in play, Electra. When I first heard it, I wasn't sure if it was right. But a greater force than my judgment has gathered around it. Now it must go where it will. Come, we have much to do."

Indeed, there would soon be more than enough for Pacifica to do, for in the past several weeks, she had set in motion events that were about to escalate and converge in a crisis of opportunity and danger. On one front, she had been busy with the Queens' initiative in Centrasia, while on another, the Visionants were picking up a following that would soon lead to an unexpected outcome. Further afield on a third venture, the Observa expedition out on the Rim had reached the edge of fresh and startling discoveries. Finally, closer to home, the conflict between the Salts and the Sugars was about to soar to an apex of folly. In the vortex of all this, Pacifica would be caught and tossed about like one of the winged future Queens riding the air currents, struggling to fulfill her mission.

Perhaps the most capricious of these turbulent air waves was the one sweeping out from Ventura and the Visionants. They had come back from the Red Ant Colony to Buranda with Natasha and their new associate and former Red soldier, Bravura. Several other old Red soldiers also came along, as well as a few Black and Yellow veterans who they met along the way. The group now looked more like a traveling road show than anything else, so when they set up camp by a large rock on the courtyard just outside the mound of Buranda, they quickly attracted attention.

Ventura moved into the role of organizer and sent her young Visionants out to spread the word that, just before sundown, an important presentation would be made. Workers coming back from their day's activities gathered around to see what was going on. Other ants from the mound, seeing the crowd, also came over. By the time Ventura climbed up on the rock to speak to the assembly, she had an audience of several thousand.

"Friends," she said, "a year ago, this place where we are gathered was the scene of bitter fighting. Some of you who were here can remember, but most of us are too young or have come from another place. But the question for all of us is the same: Are we doomed to repeat the tragedies of the past or can we think differently to create a better future? The group you see here, we call ourselves Visionants, and we have answered 'Yes' to the question of wanting to cut the future free of the conflicts of the past. It begins in knowing the connections among us. Red and White were enemies a year ago because a few distorted minds broke the bonds that bind us, and let loose a holocaust where fury had free play. It must not happen again. Cruel, unnatural dictatorships can only flourish when the rest of us allow our minds to be fed by fear. I give you now to one who knows this all too well."

Ventura stepped aside and Bravura, the old Red soldier, climbed up the rock to speak.

"My name's Bravura," she spoke out forcefully, "and you have every reason to hate me. You see my color. To many of you, it is a badge of terror. And rightly so. For I came here a year ago as part of a marauding machine, intent to take from you everything you had. I did not do this on my own. I did it as part of a collective madness, for we had given away our minds to monsters who fed us on a diet of hate. It plunged the whole world into darkness. Now that we are again in the light, we must build the relationships that will keep us there. We can do that only if together we look forward into a future where we see all of us living peacefully as equals. That is why I have joined the Visionants. In the time I have left to me in life, I want to use my thoughts and actions to secure the future for everyone. It's a new thought for me, and I am looking for those who can help me hold it."

Bravura ended, but stayed in her place on top of the rock. Natasha struggled up beside her and looked out over the crowd.

"Hello," she said. "You all know me, I think. Silly old Natasha who can't even keep all her legs together, let alone her wits." This brought some laughter from the crowd. Natasha continued: "But I'm not so daft that I can't find good friends to keep me company." Ventura climbed back up on the rock and stood next to Natasha with Bravura on the other side.

"See what I mean?" Natasha continued. "We all lost much in the war, but look at what I've found now. Friends to march forward with into the future. What's past is done. What's to come is open. Let's all step out and make it wonderful."

In her excitement, Natasha took a step forward but lost her balance, and would have tumbled off the rock had not Bravura and Ventura grabbed her and held her on either side. The crowd cheered, loving it.

"So that's our story," Ventura shouted. "Old enemies as new friends creating a free and open future together. It's a message we want to take across Antale. We need thousands to help us. If you hear the call, stay now and talk to us. Join the Visionants and change the world!"

From that day on, the Visionants became a phenomenon. Their numbers grew and word about them spread. Ventura was a good organizer. She picked her best leaders and sent them out to clone themselves, first into the more friendly territory of the White, Black and Yellow colonies, then north and south into the lands of the former aggressors—the Reds and Greens and Browns. As the movement grew, Natasha let it go and stayed close to home in Buranda, enjoying her new celebrity status. Ventura and Bravura worked together, always moving into new territory. On one of these expeditions, deep inside the former Green Ant Colony, they had an encounter that impacted dramatically on the future of Antale.

It was the end of the day and they had just finished speaking to an enthusiastic crowd. They were aware that, as they pushed south, they were under increasing scrutiny by soldiers standing at the back of the crowds. So far, no interference had been made with their activities, but this day, the presence of the soldiers was more obvious than ever, and at the end of the meeting, when smaller groups tried to form to join the Visionants, the soldiers moved in and broke the gatherings up. There was no violence, for the Green ants in the audience, when they saw the soldiers, quickly slipped away. Watching from their vantage point on their speakers' platform, Ventura and Bravura knew that they had come to a turning point. They were now deep in territory where the Salt dictatorship was controlling the affairs of the former Green Ant Colony. One tyranny had been replaced by another. If the Visionants' message was to spread here, let alone penetrate further south into actual Salt territory, it would have to take another form.

At that moment, as Ventura and Bravura turned to come down from their platform, they were approached by a small, wizened ant of indeterminate age.

"Hsst, sisters!" she said. "May I have a word?"

Ventura and Bravura paused. Their own group of Visionants closed in around them. The small ant continued speaking, her antennae twitching nervously.

"This is not friendly country for you. Not friendly. Be wary. The thugs are about to move in. It could be dangerous."

"Who are you?" Ventura asked.

"I'm called Cassandra," said the other. "I've come to warn you and show you another way. Will you come and meet someone who can help?"

"Who is that?" asked Bravura.

Cassandra crouched down low and looked around to make sure no soldiers were listening. "Her name's Democrika," she said. "She's biding her time."

"For what?" Ventura asked.

"For the start of the New Age. It's in the flow of time, but its moment has not yet come. I've been watching. Now you are here. That's part of it. But you have to meet Democrika before the next piece can happen. I have come to bring you."

"Well, what do you say, Bravura?" asked Ventura. "Should we go and meet this sister of destiny?"

"I'm not sure, yet," replied Bravura. "Just one word more, Cassandra. Tell us about the New Age."

"It comes when the walls are torn down. When the messenger returns from outer darkness. When the young ones cry out with new voices."

"Is it a good time?" Bravura asked.

"As in all times, the good unfolds from the opposite. Democrika is its potential, but she needs your help."

"Then I think we should give it to her," said Bravura.

"All right, Cassandra," Ventura added. "Lead the way."

Several soldiers had come up toward the end of the conversation and Cassandra scuttled off so quickly that Ventura and Bravura lost sight of her. Then they saw her head pop out from behind the base of a berry bush, jerking back and forth, motioning for them to follow. Ventura sent her small group of Visionants to distract the soldiers while she and Bravura slipped away to join Cassandra.

"This way, quickly, there's a path," whispered Cassandra.

"How far is it?" asked Bravura.

"Not far, follow me," replied Cassandra.

Half an hour later, Bravura asked again, "How far is it now, Cassandra?"

"Not far," she replied. "Just along here."

An hour later, the sun went down and they were still scrambling along a barely discernible path.

"How far, Cassandra?" It was Ventura's turn to ask.

"Not far," Bravura replied before Cassandra could, "just follow her."

Another hour passed and the moon came up. They had just climbed over a rocky ridge and were slithering and sliding down the other side.

"It's a good thing you told the others to go back to Buranda and not to wait for us," said Bravura. "We're on a marathon, here."

"How much further, Cassandra?" asked Ventura, "and if you say 'not far,' I'll throttle you."

"No, no, here we are," Cassandra said triumphantly, "just inside this cave."

They entered a crack in the face of a wall of rock and scrambled along in the darkness for another thirty minutes. Cassandra moved very quickly, just managing to stay out of the reach of Ventura, lest she carry out her threat. Finally, they came out on the other side of the rock face onto a broad stone platform flooded with moonlight. There, ahead of them in a circle, Ventura counted eight dark ant shapes squatting, probably asleep.

"Hello, heads up, spirits, too! Cassandra's back with company. Two more for the circle. A perfect ten. The portal is ready to open."

One of the ant shapes rose and embraced Cassandra.

"Still speaking riddles, are you, old girl," said the ant. Then she greeted Ventura and Bravura. "Welcome, I am Democrika. You have come to teach me, yes?"

"Right now, I'm not sure of anything," replied Ventura, "except that we've been following this wily rascal at full speed for three hours when we thought you were nearby."

"Ho, that's Cassandra, sure enough," Democrika chuckled. "She's never in the world long enough to know what time it is. Look, she's already left us."

Ventura and Bravura turned to see Cassandra lying flat on her back, with her legs stiff in the air.

"Good grief!" exclaimed Bravura. "Is she dead?"

"No, just in a trance. That's how she sees everything. She saw you and knew I needed your help. But come, you must be famished. We've got a great meal of cut worm here. These are my associates. You can meet them all as we eat. I'll tell you the whole story."

The whole story was a wild scheme whereby Democrika was planning to overturn the dictatorship that Bravada held in place by force across the territory occupied by the Salts. Democrika was a rebel from the mountain passes on the northern border of Salt territory. Her clan was the Barbs. They had never rested easy under the rule of the Salts and had been waiting their chance to break free. With an aging Bravada now playing dangerously with explosive technology in confrontation with the Sugars, Democrika felt that the time had come to make a move. She had gathered up seven other leaders of rebel groups and brought them all up into this mountain retreat to consult Cassandra. Democrika's clan were mountain mystics. They had always trusted in their prophets' ability to know the future. Cassandra was among their best and Democrika had unshakeable faith in her. Cassandra had spoken of the spreading influence of the Visionants and their message of equality and freedom. Democrika wanted detailed information, so Cassandra had brought Ventura and Bravura to her.

"You want us to school you in revolution!" exclaimed Ventura. "That's not what we're about."

"The teaching's yours, the method is ours," replied Democrika. "We will set our sisters free. Then they need your wisdom. Is it a deal?"

"How long do we have?" asked Ventura.

"Until the walls are torn down," said Bravura. "You heard what Cassandra said."

"What the heck does that mean?" asked Ventura. "What walls where?"

"I don't know," said Democrika, "but it's surely true. Is it a deal, my friends? Will you teach us to be Visionants and bring it to our sisters?"

Bravura and Ventura exchanged glances.

"All right," said Ventura. "It's a deal."

Back in Centrasia, Pacifica knew nothing at this time of Ventura's encounter with Democrika, but something else related had just been brought to her attention by her ever wary Captain of the Guard, Bluffasta.

"What do you mean, the Salts are building a wall?" Pacifica asked incredulously. "Ants don't build walls. The word hardly exists in our language."

"Then the Salts intend to change that," said Bluffasta. "Twenty thousand slaves picking up pebbles can build a wall, or whatever you want to call it, very fast."

"Tell the Salt ambassador I want to talk to her," said Pacifica.

An hour later, the two met in Pacifica's private quarters.

"Is it true you are building a wall across Freedom Pass?" Pacifica asked.

"Wall?" queried the ambassador. "That's a strange term. We're simply helping the local Pebble Ant population control their territory. There's too much traffic through the pass."

"But that's why it's called Freedom Pass," said Pacifica. "It's an important part of the north-south trail. It's always been open to travelers. If you close it, all that traffic along the shore of Lake Miasma will have to go down through the marshes. It will be a disaster for north-south trade—the very thing Unicol is trying to promote."

"Some members of Unicol may be trying to promote that," the ambassador retorted, "but we do not agree."

The problem exploded a few days later in an emergency meeting of the Protectorate.

"This is the most provocative, contemptuous act that any colony can commit against its neighbors, short of war," raged the Sugar ambassador.

"It's not a matter for this council," retorted her Salt counterpart. "The Pebble Ants can choose to do whatever they like in their own colony."

"We all know you Salts are controlling the Pebbles. You've got a virtual slave army building walls at both ends of the pass, simply to inconvenience the Quadrant Four Alliance. We demand that you take them down or we will regard it as an act of war."

This was the strongest language ever used in the short history of the Protectorate. Pacifica sought to intervene on the side of sanity.

"As this is a matter of policy affecting all members of Unicol, I propose we refer it to the House of Assembly for debate," she said. "Let us have no talk of war or retaliation here."

Afterward, on a private transmission to Serenta, President of the Sugar Ant Colony, she put it more bluntly. "I understand your frustration with the Salts," she said, "but I ask you to restrain your delegation from threatening war in a meeting of the Protectorate."

"I take your point," replied Serenta, "but the trouble is, Bravada has gone out of her mind. Someone has to pull her up. If you folks up there in Unicol can't do it with diplomacy, then maybe someone else will have to do it with a charge of explosive. Either way, those walls have to be torn down."

Pacifica tried to talk to Bravada, but her calls went unanswered. A few days later, the debate in Unicol began with most speakers supporting the idea of freedom of access. At the same time, all supported the right of a colony to exercise control over its territory. The debate continued over several days, during which the walls at both ends of Freedom Pass rose higher and higher.

Very little of this diplomatic maneuvering reached the mountain retreat where Ventura and Bravura were working with Democrika and her rebel leaders. In fact, they knew nothing about the walls incident until a full week after the Unicol debate began. Word was brought in by one of Democrika's contingent from the Pebble Colony. Her name was Rocha. She was part of a continuous stream of rebel leaders Democrika was rounding up to listen to Ventura and Bravura.

"You are right," said Rocha at the end of a session. "We can't go on living under a dictatorship. Our colony has always lived in peace with our neighbors. Now the Salts have us working as slaves to build walls to cut off traffic through Freedom Pass."

"What's that? Walls, did you say?" asked Democrika.

"Yes, but they won't last long. I've heard there's a squad of Sugars nearby waiting for a chance to blow them up."

A high-pitched shriek rang out from above. They all looked around to see Cassandra standing on a rock, rearing up and waving her forelegs vigorously.

"When the walls are torn down!" she wailed. "When the walls are torn down!"

"My gosh, who's that?" asked Rocha.

"That's Cassandra," said Democrika reverently. "She's already predicted what you told us. So what do you think, my friends?" she asked, turning to Ventura and Bravura. "Is it time for Democrika to act?"

"This is down right spooky!" said Bravura.

"Hold on, now," Ventura asserted. "You don't go launching a revolution because of some weird prophecy. The message needs time to spread, Democrika. We've hardly begun."

"Then we must speed up," replied Democrika. "I will send out the word. Within a week, you will have a thousand leaders to speak to. That should do it."

She turned and left to issue her orders.

"I don't like this, Bravura," Ventura whispered to her friend. "These ants aren't ready to take control of their own affairs. Maybe we should get out of here so that we don't encourage them to do something they'll regret later."

"They're going to do it anyway," said Bravura. "At least this way, we have a chance to help them."

Ventura stood thoughtfully for a moment before replying. "Of course, you're right," she said. "Perhaps we can convince them to go more slowly."

"Besides," added Bravura. "The walls are still standing. They may never get torn down."

Both of them looked up to the rock where Cassandra was standing. She was crouched down low, staring at them intently.

CHAPTER 11

Out of Control

It was the end of a long, hot, tedious, unprofitable day of debate at Unicol. Pacifica, exhausted, had retired to her quarters. The Salt strategy on the Great Walls Debate, as it was now being called, was obvious. Keep talking and keep building. If they could stretch the discussion out long enough, the walls would be finished, and Unicol would have a hard time to do anything about it, no matter how the members voted. Pacifica remembered only too well Serenta's barely veiled threat to take more direct action. If that happened, another major war could erupt. She longed to hear some good news for a change.

It came a few minutes later when Roanda, her assistant, burst in.

"Pacifica, there's a message from Mission Control. Observa's on the line. They've discovered something. She wants to speak to you."

As Pacifica hurried to the transmission room, she realized how preoccupied she had been over the past eight weeks since Observa had left on her expedition to follow the Explora probe of last year. Pacifica had received periodic reports of progress, but there had been no significant developments, and she had concentrated on other things. She wondered what the news would be.

Observa's message came in loud and clear: "We're onto something at last, Pacifica. We're right on the spot where Explora sent one of her last messages. There's a new world here, all right. Just like she said. We can see where her party went down into it along a deep ravine. It's a kind of steamy haze down there and those strange transmissions are very strong."

"That's incredible," said Pacifica, "but you must be careful. We don't want to lose you, too. Have you seen any sign of Explora?"

"No, nothing specific, but I know we're in the right place from the details in her reports. I'm not going to go down into the ravine, though. We'll work our way around the edge of the Rim to get an overall view. There's life down there, I'm sure of it, but I don't know what it is."

"Your life is the most important one, old friend." Pacifica felt herself flooding with emotion. "Take good care of it. Your news will be an inspiration to everyone here. We need to hear it, now, more than ever, to give us something to expand our view—to appreciate who we are in the universe. Bring that to us and everything will change."

"I understand," Observa replied. "I know what you are struggling with back there. We can't solve the meaning of life, but we'll bring you the best scientific data we can. I must sign off, now. Goodbye."

Pacifica stared for several long moments at the transmission control panel. Then she turned to the officer in charge. "Get me Professor Electra in Blackhall," she said.

Electra's transmission came in.

"Hello, Electra," said Pacifica. "Some good news at last. I've just spoken to Observa. She's on the edge of that same new world that Explora reported. She's going around it, mapping from the top, trying to see what's down there."

"Are those transmissions still coming in?" asked Electra.

"Yes. She said they're very strong. Why do you ask?"

"Because I think they're expressing the level of consciousness of that place."

"Higher than our own, do you think?"

"I don't know, and I don't want to speculate. We don't know how to measure these things, but I think that there's a collective level of consciousness reflected by electrical vibrations. If we could measure it here on Antale, I believe we would see it going up."

"Why do you say that?"

"This is my own piece of good news." Electra was obviously pleased with herself. "I was going to call you about it. Our initiative with the Queens is working. Anastasia was right. They understand what they can do to raise the level of consciousness in their nests. Royal households everywhere are asking for the Elixir."

"That is good news. You say everywhere. What does that mean?"

"There's no pattern. It seems to be operating independent of political jurisdiction. It's spreading through personal communications among nests. Once a Queen hears about it, she finds a way to get it. All we need is time."

"Yes, and that's a problem, Electra. How much time?"

"Well, we can't expect to see much come from this initiative until next spring, when the new generations are born."

"And we've still got half a summer of danger ahead of us." Pacifica reflected solemnly for a moment before continuing. "But that's not your concern, Electra. Your news is good. Keep me informed."

"I wish all of it was good." There was a change in Electra's voice.

"Oh? Do you have something else to tell me?"

"It's too soon to be sure, but there are some disturbing signs in our weather pattern this year. Much too hot and dry. I'm trying to see if it's a trend from past years and whether it could predict the future."

"Most of us have been too busy fighting wars and doing politics to notice. Do you think it could be serious?"

"I don't know. But it signals the need for us to pay attention to life support systems before we get caught out."

"All right, Electra. Thank goodness, we've got you looking out for us. Goodbye for now."

Roanda, who had been listening to Pacifica's conversations, made an observation: "Do you realize," she said, "the scope of what you've been talking about in the last few minutes? The discovery of life in a new world, the rebirth of consciousness on our own, and the possible disruption of weather and climate patterns? My gosh, Pacifica, that's quite an agenda."

"Yes, and yet I'm spending most of my time listening to a tedious debate about walls. Somehow, we need to get these Unicol ambassadors to enlarge their vision. That was what I hoped Ventura and her Visionants could help us with. Maybe I should bring her in to speak with Unicol. Where is she now?"

"Well, the Visionants are active in Quadrant Four, I know that much," replied Roanda. "Ventura herself seems to have dropped out of sight. She's somewhere down in Salt territory, I believe."

"Well, I hope she's safe. She's another brave soul that Antale surely needs right now."

Had Pacifica been aware of Ventura's situation at that moment, she would have found good reason to be concerned about her safety. Ventura and Bravura were standing on a rock surrounded by a sea of the toughest looking collection of anthood that one was likely to find anywhere in Antale. These were Democrika's revolutionary leaders, rounded up from nests all across Salt territory. They were raw and ribald, itching for action, and ready to overthrow their oppressors. Ventura's appeal for caution was not going over very well.

"I understand your anger and frustration," she was saying, "but you must take time to seed a new vision in the minds and hearts of all those who you say you want to set free. The best leaders lead from behind. Give your sisters a new dream to see for themselves and they will find a way to make it real."

"Yes, and have their heads beaten and their backs broken for their trouble," shouted someone from the crowd.

"Dreams are for dreamers," shouted another. "We're done with that. Now it's time to snap off some Salt heads and roll them in the dust."

"I'll tell you whose heads will roll first!" Bravura had now entered the fray. "You see me. I'm an old soldier. I know how to kill and maim. I was trained to do it. If you go head to head against the Salt troops, your workers will be cut to pieces. So much dead meat in the name of freedom. Listen to Ventura. It's not enough to run wild with passion. You have to build your strength. Train your own troops. Then, wait for the right time to act."

A loud murmur rolled like a wave across the sea of ants as they argued amongst one another about Bravura's words. Suddenly, Democrika leapt up on the rock beside the other two.

"Knowing the time to strike is what counts," she shouted. "We must make our plans. Train our sisters. Then we will know when it is time."

"When the walls are torn down! When the walls are torn down!" The message came wailing across the heads of the crowd. All eyes turned upward, searching for its source.

"Look! There she is," shouted someone, "up there, in the leaves."

Cassandra was clinging to the branch of a bush, swaying over the crowd.

"It's the old witch!" This was Rocha speaking now, from the Pebble Colony. She climbed up on the rock beside Democrika. "She's telling us it's time to act now—to tear down the walls the Salts are forcing the Pebble workers to build. This will be the signal for the revolution to begin."

"Then tear down the walls!" someone shouted from the crowd.

"I'll need your help," cried Rocha. "Who will come with me to the walls?"

"To the walls! To the walls!" roared the crowd.

Rocha scrambled down from the rock and crawled across the backs of the crowd until she reached the far side. Chanting and waving, the mass of rebel leaders slowly turned and followed Rocha out along a path.

"Democrika, this is crazy," said Bravura. "The Salts will carve them up for dinner. You'll lose all your leaders before you start."

"It's not for me to say," replied Democrika. "Cassandra is always right. If the walls come down, the revolution begins. If not, we wait." She climbed down the rock and followed the others.

"Come on, Bravura," said Ventura. "We've got to get back to Centrasia to warn Pacifica about this."

They hurried off in the opposite direction. Cassandra, perched on the swaying branch, watched them leave.

It was a hard, difficult journey, much of it over country not familiar to them. They traveled all day and through the night and came up to the dome of Centrasia early next morning. They spoke to Pacifica before the opening session of Unicol for that day. Pacifica immediately saw the implication of their news. If there was an upheaval around the walls, it would confuse the Unicol debate and indefinitely delay any resolution to the matter. Unicol needed to take some action of its own, but there was no way for the House of Assembly to act quickly. Pacifica sent word canceling the day's meeting of the House and called instead an emergency meeting of the Protectorate.

After informing the members of the news she had received, Pacifica made a proposal that the Protectorate send in a Unicol peace-keeping force to try to bring stability to the region. She quickly received the support of the Black, White and Yellow members, but the Salts and the Sugars were not receptive. The Salts, as might be expected, argued against any interference from the outside. The Sugars, strangely, seemed to support the Salts. All members wanted to get instructions from their home colonies before making a final decision. Pacifica called an adjournment, during which she contacted her own observers whom she had stationed near the walls. They reported some unusual activity among the Salt troops, who seemed to be moving around indecisively, while the Pebble workers, who would normally be under Salt supervision working on the walls, remained idle. Pacifica pondered this, wondering what it meant, but could find no answer.

It took a long time for the Salt and Sugar ambassadors to return to the conference hall, and it was late in the day before Pacifica reconvened the meeting. There was a marked change in the behavior of the Salts and the Sugars. The Salt ambassador, in particular, seemed visibly shaken. She announced quickly that they were now prepared to support sending in a peace-keeping force. The Sugars followed and said that they, too, were now in agreement with the proposal. Pacifica looked sharply at the Sugar ambassador, wondering about this sudden change of mind, but the latter betrayed no sign nor gave any substantial reason for their new position.

With the decision made, the rest of the discussion concerned the number, makeup and terms of reference of the peace-keeping force. By the end of the day, they had agreed to send in a party of two hundred, made up of forty soldiers from each of the five colonies. The troop would be under the command of Colonel Mona from the Yellow colony and its role was to act as a mediating force in any conflict that might develop. It took two more days to put the contingent together. So it was on the fifth day after Ventura and Bravura had set off from Democrika's camp to warn Pacifica, that a Unicol peace-keeping force marched out of Centrasia for the Pebble Colony and the disputed walls.

Needless to say, Democrika, Rocha and the other rebel leaders had more than enough time to reach their objective ahead of the Unicol force. They had crept into position on the eastern rim of Freedom Pass at the same time as Pacifica and her colleagues had reached agreement to send in the peace-keepers. Two days later, there was not going to be much peace left to keep.

Freedom Pass was really a narrow gully cutting through a rocky ridge that ran down to the shores of Lake Miasma. The gully was about ten feet wide, fifty yards long, and six to eight feet deep. Meandering along its bed, the main north-south trail connected Quadrants Four and Three. Along the trail on either side, the low, gritty, reddish brown mounds of the Pebble Colony sat like pimples on the dry earth.

Looking down from the eastern rim, the rebel band saw all this at a glance. But two other things captured their attention. First, the walls. They were solid masses of small rocks, pebbles, and red earth built like plugs across both ends of the pass. Already, they climbed more than halfway up the sides of the gully and at their base, they were at least six feet thick. Even Democrika's faith in prophecy took a little shaking when she realized how much work it would take to bring these walls down. The second item the rebels noted as strange was the activity going on down in the Pebble Colony. Being late in the day, it was a good time to work. Yet, there did not seem to be a single worker ant on the walls. They were all clustered around their nests, while along the trail, several thousand of the larger, dullish-gray Salt soldiers were scurrying along, backward and forward, seemingly engaged in animated conversation and giving the impression of total confusion.

"What do you make of that?" Democrika asked Rocha. "That bunch couldn't organize a ditch digging party, let alone build those walls. What's going on?"

"I don't know," replied Rocha. "I've never seen them act like that before. It's always been hup! hup! hup! Do this! Do that! Something must have happened."

"This could be our chance." Democrika was getting excited. "Look at all those Pebble ants hanging around. If we could get down there and organize them, we could jump those Salts from behind. They'd never know what hit them. Are the Pebbles up to it, do you think?"

"By the rubble!" Rocha exclaimed. "You ask me that? Give us the hope and we'll move the world!"

"All right," said Democrika. "Let's get our own team organized. We can be down there tonight and attack tomorrow."

Democrika and her rebels were not the only outside observers of the activity in Freedom Pass. At the north end of the western slope, Pacifica had her own small band of Unicol officers. They had already reported the strange behavior of the Salt soldiers, which was followed by a sudden agreement in Centrasia of the Salt ambassador to the formation of the Unicol peace-keeping force. The Sugars, too, had suddenly changed their minds. This was related to a third group of observers at the southern end of the Pass.

Colonel Alexa was one of the best Sugar campaign leaders. That was why she was chosen to lead Mission Demolition. War veteran and hero of the Acid attack on Camp Portal last year, she was well tested under pressure. President Serenta and the Sugar high command had great confidence in her ability to bring down the walls across Freedom Pass. Her judgment was now being put to the test as she watched with two of her officers the strange behavior of the Salt troops down below in the Pebble Colony.

"They've obviously received some bad news and don't know what to do about it," said Alexa. "That's why they've stopped work on the walls. They may be getting ready to pull out. Our best bet is to wait and see what happens."

"They've still got plenty of guards on the wall," said one of the officers.

"All the more reason to wait," replied Alexa. "We can't afford to have our bomb squad detected as they go in. My hunch is that, within a couple of days, we'll have our best chance. In the meantime, we'll get our second squad in place at the north wall. Once we take the southern one out, we'll use the confusion to go in and demolish the other. We just have to pick our time."

It was just as well for Alexa's strategy that Democrika's plans didn't go smoothly. If her unruly bunch of rebels had launched an attack the next day, who knows what might have happened. As it was, she found it impossible to organize her ill-disciplined group before it was well into the night and too late to move down into the Pebble nests before sunrise. So they lay under cover throughout the next day and moved down that night. Needless to say, the Pebbles were more than a little surprised to find this host from the hills descending upon them and inciting them to rebellion. It took a lot of diplomatic shuttling by Rocha among the nests to explain the mission. The result was a further day's delay before Democrika and Rocha could feel confident they were ready to attack. During all this time, the Salts' behavior had shifted from agitated animation to morose morbidity. They made no attempt to get the Pebbles back to work, but simply hung around in listless despondency. No one among Democrika's party or the Pebble Colony knew what was causing this.

At sunrise on the third day, Colonel Alexa looked down from her vantage point near the southern wall on the awakening Pebble Colony. At the same time, Colonel Mona was leading her Unicol peace-keeping force out of Centrasia. It would take them half a day's march to get to Freedom Pass.

Alexa methodically noted the placement of the Salt troops. They were settled in camps several yards apart along the edge of the trail. On the wall, two other camps were placed strategically so that sentries could see every inch of the wall on either side. Alexa had decided that she would have to create some kind of diversion to distract the attention of the sentries. She need not have worried. Democrika's rebel band was about to launch all the diversion that Alexa needed.

To her amazement, Alexa suddenly saw the whole hillside below her begin to move. At first, she thought it must be an earthquake, but the ground wasn't shaking. Then, she saw that the slope was alive with Pebble ants, each one crouched behind a small rock, pushing it with all her might, slowly getting it to move, until all at once, an avalanche of thousands of rocks was rolling down the slope onto the unsuspecting Salt camps below. The Salt soldiers in the camps never had a chance. Within minutes, they were buried under several inches of rocks and a seething mass of Pebble ferocity.

Alexa couldn't believe it. The Pebbles were a docile race. That was why the Salts had found it so easy to get them to build the walls. Now, here were these same Pebbles turning on their former masters. Then, Alexa saw the others—Democrika's ferocious followers of all sizes and colors leading charges on any Salt soldiers who had escaped the avalanche.

It had taken just a few minutes and the rebels already thought they had won the day. But then the Salt troops on the wall moved into the attack. They were only a thousand strong against many times that number of rebels and Pebbles, but these were trained warriors. Gone, now, was the listless despondency of the past two days. They had an enemy to deal with. They came down off the wall in solid fighting formation and quickly began to wreak a heavy toll on the undisciplined rebels.

Alexa waited no longer.

"Operation, go for Number One," she said calmly into her transmission box, "you're clear for placement." At the base of the south wall on the outside, a party of Sugar soldiers moved out of cover, bearing three large cylinders. Within minutes, an excavation party was digging furiously into the foundation of the wall. They worked unobserved by any Salt sentries. All of these were now on the other side of the wall, battling with the rebels.

"It will take them a couple of hours to get the bombs in position," Alexa said to one of her officers. "I'm going north to observe the situation there. You're in charge here. Send me a transmission when you reach D time."

Alexa set off along the top of the slope with the second officer. Down below, turmoil, confusion and carnage raged along the entire length of the pass. Democrika had coordinated her campaign well. The Pebbles had rolled avalanches onto every Salt camp and were jubilantly celebrating their success. At the northern end of the pass, however, the Salt soldiers had again poured down off the wall and were moving in on the rebels with great effect. By the time Alexa reached a point overlooking the north wall a half hour later, a full-scale battle was raging down in the pass. The wall, however, was clear of Salt sentries.

"Operation, go for Number Two," Alexa transmitted, "you're clear for placement." As in the south, a party of Sugars moved into action at the outside base of the north wall.

Alexa made one more transmission, this time to headquarters in the Sugar Colony. "The seeds are planted," she said. "Germination under way."

Down in the thick of the fighting, Democrika's early elation was turning to concern. The Pebbles were good workers, but hopeless fighters. With the ferocity of the Salt counterattack, most of the Pebbles had taken to the hills. Democrika's own rebels were facing the brunt of the Salt vengeance. Caught in the pincers of the two Salt movements from the north and south, the rebels slowly fell back toward the center then finally fled to the hills themselves. The Salts did not pursue them, but turned instead to digging any survivors out of the rubble of the avalanches. Looking down on the battle scene two hours after it began, Democrika began to wonder what she had accomplished. The Salt occupying force had been decimated, but they were still in control of the Colony. The Pebbles would have to come back to their mounds, and who could say what the Salts would then do to them? And the walls were still standing. How could the revolution begin in earnest while the walls were still standing? Democrika looked north and south at those immovable masses and sadly shook her head. It was then that the south end of Freedom Pass erupted in a gigantic upheaval of rock, earth and dust.

It began as a low rumble, then, as Democrika turned to look, she saw the entire south wall shaking. Something was tearing it apart from the inside. The next moment, the whole mass heaved two feet into the air, then flattened out into a pile of rubble, spreading at the edges like a broken egg. When the dust cleared, Democrika saw that the wall was gone. One half of Cassandra's prophecy had come to pass.

"Aiyee!" Democrika shouted, shaking Rocha, who was at her side, so hard that the startled Pebble thought another eruption was under way. "The wall! The wall! Do you see?" Democrika continued. "It's down! It's down! One more to go and the revolution begins!"

"By the rubble!" Rocha muttered, "I see, but I don't believe it."

Throughout the length of the pass, every ant, Salt and Pebble alike, was transfixed by the spectacle of the impossible that had just happened. For a long moment, all motion was suspended. Then, as if responding to some mysterious signal, the Pebble ants who were nearest to the destruction zone poured down from the hill slopes where they had been hiding and, like a single, seething organism, seized on the scattered pieces of the former wall and spread them out along the pass, so that all traces of the Salt monument to audacity and belligerence rapidly began to disappear. The remaining Salt troops, in their turn, huddled together, immobile to the point of paralysis, completely uncomprehending the misfortune that had befallen them.

About a hundred yards north along the trail to Centrasia, Colonel Mona and her Unicol peace-keeping force were clipping along at a good pace when they heard a low rumble some distance to the south. They paused, straining to see, then noted a plume of dust drifting in the air above the hills near Freedom Pass.

"That's strange," Mona said to her second-in-command. "I wonder what caused that."

Half an hour later, the peace-keepers were coming up to the pass with the north wall in full view. Mona was just considering what path they would take to get around the wall when a violent, concussive shuddering shook the ground all around, and before their eyes, the wall in front of them lifted into the air and a shower of rocks and earth came crashing down upon them. The peace-keepers dove for cover.

When they lifted their heads a few minutes later, all that they could see, where once the wall had stood, was a huge pile of rubble. Then, as they watched, dumbfounded, a horde of Pebble ants appeared from nowhere and began hauling the rocks away.

"Thunder and blazes!" Mona exclaimed. "Someone's cut loose with a mega bomb. Who in the hell could do that?"

Up in the hills, Colonel Alexa, looking down on Freedom Pass without walls, sent a cryptic transmission to Sugar headquarters. "Harvest time. The crop is in."

Colonel Mona likewise transmitted to Pacifica: "Someone's blown up the north wall. The Pebbles are everywhere. We're going in."

As they scrambled into Freedom Pass over rocks and around jubilantly jabbering Pebble ants, the Unicol peace-keepers' eyes grew wider with astonishment. The whole pass seemed to be an elongated burial mound, for they could see the remains of countless Salt soldiers protruding from piles of rubble all along the trail. As if there could be no end to the extraordinary, when they reached midway along the pass, they stumbled into an astonishing scene.

Huddled together in a tight defensive fighting square, the last of the oncemasterful Salt occupying force was making a final stand. Surrounding the Salts, but keeping some distance back, a multitude of Pebble ants looked on. Between the Pebbles and the Salts, a rag-tag circle of other ants stamped and jeered defiantly at the Salts. One of these was standing on a large rock, delivering an ultimatum:

"In the name of the democratic revolution now begun, I call upon you all, Salt offenders, to give up your brutal aggression and join our freedom fighters. You have seen our awesome power. The walls are torn down! It's just the beginning. Now the flames will spread and sweep as a fire of freedom across the land. Join us in the vanguard of our great cause or perish in the next conflagration we will bring upon your heads."

It was Democrika's best speech ever. Her rebels cheered enthusiastically. Then, Colonel Mona and her peace-keepers came marching through the line.

"Hold up a minute, there, sister," she said. "I'm Colonel Mona, commander of this peace-keeping force dispatched to Freedom Pass under the authority of the Protectorate of Unicol. It seems you've had quite a killing party here. Before there's any more of that, let's see if we can talk this out." Without waiting for an answer from Democrika, Mona turned to the Salts and shouted: "Who's in command, there?"

A Salt officer came out from the square of soldiers. "I'm Lieutenant Serba, Colonel," she said. "I'm in command now. All the other officers are dead."

Mona signaled to Democrika to join her and she took the two of them, rebel leader and Salt officer, a short distance apart from the others to talk. Then, for the first time came an explanation to the outside world as to why the Salt forces had relaxed their control and lost the pass. Bravada, Supreme Commander of the Salt Dominion as she had called herself in the last days, was dead. The word had come through to the Salt troops in Freedom Pass five days ago, and with it, further news of a power struggle in the military that had left the forces in the pass cut off and isolated. Not sure about continuing support, they had stopped construction on the walls and waited.

"Providence, sister, providence!" Democrika said excitedly. "The despot is dead. The walls are down. Join the revolution and we'll create the new age of freedom."

"Yes, I think we can talk about that," said Serba.

"Hold on," Mona intervened. "Revolution never settles anything. Support the structure we've got in place at Unicol, and one day you'll have your freedom and peace with it."

Democrika looked solemnly at Mona.

"Unicol lets the despots rule, Colonel. You are a good soldier, I'm sure. Keep what peace you can. But understand this: The walls are down and the revolution's begun."

Democrika and Serba walked away together. Mona returned to her troops. A short time later, Pacifica in Unicol headquarters received a full report from her peace-keepers, including the news of Bravada's death and the talk of revolution among rebels and disillusioned Salt soldiers. Suddenly, she realized that a whole new set of turbulent forces were about to be unleashed. Where and how in all this, she wondered, could the goal of universal peace, for which she longed with all her heart, be found and won.

CHAPTER 12

Adrift with Delusions

IN THE GOLD HOUSE IN THE SUGAR Colony, President Serenta was enjoying her moment of triumph. Flanked by her chiefs of staff, she was tying a braid of dried grass stems as a ribbon of honor across the shoulders of a proud Colonel Alexa, standing stiffly at attention.

"Took them right out, eh, colonel?" the President chuckled. "Now you see them, now you don't. Very good, very good. And getting those Unicol peacekeepers there right on cue—master stroke, that. We take out the walls and leave Unicol to keep the peace. A good day's work all round."

Serenta embraced Alexa, then turned to her officials. "Now what's the fallout from Bravada's death?" she asked. "Nasty piece of work, that one. Never did like her even when we had to work together in the War. Who's in line to take over now she's gone?"

General Domina, chief of military forces, replied. "According to intelligence reports, there's a lot of confusion right now. Several military commanders are ready to fight for power. Also, we've just heard about some kind of revolution breaking out in the north."

"Sounds like the Salts are going to be tied up in knots for a while," mused Serenta. "Gives us a good chance to strengthen our trade to the north. Now those infernal walls are down, we can get things moving again. What about the west? This is a good time to try to civilize those savages in the Dark Country. And what about the Dragons? How can we sit here in this modern age and have no contact with those hordes of nests we know are out there in the shadow of the Rim? This is the time for the Sugars to reach out. If we act decisively, we can get our products and technology into every colony in Antale. We've had our problems in the past few weeks, but we can still make this the Year of the Sugars. What do you say? Is there anyone who can give me one good reason why we shouldn't move now at full speed?"

Serenta had warmed to her theme. This was her third year in office. She knew she did not have much time left. The War and the power struggle with the Salts had kept her preoccupied for a long time, but they had also opened her eyes to the possibilities for Sugar domination in the world—not by War, as the Reds had tried to do it, but by ideas and influence, by products and technology. They had the force, too, and could use it, as they had just shown by blowing up the walls that stood in their way. This could be Serenta's greatest year. She did not want to lose it.

However, there was one major problem. Everyone in the oval office that morning knew about it. They all waited for someone else to speak. Finally, Secretary Helena, Chief of Social Stability, stepped into the breach.

"No one can deny that this is our time of opportunity to become a great power," she said, "but to do so, we must be strong at home, in our nests. We have a problem there and it's getting worse."

Serenta shuffled about irritably. She did not want to hear this. "You're going to bring up the beetle thing again, are you, Helena? I thought we dealt with that. We sent in the guard and cleaned them out."

"It's not so easy, Ma'am," Helena replied. "The beetles have laid eggs in more than half our nests. Our own workers look after them and now there are hundreds, maybe thousands, of beetles being born. Most of them are hidden away in secret tunnels. It's organized drug addiction. Our youngest workers are particularly vulnerable."

"What do you mean, organized?" Serenta asked testily. "This is just a damn weakness that should have been stamped out. I don't know why we haven't done it."

"With respect, Ma'am, we haven't done it because we haven't paid enough attention to it. We've been too busy on outside affairs. Now we have an internal epidemic to deal with. And it's run by a group calling themselves the Nirvanists. They have a leader, a kind of pop idol, named Esoterica."

"Well, blistering blazes!" Serenta exploded. "If you know all this, why haven't you cleaned them out?"

"Because the workers support and protect them. It didn't matter too much at first. Most of the ants just took a sip of the beetle juice and went on their way. But it's addictive. They keep coming back for more. Now, I'd say, we've got twenty percent of our workforce with a serious drug problem, and it's getting worse."

"I don't believe this! I just don't believe this!" Serenta was storming up and down. "We've got the greatest colony in Antale here. Look at our technology. Look at our military. Look at our sugar plantations. There's no shortage of food. Maybe we do have a few idle loafers who like to get high on beetle juice. But that's not who we are. This is the Sugar Colony. We won the War. We've held out against the Salts. How can you stand there and say twenty percent of our ants are drug addicts? Domina, Alexa—you're military leaders. Do you think we've got a drug problem in the military forces?"

"No, Ma'am," Domina replied, "we've got the cleanest, sharpest fighting force you'd find anywhere."

"Well, then," said Serenta, calming down a little, "I suggest you and Helena get together and figure out a way you can use our fine military troops to clean up this beetle problem. The rest of you, I want you to think about what I said before. We've got two good summer months left to expand our interests. We'll meet again tomorrow. I'll hear your suggestions then. And, Helena, one thing more. This Esoterica. Find her! Get rid of her! Shut her down! I'll see you all tomorrow."

Serenta turned away and the chiefs of staff left her office.

Only a hundred yards away in a different oval office, another leader was looking with a similarly ambitious gaze at an alternative idea of world domination. Esoterica was a strikingly distinctive Sugar Ant. Born last year as a sexual, she had returned from her mating flight unfertilized. The usual fate for such a one is a lonely death, but she had alighted near Paradise Beach, where a bevy of Sugar Ants whiled away their time under the influence of the delusory beetles. This was the same beach that Wiseria, Pacifica and Roanda had stumbled upon, to their great surprise, during their journey around Lake Miasma last year. Esoterica had come on the scene several weeks after that, and because of her striking appearance, had been received by the deluded patrons of the area as a gift from their mythical realm of Nirvana. At that time, she was still bedecked with her glorious golden wings, and her bulk of twice the size of a normal worker ant gave her the presence of a Queen. Denied by fate the normal role of a dedicated broodmother, she had quickly slipped into the role of Queen of Paradise Colony. She laid no eggs, but built her nest by capturing the loyalty and service of her disoriented followers. While the rest of the Sugar Colony was struggling with the burdens of the Great War, the denizens of Paradise Beach and their surrogate Queen created their own nest of illusion.

It was a veritable magic queendom. Esoterica had personally supervised its construction deep under the ground with no visible sign on the surface. Access was by several hidden entrances spread over an area of several square yards. The long tunnels connecting their entrances to the main complex also provided many means of escape, should the nest ever be discovered.

Esoterica had learned early on how to enjoy the stimulant of the beetle secretion without forming an incapacitating addiction. Her mind instead was a continuous haze of munificent expectation. She saw a vision of a blissful Nirvana all over Antale and dedicated her life to create it. She began with her own domain. Instead of the usual stark austerity of an ant nest, her chamber was a crystalline fantasy land, lined with the finest grains of polished silicon and quartz that her followers could gather. She presided in this subterranean oval royal repository, twice the size of President Serenta's office in the Gold House, and from here, carefully orchestrated her plans to realize her vision.

The key was to expand the number of delusory beetles inside the Sugar nests and then beyond. The Sugars had always shown some weakness in this regard, but in the past, the authorities had continually driven the beetles out. Paradise Beach had been the collecting spot, where beetles and ants passed their idle days at the mercy of marauding birds and other predators. Esoterica soon brought a change to that and used her underground queendom as a breeding place for delusory beetles. Their eggs were carefully transported to other nests by dedicated workers and mixed in the nurseries with Sugar eggs, so that when the young larvae or grubs were born, they were looked after by the Sugar nurse maids. The result of this enterprise a year later was an epidemic of drug addiction, as Helena had accurately reported to Serenta.

But Esoterica was not content to rely on a single strategy to achieve her goals. To gain release from the stress of their hard working lives, ants needed a variety of stimulants, and Esoterica had established a research program to produce other possibilities. The most promising was an alcoholic elixir being developed by her chief researcher, Rotunda. This morning was an auspicious day, for Rotunda had come to the royal chamber to report her success.

"I think we've got it this time, Maj," she said. Rotunda was a short, stocky ant with an unusually large, round abdomen. It heaved and trembled now in her excitement. "The main problem was the container, but we've adapted that cocoon the Acids used for their poison gas. Works like a charm. We've got a batch in storage, if you'd like to see it."

"Why, Rotunda, your news is a wonderful revelation," Esoterica replied in her usual flowing rhetoric. "If we can bring this elixir to the masses, it will be a gift from the magic vales. Come, show it to me. Lead the way, my dear."

Esoterica lifted her large bulk rather clumsily. Several attendants scurried around stabilizing her, then she lurched in a wobbling gait after the puffing Rotunda. They went down a passage just barely wide enough to accommodate the Queen and came eventually into an open chamber.

"I don't see anything, darling," said Esoterica, "but what is that tantalizing aroma?"

Rotunda had paused beside a small rock blocking a tunnel. She suddenly seemed a little unsure of herself. "It's the juice," she said. "Fermentation causes the smell. It shouldn't be so strong, though. The containers are stored in the cellar behind this rock. I'll just move it aside. Easy does it, now."

These were the last words Rotunda said before the deluge enveloped her. As she pushed the rock away, a thin trickle of slime came with it, then a stream, then a flood, and finally, a dam-burst of foaming fermentation, as a whole cellar full of her famous elixir rushed out to engulf her and the astonished Queen. The release of pressure allowed more containers to explode and the sea of foam surged out to the accompaniment of a volley of detonations. Rotunda disappeared under the waves, while Esoterica went surfing out with the fermenting tide, back along the passage to the royal chamber, where her startled attendants saw the apparition of their Queen floating along in foaming splendor. Before the flood subsided, it had covered the entire floor of the royal chamber. Queen and attendants inhaled and drank themselves into delicious delirium. They hardly noticed a few minutes later a very unsteady and apologetic Rotunda stagger back into the chamber.

"I guess it has more pressure than poison gas," she muttered. "We'll have to strengthen the cocoons. I'm sorry, Maj. I'll get some workers to mop this up."

"No, no, don't waste it, darling," murmured the Queen. "We'll make it a royal open house. It's the birth of our new Heavenly Tide, so everyone can come and sample. You go back to your laboratory, dear. Soon, we'll have something to deliver to the whole world."

So it was that, in the late summer of the year, the great undeclared contest began between Esoterica and Serenta to capture the minds of the ant world. Inevitably, this would become a problem for Unicol and, therefore, Pacifica, to deal with.

In the meantime, however, Pacifica had more than enough problems before her, stemming mainly from the collapse of the Salt Colony. While true that the threat of war between the Sugars and the Salts had now disappeared, Unicol's quest for peace was shattered by the outbreak of violent internecine conflict among nests formerly under the domination of the Salt army. Bravada's iron rule had prevented ants with a history of aggressive rivalry over territory from attacking each other. But now the Salt troops who had kept order were withdrawn to fight amongst themselves under the command of competing generals. This left the nests to raid and pillage their neighbors at will. "Species cleansing" became a catchword to describe terrible atrocities. Added to this was Democrika's unfocused revolution that encouraged rebels to overthrow Bravada's former petty despots in the nests, but failed to provide any stable governing councils in their place.

Viewed from her perspective as Conductor of Community, Pacifica felt devastated at this collapse of a large part of Antale into anarchy. She worked tirelessly to try to persuade other colonies to help bring order, but they always did this with reluctance, fearing similar unrest would break out at home if they paid too much attention to what was going on elsewhere.

To her credit, Pacifica successfully established the practice of raising troops from various colonies to go into trouble spots as Unicol peace-keepers. The problem was that, more often than not, very little peace could be found to keep, and all too frequently, they were caught up in the fighting. As the summer wore on, Pacifica found herself longing for the coming of winter so that the period of hibernation would set in, and after that, the hope of a new spring and the birth of a new generation with a deeper consciousness of how to live in peace and cooperation.

Indeed, the news she received consistently from Electra about the spreading acceptance of her initiative among the Queens was Pacifica's greatest source of hope. It seemed that, even in nests in the most troubled regions, there was a common bond among the Queens, an awareness of a lifeforce that must be preserved and enhanced. Their envoys were coming in a continuous stream to Blackhall to secure quantities of the Royal Elixir and receive training in its use.

So, in the midst of present unrest, Pacifica kept her attention focused on the future. She understood that the new generation would need mentors with different mindsets from those brought up on a history of warfare. She encouraged Ventura to redouble her efforts to establish pockets of Visionants wherever she could, so that their voices of optimism would be there, even though for now, they might have to remain silent in seclusion. At this time, Pacifica knew nothing about the other voice that was rising in the south, out of the mystical Paradise Colony, from the surrogate Queen Esoterica, mistress of fantasy, whose passion to spread her own elixir and gospel of indolence among the nest of Antale knew no bounds.

It was in the closing weeks of good weather that everything came to a head. The nights were already cold and the days shorter and cooler. Ants were staying closer to home, preparing themselves and their nests for the coming winter. Those leaders who were trying to impose their influence on the larger ant world of Antale were making their last concerted effort to do so.

Ironically, Serenta's vendetta against Esoterica gave the latter the acceleration she needed. It began with a raid one day on Paradise Beach, shortly after Serenta had given her orders to "clean up this beetle problem." Soldiers swept in with a vengeance. Beetles, sunbathers, daydreamers, were all upended, shaken about, then herded unceremoniously together and driven down into the lake. The beetles were decapitated and their bodies pushed out among the reeds. Unremitting soldiers held hundreds of panic-stricken ants in the cold water until their bodies stiffened, then they dragged them through the sand, forcing life back into frozen limbs, and finally scattered the bewildered "paradisers" in every direction away from the beach. The soldiers then tore the place apart, shredding every vestige of the former cove of indolence and looking for secluded hideaways. They found a few surface nests, but failed to discover any of the entrances to Esoterica's cavernous domain. Satisfied, the soldiers withdrew and continued making similar lightning raids on pockets of beetle infestation throughout the colony.

Though Esoterica's followers never returned to Paradise Beach, their numbers in the nests were not greatly diminished by the efforts of the soldiers. Workers protected their beetles by the most cunning subterfuges, and there could never be enough troops to round them up. In the meantime, Esoterica's Paradise Colony enjoyed greater security because the soldiers never thought to come back again once the beach was destroyed. From this base, an expanded operation swung into action.

Rotunda soon overcame the problem of the exploding cocoons and a steady stream of Heavenly Tide began to find its way into the Sugar nests. This had a much wider appeal than the beetle secretions, and was a lot easier to get to the customers. Soon, there was a sufficient supply for half the ants in the colony to have a daily portion. After a few weeks, it was not unusual to see many workers wandering around aimlessly or darting about in short staccato rushes that seemed to achieve no purpose.

In the meantime, Serenta's initiative to increase Sugar trade among the other colonies was also enjoying good success. Missions went out bearing samples of Sugar products and orders came in for more of the same. Soon, a lively "caravan" industry developed and the ant trails out of the Sugar Colony became a continuous stream of Sugar entourages going out and outside missions coming in, bringing all kinds of new products into sugar marketplaces.

Needless to say, it was not long before Esoterica's Nirvanists discovered how to use this trade to their advantage. When a few samples of Heavenly Tide mysteriously got included in the inventory of official trade missions, orders came in from far and wide for this wonderful elixir. Toward the end of summer, as much as ten percent of all the produce traveling out of the Sugar Colony came from Rotunda's unpretentious cocoons. Manufacturing and distribution sources were set up deep inside most nests. Extensive sections of the sugar plantations, which provided the raw material for the product, were now devoted to this purpose. Esoterica's elixir had suddenly become big business for the Sugar Colony and a highly sought after product in much of Antale.

Of course, the Sugar trade officials knew what was going on, though they never tracked the original source of the product to Paradise Colony. Not that they tried very hard, either. The steadily increasing trade figures matched the speeches their President was making, both inside and outside the Colony, so who were they to raise questions about the legitimacy of their most popular export item. It was not until a devastating discovery was made that the matter finally came back onto the agenda in the Gold House.

Ventura was the one who set the chain of events in motion. She was on the road north of Lake Miasma, near the Wood Ant Colony, with a party of Visionants. Over a rise, they saw coming toward them a large Sugar caravan. High-stepping, golden athletic soldiers led the way followed by a long train of workers loaded up with produce. Some carried their burdens in their mouths, others on their backs, while others pulled various assortments of leafy vehicles piled high with products.

"Hello, there," called Ventura as she and her party came abreast of the leaders.

"What ho, yourself, travelers," replied a cheerful Captain of the Guard. "It's a beautiful day."

"To be sure," said Ventura. "You're a long way from home."

"All Antale is home to the SOTs," said the Captain.

"SOTs?"

"Yeah—Sugar Opportunity Traders. We're the salesants to the world."

"Look out, Captain! Here she comes again!"

The last excited cry came as a warning from one of the guards. Even as she spoke, the whole caravan shuddered under the wind draught of a dive-bombing black bird who swept in and passed along the length of the party. She scooped one unfortunate group of ants up in her beak and headed off into the trees. Everywhere along the caravan, ants and their burdens were upended. The guards rushed about trying to help and Ventura and the Visionants joined in. Eventually, order was restored and the traders set off again, this time with the guards keeping a much closer look out.

Ventura and her group watched them go, then turned in the direction of Blackhall. At that moment, something in the grass caught Ventura's attention. Three cocoons were lying there. They must have spilled off one of the carts. Curious, Ventura rolled them over. They all looked identical, but one was much lighter than the other two. Ventura decided to take them back to Blackhall for Electra to examine.

They brought the cocoons to the old scientist's laboratory. After poking them for a while, Electra sliced them open. She immediately jerked back, her antennae waving frantically.

"If this is what I think it is, Pacifica needs to know right away," she said.

A few minutes later, she was in touch with Pacifica by transmission to Centrasia.

"I think we've got a problem," said Electra. "A big one."

"What's up?" asked Pacifica.

"We've got some samples here of cocoons that the Sugars are trading around the country," replied Electra. "Two of them are filled with that alcoholic juice we've been hearing about, but the other one is stacked with eggs—beetle eggs."

"What kind of beetles?" Pacifica asked, her heart sinking in anticipation of the answer.

"Delusory beetles," said Electra. "It looks like the Sugars are exporting their problems to the world."

"I can't believe it. Serenta may be pushy, but she would never do a thing like that."

"Then I suggest you ask her who is, because these cocoons came off one of her caravans."

When Serenta confronted her chiefs of staff in the Gold House a short time later, the rage that shook her body seared out across the room.

"This was to be our greatest year," she stormed. "But now it's shattered! The most successful trading operation the world has ever known, and it's infiltrated by those slobbering Nirvanists. Right out of our own colony, they're spreading their soldiers into the world. We've got to shut everything down! Every single caravan must be stopped and searched and the ones already out there tracked down. All the colonies we traded with have to be warned. What a disgrace! Where in the name of all that's decent is this filthy stuff coming from? I told you, Helena, to clean it up! And you, too, Domina—you let me down. Our soldiers can go out and win a war, but they can't round up some loony bunch of weirdos here in our own nests! Thank all the stars that winter's coming on and we can hide our shame. But next spring hardly can be thought on, when all those parasites will hatch. I don't think I want to live to see it!"

Though Pacifica did not share the remorse and guilt that shook Serenta, she also had lost some taste for the thought of next spring's birth. Her initiative with the Queens was now in jeopardy, threatened to be overwhelmed by an infestation spread unwittingly by the Sugars. Added to that was Electra's other news that the weather patterns showed the portent for a dry and dusty spring when food supplies might well be short. It was too late to do much about it now. The Salt revolutionary wars had sapped all their energies. Unicol had disbanded for the year. The ambassadors had all gone home. And now, this last blow from the Sugars. What else could go wrong?

Only the Observa expedition. Word came in from Mission Control that, though the party was believed to be safe, they had not been able to get all the way around the crater they were mapping. They would have to winter on the Rim. No ants had ever been known to do that before. Moreover, they were out of contact. Either distance or some impenetrable barrier on the far side of wherever they were was blocking the transmissions.

Pacifica had to go into winter hibernation with all these unanswered questions waiting for another year for solution.

YEAR 3

RENEWAL

CHAPTER 13

Famine

The winter was long and very cold. Deep underground, the ants sensed that some new condition gripped their land. The soaking rain that normally would freshen the earth failed to fall. Instead, wisps of snow as powder and rock-hard pellets blew about, collecting in the bushes and the leaves, smearing the ant mounds with a gray thin blanket that served neither to warm nor moisten the waiting soil. Winter waited out its time in listless temper tantrums and spring crept cautiously in, more fearful than inspired.

In the Gold House, Serenta caught the chill of her approaching death. Through long winter weeks, she had clung to lingering life among the ant mass in her nest. But she found little warmth now either in the collective body of her peers, or in her own sad thoughts of enterprise betrayed. Nearby, her old friend, Domina, sensed her President was leaving. She held Serenta close and signaled Helena on the other side to come in nearer.

"Ah, Domina," said Serenta. "You and I have seen a few campaigns. The old soldier and the prattling politician. I think we did some good, but I have lost the heart for it now. There's a hard time coming, and I would rather slip quietly away than stumble like an old fool into folly. The Sugars will need a younger spirit at their head this coming year. Not too young to still not know the deeper currents that move us, but not too old to hold onto worn out ideals. The ants and their governing councils will decide, but I want you to know that Alexa would have my vote. She's a soldier and a compassionate spirit. Perhaps that's what we'll need to see us through."

Serenta turned her head wearily toward Helena on the other side. "I think, Helena," she whispered, "Alexa will better understand what you tried to tell me and I couldn't hear." With that, Serenta fell silent and allowed herself to float unconsciously with the rhythm of the ant mass moving gently. When it came time to go above to the activity of the new year, she was among the older ants whose life had left their bodies. A saddened colony heard the news and began the year by burying their leader.

In Centrasia, Pacifica by contrast stepped into spring with vigor and determination. From a year in office, she had learned to pace herself. She used the winter months this time to relax her body and still her mind. More than anyone else, she understood the difficulties that lay ahead, so she rested and prepared herself, then moved swiftly on her new agenda.

When the warm weather arrived, it changed soon into unseasonable heat with no rain. Pacifica understood from Electra's briefings that this was just the foretaste of a bitter meal to come. She sent out word to convene the first session of Unicol two weeks earlier than planned. Then news arrived of Serenta's death and Pacifica set out right away to join other leaders in tribute at a memorial service in the Gold House. Though the occasion was solemn and disconcerting for the Sugars, it gave Pacifica a valuable opportunity to speak informally to heads of colonies and warn them that a time of trial was coming. When Unicol met a short time later, she picked up the same theme in her opening address to the delegates.

"We had last year to learn our worth as a vehicle and a voice for sanity in the world," she said. "We know our record. Some good, some bad. That we couldn't find the will to place the well-being of Antale above the self interests of our colonies does not stand to our credit. That we moved, nevertheless, on many cooperative ventures and peace-keeping efforts is a better sign. Now, this year, I believe we will be challenged as never before in living memory to respond to crisis. Not even the perils of the Great War will match what I foresee to be coming swiftly upon us. Three things stand out: two potentially devastating and the third our best hope for the future.

"First, we are apparently entering a period of prolonged drought. At best, it will seriously disrupt our food supplies. At worst, it will plunge us into famine. To the extent that we can work together to conserve and share what we have, we will find a way through this time with the dignity and compassion that befits our sense of who we are. If we fall to selfish hoarding and protectionism, and even worse to attack upon others for what they have, then we will plunge into a dark time of terror. I will ask Professor Electra to speak to you shortly about this issue, so you may understand it clearly.

"Second, you now are all aware of an infestation of beetles in most of your nests which you can expect to see break out a few weeks from now. None of us knows the extent or the potential devastation of this problem, but we do know that it was deliberately planned and perpetrated by misguided zealots who seem to have made inroads into many nests. Presumably, their intent is to swell their numbers by luring our workers into a life of indolence. Given the other challenge for survival that will be upon us, this could not come at a worse time. Again, we stand a much better chance to combat this affliction if we work together on its eradication. Assistant Conductor Roanda will present a proposal to you to establish a special agency to attack this problem.

"The third matter is both a hope and a contradiction. Being born in our nests right now is a new generation of ants who will immediately stand shoulder to shoulder with us in dealing with the two challenges I just described. I expect we will find their energy and their outlook strong and refreshing. They are being nourished in their nurseries to be cooperative and peaceful. This does not mean that they will not be bold. Indeed, I expect them to challenge the rest of us in initiative. That is where we may find the contradiction. We live in a time of transition and cannot expect it to be smooth. Creative tension between the generations in our nests, while not comfortable, should be seen as positive, as long as the outcome is toward cooperation and peace. These are the principles on which this House is founded. I ask that we all remember them in the difficult days ahead."

Pacifica knew that many of the delegates would find her last remarks confusing. Some old minds were not ready for the waves of energy and thinking that the new generation would release into the nests, but at least if they were alerted, the tension might more easily be managed. In her opening address, Pacifica had done her best to prepare the delegates for what she saw was coming. Unfortunately, she had not foreseen the worst of it.

The hot, dry weather persisted for the next four weeks. At first, the ants did not suffer all that much. In fact, as other species died, there was more food than usual for them to scavenge. They filled their larders with the remains of insects and small animals and generally held out well against the worsening conditions. In the war-ravaged territory of the former Salt Colony, the old conflicts flared to life, intensified rather than ameliorated by the weather. The threat of future shortages just gave the combatants more to fight about, and the clear hot days meant that battles could go on uninterrupted. Pacifica maintained the Unicol peace-keeping efforts and tried to bring warring leaders to treaty conferences, but none of this did much to stem the flow of conflict and the misery it inflicted on the nests.

About this time, the beetle infestation struck. The outbreak was centered in the colonies where the Sugars had done their trading, which meant that by the start of the true summer season, Antale was split between nests struggling with the internal beetle problem and others carrying on their internecine warfare, all this continuing under weather conditions that got more oppressive every day. Presiding over it all at Unicol, Pacifica began to wonder whether any of her efforts would in the end prove worthwhile. But she never gave up hope. It wasn't yet any worse than she had anticipated.

Being forewarned about the beetle problem, governing councils in the nests could act swiftly at the first sign of trouble. The Unicol special agency headed by Roanda provided a useful information service. That was on the upside. On the downside, however, the infestation was so widespread and deceptively pleasing to the victims that it took a tremendous amount of effort to drive the beetles out and get the affected ants back to work. All this meant that the normal functions of the nests were severely disrupted at a time when it could be least afforded.

Also, by now Pacifica's third factor was coming into play. In nests all over Antale, the new generation of ants born under the nourishment of the Royal Elixir were taking their place in the social structure. Even where the fighting was going on, some Queens had managed to join their sisters' initiative in the free colonies, so that from the inside, new voices asking different questions were being raised. It was not at first a very tangible difference, certainly nothing dramatic, but it had the potential to bring the change that Pacifica and all those who thought like her longed to see. The question in midsummer was whether this new energy could grow or whether it would be overwhelmed by the other compounding forces. The answer to that was impacted quite suddenly by a totally unexpected development.

The first whisper of it blew in on a hot dry wind out of the Dark Country. A routine Sugar patrol resting in the shade on the eastern bank of Cruel Creek by the log bridge was the first to know. As they watched the brittle leaves and branches on the other side of the bridge whip and dance in the wind, they were amazed to see a cascade of Tiger ants shower down out of the bushes and hit the bridge running. There were several hundred of them, and in short order they made it to the Sugars' side and leapt again from the log onto the bank. They landed a few inches away from the startled Sugar patrol.

"Hold on, there, Tigers!" shouted the Sugar platoon leader. "What's the panic?"

The leading Tiger ants stopped in their tracks. The remainder already in midair crashed on top of them. From the confused jumble of flashing legs and bodies, a dozen ants screamed in reply.

"Yuk-a-ducka-ducka-ducka-do!" they wailed.

"The beasts! The beasts!"

"The hooded hordes!"

"Tigers one! Tigers all!"

"What a stew! What a stew!"

"What are you jabbering about?" yelled the Sugar officer. She knew the Tigers were an excitable lot, but this was sheer panic. "What's happened? What devil is chasing you?"

"Oh-aah-aah-aaaah!" groaned the Tigers.

"Omigosh, lieutenant! Will you look at that!" One of the Sugar soldiers had grabbed the officer and was waving excitedly toward the other bank. Then they all saw it.

A solid wave of mottled green and gray ant mass rolled out of the grass on a twenty-yard front and spilled down the bank to the water's edge underneath the log bridge. The Sugars, like the Tigers, were transfixed by the sight. Though the mass was a single blanket of indistinguishable ant bodies, the few leading ones could be seen plain enough. They ran over the rocks and hit the water, then reared up onto their hind legs and looked right across at the Sugars, no more than five yards away on the other side of the creek. The Sugars had never seen their like.

They were not large, at least not their bodies, but behind their heads, where on a normal ant a slender neck links head and thorax, a broad thin band of gray muscle arched up and around like a hood. It made them seem twice the size they really were. The rest of the body was a dullish green shade like the rough marble in the rocks on some parts of the Rim. For the first time, the Sugar soldiers were looking at the mysterious Dragon ants that had long been rumored to live in the shadow land behind the Dark Country, but whom the Sugars had never seen.

"Hello there, strangers," the Sugar officer called out uncertainly. "Who are you and where are you headed?"

One of the Tigers grabbed the Sugar and said, "Don't talk! Don't talk! Just hiss!"

"Hiss-iss-iss!" repeated all the Tigers together.

"Hiss-iss-iss-iss-iss!" swept over the creek from the hordes on the other side.

"Hiss of the Dragon! Hiss of the dragon!" wailed the Tigers.

"Zit! I don't like this," said the Sugar officer. "Cota and Runta," she continued, speaking to the two nearest soldiers, "get back to base. Tell the colonel, and bring a company with a detonation squad. We may have to blow the bridge."

The two soldiers scurried off. The officer spoke to the Tigers: "Now, will one of you just tell me what's going on?"

The Tigers all jabbered at once.

"One at a time!" roared the officer.

"Hiss-iss-iss-iss-iss!" came from the Dragons.

The nearest terrified Tiger spoke up. "They came down for food," she said. "Gobble everything up. Now try to eat us."

"Good grief!" said the Sugar. "Can't we speak to them? Tell them we can help? They don't have to behave like that."

"Don't talk," said the Tiger, "just eat and hiss. Eat and hiss."

By now, the Dragons appeared to be getting angry. Stopped by the creek, the back ranks were spreading out along the rocks exposed by the low water level.

The line now stretched for more than thirty yards on either side of the bridge. At the rear, others were crawling back up the bank toward the bushes hiding the end of the log bridge. All this was accompanied by their continuous loud hissing.

"If they find the bridge and come over, we'll never stop them," said the Sugar officer. "Let's hope help gets here in time."

A tense thirty minutes passed. A few Dragons found the bushes near the bridge, but dropped off in the gusty wind before they discovered the log. But others were getting closer. It was only a matter of time. Then a company of Sugar troops arrived. The colonel in charge quickly appraised the situation and didn't hesitate to get several bombs in place at the end of the log bridge, where it dug into the bank on their side. This took some time, during which the Dragons got closer and closer to finding the other end of the bridge. The colonel tried speaking to them, but with no more success than before. Then, aghast, they saw a group of Dragons on the log starting to cross. A great hiss arose from the other Dragons and the tide turned up toward the bridge.

"Are you ready, down there?" the colonel called to the bomb squad.

"Just a few more minutes," one of them replied.

By now, a solid line of Dragons was coming cautiously along the log.

"Company! On the bridge and terrorize them!" ordered the colonel. Several hundred Sugar soldiers rushed out on the log, shouting and waving legs and antennae. The Dragons stopped short, hesitating.

"Okay, Ma'am," said the leader of the bomb squad.

"Back!" roared the colonel above the hollering of her soldiers. As one, they turned and wheeled, rushing back over the log.

"Blast!" ordered the colonel while her troops were still spilling off the end of the bridge. The last of them leapt for safety as the bombs went off. The end of the log flew three feet into the air, then twisted around and fell into the creek. The Dragons on the other side stood terrified by the blast and the sight of several hundred of their group disappearing down the creek on the log. Then as one, they turned hissing up the bank and fled into the grass as quickly as they had come.

Pacifica heard the news directly from Alexa, who had now been elected President of the Sugars. She spoke by transmission from the Gold House.

"We don't know the size of the problem yet," said Alexa. "I've deployed troops all along Cruel Creek in case they try to cross again somewhere else. We've also sent scouting parties into the Dark Country. There's no sign of the Dragons, but the land is stripped bare. My guess is that they're headed north. Hordes like that could clean out every colony they come to. We need an emergency session of Unicol to decide what to do."

The delegates at Unicol were not at first convinced they had a serious problem to deal with. So far, only the Tigers had been affected, and though their ambassador made a passionate plea for help, the other colonies, plagued as they were with the beetle infestation and their own food shortages, were not eager to get involved with anything else. The colonies in the territory formerly controlled by the Salts were so embroiled in their internal warfare that they were not even participating any more at Unicol. For most colonies, the Dragons were only a mythical species. They had never been a problem in the past. The current reports of their emergence were probably exaggerated. They had not been seen since the incident at Cruel Creek and had likely gone back to wherever they came from. This was the tenor of the discussion during the first few days of debate. But all that changed when an emergency transmission came in from the Rocky Mountain Ants. Hordes of the gray-green Dragons were coming out of the Dark Country and crawling slowly across the hillsides between Lake Miasma and the Rim. In two days, they would be at Escarpment Slope.

The matter was now too urgent for the House of Assembly. Pacifica called an emergency session of the Protectorate. With the Salts no longer participating, the other four colonies quickly reached a decision to send in a joint defense force. The trouble was that it would take several days to assemble and get to Escarpment Slope. Pacifica decided to take an initiative of her own to buy time.

She put Roanda in charge of raising the main defense force and asked Bluffasta, the captain of her personal guard, to assemble an expanded Unicol unit to accompany her to the Rocky Mountain Colony. Pacifica was going to try her own peace initiative with the Dragons.

"By the force!" exclaimed Bluffasta when she heard about it, "now we fight Dragons, eh? Ants with hooded heads, you say? Whoever heard of that? Sounds like those Sugars were drinking too much of their joy juice."

Pacifica also spoke to Ventura about the expedition.

"I would like you to come along," said Pacifica. "I'm not sure what we can do, but I need someone who can make an opening for me. We need to find out how to communicate with these ants."

"I suggest we bring Bravura, too," said Ventura. "She's good in situations like this."

"All right, tell her to come."

"And there's someone else," added Ventura. "She's one of the new group. She's a Red ant, born only a few weeks ago, but already organizing a peace team throughout the colony. I've been intending to speak to you about her."

"Okay, it should be good experience," replied Pacifica. "Get our group together. We leave in a few hours."

When they finally set off, Pacifica's party had a guard of a hundred soldiers from various colonies, now operating under Bluffasta's command. It took them a day's travel to get to Escarpment Slope. The country they crossed was parched and hot. Very few ants were out, and the ones they saw looked weak and fearful. This was a troubled land. They certainly did not need the assault of a vicious enemy to add to their misery. Seeing this sad picture, Pacifica understood more clearly than ever Unicol's role in support and protection. Another strong test was about to be taken.

The party had traveled all night and came to the foot of Escarpment Slope in early morning. Not yet hot, the air was sharp and fresh. The sun shot long bright rays over the eastern edge of the Rim and brought the rough country of the west into sharp relief. Clambering over rocks toward higher ground, Pacifica and the others searched for some sign of the Dragons.

They found the Rocky Mountain Ants first. Usually alive with brisk energy, these Keepers of the Slope were strung out in long, forlorn lines, clinging to every vantage point, clustering together, all staring down toward the lake. They barely noticed the Unicol group arrive.

"Ho there, you mountain scramblers," called Bluffasta to the first group they came upon, "Unicol's here to help. What are you looking at, eh? By the force! What in the name of all anthood is that?"

The sight that had brought the last exclamation was one never likely to be forgotten. The rolling ground below Escarpment Slope to the south and west should have been an open vista of grass and red rock. Instead, it was a greenish gray slab of crawling matter that moved ever so slightly in the early morning sunlight, forward and sideways, blanketing every square inch like pus oozing out of a festering sore. It was about two hundred yards away and, at the pace it was traveling, would take more than a day to reach the Slope. Whatever was to be done to stop it had that much time.

"We have to go down closer," said Pacifica.

"No go! No go!" exclaimed a bevy of Rocky Mountain ants who were now clustering around the Unicol party.

"If we wait until our troops get here," Pacifica continued, "there's likely to be mass slaughter on both sides. We have to make contact with these Dragons somehow."

"Like stepping into fresh doo dung," said Bluffasta. "Thick and rotten."

"Come on," said Bravura, who was listening. "These are ants. There's got to be intelligence down there. They must have scouts. If we can nab some, maybe we can talk to them."

"You want to do that, little White ant?" Bluffasta asked Pacifica.

"Yes," Pacifica replied. "We have to try."

"All right," said Bluffasta. "We go in two groups. Bravura, come with me on a raiding party. You philosophers trail along behind with the rest of the guard.

If these Dragon hoods eat us, you can still live to think of something else. By the force, the old Salt and Pepper days look good right now!" She turned to the Rocky Mountain ants. "You want to come, too?"

"Oh, no! No go!" chirruped the little red ants. "Mountains home. Dragons never come. Roll rocks down. Roll rocks down."

"Ho, so that's your game," said Bluffasta. "Might work, too. Just don't bury us while you're at it. Come on, troop. We've got some Dragons to catch."

Bluffasta and Bravura led their raiding party off down the hillside toward the slowly advancing mass of Dragons. Pacifica and the others followed in a separate group. Two hours later, the raiders were close enough to hear the strange hissing sound of the Dragons as they moved over the ground, like the gigantic mouth of some marauding monster sucking up every vestige of food it could find. Bluffasta and Bravura peered out from behind a rock, trembling at the sight.

"By the force!" Bluffasta muttered. "If I didn't see it, I wouldn't believe it. It's a walking wall. How do they stay glued together like that?"

"Yes, but look," whispered Bravura, "they have their scouts, just like I thought they would. See, over there, coming up that gully, there's a party of twelve or so well out ahead of the rest. We can pounce on them from above."

Bluffasta and Bravura moved their soldiers carefully into position on the lip of the gully and watched the party of Dragons slowly come up until they were right below them. The Dragons never looked up. Their attention was totally focused on the ground around them, which they swept continuously with their antennae. Suddenly, the Unicol troop dropped down as if from nowhere and, in a matter of seconds, they paralyzed the Dragons with sharp stings, then rolled them over and loaded them onto the backs of a few soldiers who dashed off with them up onto higher ground, where Pacifica's party was waiting.

The Dragons were dumped unceremoniously into a heap while the Unicol troops gathered around, staring curiously at these strange hooded ants from beyond the Dark Country. They slowly stirred back to life, then snapped into consciousness as they became aware of the soldiers surrounding them. They backed into a tight circle and reared up on their hind legs, hissing and waving their forelegs and antennae menacingly at the strangers.

Pacifica stepped forward. She focused all her powers of transmission on the Dragons, searching for some intelligence she could communicate with. She could sense very little. She tried speaking quietly. "Don't be afraid," she said. "We won't hurt you. We want to speak."

The Dragons settled down a little, but showed no signs of understanding. Then one of them came forward, staring hard at Pacifica, waving her antennae.

"Hello," said Pacifica, nodding and straining to communicate. She sensed a glimmer of receptivity in the Dragon.

"I am Pacifica. What is your name?"

"Urrah!"

It was the faintest of intelligent signals, but it meant nothing to Pacifica.

"I want to speak to your leader," said Pacifica. "Your leader, chief. Do you understand me?"

"Urrah, rrah, urr," came back from the Dragon. It was definitely a signal, but Pacifica could make nothing of it.

"Excuse me, Ma'am," said an ant just behind Pacifica. "May I try?" Without waiting for a reply, she came forward. It was the young Red ant that Ventura had brought along. She went forward toward the Dragon very slowly. The latter rose up, hissing, menacing, but the Red ant kept coming until almost within reach. Then she stopped and extended both forelegs toward the Dragon. The hooded ant stopped hissing, then slowly came down from its attack position and reached forward with one foreleg. The two ants touched, first one foreleg, then both, and they stood looking at each other. All around the circle, the Unicol troop could feel a relaxing of the tension. The Dragons were somehow no longer unintelligent creatures, but ants—strange ones to be sure—but ants, nevertheless.

"My name is Futura," said the Red ant. "What is your name?"

There was a long pause. Then came a reply, barely distinguishable, but clearly received by Pacifica and others nearby. "Oora," said the Dragon. "Name is Oora."

"Hello, Oora," said Futura. "This is Pacifica, my leader." Pacifica came forward and extended her forelegs as Futura had done. Oora reached out and touched Pacifica.

"We want to speak to your leader," said Futura. "Who is your leader?"

"Not here," said Oora.

"I know," said Futura. "Can you bring her here?"

"You come," said Oora.

"Oora," Pacifica intervened, "we must speak to your leader here."

"You come," repeated Oora, looking at Futura.

"All right," said Futura. "I will go with you to bring your leader here." Futura turned to Pacifica. "Do I have your permission to go with Oora, Ma'am?" she asked.

Pacifica felt uncomfortable, but she sensed that this was probably their only chance to contact whoever was in charge of this mass migration. "Yes, my dear, but take care. We will wait for you." Pacifica spoke to Oora. "Futura will go with you. Also one other." Pacifica looked around. "Bravura, will you go, too?" she asked.

"Why not," said Bravura. "You never know, I might learn something."

Pacifica turned back to Oora. "You may take one other of your party. The others stay here with us until you return. Do you understand?"

Oora nodded. She motioned to one of her companions, then the two of them accompanied by Futura and Bravura set off for the Dragon lines.

"By the force!" exclaimed Bluffasta, watching them go. "There's two brave ants. Those Dragons better bring them back alive!"

The Unicol party stayed in position throughout the day. The Dragon's front line was still about a hundred and fifty yards away, moving very slowly. By nightfall, Futura and Bravura had not returned. Pacifica was nervous and apprehensive. During the night, she received a transmission to say that a Unicol defense force armed with explosives was on its way and would be on Escarpment Slope some time the next day. Morning came. There was still no sign of Futura or Bravura. Noon. Word came that the Unicol forces had arrived—a full division of ten thousand soldiers made up units from the Sugars, Whites, Blacks and Yellows. Pacifica looked up to the Slope and could see them gathering. She sent word that they should place some explosives in position, but come no further and wait. By now, the Dragons were less than a hundred yards away. Time and distance were running out, but Pacifica stayed where she was, waiting.

Several more hours passed. The Dragons were getting dangerously close. The Unicol commander on the Slope sent word that they had mined the whole mountainside. Bluffasta had posted guards all around and they were reporting Dragon scouts no more than twenty yards away. It was time to pull out.

Pacifica stood with Bluffasta and looked down on the green-gray ocean of Dragons now just below them, swallowing everything in sight.

"Well, we tried, Bluffasta," said Pacifica. "I thought we could do something to avoid what's coming. But all I've done is send Futura and Bravura to their deaths. When we got through to Oora, I really thought we had a chance."

"And maybe you still have, little White ant," Bluffasta replied excitedly. "Look down there, coming up the hill. Is that what I think it is? Yes, by the force! It's the Head Dragon Hood herself or I'm a Salt ant grandmother! And there's your spunky little Futura with Bravura! They're back in the nick of time. You've still got your chance, little White ant. Go for it!"

A few minutes later, Pacifica found herself facing the most overpowering ant she had ever seen. A full two inches long, with a head half an inch across and, behind that, the thick Dragon hood, the creature looked like a gnarled tree branch on legs. And what legs they were, too! Solid, thick, bulging with muscles and bowed out as if ready to leap forward and launch the powerful hooded head into battle. Pacifica stood her ground, while Bluffasta signaled the whole Unicol guard to press in close behind to give them some support. Futura, hopelessly dwarfed by the huge Dragon, spoke up first.

"Pacifica, Ma'am," she said. "This is Commander Supreema, leader of the Dragon Colony. She has agreed to talk with you."

Pacifica could only imagine what miracle Futura had worked to get this towering giant to agree to discuss anything. Supreema's first words, or more accurately, animated signals, confirmed this.

"So, what, you, think, hey, stop, here, no. Dragons, hungry, take food, go." It all came out as a rush as the huge ant towered over Pacifica.

"Hold on!" shouted Pacifica. "You might be hungry, but you can't just walk over the land. There are other ants here, too."

"Dragons eat other ants. All the same. Go back when full."

"Listen to me!" warned Pacifica. "Up there on the Slope, there are many ants with powerful weapons. They can bring the whole mountain down on top of you. You must stop and go back. We will bring you food."

"Nothing stops Dragons."

"Do you remember the bridge? Log! Creek! Bang!"

Pacifica had resorted to the same wild communication as her antagonist. It seemed to work. Supreema stepped back a few paces, apparently thinking. "Now look again!" Pacifica shouted. "Bluffasta, tell them to set off the first charges."

Thirty seconds later, a portion of the higher part of Escarpment Slope erupted and an avalanche of rocks and debris came rolling down. It was only a demonstration, but several rocks crashed among the leading ranks of Dragons, causing a wild uproar. One boulder came rolling down perilously close to where Pacifica's party was standing. Supreema, dumbfounded, watched it go hurtling by.

"Ha! You great thick-headed Dragon," Bluffasta shouted. "See what's waiting for you? You want some more, eh? Just keep coming and, by the force, you'll get it."

"That's enough, Bluffasta," ordered Pacifica. To Supreema, she said, "Look, Commander. We want to give you food, not bombs. But you must stop and go back to your own land."

Supreema, for all her bulk and bluster, was now clearly afraid. Tiny Futura stepped up to her and spoke quietly. "I will come back with you," she said. "You listened to me once and it has saved you from a terrible punishment. Listen to me again. We will not let you down."

Supreema hesitated for a while longer, then signaled to Oora to send word out to the scouts to stop the Dragon advance. It would take some time to turn such a mass around, but the order was given. Supreema turned back to Pacifica.

"Bring food quick. Next time, no stopping," she said. To Futura, she added, "You come now."

"Just a moment," said Pacifica. She took Futura aside and spoke quietly to her. "You've done very well for Antale today. Supreema seems to trust you. I hate to let you go back with her. You don't have to, you know. I would never ask you to do that."

"I know," replied Futura, "but it's the best chance we have to avoid slaughter. These Dragons are not looking for war. They're just hungry. If you can get supplies quickly to me on the inside, we may be able to get them to stay on their own land."

"I'll do my best," said Pacifica. Then she spoke to the rest of her party. "I'd like ten volunteers to go with Futura."

Bravura spoke up immediately. "I'm getting a taste for this. I'll go. Always wanted to see the inside of a Dragon's nest."

"Thank you, Bravura," said Pacifica. There was no shortage of other volunteers. Futura picked another nine. Pacifica had one final word with Supreema, who had been watching all of this intently.

"I am entrusting my comrades to your care, Commander," said Pacifica. "Food will follow. When these hard times are over, you and I will meet again."

"Dragons eat first, then talk boom!" was Supreema's cryptic reply. She set off with Futura and the other Unicol volunteers. As Pacifica watched them go, she spoke wistfully to Ventura and Bluffasta.

"There goes the next challenge for Unicol," she said. "We know about them now. We can't pretend they don't exist. They have to be brought into the world of Antale."

"That big one will be back," said Bluffasta. "She wants to know how to make the boom."

"We have to give them better reasons than that to join the world," said Ventura.

"And we will," replied Pacifica. "Futura and the others are risking their lives to get started. But we have to get the food lines moving. If we can't send food to those starving ants, nothing else counts. That's going to be challenge enough for us now."

CHAPTER 14

The Return

Pacifica had a Unicol defense force of ten thousand soldiers armed with explosives, but what she really needed was a convoy of carriers and the food to go with them. She knew she had no chance of getting approval through Unicol in time to meet her commitment to Supreema and the Dragons. So she appealed directly to Alexa. Back up on Escarpment Slope, she sent a transmission to the Sugar President in the Gold House.

"The Dragons are on their way back to their colony," she said. "They need food immediately. Can you help?"

"Absolutely," replied Alexa. "We'll send a supply line over Cruel Creek right away."

"Thank you, Alexa. I'm going to try to use this defense force to move supplies in from the north. But I need to find the food. The other colonies will have to agree."

"You've got my support on that," said Alexa.

"Thank you again," replied Pacifica. "I'll keep in touch." She left instructions for the bulk of the defense force to stay in place on Escarpment Slope and returned to Centrasia with the remainder. On the way, she discussed the situation with Ventura.

"This will be the first test for our new generation in the nests," she said. "I want you to use the Visionants to get them mobilized. Start with Futura's Peace Team in the Red Colony. With her life on the line, they'll have an added incentive to get moving. Then get the word out everywhere else."

"We can use the Queens' network," said Ventura. "We know how well that works."

"Good idea," replied Pacifica. "We have to prime the nests with new thinking. I'm going to try to get a special resolution through Unicol for every nest to allocate ten percent of its food reserves for others. If the Assembly passes it, that will put pressure on the nests to act. With a Peace Team in place in every nest, we have a way to get things moving. The Dragons can be the first to receive help."

How to get ants who were already short of food to agree to send some of what they had to an unknown and possibly unfriendly neighbor—that was the challenge facing Pacifica as she addressed the House of Assembly at Unicol twenty-four hours later.

"Two days ago, I stood facing the front line of a terrifying prospect," she said. "I saw a flood of ants driven out of their nests by hunger. They seemed strange and different. By all appearances to us, they are primitive. We could have used our technology and buried them under a mountainside of rubble. But what would that have said about ourselves? The Dragons have come to remind us that the first principle of a successful society is compassion. We know only too well what happens when we treat each other badly. So we have an opportunity here in the midst of this terrible drought to act another way. We could say it is all too much. We could say we should not deprive ourselves, because we have already suffered more than we should. But who are we to know when our needs might exceed our means and we will find ourselves as desperate as our sisters who need our help right now? They have agreed to return to their nests if we will send them food. Some of my comrades went with them in the belief that we would not let them down. The Sugar Colony has already responded. Now, here in this great assembly, we have an opportunity to act. We cannot, we must not turn away. If we do, we are turning away from ourselves, and we have learned nothing at all about how to live together. I ask you today to approve the resolution before you and open your storehouses to send food to the Dragon Colony."

It was not a unanimous decision. It was certainly not a harmonious debate, but at the end of the day, Pacifica's resolution passed. The decision to act still lay with the leaders or governing councils in the individual nests, but with the force of the Unicol resolution in place, and with a rising energy among the Visionants and the Peace Teams of young ants, gradually, one by one, over the next few days, a majority of the nests began to make some food available. The defense force, sitting idle on Escarpment Slope, was pressed into service as food carriers, and soon, long lines of ants were stretched around the north and west shore of Lake Miasma, bearing all manner of food down to the Dragon Colony.

Reports began to filter back to the nests about terrible devastation among the Dragons: thousands of ants lying around, too weak to move and countless more staggering out to meet the food lines. Once revived, however, the Dragons immediately shared the burdens with the Unicol troops and brought the food back to their starving companions. The soldiers told stories of how these strange hooded ants soon lost their fear of strangers and welcomed their benefactors into their rough nests among the hard, rocky terrain in the shadow of the Rim. Peace was restored, too, with the Tigers, who had earlier fled from their nests when the waves of Dragons passed through. As they also had lost their food supplies, the Unicol rations were shared with them. Within a week, the whole of Quadrant Two in the southwest corner of Antale was rescued from devastation to stability. It was, for the moment, Unicol's greatest achievement. The colonies had shown, in the face of harsh adversity, a capacity to respond to a neighbor more afflicted than themselves.

Working actively in the midst of all this was Futura. She had held things together during the early days of the rescue mission and soon established a reputation as a tireless and capable organizer. Her enthusiasm and ability won the confidence of the prodigious Supreema, who liked nothing more than to stride about her colony looking important, while the tiny Red ant scuttled around, keeping things moving. Futura was later joined by a company of her friends from the Peace Team in the Red Ant Colony and, together, they set up activities to help the Dragons with the communication difficulties that had almost brought them to disaster in their first encounter with the Unicol forces before Escarpment Slope. A history of isolation had cut them off from the development achieved by the rest of the colonies in this area. Bravura, the old soldier who had been with Futura at the beginning, became one of the most popular participants, as she went around teaching boisterous ballads from her soldiering days. The peace workers found that the Dragons, despite their initial fierce entrance into the outer world of Antale, were really a shy and retiring race. In all, the experience of the first few weeks of the Dragon Project, as it came to be called, was a boost to morale throughout Antale and a justification for Pacifica's determination to focus Unicol's work on compassion and cooperation.

But the drought persisted. The long hot days came in with grim monotony. Food supplies were shrinking everywhere. The workers in the nests searched longer and harder just to survive. The ability to continue to share resources with the Dragons or anyone else was being threatened. Compounding this was the other problem that the authorities in the nests were still struggling with. The situation was approaching overwhelm.

The infestation of delusory beetles could not be eradicated. It just went deeper underground. Throughout the summer, the problem had been kept under control, but with no end to the drought, more and more workers began to lose hope and turned in greater numbers to the delights of delirium. This in turn weakened their condition, so the problem compounded until, in some nests, it reached the critical point where there were just too few capable workers to keep things going.

Presiding over this moral and physical decay from a distance in her fantasyland queendom in Paradise Colony was the great grande dame of delirium, Esoterica. Throughout the steadily deteriorating conditions of the past four months, she had continued to live in the comfortable isolation of her underground fun palace. Well supplied with food and adulation from her followers, she maintained her aura of beatific wisdom. At first, she received no word of drought or devastation, but as the situation in the nests worsened, the news slowly began to reach her. It was Rotunda, her corpulent and cheerful head of research and development, who finally decided that the Queen should be told something at least approaching the truth. They were relaxing in Esoterica's garish chambers when Rotunda broached the matter.

"Half of anything is better than nothing," she said, "but how many times can you halve something before you have nothing?"

"Why, darling," replied Esoterica, "whatever are you talking about? Are you trying to practice your tedious mathematics on me?"

"No, Maj, just reflecting. The word is that all nests have had to cut consumption by half. Because of the drought, you know."

"Oh, well, then there's no loss," Esoterica said sublimely. "You just substitute hope for the missing portion. It's called the Law of Divine Replacement."

"How's that go again, Maj?" Rotunda asked.

"You're a scientist, darling. You should know about such things. If the ants are hungry, then they just substitute hope for food. The less food, the more hope. It's really very simple."

Rotunda considered this for a moment. "But what if the ants starve to death because they run out of food?"

"Then they have ultimate hope," said Esoterica, and she waved her antennae expansively. "It's called faith."

"Faith in what?"

"In the grand ant world. It's beyond the Rim."

"Oh, has anyone told them?"

"Why, everyone knows it. We sent the great Explora out to find it."

"But she got lost."

"Who says so?"

"I don't know. I heard it somewhere."

"The trouble with you, Rotunda dear, is that you have too much food and not enough hope, not to mention faith. Explora's not lost. One day she'll return and she'll bring wonderful news of the grand civilization that will come to help us build Paradise on Antale."

"Oh," said Rotunda, thoughtfully. "I wonder if the starving ants know this."

"If they don't, you should see that someone tells them, darling." Esoterica turned her most munificent gaze on Rotunda. "I'm sure that's part of what a good research director should do."

Rotunda was nothing if not responsive to her Queen's desires. Over the past months, she had established a very effective transmission network with her contacts in nests all over Antale. Within hours of her enlightening conversation with Esoterica, she was spreading the message of hope across Antale that Explora had discovered a grand civilization beyond the Rim and was even now returning to bring the news. The fact that she had embellished on what Esoterica had said with the last part did not bother Rotunda one whit. It was her contribution to add some increased excitement.

When the message came to Pacifica's notice a few days later, she was more furious than anyone had ever before seen her.

"Who are these despicable creatures that would spread such lies?" she stormed at Roanda, who had brought her the message. "It's not enough that we've lost Explora, it's not enough that there's been no word from Observa for months, it's not enough that our ants are starving everywhere—now someone has to spread this garbage and create false hope."

"The delusory sect is behind it," said Roanda. "It's very seductive to workers who are tired of going out every day and grubbing for nothing."

"Exactly," said Pacifica. "So they turn on to the beetle juice and lie around, waiting for the savior. We've got to do everything we can to counteract this."

Pacifica launched a full scale effort through Unicol to put out the truth about Explora, but it was not nearly as appealing as Esoterica's version. As three more hard weeks of drought went by, more and more ants turned to the hope of delusion rather than face the misery of each passing day.

It was then that things took a most ironic twist.

Since early spring, Pacifica had made a practice of checking regularly with Mission Control about news of Observa. The last word she had heard was at the beginning of winter, when Observa reported that she had run out of time and would have to spend the winter on the Rim. After that, Mission Control had lost contact. When still no word had been received by late spring, Mission Control had recommended sending out a search party. But by then, the first bite of the drought was being felt and the infestation of beetles broke out, so that the attention of Unicol was diverted to managing affairs on Antale. There was no enthusiasm for sending another mission across the Rim. Two failures were enough. Wait and see. Maybe Observa would reappear.

When still no word had been received by midsummer, Pacifica made another attempt to get approval for a rescue mission, but by then, conditions on Antale had deteriorated so far that there was even less support than before. In fact, the apocalyptical idea that the colonies were being punished for going out on the Rim, where they had no business to be, was brought up by some of the most vocal fundamentalists in the Assembly, and it gained a fair amount of support. Then, the crisis with the Dragons intervened and thoughts of Observa and Explora, lost somewhere out on the Rim, passed from general consciousness. That a reminder was now being brought back in a self-defeating way by the delusory sect was bitter medicine for Pacifica to take, and explained why she was so furious about it. She blamed herself for not having tried harder to send a third mission, and now it was too late, and she had nothing but chaos and despair waiting for her at every turn when she woke to the business of the day.

However, all that suddenly changed when, late one evening, she received an urgent transmission from Mission Control. It was Constella, the officer in charge.

"I'm sorry to call so late, Ma'am," she said, "but I have news I thought you would want to know immediately."

"What is it?" asked Pacifica.

"One of our routine search patrols has just come in from the Rim," said Constella. "They found someone and brought her back."

"Yes, yes," said Pacifica, her heart suddenly thumping strangely. "Who did they find?"

"Prepare yourself, Ma'am," Constella was hesitating. "It's what we hoped, but then, not altogether so."

"For mercy's sake, Constella," exclaimed Pacifica, "tell me who you've found!"

"It's Observa, Ma'am."

Pacifica's body shuddered. Her mind whirled with a thousand questions. Constella continued: "But she's not, well, herself, Ma'am. I think she's been traveling on her own across the Rim, probably for weeks. She's almost dead from exhaustion and starvation. But there's something else."

"What are you trying to tell me?" Pacifica asked.

"It's her mind, Ma'am. I think she's had a terrible experience. She seems deranged."

"All right, Constella. You look after her as best you can. I'll come right away and bring help."

Pacifica immediately called Electra and told her the news. "I'm leaving for Mission Control first thing in the morning," she added. "I'd like you to come, too, if you feel up to it. We need medical help as well. Who do you suggest?"

"I'll bring Hedra," said Electra. "She's the best there is. We'll meet you at the land bridge at first light."

Pacifica told no one but Roanda where she was going. She brought Bluffasta and half a dozen others as her personal guard. At daybreak, they met Electra and Hedra at the land bridge. The old scientist was still alert and active despite her age. Hedra, a young Black doctor, was eager to go. She had brought a package of herbal medicines wrapped in a leaf. One of the guards picked it up and the party set off.

They tried not to attract attention as they went, but the day was cooler than usual and many ants were out, a lot of them lying around idle, seeming to have little more to do than speculate where this official party was going in such a hurry. By the time they reached Escarpment Slope at the end of the day, the whole underground network across Antale was buzzing with speculation. It reached Rotunda in Paradise Colony, who began to wonder if her powers of prophecy were as good as her research skills. When she heard that Pacifica's party had continued through the night to the top of Escarpment Slope and was last seen heading in the direction of Mount Opportunity, Rotunda was sure some momentous news was about to break. She put her whole underground network on alert.

Pacifica, unaware of all the gossip, pushed her group on without a break. She was concerned about Electra, but the old scientist held her own. Toward dawn of the second day, the party reached the top of Mount Opportunity, where they were met by a team from Mission Control, who escorted them in.

Pacifica remembered well her last visit here with Wiseria, almost two years ago, when the old Black warrior had died during the night. They had been greeted then by the young, affable and athletic Colonel Observa, who was in command of the facility. Now Observa was here again, but after more than a year out in the vastness of the Rim. What would they find when they met her? Pacifica had thought of little else since she had received the transmission message from Constella.

She met Colonel Constella for the first time as they entered the large room which was the general quarters of Mission Control. The commander was courteous and warm. "You've traveled hard," she said. "Can we offer you refreshments?"

"Thank you, no," replied Pacifica. "Electra and Hedra and I would like to see Observa right away. The guard, I'm sure, could use some food and rest."

"Come this way, then," said Constella. "Observa is in my personal chamber."

The room was spacious and bare, one side of it opening out into a broad passage that led to the observation platform, where a few pale stars could be seen winking in the early evening sky. Of much more interest, however, was the pale body lying on a bed of fresh leaves in the center of the room.

Pacifica was shocked to see how her old friend had faded. The strong, agile body was now bent and crumpled and the former healthy golden glow of her Sugar complexion had dimmed to ghostlike translucence.

"Observa," she whispered, coming close and gently touching the body on the leaves, "old friend, it's Pacifica. Welcome home. It's wonderful to see you."

"Ah ha! You think so, eh?" Observa tried to straighten her twisted limbs and pulled back from Pacifica's touch. "Dark holes are deep wherever you find them. Good for hiding in, you know. But it's the eyes that find you out. You can't take back the sight of it. You never can, you never can."

The last words trailed away and Observa's body folded up like a crumpled leaf.

"She's been like that ever since we found her," said Constella. "Seems to be in shock. She hardly knows where she is. Her mind is somewhere else. Somewhere horrible."

"Let me see if I can help," said Hedra. The doctor carefully unwrapped the package of herbal medicines she had brought, mixed a potion with a drop of water and carefully touched it to Observa's mouth. After a time, the crumpled body stirred into a more natural shape and Observa appeared to have fallen into a deep sleep.

"She needs rest and nourishment more than anything else," said Hedra, "then we'll find out if she can tell us what's in her mind."

Under Hedra's care, Observa slept for two days with only fitful periods of consciousness and little coherence. Then, late in the afternoon of the third day, she snapped back into awareness and recognized everyone around her.

"You all want to know what happened, don't you?" she asked. "You want to know what's out there on the Rim. And you know something, so do I. But right now, I can't remember. I can't remember a damn thing."

"Don't worry, Colonel," said Electra. "It will come back to you in time. Of all the ants in Antale, you are the only one who knows the ultimate mystery. The rest of us can only speculate. Your mind cannot lock such secrets away forever."

"I hope you're right, Professor," said Observa. "You know, I'm a damn good observer. That's my name, isn't it? I have this feeling that I've got it all down, but I can't reach it."

"You can take all the time you need to remember," said Pacifica. "The most wonderful thing is that you're back. Now, you must get well. Then you can tell us what you found and what you know about Explora."

"Explora," Observa repeated. "Explora—there's something ...." She broke off, trying to remember. Then she jerked upright. "Where is it? Where is it? I had it. Someone's taken it. Where is it?" Observa had now gone into a wild panic and was suddenly plunged back into the same distraction as before. She struggled to stand up, looking furiously around, crying out continuously "Where is it?"

"Where's what, Observa?" asked Pacifica. "What are you looking for?"

But Observa was now incoherent, thrashing around, searching.

"It's the package," said Constella. "She had a package when we found her. I put it aside for safekeeping. Here it is." Constella produced a tightly wrapped leaf package. "It is sealed with her seal," said Constella. "We did not open it."

Observa saw the package and snatched it from Constella. She clutched it to her and then rocked back into the same incoherent muttering as before.

"I've done as much for her as I can," said Hedra. "We need to get her back to Centrasia where she can be properly cared for."

"All right," said Pacifica, "we'll leave tonight and get across to Escarpment Slope under cover of darkness. You can rig up some kind of transportation for Observa."

Preparations for departure were hastily made. While they were going on, Pacifica took Constella aside. "How is it you never mentioned that package before?" she asked.

"I'm sorry, Ma'am," replied Constella. "She was gripping it so tightly when they brought her in, the only way I could get it off her was to promise that no one else would see it. I was waiting for her to remember before I mentioned it to you."

"All right, I guess there's no harm done," said Pacifica, thoughtfully. "Whatever's in it was strong enough to jolt her memory. We'll let her tell us in her own good time."

The return journey was much slower than the outward one. The guards carried Observa on a leaf bed and had to watch their steps. Pacifica remembered only too well a similar return two years ago, bearing the body of Wiseria. This time, there was no crowd of idolizing ants grateful for the end of a cruel war. However, to Pacifica's surprise, an ever-thickening number of ants were lining the path as they came closer to home. It seemed that the word was going on ahead and the curious masses were coming out to watch the party go by. Pacifica had still made no release of information concerning Observa's return. She wanted to announce it first to the House of Assembly in Unicol. Why, then, was there such interest in her party?

If she had been aware of the messages now beginning to be broadcast by Rotunda from Paradise Colony, she would have been amazed. "The prophecy is fulfilled," went the gist of it. "Explora has returned. Come to a grand assembly at Centrasia to hear the message of the great Explora. Paradise is coming. The messenger has returned from outer darkness."

It took two days for Pacifica's party to reach the land bridge and by then, they could see crowds swelling along the remaining distance to Centrasia.

"By the force!" exclaimed Bluffasta. "I knew I was popular, but this is getting ridiculous. We need reinforcements or we'll never make it." She called ahead and soon a guard of a hundred Unicol soldiers came down along the road from Centrasia. They pushed the crowd back so that Pacifica's party could get through. A chant of "Explora! Explora! Explora!" went up.

"My gosh," said Pacifica, "they think Explora's returned! How did that rumor start?"

"No matter how it started," said Bluffasta, "it's how it finishes that counts. We better get inside the nest before they find out there's no Explora. Those ants are crazed with joy juice. They could go berserk."

It was late in the day when they finally entered the mound. Outside, the courtyard was packed solid and more ants were pouring in by the minute. But the travelers were home safe and a relieved Pacifica saw that Observa was immediately taken to the infirmary. She was conscious, but not particularly aware of what was going on around her. Like before, she seemed to be reliving some dreadful experience in her mind, running it over and over, but not including anyone else. Her forelegs were wrapped firmly around the mysterious leaf package. It had not left her grasp since the party had set out from Mission Control.

Once Observa was settled in the infirmary, Hedra acted immediately to prepare a potion. "I think this will help," she said. "It's a powerful narcotic derived from the leaves of the arcana bush. It sends the nervous system into shock. She'll sleep for about twelve hours afterward, but there's a good chance then she'll have at least some of her memory back."

"Is it safe?" asked Pacifica.

"As safe as any medicine of this kind," replied Hedra. "Observa has a strong constitution. She could never have survived if she didn't. I believe this is the best treatment we can give her."

"What do you think, Electra?" asked Pacifica, turning to her old friend.

"I have complete trust in Hedra," replied Electra.

"All right, then," said Pacifica. "Go ahead and give me regular reports on her condition."

Pacifica then turned her attention to Unicol. The delegates had already assembled, summoned by Roanda when Pacifica had called ahead. There was not much she could tell them about Observa. There was likely to be more news tomorrow. The other question was what to do about the crowds outside. They decided to send messengers out to say that it was not Explora who had returned in the hope that the ants would disperse. Then Unicol adjourned, waiting Pacifica's further call.

The strategy with the crowd did not work, for the event had already gathered the momentum of a happening. Throughout the night, instead of leaving, the crowds kept coming. Under a bright full moon, their celebrations picked up gusto. Copious quantities of Rotunda's Heavenly Tide were passing around, then later on in the early hours of the morning, a herd of delusory beetles were driven in from somewhere, and a full scale love-and-drug-in developed.

Bluffasta watched all this with mounting disgust. "By the force, just say the word," she exclaimed, "and I'll take a few Peppers down there and scatter that hooch-happy bunch into the breeze. They want oblivion. I'll give it to them."

But Pacifica restrained anyone from taking violent action. She hoped that, in the heat of the coming day, the crowd would eventually pay attention to the messengers and disperse. However, by noon, when the sun was beating down intensely on the ants in the tightly packed courtyard, there was still no sign of anyone leaving. Pacifica began to fear for the condition of the ants. None of them were strong. Most were close to starving, and though the delusory beetles had now disappeared, the majority of the ants were undoubtedly under some form of hallucination. They wanted a show, so Pacifica decided she would have to give it to them. The last word on Observa's condition was that she had had a comfortable night, and was still sleeping soundly. Pacifica, like everyone else, still knew nothing about what had happened out on the Rim. If she told the ants that, would they believe her? She did not know, but decided she would have to try.

Unknown to Pacifica, down on the courtyard, a new development was occurring. Ventura saw it first. She was coordinating the effort of the messengers to try to get the crowd to disperse and was standing on the mound, looking out over the mass below. She suddenly noticed a new group arriving at the back. She could not be sure, but they somehow seemed familiar. Pushing her way down, she went over toward them. Then she saw why they looked familiar. They were not the half-starved followers of the delusory sect, but rather the well-fed members of a band of freedom-fighters. She recognized several of them from the gang that Democrika had assembled for her and Bravura to train last year. Since then, they had become the leaders in the rebellion that was still rampaging across the whole of the old Salt territory. What were they doing here on the courtyard of Centrasia? Then Ventura saw Democrika.

The campaign must have been treating the old leader well, for she looked prosperous and hearty. When she saw Ventura, she treated her like a long lost friend.

"Ho, there, old mentor," she called.

"You're looking good, Democrika," returned Ventura. "It's been a long time."

"Too long," said Democrika, "but we're keeping to the vision. You taught us that. You should be proud."

"I don't remember that you ever had a vision," said Ventura. "Just charge right in and see what happens."

"Ho, but we've learned a thing or two since then," Democrika replied proudly. "Do you remember the walls?"

"How could I forget? Cassandra's first prophecy: 'When the walls are torn down.'"

"You are right. Good memory. Well, the walls were torn down and we joined forces with some of the Salt troops. We did like you said. Developed a plan. Now we have won back half the country."

"There's a lot of bloodshed in that," said Ventura. "I never recommended that."

"Not yours to say, old friend. We know our way. It's following the call. The walls are down. That's one of three. Do you remember the second?"

"Are you talking about Cassandra's prophecies?"

"Just so."

"I don't know—something about a messenger, I think."

"'When the messenger returns from outer darkness,'" Democrika announced proudly.

"My gosh," Ventura exclaimed, suddenly seeing the implication. "Is that why you're here? You think the messenger has returned from outer darkness?"

"Exactly so. Cassandra sent us. We've come to hear the message."

CHAPTER 15

The Message

IF THERE ARE SOME WHO KNOW THE future, so be it. Whatever was happening that day on the courtyard outside Centrasia was far beyond the power of the central players to control. They could only press on, following their best sense of how to act, to hold a course among swirling currents. Pacifica, as usual, was trying to steer the raft. Inside the mound, she had decided on another strategy to help defuse the situation with the crowd. She went to Queen Anastasia.

"The ants all love you, Ma'am," said Pacifica. "Even those not from our nest know of your wisdom and strength. They are looking for a message. There's none to hear, I fear, from Observa. Will you come and speak to the crowd?"

Queen Anastasia agreed. Pacifica also urged the Unicol delegates to make an appearance. A short while later, the crowds on the courtyard stirred to the sight of the Unicol ambassadors emerging and lining the lower levels of the mound. Roanda came out. She spoke to the crowd, settling them down, then announced that Pacifica would address them.

"Dear friends," Pacifica began, "you have come to hear a message. In the hard, hot days of our terrible drought, what would you like to hear? That the time of our affliction is at an end? That we can somehow miraculously change the weather and rebuild the former comfort of our nests? I can give you no such message. But I can point to the indomitable spirit that stirs within all of you, that has so far sustained us, that has enabled us to support one another and share what we have, to hold fast to the firm conviction that no matter how difficult the times are now, or will be in the future, we are stronger than the times, and will endure in the face of all adversity, until the rains come and our land is restored."

"Explora!" someone in the crowd shouted. "Explora!" a hundred others picked it up. "Explora!" the whole compacted mass of ants called out. "Explora! Explora! Explora!" the chant went up. Pacifica waved it down. The chant subsided. She spoke again.

"Explora is not here. We do not know where she is. The wonderful news I can share with you is that the leader of our second expedition, Colonel Observa, has returned. Even now, she lies in our infirmary, too ill from her terrible ordeal to speak to you. But you have my word that as soon as she is well, you will hear her report. For now, we must focus on life as we find it here, day by day, and search for the strength within to endure and to ultimately triumph over adversity."

"Explora! Explora! Explora!" the chant started up again. Bluffasta, watching from her vantage point high on the mound, gave the signal to her guards for full alert. Pacifica was not holding the crowd with words. It looked like some heads would have to be broken. But Pacifica was not finished yet. She waved the chanting down again.

"I cannot give you Explora! I cannot give you Observa! But I can give you one who shares a place in all our hearts as deep as any love can stir. I ask you all to acknowledge our most gracious monarch, Her Majesty Queen Anastasia!"

It was a bold gamble and a deadly risk for Pacifica and Anastasia to bring the young Queen suddenly in front of a chanting, disoriented crowd. But the magic worked. The Queen stepped out from behind Pacifica and came forward to the very front of the platform. She stretched to the full height of her lithe and magnificent white shining body and waved to the massed assembly below.

"Long live the Queen!" someone shouted. "The Queen! The Queen! Long live the Queen!" Everyone picked it up, until the whole packed courtyard rocked with the acclamation. Anastasia stood graciously for several minutes, waiting for the tumult to subside, then reached with the quiet dignity of her spirit into the hearts and minds of every ant there.

"I stand before you as your Queen and feel my heart swell with love for the life that binds us all. You have come seeking a message. But what is that? Some words? Some brave symbols of hope? Some ideas that might stir you, somehow move you, to do something, you know not what? Yes, you have come seeking, but let me say this to you: whatever it is you are searching for already lives in the bonds that hold us together.

"We do not have to look for truth in another world. Whatever we may one day learn from our brave adventurers who have gone out to seek beyond the Rim, we can be sure it can never replace the truth we already know. We are one life. We are one great family. The energy of the stars, the sun, the moon, the streams, the soil—of everything we know or can ever know—it is all one energy and it is all of us together. There is no greater truth than that. The challenge for our individual lives is to use this knowledge to build a safer, kinder world within our nests and between our colonies.

"Perhaps, when our brave Colonel Observa, who has miraculously returned to us, can speak, she will tell us of others who have learned better than we, how to do that. Perhaps not. But, whatever the message might be from beyond the Rim, this I know for certain, the secret of life abundant lies here in our own world, waiting for all of us to find it."

A deep stillness had settled on the crowd as Queen Anastasia spoke to them. In the blazing heat of the noonday sun, they stood silently looking up to her. What further she might have said, or how she might eventually have sent them away, would never be known. For at that moment, another force intervened and swept every eye to its attention. Above the Queen, almost near the top of the mound, in full view of everyone, a shower of leaves came cascading out of a large entranceway. They floated down lightly in the still, hot air, then whipped and danced a little, as a warm current caught them and whirled them away. Behind the leaves, straining to stand and find a secure grip on the mound, the lean, light figure of Observa appeared. She had struggled from the infirmary near the top of the mound and pushed her bedding of leaves out the entrance to attract attention.

And attract attention she surely did! A gasp, then a collective "ooh! aah!" exhalation arose from the crowd. "Look! Look!" someone called. "It's Explora! She's here! She came back!" Queen Anastasia turned and looked up. Likewise, Pacifica behind her, and every Unicol dignitary on the mound. They stared, amazed, completely taken by surprise by this appearance.

"Your Queen has spoken true!" Observa's trembling words came floating down, like the leaves that preceded them. "There is no secret of the universe outside Antale. If you want to know the truth, you must find it here. You wanted someone from beyond the Rim to bring you a message. Well, I am here, and this is it. No, I am not Explora, but I can tell you what she told me. That's what you came to hear, isn't it? A message from one who dared to go beyond the known? Well, I have been there with Explora and I can tell you what she found."

Pacifica, like all the others hearing this for the first time, trembled in anticipation of what might be told. She marveled at Observa's recovery and feared for her strength, hoping above all else that her mind would not snap again. For the present, though, Observa was fully in control.

"I am Observa. I was sent last year by Unicol to search for Explora. We traveled for weeks across the Rim. From here it seems a vast and empty wasteland, but out there, you soon discover something else. We traveled by night, and were never alone, because the sky is filled with stars that cluster in their millions to light the way. But more than that, the air trembles and pulses with strange vibrations, almost messages, but not quite, leading us on, night after night, growing stronger, until we were there, at the place where Explora had been before us.

"It was a deep ravine, filled with steaming vegetation, hiding under a haze thicker than any fog we'd ever seen, and the air pungent and filled with those vibrations, stronger, louder, denser almost than the fog that covered where they were coming from. We didn't go down. We tracked around the edge and found that we were following a never-ending precipice, the Rim butting up to another world like Antale, but then nothing like Antale, ten times the size and covered entirely with that cloud. Above us, the sun could blaze as it does here today, but below that cloud, it must have been a world of unending gloom.

"We continued on, week after week, trying to find an end to it, but there was no end, for we were circling a cavernous hole. We were at the end of summer. Winter was coming on and it caught us on the other side. The wild transmissions from the world below blocked our own transmissions back to Antale. We kept on going, alone now except for whatever was down there. But it soon became too cold to move. We crawled into some holes on the edge of the cliff, where the hot air from below kept us warm enough to stay alive while howling gales blew across the Rim outside.

"Then, finally, warm days returned and we could move again. You might call it spring, but that word has no meaning when all you have is rock. Our provisions were exhausted, but we stayed alive by catching beetles and anything else that crawled up from time to time out of the hidden world below. Something had gone wrong with our transmission equipment and we never regained contact with Antale. We continued on like silent outcasts from the world we left and fearful travelers to this other, hostile place. The one thing that kept us going was the certainty we were traveling in a circle and must eventually come back to where we started. And finally we did. Below us was the very ravine where we knew Explora had gone down. It was the only way in. The transmissions had led her there and she had gone down and never came back. What were we to do? Head homeward to Antale and report what I have just described, or make at least some small attempt to see what lay beneath those clouds, and perhaps find out what had happened to Explora. It was my decision. I was the one who had to make the choice."

Observa paused in her story, catching her breath. Pacifica wanted to go up to her, to ease her pain, to say that she did not have to do this. But the crowd was there and waiting. Observa had opted for a full performance. She would either falter or see it through.

"I decided that we must go down. I left two of my party on the top and led the others in. Almost immediately, we felt the place sucking us under and once beneath the clouds, the gloom settled on us like hot, stale breath. We could barely see our way, but those infernal transmissions led us on. We were in thick, dense jungle, but on a path tramped clear and hard. I wondered what could have made that track. I should have listened to my inner sense that said 'go back.' But as yet, we had nothing to report, so we carried on.

"Some time later, I don't know how long, several hours certainly (how can you tell in a place like that?), we came out of the jungle. The path stopped there. We were on flat, hard rock. The fog was thicker now and the air rank with sulfur fumes. So now we knew what caused the fog. We have a trace of that on Antale in the Dark Country, but nothing like this. The whole place was one great lake of bubbling mud and rotten gas with narrow rock bridges winding in and out among the pools. You could be lost in there in a minute. If Explora had come this way, there was no point looking further. The whole party could have been caught in a mud spurt and cooked alive. We turned to get out of there.

"But then a puff of air whipped the fumes aside and, right in front of us, on the edge of a pool, we saw a pinnacle of some sort, about six feet tall and crusted over with the yellow sulfur deposits. No sooner had we seen it then it was gone again, behind the fumes. We went in closer, and when we got up to it, we saw there wasn't just one of them, but a whole colony.

"It was the most eerie, forlorn, empty, gloomy place you could imagine. Yet some living creatures must have built those mounds. If so, what, and where were they now? The other thing that made us sure there was intelligence somewhere in back of this was that those mounds, or pinnacles, or whatever you might call them, were the source of the transmissions. It was a nightmare of frenzied signals in there. Every one of the mounds was acting like a transmitter, but none of it made sense, just a distorted mumbo jumbo of mixed transmissions, as if they were all switched on and left running.

"We should have left, but one thought nagged at me. If these pinnacles were the products of intelligent minds, what marvels might there be inside? We must at least attempt to find out. We approached the base of the first one, searching for an entrance. We did not find one. Instead, we found Explora."

A collective gasp went up from the crowd. Observa stopped speaking. She seemed to become lost in her thoughts. Then, she did something strange. She turned and picked up a bundle in her mouth and began to make her way down the mound. Pacifica recognized the leaf package that had put Observa in such a frenzy when she had thought she'd lost it back in Mission Control. Now what was she doing? Observa found a place to stand on the mound, still a few inches above Pacifica and the Queen. She put the package down and spoke to the crowd again.

"Explora was already half out of her mind. She had been wandering around, lost in that place, for almost two years. The rest of her party had long since died, either by accident or starvation. Somehow, Explora had found enough slugs and worms, or whatever else was still alive in that infernal spot, to live on. When she finally came enough into her wits to realize who I was, she said she would take us inside the mound.

"It was an architectural and technological triumph. You cannot begin to image the splendor of it. Explora knew every inch by memory. She led us up through spiral passageways and great chambers until we reached the very top of the mound. This was the command center and transmission room, filled with equipment far beyond anything I could begin to understand. This was where the transmission signals we can hear at Mission Control were coming from, and from the other mounds, too. They were supplied by some unending source of power—I don't know what. All this, and no inhabitants. We had seen no intelligent creature besides Explora in the whole place—and she had found the reason why.

"She led us back down through the mound by a different route. We passed through chambers that looked like storage rooms and chemical processing plants and agricultural complexes, until we were down deep underground, far below the base of the mound. Explora stopped by a bare wall and warned us to stand aside. Somehow, she swung open a huge opening in the wall and suddenly, a belching bubble of slime and gas leapt in to engulf us. It was more than Explora had expected. I heard her cursing as she struggled to close the opening. I was swept up into the back of the room. I heard my three companions scream and, then, silence. When finally the fumes had cleared enough, I crept forward again. There was no sign of Explora or the others. The wall was still wide open and I looked down into a cavernous black hole, where the sound of boiling mud raged below. When I understood that my companions and Explora had perished in that pit, I almost lost my mind."

Observa stopped again. A deathly silence hung over the packed courtyard. As before, she stooped to pick up her leaf package and this time, carried it down to the platform where Pacifica and Queen Anastasia were standing. Pacifica saw the strain in every muscle of Observa's body, but like everyone else, she was too transfixed to move. Observa put her package down and continued to tell her story from the platform standing beside Queen Anastasia.

"But Explora was not gone. I heard her cough and found her pinned behind the rock that she had pulled aside to open the wall. I dragged her free and somehow stumbled back the way we had come, carrying her out of that place, out of the mound, away from that colony of horrors, and back along the path where we had come in. As we went, Explora regained her senses enough to tell me what she had come to understand from being in that place for as long as she had.

"The ants who had built those mounds had discovered a powerful explosive force which they continually tested underground. They must have been doing it in all the mounds and who knows in what other colonies as well. Explora found details about this recorded somehow in the transmission room. Her conclusion was that, with these explosives and other technologies they were using, they set off a chain reaction that broke the slender membrane between their beautiful world and the poisonous inferno that lay beneath. They were too preoccupied with their technology and competition to notice they had pushed the tolerance of their world beyond its limits. They poisoned their home and themselves along with it. All this must have been many thousands of years ago. Some of the jungle is growing again. The air is less poisonous. A few simple animal and insect species are coming back, but so far, no ants.

"You wanted to know the story of what Explora found. Well, now you have it. She died before I got her back to the top of the Rim. I found my two companions waiting and we set off to make our way back to Antale. But without our transmission equipment and weak from lack of proper food, we got lost out there. One at a time, my companions died, but somehow, I carried on. By grace or good fortune, I don't know which, I was found by Mission Control. I guess they brought me home and now I'm here.

"That's probably not the story you hoped to hear, but there it is. You also wanted a message from Explora. Well, I have one word more for you from her. Before she died, she told me to tell you this: 'Tell the ants of Antale,' she said, 'to love their world, for that is all they have. Tell them to care for one another, for that is the only way to sustain their world.'"

"That is what she said—except for one last request."

Observa stooped and began to unroll the leaf package. She continued speaking as she carefully laid it out on the platform. "Before she died there in that steaming half world, she said if I would do one last thing for her, she might die easier so far from the home she loved." Observa stooped to lift the contents of the leaf package gently in her forelegs. "You came to welcome Explora home. Now you have your wish. Explora asked that I bring her body back to Antale and I have carried out my promise."

Observa stood before the packed crowd of ants on the courtyard of Centrasia, holding the fragile shell of the body of Explora. She stood up tall for as long as her failing strength could bear, then gently placed the body on the platform and knelt beside it, mourning. Queen Anastasia and Pacifica came in close in grief. Explora was home. The messenger from outer darkness had returned.

CHAPTER 16

Fire

No ant who was there that day on the courtyard at Centrasia and heard Observa's story could ever view the world the same again. No worker who had come hoping for good news to ease her life of toils. No frothy follower of Esoterica who had sought a path to paradise. No delegate of Unicol who wanted simple answers on how to govern the ungovernable. No wild-eyed rebel bent on overthrowing those in power. None of these could leave with their convictions still intact. The one clear message they all had heard was that no outside power would come to sustain Antale. They were alone.

Queen Anastasia's final words after Observa's dramatic revelation closed the chapter. "We sent our adventurers to seek unknown worlds," she said. "What they have found must now take all of us on a journey to find our common soul. I am as amazed and shaken as all of you by what we have heard just now. We will honor in death our great Commander. We will nurture back to health our gallant Colonel. And we will go from this place to dedicate all our strength in service to each other and to Antale. Go, my dear ones, and may you soon find good fortune from your labors. We leave with greater wisdom than we came. Go now with the blessings of your Queen."

Next day, Explora was buried with full honors. Observa returned to the infirmary for recuperation. And Pacifica sent the Unicol delegates home.

"The place for us now is not in debate," she said, "but back in our colonies to report what happened here. The crowds came out looking for escape from suffering. They didn't find it. Now things can go either way—despair or determination. Queen Anastasia has given us our cue. Our task is to be the same voice of hope in all the nests."

So the Unicol delegates went home, as did everyone else who heard Observa's story. The news spread quickly. It swept from nest to nest like a brush fire before the wind. Observa was back. Explora had perished in a dead world still beaming its forlorn messages across the empty Rim. Antale was alone and gripped by its own fierce punishment of drought. What did all this mean?

As many as the discussions that now ensued, so were the answers and opinions, but at back of all was one clear fact. The ants alone did not control the outcome. They were leaves hanging in the forest. If the trees, the soil, the world could not support them, they were gone and all their technology and social systems with them. Already, there was fear that this unheard of drought had been caused by their own abuse of their world. Electra had suggested as much. Now Observa's story raised the specter more. If this were so, what could they do to change it? The terrible truth that began to settle out was that they could do nothing to alter larger systems. If these were upset, the ants would have to live with the consequences. The choice they had was in how well they might do the living. The way that choice unfolded was now dramatically impacted by a new development.

When Democrika left Centrasia, her thoughts were mixed and more than a little uneasy. She found no comfort in the outcome of Cassandra's second prophecy. When she spoke to the wily priestess a few days later, she said as much. Cassandra was swinging on a leaf and listened to the outburst unmoved.

"What game are you playing with me, eh?" Democrika complained. "When walls come tumbling down, that's pretty clear. But this messenger from outer darkness is not so good. I don't know what to make of it. She told one ugly story, that's for sure. But what's that mean for me? We've got those old Salt generals bottled up. One final push and everything is ours. We'll have a new republic. Why did you send me to hear some wild story about ants blowing up their world? That's not so good, you know."

Cassandra let her leaf swing easily in the breeze. At each pass, she made a clipped reply. "One is to start." The leaf swung out, then came back again. "Two to go." Away she went once more. When the leaf came back the third time, she dropped off and landed right in front of Democrika, fixing her with a penetrating stare. "Three is the end."

"That's no answer," stormed Democrika. "I remember number three well enough: 'When the young ones cry out with new voices.' What young ones where? There's no one on the front but old soldiers and us free thinkers slugging it out."

"And so time flows," said Cassandra. "It's ending now. Fire and storm will bring the New Age in."

With that, Cassandra walked away. "So it's fire and storm as well, is it?" Democrika called after her. "And what about the young ones, then? Tell me that." But Cassandra paid no heed. "Crazy old witch," Democrika muttered to herself. "What's she want me to do? Blow up a nursery?"

Just then, one of her rebel leaders came up.

"We can't stay here any longer," she said. "The force is getting restless. They've been waiting two days for you to come. If you don't give the order soon, they'll storm the place themselves."

"Ah, ha! Then maybe that's the storm!" exclaimed Democrika. "Is there a nursery in that place?" she asked as an afterthought.

"What the hell are you talking about?" asked the other. "It's a factory filled with bombs. There's no nursery in there."

The subject of this last discussion was a mound deep in the heart of old Salt territory. As Democrika's rebels had gathered strength throughout the months of war, and been joined by deserting soldiers in outposts all across the colony, they had thrown a circle around the hard line military command and pinned them down in this one last strategic mound. The problem for the rebels was that this was where the Salts had made their bombs. No one knew for sure how much destructive power was buried in those chambers, but they guessed it was immense. With the generals on the inside in control, and the rebels on the outside itching to get in, it was, to put it mildly, an explosive situation. Knowing this was what upset Democrika so much with the end of Observa's story. Was she sitting on a potential Antale holocaust that could tear their world apart? She did not know. And Cassandra had been no help at all.

Democrika hurried back to her command. When she arrived, it was early evening and she found her forces holding a noisy bivouac around the mound. On top, a cluster of old Salt troops looked down defiantly on the rebel hordes. All other entrances to the mound were closed. The only way in was through the top and the Salts controlled it.

"Well, that's no problem," said Democrika, sizing the situation up. "We'll tunnel around the base and lift the top right off."

She gave the order and, under the cover of darkness, the operation began. They had barely worked ten minutes before some objects came rolling down the mound on all sides. A series of blinding flashes lit the night as the objects reached the bottom and detonated among the workers. The rebels howled in terror and fell back.

"The devils are using ball grenades," Democrika cursed. "We can't compete with that."

"Then we'll have to starve them out," said one of her leaders.

"That'll take too much time," replied Democrika. "We'll lose all the old Salt troops if we don't take the mound right away. They'll defect back if they think we can't get to those bombs inside."

"Then let's storm the bloody thing right now," said someone else. "They can't stop us if we take them in a rush."

"I don't know," Democrika was hesitating. "We don't want any of those grenades rolling back inside. It could set the whole pile off and blow us all to the other side of the lake."

"Garbage!" another leader shouted. "The generals are down in there. Do you think they'd blow themselves to pieces?"

"Let's take it now! We've been too long at war."

"Storm the mound!"

"Finish the Salt heads off!"

Democrika was besieged by a chorus of angry rebel leaders who wanted done with it. She gave the word and a seething mass of roaring rebels rushed up the mound.

What neither Democrika nor any of her rebels knew, however, was that the generals were not in the mound. They were under it. The explanation went back to the days when Bravada stole the secret of explosive technology from the Sugars. She knew it meant the possibility of violent conflict between their colonies and the threat that the Sugars would make an explosive strike against the Salts. Bravada acted to protect herself and her high command by building a shelter deep underground. It was called the Bravadabunker.

It was a large, round chamber tunneled out of rock and covered on the top by twelve inches of hard-packed clay for added strength. Above, they had built a normal mound which was used as a military base. Very few ordinary ants knew about the Bravadabunker. It was buried three feet underground and sealed with a large rock. Inside, a separate vault with walls of added thickness served as a storehouse for enough bombs to launch an overpowering military attack on an aggressor. The thinking was that, if the Salts were overrun by the Sugars, this secret base would remain intact with its command force and supply of weapons to strike a counter blow. Well stocked with food, the bunker could support a force of several hundred troops for at least three months. In addition, secret tunnels provided alternative routes in and out.

Bravada had never used the bunker. Now, her old generals had taken it over to make a final stand against the rebels. When they knew their attackers were closing in, they put a skeleton resistance force in the mound and retreated with a company of several hundred soldiers into the bunker. The mound above was mined with a chain of the most powerful explosive charges the Salts had ever built. It was set up as one colossal bomb. If the rebels overran it, the generals could blow it up. They would then be sealed safe for the time being in their bunker and live to fight another day. At least, that was the strategy. And it may have worked, had not the generals (and Democrika and everyone else), overlooked another factor. Natural forces are not benign in the affairs of ants, and will exact their due.

Outside on the mound, pandemonium raged unchecked. Thousands of rebels were charging up the slope against an avalanche of fiery grenades. The carnage was incredible, but the rebels paid little heed, because now they were on their final assault. The top of the mound was the climax of their cause. Just a few inches more and they would have their prize. No wall of death could stop them now. They reached the top. The Salts disappeared inside. Ten thousand cheering rebels packed the mound and shouted their triumph to the skies.

It was then that the generals set off the charges.

Never before had such an eruption torn at the fabric of the land. A thousand times the power of the single bomb the Sugars had first exploded two years ago, it now wrenched the entrails of the Salt's last bastion, and hurled a holocaust of death a thousand feet away. Rocks and soil shot skyward, taking the rebels with them, and cascaded as a shower of white hot sparks onto the drought-dried grass and shriveled shrubs of the surrounding land. In an instant, the grass and leaves exploded into flame. Nature took over from what the ants began and a brush fire sprang to life, licking and leaping its way outward in a circle, seeming to pause a moment before deciding which way to go. Then a freshening northeasterly breeze took charge, whipped it up, and drove it as a wall of flames southwest toward the Sugar Colony.

Democrika and those around her had survived the blast. Scorched and shaken, they huddled under rocks, peeping out in terrified dismay at the aftermath of their glorious assault.

"Fire and storm!" Democrika gasped. "By thunder, the old witch didn't tell the half of it!"

Inside the bunker, the generals stared at each other blankly. Down there, the world was absolutely silent. When the bombs went off, the shock waves had thrown them around, but after that, absolute stillness, the silence of the tomb.

"Do you think it worked?" one of them asked.

"Of course, it did," said another. "You felt the shock."

"But what did it do up there?" the first one asked again.

"The only way to know would be to be up there," said someone else.

"But, then we'd be dead."

"Instead of being safe down here."

"Not knowing what happened up there."

"If only it wasn't so quiet. I didn't think it would be so quiet."

"When you set off the largest explosive in the world, maybe you should know what will happen!"

"How can you know when it's never been done before?"

"Then maybe you shouldn't do it."

"But then we'd be dead."

"That's true."

"If only it weren't so damn quiet."

As they spoke, what none of the generals knew was that the roof of their bunker had been damaged in the blast. Even then, a pocket of acrid smoke from the explosion pushed by a down draft was just beginning to find its way inside their shelter.

Half a mile away in the Gold House, President Alexa was summoned by an aide to come to the observation deck on the top of the mound. Away to the northeast, they could see a strange glow lighting up the sky. A group of senior staff were already discussing it.

"Well, what do you think it is?" asked the President.

"No one has ever seen one before, Ma'am," one of the staff replied, "but we kinda think it's a wild fire."

"What do we do to stop it?" asked Alexa.

"Ants don't stop wild fires, Ma'am," said the other. "You just try to block the entrances and get down deep inside the nests.

CHAPTER 17

Rescue

From the heart of Dragon country, another half mile further west, Futura and Bravura also saw the glow.

"That's strange," said Bravura, "the sky's a flood of moonlight, but where's the moon?"

Futura scrambled to the top of a boulder to get a better view over the bushes. "It's not the moon," she said, "but it's just as bright. I wonder what it is."

"Big fire, whoosh!" grunted a voice behind her. She turned to see the bulk of Supreema laboring up the rock.

"What did you say?" asked Futura.

"Big fire, whoosh," repeated Supreema. "Been here before in Dragon land. Very hot. Cooks everything. No good for ants."

Futura had now been joined by fifty of her Peace Team. They were all too young to have ever seen a brush fire. Supreema's cryptic words meant nothing to them. "Coming over Sugars." Supreema was now on the top of the rock beside Futura. The Peace Team gathered round. "You young ones not know," Supreema continued, looking worried. "This is very bad. Will kill everything. Must go help."

Supreema turned and gave a long, loud hiss. Immediately, it was picked up by several thousand Dragons who had been lying around on the rocks in the cool of the evening. They moved forward as a sheet, hissing, and Supreema lumbered down to lead them. "Come, Red ants," she said to Futura and Bravura. "You will see. Dragons go to help their friends."

"I saw fire flashes in the war," said Bravura. "But nothing like this."

"Supreema seems to know what she's doing," said Futura. "Come on, everyone," she called to her Peace Team, "let's follow and see what's to do."

Supreema had guessed the fire would be stopped by Cruel Creek, and she was almost right. When they got to the creek bank two hours later, the fire was already burning itself out in the low bushes on the eastern side. But it was still a terrifying sight to ants who had never seen the like before. Tongues of flame cracked and sizzled in the tinder dry brush. Burning branches fell in the water, sending up clouds of steam like an angry breath from the fire because it could not cross. At least, that's what they thought at first, then Supreema saw something that froze her stiff in fear. The new log bridge the Sugars had built to bring supplies across had caught alight, and a band of fire was already halfway over, burning along the bark of the log. If it reached their side, the nearby bushes would catch and the whole forest would go up in flames, wiping out the Dark Country and the Dragon lands, not stopping until it hit the Rim.

Supreema saw they had one chance. "Cut bushes down!" she shouted. Thousands of Dragons threw themselves into the bushes and began chewing at the branches. "Strip off the bark!" Supreema ordered again. Another brigade attacked the log and chomped at the bark. Futura, Bravura and the Peace Team looked on, amazed. "Wet the branches!" came Supreema's next command. The cut branches and their leaves walked on Dragon legs, stumbling over rocks down to the water's edge. "In the water! In the water!" yelled Supreema. The Dragons rolled and tumbled the branches over until the leaves were thoroughly wet. "Back to the log!" cried Supreema. The sodden bushes wobbled back up the bank onto the log. "Beat out the flames!" Supreema ordered. The Dragons who had been chewing on the bark made way for the fire brigade, who now marched out along the log armed with their wet beating brands and attacked the leading edge of the flames. As the front line collapsed from exhaustion and fell off the log into the creek, still clinging to their branch, another line came up and repeated the process. Meanwhile, the bark chompers went back to work. The Dragons kept at it for over an hour, but they held the flames at bay until, finally, the log burnt through and fell into the water.

The Dragons were too exhausted to cheer, so the Peace Team did it for them. "Supreema, you're supreme!" shouted Futura. She tried to hug the Dragon giant, but could barely reach her knees. The others gathered round and swarmed all over Supreema and her fire fighters. It was Bravura who brought them back to attention.

"We've got to get across to help the Sugars," she said, "but now the bridge is gone. Supreema, can your crew build a dam?"

The Dragon leader nodded. Though the team of workers, who were still on half rations from the drought, were not fit to begin with, what they lacked in strength they made up for with energy. They all nodded likewise, looking questioningly at Bravura. She pointed out a clump of rocks just a short way downstream that were showing above the surface of the creek because of the low water due to the lack of rain.

"If we cut some larger branches and float them down," she said, "they should catch on those rocks. Then we can crawl over the branches to the other side."

And so it was done. An hour later, Bravura was the first to cross, followed by Futura and the Peace Team. After them, Supreema led her army of Dragons over.

On the other side, the burnt grass was still hot and dangerous. Acrid smoke choked and blinded the ants as they moved carefully forward. The night was as black as the scorched earth. Bravura, at the head, found a well-worn path safe enough to travel on, except for half-burnt sticks that had fallen from burning bushes. She inched her way ahead with Futura and the Peace Team following, and after them, Supreema and a long line of Dragons. Progress was very slow, and it took the rest of the night before they reached the outskirts of the Sugar Colony.

The ground was much cooler now, so the ants could spread out on a broad front. Bravura called a halt and spoke to Futura and Supreema.

"I don't know what we'll find," she said. "Let's take a look at this first mound over here."

Before the fire, the dry grass had been growing right up to the base of the golden mound. Now, all the grass was burnt black and the mound sat, blotched and dirty, like burnt skin where the fire had raced over it. It was one of a dozen ugly sores they now could see on the face of the blackened ground in the early morning sunlight. There was no sign anywhere of any Sugars.

Futura was the first to find an entrance. She pulled some debris aside, then reeled back in horror. The tangled matter she was tugging at was a sticky, fused mass of burnt ants. Her head and forelegs were covered in the golden slime. She collapsed, retching, as similar cries of anguish went up from other members of the Peace Team, who were probing other holes. The young ants could not bear to dig their way in.

Supreema, watching, shook her big head sadly. "No good for you," she said. "Too horrible. Dragons will do it."

She did not have to issue orders. The Dragons somehow seemed to know what to do. They fanned out in a somber pack and began the grisly task of opening up all the nests that they could see.

It seemed the Sugars had tried to plug the entrances, but had underestimated the forces released by the fire as it swept over the mounds. The plugs were either consumed by the heat or crumbled inward, no doubt allowing smoke to get into the nests. In a frantic attempt to reseal the entrances, Sugar workers had rushed to the surface, where they were cooked alive, unwittingly sacrificing themselves as their burned bodies piled up and resealed the entrances. It was this congealed mass of ant flesh that the Dragon workers were now pulling aside to get through to the Sugars still hiding below.

The first breakthrough came after about half an hour of grisly work by the Dragons. Futura had recovered her composure enough to volunteer to be the first to go down inside. Her slim frame had no difficulty sliding in through what still remained of the burnt bodies, until she was clear of the mess and moving along an open passage. The smell of smoke was strong and made her gasp. She called out, "Hello! Is anyone there?" No answer. She moved on. The smell was strong, but not overpowering. "Hello!" she called again. "Friends are here to help. Where are you?"

The passage opened out and she found the first Sugars. They were alive, but very groggy from the smoke. "Come on," said Futura, "you've got to get out of here into the open air." She pushed a few toward the entrance. The fresh air coming in seemed to revive them a little and they began stumbling out. "That's it!" urged Futura, "up you go. Move along, the rest of you. It's safe outside. You must get out of the nest." The word passed down to the mass of ants huddled in deeper chambers. Less affected by the smoke, they eagerly pushed up toward the surface. Futura found herself swept along by the current and was carried back out of the nest. When she got to the surface, she saw dazed Sugars now pouring out of several entrances cleared by the Dragons. The latter, now that their work was done, had shyly retreated into a huddle at the base of the mound. When the leading Sugars saw them, they stopped abruptly. Some fell back in fear, but the soldiers pushed through to the front and immediately formed into a threatening military line.

Seeing what was happening, Futura rushed down the mound toward the Dragons. Bravura was there, too, and several of the Peace Team. They formed a tiny guard facing the Sugars, who were unknowingly about to attack their saviors.

"Hold on!" shouted Futura. "The Dragons are your friends. They have opened up your mounds. Look around. They stopped the fire from spreading further and now they've come to help. They are your friends!"

The Sugar soldiers paused, uncertain what to do. Who were these puny few Red ants facing them? And who were these strange ones behind? And what had happened to their world? Where was all the grass and trees and bushes? What was this ugly scene of blackened desolation all around?

Futura cried out again. "The world has suffered a terrible blow," she shouted. "But you have survived! The Dragons have freed you from your prisons. They are here to help you rebuild, just as you helped them survive the drought. I and my friends are a small Peace Team. We will also do what we can to help. But your true friends and heroes are the Dragons."

Futura's earnestness saved the day from further suffering. A Sugar captain ordered her troops to fall back. She approached Futura. "I believe you speak the truth," she said. "My name is Centura. Where is the Dragon commander? I would like to thank her."

All this time, Supreema had been out of sight, busy at a neighboring mound. Bravura looked around and saw her hunkering toward them. "Ho, there, Supreema!" she called. "Come and meet the Sugars." A collective gasp went up from all the Sugars on the mound at the sight of this giant creature plowing through the blackened grass, kicking up a dark cloud as she came. By the time she arrived, her great Dragon hood was encrusted with a layer of soot and grime. She towered over them like a tarnished colossus.

"This is Captain Centura," said Futura. "I've explained what you and your Dragons have done to rescue them."

Centura, still intimidated, saluted Supreema.

"We are much obliged to you and your troops, Ma'am," she said.

"Humph!" Supreema puffed, clumsily acknowledging the salute. "You help us. We help you. Fire very bad for ants. We help you clean up."

"Thank you, Ma'am. I'll send word to the other nests so everyone will understand."

Centura issued some orders to her soldiers, who then disbanded. Supreema, in the meantime, had suddenly become very alert. She raised her large head even higher, and twisted around, her antennae searching the air.

"Beetles!" she exclaimed. "Smell beetles. No good. Where are they?"

Without waiting for a reply, she moved surprisingly quickly over to a nearby entrance in the mound, tore at the hole to make it larger, and thrust her head inside up to the hood. Everyone watching saw the rear end of her large body shake violently as she wrestled with something inside the hole. A moment later, she stepped back and her head came out, bearing a large and very startled delusory beetle in her jaws. As they watched, she snapped the creature's head right off and flung the rest of the body aside like a squashed leaf.

"Beetles bad news!" she exclaimed. "No good for nests."

Centura had looked on, amazed. "You could smell that thing?" she asked. "That's terrific. Our nests are full of them. Can all your Dragons do that? I mean, could they go down in the nests and find all the beetles?"

"Dragons kill all beetles," said Supreema. "Good to eat. Bad to keep around."

"Their juice doesn't affect you?" asked Centura.

"Ha!" snorted Supreema. "Dragons too strong for beetle juice. Hoods soak it up. No problem for us."

"Well, I'll be darned," said Centura. "Commander, Ma'am, with your permission, I'd like to have some of your troops go down inside the nest to see what they can find. This could be your second great service to us today."

Centura's words were nothing short of prophetic. Before the day was out,

Sugars and Dragons were working together in every mound. They cleaned up debris from the fire. They recovered the remains of Sugars who had perished in the blaze. But, by far the most spectacular, the Dragons sniffed and searched their way through every nest and herded hundreds of delusory beetles to the surface. The last the Sugars saw of their unwelcome guests, they were huddled together in a corral of Dragons, waiting to be driven away for execution. Out of the disaster of the wild fire, the Sugars had found a totally unexpected measure of salvation. It was recognized as no less than that by a grateful Gold House.

Like all the other nests, the President's mound had taken its share of punishment from the wild fire. Alexa and her governing council had gone deep underground for safety, barely escaping from the oval office at the top of the mound before it had collapsed under stresses set up by the fire. In the morning, a shaken President had emerged to the scene of her devastated colony at about the same time as the Dragons were opening up the nests not far away. When she received the news, Alexa set off immediately to greet their benefactors. She arrived to find Futura, Bravura and Supreema standing with Centura, watching the first of the beetles being brought out of the nest.

The two leaders, as different from each other as their colonies, were meeting for the first time. It was an emotional moment. Stranger neighbors could hardly be imagined, but all that was set aside. Both knew how much they owed each other during the time of crisis that had gripped their world.

After watching quietly for a while, Futura made an observation. "It's no coincidence we're all here together," she said. "The fire was a cleansing. I think Antale is being given a chance to start over, and it's beginning here with your two colonies.

"Redemption by fire. Is that what you mean?" said Alexa. "It's a hard lesson."

"Fire not start from nothing," said Supreema.

Alexa looked sharply at the Dragon leader. "Well, that's true enough. But are we talking about hidden causes, here?" However, Supreema said nothing more.

"Yes, I believe we are," Futura replied instead. "I don't know anything about fires, but I have a sense we're meant to look further for an answer. That's what I'd like to do now. There's no good reason for our Peace Team to stay here any longer. We will go east to see if we can find out what started the fire. Will you come, Bravura?"

"Yes," said Bravura. "I already have a theory."

"What's that?" asked Alexa.

"I think those rebels fighting over the old Salt lands set something off. They're a wild lot, you know. More stars in their eyes than brains in their heads."

"If you're going into that country, you should take a guard," said Alexa. "I'll give you one."

Centura jumped in. "With your permission, Ma'am," she said. "I'd like to do it."

"All right, Centura," said Alexa. "Pick some troops and keep me informed directly on what you find." To Futura, she added, "Take good care. You young ones are our best hope for the future."

"Thank you, Ma'am, we will," replied Futura. She turned to Supreema. "It's been wonderful to know you, Commander. We'll come back again soon."

"Watch out for big boom," said Supreema. "Not so good now as I first think."

"Well, that's progress," said Bravura. "Don't worry, Commander. There's one old soldier here who has no desire to see any more big booms. I'll keep them out of trouble."

Shortly afterward, the Peace Team took its leave, heading eastward across the blackened landscape.

CHAPTER 18

A Grim Discovery

At Unicol headquarters in Centrasia, Pacifica had received a stream of reports throughout the night about the fire. They came as frantic transmissions from nests about to be overrun—and after that, silence. When the same thing happened for the entire Sugar Colony, she knew the devastation must be enormous. From the observation deck on the top of the mound, she could see the glow of the fire to the south. Thousands of ants in the White Colony were out watching. No one had ever seen the like of it before. After several hours, the glow faded, then disappeared. The curious ants gave up their watching and retired. Pacifica alerted the other members of the directorate to her concern about the Sugars and they all kept an anxious vigil through the night. Finally, Pacifica received a transmission from Alexa about an hour after sunrise.

"We've been hit really hard," said Alexa. "You can't believe the devastation. It's like the end of the world. If it wasn't for the Dragons, half of our population could have been suffocated in their nests. And now, they're bringing out those infernal beetles, too!" Alexa explained how the Dragons were rounding up the delusory beetles. "The other thing you should know," Alexa continued, "is that Futura and her Peace Team are heading east to see if they can find what started the blaze. I've sent a guard to accompany them."

Shortly afterward, Bluffasta spoke to Pacifica. "There's no news from the Peppers," she said. "Transmissions are cut off. That's not good. I have to go and see what's up."

"I understand," replied Pacifica. "I need a reliable report on what's happening down there, anyway. Take your guard and go. Don't worry, I'm sure you'll find the Peppers are all right."

"Hot enough already, by the force," exclaimed Bluffasta.

"Yes, something like that," Pacifica smiled a little, despite her anxiety. "Keep a look out for Futura and the Peace Team. I don't know why they haven't reported in."

The reason for Futura's silence was simple enough. Somewhere in the rough and tumble of the fire fighting at Cruel Creek, their transmission equipment had been damaged. They did not discover it until several hours out of the Sugar Colony. Centura could communicate with her base, but could not raise the frequency for Centrasia. For the time being, Futura and the Peace Team were out of direct contact with Unicol.

Had they been able to report, it would have been a grim description. They picked their way across a land of blackened devastation. As if to outdo the inferno of the fire, the sun blazed down from a mercilessly clear sky, heating the bare soil and rock until it was almost too hot for any living thing to move. Not that there was much life left, anyway. Dark skeletons of trees gave no refuge for any bird, and the still smoldering carcasses of logs and bushes had become the smoking crematoria for the insects and small animals in the incinerated ground cover. A hot and heavy stillness gripped the land. A black, unending stretch of soot and ashes challenged the small party of ants at every step.

None of them had ever been this way before. They crept blindly on, keeping to what shade they could find along a rocky defile that twisted like a snake east and north from the Sugar Colony into the old Salt lands. Because they came along the gully, they saw no ant mounds. These were located some distance off on both sides. Futura's team might well have traveled for days and discovered nothing had they not met another party who had sought refuge in this same rocky defile.

When Democrika and the other few survivors from the original explosion first saw the fire, they truly believed they had triggered the end of the world. Stunned by concussion and shock, they stared paralyzed at the inferno now blazing in a leaping circle of death outward from the centre. They stood fixed and motionless for hours, totally mesmerized by the awful tragedy they had unleashed. The mound that had been the object of their assault, the glorious monument to their successful revolution, was now a gaping, smoking hole in the ground. Their ten thousand comrades, who had stormed triumphantly to the top, were gone, evaporated by the blast. Of all that exuberant force of freedom fighters, only six half-crazed survivors remained. At dawn, they looked out disconsolately on a world in ruins and sought simply to crawl away.

They had no idea where they were going, but looked for the path of least resistance through the hot and smoking terrain. They found it in a rocky gully running south. The fire had leapt over the top of the defile, sprinkling it with ash and other charred debris, but otherwise leaving it alone. It was a winding, dry river of rock through the scorched remains of rich countryside. It was there, staggering and incoherent, that Futura and her party found them toward the end of the day.

"What, ho there, ants!" challenged Bravura, who was the first to see them. Then she looked more closely. "By all the ant legs!" she exclaimed, "it's Democrika."

The rebel leader stared blankly at Bravura.

"What's wrong, you old firebrand," said the latter, "don't you recognize me?"

"Aiyee!" Democrika shrieked. "Firebrand! That's true enough. I've set the whole world alight!" She covered her head with her forelegs and crouched, trembling.

"Who is it, Bravura?" asked Futura, who had now come up. "Do you know her?"

"Yes, I know her well enough," replied Bravura. "It's Democrika, the rebel rouser. I think my theory might be right on the mark." She addressed Democrika's companions. "What about the rest of you? Can you talk? Did you lot cause this mess?"

Slowly, the truth came out. The Peace Team crowded round and listened, aghast, to the incredible story told haltingly by the survivors.

"This is where we come to when we think we're greater than we are," said Futura. Her eyes blazed fiercely in anger. She shook Democrika into comprehension. "What about the Salts? Did any of them survive?"

"Can an ant live on a red hot coal?" asked Democrika. "They were in the heart of the holocaust. Cooked alive!"

"No doubt," Futura nodded, "but we'll see for ourselves. I want you to take us there."

Democrika and the others began to wail in protest.

"Now!" roared Futura, in a fury no one had ever heard from her before. "You sought to be a ruler. Now take us to what's left of your empire."

Futura forced the reluctant rebels to march all night, and they came to the site of the blast early next morning. From the rim of the gully, they stared down to an acre of ground that looked like a white eyeball in a blackened face. The force of the explosion had flattened everything in its path. Trees and shrubs were uprooted and flung around in a tangled mess. Beyond that, the fire had started, but strangely, not burned back into the circle. This left the dry, yellow grass and the leveled foliage covered with a light sprinkling of white ash, while all around the land was black and burnt. In the centre of the circle, the tell-tale hole of the former mound gaped open, three feet deep.

The Peace Team and Centura's troop of soldiers looked silently and solemnly down on the grim spectacle.

"Look closely, friend," Futura said softly. "This is what lies in store for all Antale, if ants of like mind have their way."

"It doesn't have to come to that," objected Centura. "These were rebels, not professional soldiers. A trained military command would never let this happen."

Futura turned and fixed her calm, soft eyes on Centura. "It was the Salt military command that placed the charges. The rebels were the poor fools who tripped the trigger."

Before Centura could protest further, Bravura intervened. "Say, look at that," she said.

"Look at what?" asked Futura.

"That hole in the middle, where the mound was. Look at the bottom of it. It's flat. Don't you think that's strange?"

"Must be a rock base," said Centura. "The explosion couldn't crack it."

"But why would the Salts build their strategic command over a rock base?" asked Bravura. "It limits the depth of their underground construction."

"Unless they built something under the rock," said Centura.

"Precisely," said Bravura. "Let's go and take a look."

When they got to the hole, the team of ants clambered down to the flat base and spread around, examining it. Democrika and her rebel companions stayed back in horror with a couple of Sugar guards watching them.

"This is not rock," Bravura announced. "It's hard packed clay. The Salts deliberately built this."

"Must be damn thick," said Centura, "otherwise it would've been blown to pieces."

"Look, it butts up to this ring of real rock," said one of the other ants, who had walked half way round the circumference.

"By gosh," Bravura declared, "I think what we've got here is a cap over a giant cavern. If I'm right, what do you think those Salts would have gone to so much trouble to hide away?"

"It's a bunker!" shouted Centura. "I'll bet it's filled with bombs!"

"And old Salt generals waiting to fight another day," said Bravura.

"Did I hear you right?" asked Futura, her eyes wide with amazement. "You think there are ants down there? Generals? Military leaders? Would they build a hole like that and hide in it with their bombs?"

"You bet," replied Bravura. "It's a perfectly good military strategy—crazy, but deadly."

Futura turned back to Centura. "So, there we have the thinking of the military command," she said. "What did you call this thing? A bunker? How many bunkers do the Sugars have filled with bombs?"

Centura shuffled and did not answer. Just then, another searching ant shouted excitedly. "There's a crack here!" she cried. "I think we can get inside." Everyone crowded around.

"This must have been the entrance," said Bravura. "The explosion fused it, but sent out a stress line through the clay. If it goes right through, we can get into the bunker. We need a search party to go down. It's a narrow crack. I don't think you Sugars can make it, but a few of us Red ants should be able to squeeze through. I'll go first."

Bravura picked a dozen Red ants from the Peace Team to go with her. Futura said she was going with them, too. "You look after things up here, Centura," she said. "We'll string out in a line to let you know what we find."

Centura was clearly not happy with the arrangement, but had no choice. The Sugars were all too large to go down the crack.

Futura followed close behind Bravura as they crawled into the darkness of the hole and began to make their way slowly downward. It was a torturous, uneven cavity. They went down three inches, but then had to crawl horizontally for several feet before they could go down again. This was repeated several times, with many blocked passageways and false starts. Bravura sent word back up along the line to get more ants into the string, to keep contact with the surface. Otherwise, they might never find their way out again. Finally, after almost half an hour of this twisting and turning, Bravura and Futura burst together into the underground domain of the Salt High Command.

"By all the ants in outer darkness!" exclaimed Bravura, "look at what we've found. The hell hole of the damned!"

Bravura's morbid imagery told its own truth. Below them was the main floor of the bunker, a large round chamber about six inches deep and two feet in diameter. In the centre of the room a cluster of Salt generals sat in a circle, as if in conversation. Around them, spread-eagled in various positions of agony and desperation, were several hundred Salt soldiers. Not one of them moved. Every one was a corpse. Futura and Bravura were looking down into the involuntary burial chamber of the last inhabitants of the Salt empire. It was one colossal tomb.

"What do you think happened?" asked Futura.

"Suffocated or poisoned. Possibly both," replied Bravura. "I expect some noxious fumes from the explosion seeped down through the crack and killed them all before they knew what was happening."

"But the air seems clear now."

"Must be a ventilation shaft somewhere. It's had time to work now, but couldn't save these poor devils. Let's go down."

Futura, Bravura and a few of the other Red ants who were following them crept down among the bodies strewn on the floor.

"I wonder what they were talking about," said Futura as she looked at the corpses of the generals, surprisingly life-like in their positions.

"Probably planning how they were going to conquer the world," replied Bravura. "You said it all before to Centura. The military mind doesn't give up until it tosses the last bomb. Speaking of which, let's see where they are."

It did not take long to find the storehouse of bombs. The entrance was not even sealed. It opened off the main chamber into another, more strongly reinforced, cavity about twice the size of the other. Subdivided into neat compartments, with passageways in between, it was stacked from floor to ceiling with white cylindrical cocoon bombs. Could Democrika have seen it, she would perhaps have recognized the irony. She had wondered if there was a nursery in the nest. Here it was—a nursery of death!

"What could the Salts have done with this?" asked Futura.

"Oh, probably wiped out a third of the ants in Antale," Bravura replied. "The Sugars can take out another third. That leaves the rest of the power block—Whites, Blacks and Yellows—to wipe out everyone else."

Futura stood silently gazing at the ghastly chamber, then looked again at the morbid tomb behind.

"It has to stop now, Bravura," she said. "We must raise one collective voice in all Antale against such insanity!"

They returned to the main chamber. Bravura called to several other members of the Peace Team who had made their way down from the crack in the roof. "Let's see if we can find another way out of here," she said. "Look for a pile of bodies heading in the same direction. I expect a lot of them would have tried to escape before the fumes got to them."

Sure enough, a short while later they found a heap of dead ants partially blocking the entrance to a passageway. A stream of bodies littered the route, gradually thinning as they went, showing how the fleeing ants must have slowly succumbed to the fumes before they could get out. They passed the last of the corpses and continued on until they reached an opening three-parts blocked by debris. After pulling the rubble away, the party emerged into the open air with Futura and Bravura in the lead. They were about six feet south of the mound. Before heading back to find Centura and the others, Bravura whispered a word of warning to Futura.

"You know, we've got a delicate situation here," she said. "Right now, you and I are the only ones who know about a cache of bombs large enough to wipe out almost half the world. Once we tell Centura, then another superpower will know where to find them. Maybe we should think about that."

"Well, the solution's clear enough," said Futura. "Unicol will have to take the bombs and destroy them."

"That may be clear to you," replied Bravura, "but don't assume the same for Centura. She's a soldier and has a loyalty to her President."

The next hour proved Bravura only too right. When Centura learned about the bombs, her attitude suddenly changed toward Futura and the Peace Team.

She took command of the situation by posting guards down in the bomb chamber as well as at the entrance to the tunnel. She refused to let Futura or any of her team back inside.

"This is a military site," she said. "I'm sealing it off until the High Command arrives. I have informed the President by transmission."

"You mean the Sugar High Command," said Futura. "They have no authority here. This is a matter for all of Antale. Unicol must be informed."

"That's not for you or me to decide," Centura replied, testily. "I am responsible only to my President."

"Damn it, Centura!" stormed Futura. "You're responsible first to the world. Look around you. A fraction of the power down in that hell hole did this much damage. And it was a military high command that gave the orders. They killed themselves and devastated a quarter of the world. How much further do you want to go down that road?"

"That's why I've secured the site," Centura replied evenly. "There'll be no more mishaps here."

A quarter of a mile away, someone else was reflecting more bitterly on mishaps. Bluffasta had traveled hard from Centrasia to get to the Pepper Colony. The last half of the journey turned into a growing nightmare of despair. The fire had burnt only irregularly to the north, for the wind had carried it south and east. Nevertheless, Bluffasta's party encountered many pockets of devastation where the ants were just beginning to crawl back out of their nests, trying to figure out what to do to restore their life. It became worse as they approached the Pepper Colony. Around the few Pepper mounds, the ground was a blackened scar. They had taken the full fury of the early blaze, and when Bluffasta's party arrived, a deathly stillness hung over everything.

Bluffasta ran up onto the shell of the first mound she came to. She found an entrance and was about to go inside when something made her look around. Startled, she saw a group of a few hundred Peppers sitting on a rock a few feet away, staring at her.

"Ya! Ya! Sisters!" she called, "how are you?"

No one answered. Bluffasta went over and recognized an old friend. "Provaska!" she cried. "Look at you. By the force, I've never seen a face so long. How goes it with you?"

"They send you from the north to ask such questions," replied Provaska. "Better you bring some answers. What happened to the good life we had before the world went mad?"

"Too many leaders tried to have their way," replied Bluffasta. "But that's not your trouble now. I can see it's bad here. How bad?"

"Some things no one needs to know. Who wants to count the dead? We have our Queen, so we can start again. We'll bring the cocoons out later. They were safe enough. But there are few of us to forage now."

The full truth hit Bluffasta hard.

"You mean that this is all there is? Just you few clustered here? How could it be so bad?"

"It came too fast," Provaska remembered painfully. "First the blast, then the fire roaring through. The workers were caught outside. The rest suffocated in the nests. We few stragglers somehow forgot to die."

Bluffasta suddenly felt sick in her heart. All of her friends and sisters, the wild and audacious Peppers who had stood their ground against the Salt extravagances, who loved nothing more than the freedom of their fields by day and the warm comfort of their nests by night, to work hard when they should, to play and wrestle when they might—all these fine friends of her youth and later life—could they be gone? Reduced to the lost and lonely few she saw before her here? If ants could weep, this would be the time for it now. Bluffasta came down from the mound and embraced Provaska.

"You said there was a blast," she whispered. "Where?"

"Not far," replied the other. "I think it was the Salt's old Sentinel—the place where they made the bombs."

Bluffasta called her guard and hurried east. She knew the place quite well. As she went, she sent a transmission to Pacifica. "No natural force set this thing off," she said. "Some Salt stupidity's at work. I'm going to find out what and who, and then I'll break some necks."

Pacifica sent a transmission to President Alexa. "I've heard from my team," she said. "They think the Salts might have caused the fire. Do you know anything about that?"

Alexa had just heard from Centura. She knew about the horde of Salt bombs in the bunker. Her senior military staff were already on their way.

"Nothing definite," Alexa told Pacifica. "We're still checking things out."

CHAPTER 19

A Shift of Energy

BLUFFASTA STUMBLED ON THE DETONATION ZONE ABOUT noon. Her team crept cautiously across the white area toward the hole in the middle. At the lip of the crater, they bumped into Futura and Bravura.

"By the force!" exclaimed Bluffasta. "Where did you two spring from?"

"Bluffasta!" Futura cried, embracing the old Pepper warmly. "You've come to save the day. Can you connect me to Pacifica?"

When Pacifica heard Futura's story by transmission, her anger and anxiety soared to new heights. She connected the Protectorate Heads of Colonies—the Sugars, Blacks, Whites and Yellows—on a conference transmission, and gave full vent to her frustration.

"It's not enough that the whole world is dying from drought," she raged. "It's not enough that a quarter of it has been burnt bare by fire and millions of our sisters burned alive or suffocated in their nests. None of that's enough for us to change our ways. We still want to play with bombs like soldiers with their toys." Her next words were aimed directly at Alexa. "You knew, Alexa, when we spoke just hours ago—you knew about the horde of Salt bombs discovered by the Unicol Peace Team. Yet you denied it. In the meantime, your soldiers take possession in your name."

"Now, hold on —," protested Alexa.

"No, I won't hold on!" Pacifica shouted back. "I'm tired of holding on while soldiers play with the future of the world. It's time to renounce this governance by the military mind. If we are leaders, then we must be champions of the heart. This situation in the Salt lands is more dangerous than we can imagine. I am leaving now to personally take command. I expect you all to join me there. It's too important to leave to ambassadors or generals."

As this was the first that the leaders of the other colonies had heard about the new discovery, anger and confusion filled the next few minutes. Eventually, however, they all shared the same information, though not necessarily the same conclusions. No one but Pacifica took the larger view. However, when she pushed hard for a special meeting of the Directorate on the Salt site to decide what to do about the bombs, no one was prepared to stay away. So the leaders and their delegations set out.

But the world does not wait for leaders, however powerful, to decide its future. The flow of life continues its unpredictable course, as many other actors contribute to the script. Bluffasta, in her grief and anger, provoked the next situation.

"Show me where the bombs are," she said to Centura. "I intend to place a guard on them in the name of Unicol."

"I can't permit that," replied Centura. "I am acting on orders from my President."

"Then get new orders or, by the force, you'll need new heads," snapped Bluffasta. "Tell your guards to stand aside. I'm going in." Bluffasta signaled to a dozen of her troop to follow, and she headed toward the entrance tunnel.

"Stop right there, Captain!" ordered Centura.

"In your Sugar pie!" rejoined Bluffasta, starting to push past the Sugar guards, who weren't sure what to do.

"Detain those ants!" roared Centura to her troop.

The Sugar guards pushed Bluffasta back. She retaliated by grabbing the nearest one around the neck and tossing her aside. In moments, a furious scuffle ensued. The Sugar guards at the tunnel mouth were no match for Bluffasta's hardened team, so Centura brought in extras. She had another dozen soldiers keeping guard over Democrika and the rebels, and she waved them into the fray. They pounced on Bluffasta's troop from behind. The startled Unicol soldiers turned and fought like demons until the whole area around the tunnel mouth became a flashing sea of legs and bodies. No one was aiming for the kill, but the pent up stress of the ugly situation came out in fury as ants who should have been friends tore at each other. It took a full-scale intervention by the Peace Team to pull the combatants apart. Even then, the process may have been difficult to stop had not Futura noticed something else and screamed for Centura's attention.

"The rebels!" she shouted. "They're gone. You've let them get away!"

Eventually the significance of this set in. Centura called her soldiers back and even Bluffasta stepped aside. The battered antagonists limped away from each other and began searching for the rebels.

"There they are!" cried someone. She had spotted them fleeing up along the gully where they first were found. Both Sugars and Unicol guards set off in pursuit. The rebels, half starved and exhausted from the past few days of turmoil, were soon caught and brought back. Bravura, watching from the sidelines, then noticed something missed by all the others.

"Hey, where's Democrika?" she called to Centura. "You've let the chief rogue slip away."

Centura stormed with fury and ordered her troops to scour the area. The Peace Team and the Unicol soldiers joined in and spread out in a net to catch the rebel leader. However, the prey was not about to be trapped like a fly in a web, for at that moment, the wily Democrika was on another plane. She had slipped past Centura's guards at the tunnel mouth as they battled with Blufasta and was scuttling along the underground passage toward the bunker. No clear idea controlled her mind, just a crazed notion she had another job to do, some unfinished business from before.

As she stumbled past the bodies of the Salt troops who had been poisoned by the fumes, a desperate plan suddenly flashed upon her. She had heard the rumors running around among the guards above, that there was a horde of bombs down here and a bunker full of dead soldiers. The last of the Salts were gone and she could now capture their vast arsenal of power. She may have lost ten thousand of her comrades on the mound, but she could still claim the ultimate prize. The world would have to listen to her then. Her glorious new republic was still within her grasp. She just needed to get the bombs.

When she reached the bunker, she gaped at first in fear at the chamber full of horror, then grew braver as she told herself that she alone in all that pile of death was alive and in command. She came up to the generals in the center and gave them a mock salute. Then one of them fell over and that was all it took to send her into a paroxysm of fear. She leapt two inches in the air and crashed back among the others. They all slipped and toppled down around her, burying her in a heap of bodies.

"What's that? Who's there?" It was one of the two Sugar soldiers guarding the bombs.

"What is it ...?" That was the other guard. They both came running out of the vault, then stopped, staring fearfully around.

"My gosh, I think that body moved," cried one of them.

"Don't be crazy," said the other. "They're all as dead as stones."

"But I heard something. I'm sure I did."

"Yeah, your heart jumping out of your skin."

Just then, Democrika leapt up, holding one of the dead generals in front of her. The first Sugar guard collapsed in terror. The other fell back, screaming. Democrika grabbed the second one and broke her neck. She pushed past her into the vault and grabbed a bomb. Moments later, she was back, shoving the bomb against the remaining Sugar guard, who backed up, terrified, against the wall. Democrika put the bomb down carefully and sat on it.

"See what I've got," she sneered at the guard. "One snap of my jaws and this thing goes off and every last one of that lot in there. That'd be the bang to end all bangs, wouldn't it? Get out of here and tell that Commander of yours up there that Democrika's in charge of the bombs now—and I want to talk to her."

When the Sugar guard came stumbling out of the tunnel screaming Democrika's message, Centura and Bluffasta looked at each other in utter disbelief. Futura and Bravura, standing by, were equally astounded. Then Futura spoke up angrily.

"This is what we get for fighting among ourselves. Come on. If the four of us go down, maybe one of us will think of something."

They found Democrika sitting in the entrance to the vault with a pile of bombs all around her and a supply of Salt bodies for food.

"Nice of you to come to my party," she said. "I didn't expect so many guests. No matter. There's plenty of food and entertainment here."

"What do you want, Democrika?" asked Centura.

"That's nice, straight to the point," replied the rebel. "All right. I'll tell you. I want you to send the word out to my comrades that Democrika's got the bombs. I want you to clear those filthy bodies out of there and make way for my companions to join me. We'll start our new republic in the old Bravadabunker. Hey, that's good, isn't it? Really good. Get cracking, now. I don't have much patience left. Don't try any tricks or I'll blow this whole lot up. It's all or nothing now. Democrika's last stand. Hear me good. Now go."

Centura was about to speak, but Bravura intervened.

"Hey, remember me, old warrior?" she asked. "You wanted to listen once. Do you remember? We told you, Ventura and me, we told you to take it easy. Now look at you. You can't build a new republic on a pile of bombs. Come out of there and we'll help you find a better way."

"No tricks, I said," Democrika replied. "Yes. I remember you. I remember the walls, too. They came down, didn't they? And the messenger—she came back. But what about the young ones, where are they? I don't know. Maybe I have to blow the whole thing up before they'll come. Maybe that's what the message was. I'll wait, but not much longer now."

"What are you talking about?" asked Centura. "You don't make sense."

At that, Democrika got really excited. Bravura hastily intervened again. "All right, all right," she said. "I understand. Don't worry, we'll find the answers for you." To the others, she whispered, "Let's go outside. I'll explain it to you then."

"I'm staying here," declared Bluffasta. Then she spoke to Democrika: "You can use some company. Bombs and bodies are not much fun, by the force. Do you want to leg wrestle?"

"Stay back, buffoon," cried Democrika, "you're only moments from eternity!"

"That's nothing new for me," replied Bluffasta. "But, still, we don't want a tragedy. There's been too much of that already. All right, I'll keep my distance. I'll just move some of these dead Salts away. They were blockheads in life. As corpses, they're disgusting. Go on, the rest of you, and send some soldiers down to help. We'll clean this place up for our friend, here."

Once outside, Bravura explained the Cassandra prophecies to the others.

"Where's this Cassandra now?" asked Centura. "Maybe if we could get her here, she'd talk some sense into that idiot down there."

"It's worth a try," replied Bravura. "Ventura might be able to find her."

So Bravura sent a transmission back to Centrasia and eventually reached Ventura, who listened carefully to the story. "All right, I'll leave right away to see if I can find Cassandra," she said. "Pacifica and the Protectorate leaders are already on their way down there. Someone better warn them about what's going on."

"We'll take care of that," replied Bravura. "Good luck with your search. Keep in touch. The whole outcome of this mess may depend on you."

As Ventura prepared to leave, she spoke to a group of Visionants. "Spread the word to do some earnest visioning," she said. "Antale has never needed it more."

Not long afterward, word reached Electra in Blackhall. "This is the moment we've been preparing for," she said to her assistants around her. "The voices of the young ants nourished on the Royal Elixir have got to be heard now. Futura's already down there with her Peace Team, but that's not enough. The young ants have got to come out of their nests to save the world. Send out the word. All who feel the call to go must leave immediately. I am going now."

The word spread quickly from nest to nest, in all the colonies, wherever the Queens had responded to the universal cry of motherhood to preserve Antale from the destructive forces that were tearing it apart. The young ants knew at once what they must do. They left their work by thousands—from the fields, from the granaries, from the forests, from the nurseries—by tens of thousands, they headed across the drought-drained land toward a rendezvous with the future, toward the demolished old Salt Sentinel, where one crazed rebel sat confused in a bunker of death, ready to unleash the holocaust.

Meanwhile, another of the agents of Antale's despair also sat confused in her underground domain. Esoterica's large round head cocked quizzically as she listened to the news from Rotunda.

"It's like the night has stolen the day out there." The corpulent Director of Research was panting from exertion. She had just rushed back to her Queen from a quick visit outside. "The fire cooked everything to a crisp. The whole land is burnt as black as death. But that's not the worst of it. There's a horde of great gray and green monsters crawling around. Dragons, they're called. They're dragging our beetles out of the nests and killing them. It's a massacre. They seem to be able to smell them. What are we going to do?"

"You're the scientist, dear," Esoterica said. "Can't you concoct a potion to feed these Dragons to make them see the truth? You're awfully good at that sort of thing."

"Damn it, Maj, you don't understand!" Rotunda wailed. "The Dragons are at our door. They'll smell us out, too. We've got to get out of here! Leave! Vamoose!"

"Leave?" Esoterica said slowly, as if this was a totally new idea. "Leave? Whatever do you mean? This is Paradise. No one leaves Paradise. It's where everyone wants to come."

As if to confirm Esoterica's last remarks, a great commotion suddenly broke out at one of the several entrances to the chamber. A number of Esoterica's attendants fled in terror from half a dozen hooded Dragons, who came pushing in. When the intruders became aware of the huge bulk of the Queen of Paradise, they stopped and stared, uncertain what to do. Remembering the great size of their own leader, they sensed they were in the presence of someone important. A hurried consultation sent one of them back outside. In the meantime, the others crawled around the garish fun palace, inspecting everything and watching Esoterica and the others clustered around her very closely. A few minutes later, a heavy scraping at the tunnel entrance announced a new arrival. Everyone turned to see the enormous head and hood of Supreema pushing through into the room. This was eventually followed by the rest of her large body. Shaking herself free of the dust of the too narrow entrance tunnel, she moved over to face Esoterica, two prodigious inhabitants of the ant world confronting each other.

"Who is you?" Supreema wheezed.

"Why, I might ask the same," replied Esoterica. "I am Esoterica, Queen of Paradise. This is my palace. I can't say you're welcome here. You have intruded rather rudely."

"You send beetles into nests. Thas no good for ants. You are very bad Queen."

"Oh, no," laughed Esoterica. "I am a very good Queen. Just ask all the ants we've helped find a little bit of happiness in an otherwise miserable life."

At that moment, a group of Sugar soldiers burst in. "Jeez, will you look at this setup!" exclaimed their captain. "Looks like you've nabbed the chief weirdo, Commander—the high priestess of hallucination herself. She was right under our antennae all the time, and we didn't pick her up."

"Dragons will find all her beetles," said Supreema. "Take them out and kill them. Seal her up in here. Too fat to go outside. I will tell your President."

"You must come again, darling," Esoterica called to the departing Supreema. "You're far too gloomy. We can brighten up your day for you. Come anytime."

When Supreema was outside again, the Sugar captain informed her that President Alexa was no longer in the colony.

"Where she go?" demanded Supreema.

"I'm sorry, that's a military secret," replied the captain.

Supreema was furious. "No secrets from Supreema!" she stormed. "Too many secrets cause all this death. You want Dragon help, you take me to your President."

A hurried transmission reached Alexa on her way to the leaders' meeting at the Salt Sentinel. The technology of transmission was new to Supreema, but she soon got the hang of it. "I have nabbed chief weirdo and you not here. Very insulting!" she said. "Where you go?"

"I'm sorry, Supreema," said Alexa. "You're right. It was wrong for me to leave without telling you. We are very much indebted to you."

"Where you go in this box?" repeated Supreema, tapping the transmission box.

"We think we've found the source of the fire," said Alexa. "It was a bomb. The leaders are meeting to decide what to do."

"Supreema is leader of Dragons. I am coming, too."

Alexa paused for a moment at her end of the transmission. Then she replied, "Of course, you're right, Commander. Please join us. My soldiers will escort you."

So another leader of a large ant colony was on her way to the meeting at the old Salt Sentinel.

Meanwhile, Pacifica had heard what happened in the Bravadabunker. She was close to despair. She confided as much to Roanda, who was accompanying her. They were still a half-day's march away from the bunker. "It seems we're being given the tests one after the other," Pacifica said, "and every time, we fail."

"Not completely," replied Roanda. "You're holding everyone together. In the darkest hour, they'll maybe find the light. It's your job to give the world that chance—and you are doing it, in spite of everything."

"Let's hope you are right," said Pacifica. "We've never been closer to the brink."

Down in the Bravadabunker, the same thought was never far from Bluffasta's mind. While she kept a close watch on Democrika, she supervised a rather reluctant party of soldiers who were hauling out the Salt bodies. The tension was thicker than a mud hole.

"Well, how's it look, Your Excellency?" she said mockingly to Democrika. "Too bad we can't spruce it up a bit for you with flowers. But they all got burnt in the fire, you know. You'll have to launch your new republic with bare walls."

Democrika was not amused. She picked up a bomb and rushed a few steps toward Bluffasta with it in her jaws. This caught the perky Pepper off guard. She hastily retreated. "Now, don't get excited," she exclaimed. "By the force, it was only a joke!"

"One joke closer to eternity," retorted Democrika, going back to her pile of bombs.

"All right, no more jokes, then," said Bluffasta. "How about a story? It'll pass the time, you know."

Democrika did not reply, so Bluffasta continued.

"My home's not far from here. I'm a Pepper, you know. We were always playing tricks on those upstart Salts. I remember one day, a patrol came by looking for food. My party had this beetle we were eating. So I called the Salts over to share it. But before they got there, all my soldiers crapped inside the beetle. The Salts rushed up and pushed us away and started chomping into the beetle. You should've heard the roar when they bit into that Pepper dung! I said to them, 'What's wrong? Don't you like good food? Maybe we should've put a bit of salt on it.'"

Bluffasta doubled up, laughing at her own story. Democrika laughed a little too, despite herself.

"Yes, those Peppers were good friends," Bluffasta continued, more quietly. "Good fighters, too. But they're all gone now, you know. They were caught in the fire."

Bluffasta and Democrika looked at each other across the immensity of space between them.

"You're a fighter, too, I know," said Bluffasta. "From the north, aren't you? And all those comrades of yours—blown to pieces in a war you still can't finish. It makes you wonder, doesn't it, whether we soldiers shouldn't step aside and let the peacemakers have a try. Why don't you just walk out of here with me and let someone else decide what to do with those bloody bombs."

For a second, it seemed that Democrika was going to do it. But at the last moment, something held her back. "I'm not so big a fool as that," she said. "I know my destiny. The young ones will come—then I'll have my new republic. You get out now. Go and tell your friends that Democrika's getting impatient."

"All right," said Bluffasta. "I'll leave you. But think about it, old girl. Think about how these bombs will be any better for you than they were for those poor devils we just pulled out of here—and for your comrades on the mound. Think about it. You've got lots of time for that."

Bluffasta turned and left the bunker.

Up above, Centura had cleared the area for several hundred yards around. She had settled all the ants behind a rocky bluff for added safety. Of course, no one knew for sure what would happen if Democrika detonated the bombs, but at least this was some protection. They waited here for the Protectorate leaders to arrive.

Pacifica's party was the first to get there, then shortly after that, the Sugars. A few hours later, the Blacks, Whites and Yellows all arrived in a single party, having traveled together from the north. It was late in the day, but the leaders wasted no time before convening a meeting in the shelter of a large boulder, while their attendants and officials settled down in a large circle a little way off. As she looked at the four leaders now facing her in this rough setting, Pacifica could not help but recall a similar meeting held two years ago by the old Federation to plan a strategy to win the Great War. Now, here they were again, different players, facing an even greater peril of a world on the brink of exhaustion from drought and fire, with the added threat of a half-crazed rebel prepared to detonate an unknown arsenal of bombs created by ants to destroy one another.

Pacifica remembered the old leaders: the great Wiseria, buried now under the cairn by the land bridge over Copper Creek; Serenta, President of the Sugars, who had died last winter in despair for the ills her policies had let loose in the world; Bravada, leader of the Salts, whose unmourned death had released the rebellious forces that had unwittingly triggered the blackened devastation now everywhere around. All these were gone, replaced by new leaders, but whose minds were still captive of the old ideas: Alexa, President of the Sugars; and aging Monta, former hero from the Great War, now President of the Blacks; Aristica, also an old wartime leader who had succeeded Appesia as President of the Whites; and finally, Valencia, one of the generals from the Yellow forces, who had replaced Antonia, the leader of the Yellows during the Great War. Pacifica, now no longer young herself, looked at them all and wondered if they were the ones who could lead the world away from the precipice.

"The question we have to ask," said Pacifica at the outset, "is what kind of a world do we want?"

"It's not that simple," interrupted Monta. "You can wish all you like for peace and harmony, but it won't ever turn out that way."

"We don't control all the pieces," said Aristica. "The best you can hope for is to muddle through."

"You can try to plan the future," said Valencia, "but you must always be on guard against despots like Aggressa. The only way to do that is to be strong yourself."

"I know that military power is not the complete answer," Alexa was the last to speak, "but it's the best protection we have. It saved us in the War, and it's kept the balance since."

"Which brings us to where we are," Pacifica rejoined. "Four frightened leaders and an impotent Unicol official cowering in the shelter of a boulder. Down there in a military bunker, a lunatic is prepared to blow the world apart—with the bombs you say are meant to protect us. And look around—nothing but devastation from drought we probably caused ourselves, and a fire unleashed by the last explosion. Do we continue down this path or find another way?"

"Damn it, Pacifica!" Monta exploded. "There is no other way! Do you think if there was, we wouldn't have found it? It's not the way that's wrong, it's the sloppiness of our controls. We need better systems."

"Most ants are just pathetic creatures," put in Aristica. "They'll go whichever way their bellies take them. And look at how they've succumbed to the delusory beetles. Their minds are weaker than their backs. The only way to manage them is firm control from the top."

"If that's your view, it's no wonder we've got to where we are," replied Pacifica, her fury rising. "You get what you expect. Don't you remember anything from the War? Our troops came back from nowhere to win the day, because Wiseria expected them to do it. We're fighting a different war now, but the capacity of ants to rise to the occasion hasn't diminished."

"Yes, I agree with Pacifica on that," said Alexa. "The potential is there. It just seems to keep slipping from our grasp."

"Because we're trying to control from the top," Pacifica continued. "As leaders, we're using a technology of fear. So what do we get? The stronger the technology, the greater the fear. So now, we have the greatest fear of all—that we will soon destroy everything, because we couldn't find another way. If that's the only leadership we can bring to the world, then we're no better than the crazed rebel down there who's ready to blow it all apart."

A deathly silence settled on the group. No one had a rejoinder for Pacifica. The silence of their anguished thoughts was as deep as the emptiness of the burnt out land around them. Night had now closed in and its blackness fell heavily on their fears. Finally, Pacifica spoke again, more softly now.

"There is one ray of hope I see," she said. "It began a year ago when, with Electra, I enjoined the cooperation of our Queens to raise the consciousness of a new generation in our nests. They are with us now, ready for the challenge, if we will give them the opening. One of them is in our circle here. I would like her to speak to us."

None of the leaders objected, so Pacifica waved Futura forward to join them. She had been listening from the outer ring of officials and soldiers.

"Perhaps not all of you know Futura," said Pacifica. "She formed a Peace Team of her fellows and has been working for the past few weeks to help with the famine in the Dragon Colony. We are trying to find our way ahead, Futura. How would you advise us?"

"The only thing I know," said Futura, looking steadily around the group of grave-faced leaders, "is the courage that grows in a team when they are given the freedom and the choice to do what's right. If they begin with a belief in each other's worth, and extend that outward to all other teams, no matter what their color or their nest, then a wave of universal compassion and respect begins to swell. We have only just begun to know this in our own small team, but my sense tells me that there's a bigger, stronger wave building up out there in all the nests. If we can call it up and let it grow, my hope is that it might soon fill all Antale with a new energy for the future."

That was all Futura said, but her words seemed to bring a faint glow of light into the darkness around the group. Perhaps it was the change of energy she brought into the circle that caused a shift in the outer energy of the world, or perhaps it was mere coincidence, but at that moment, a flicker of lightning licked along the edge of the Rim in the dark western sky. All heads turned to look, and as they did, they became aware of a new feeling in the air. It was a sensation that Futura and the younger ants born that spring had never known. It was a feeling the older ants had not experienced in more than a year. It was the breath of a rising storm, a shift in the atmospheric pressure, a harbinger of change. As they watched in silence, the lightning show came dancing in with growing speed, every successive minute more spectacular than the last, until the first dull roar of thunder shook the air, then grew in volume until all Antale resounded like a drum to the beating of the fiery fingers on the Rim. For the first time this year, Antale was in the grip of a wild electrical storm.

CHAPTER 20

Resolution

THE STORM RAGED ROUND THE RIM FOR several hours. To the tiny ants peering up fearfully from the ground, it looked as if the sky was tearing itself apart. Great jagged bolts of lightning ripped across from side to side, scoring rents in thick, black, angry clouds. But for all their fury, the bolts could not shake loose the rain. They tore holes in the clouds. The thunder crashed in deafening detonations. A wild wind whipped across the land, whirling the blackened ashes in swirls of soot that darkened more an already black night. But still the rain would not come.

The terrified leaders knew enough to fear the second holocaust the lightning bolts could cause. If they struck the ground in the tinder-dry forests of the north and west, the rest of Antale would join the already-devastated south and east in obliteration. There would be little enough life afterward to ponder then. But for reasons unknown, the fury of the storm passed over the northern quadrants and hurled itself directly at the leaders cowering by the old Salt Sentinel. Time after time, lightning bolts hit the hard rock of the Rim just above them and sent cascading charges of brilliant electrical energy dancing around like angry hornets. At the height of the storm, a tree trunk partly burnt by the last fire was hit no more than twenty yards away. The explosion was incredible. It ripped the tree apart and flung the shattered fragments for a hundred yards around. The ruling elite of the ant world of Antale crouched in abject terror at the fury of the elements.

They had plenty of time to think and ponder their situation, for the storm raged most of the night, coming and going, like an angry mistress determined to discipline her students, driving first one lesson home, then another, and another, until at last, their dull wits might catch the message. For all their protestations of power, they were as tiny specks of dust in an angry wind. They had nothing but what the universe chose to give them. It could all be swept away in a single blast of infinite power. This was the reality. It was time to learn it now.

At the height of the storm, the concussions shook the ground and reverberated in the hollow of the Bravadabunker. Democrika was knocked from her perch astride her pile of bombs, and the remainder of the deadly arsenal crashed down from its neatly-piled stacks. Democrika held her breath and waited for the blast that would carry her to eternity. But the explosion never came. The white cocoon-like bombs lay innocently around, retaining their destructive force for another day. Democrika returned timidly to her perch, wondering what was happening outside.

Suspecting that the rebel would be nervous in her underground isolation, Bluffasta had taken off in the middle of the storm from the shelter of the rocks and raced for the tunnel entrance. With lightning dancing all around her, she reached the protection of the shaft. Minutes later, she entered the empty bunker just as Democrika regained her perch on the bombs.

"By the force!" exclaimed Bluffasta. "If you think you have a powder party going on down here, you should see what's playing up above."

"What's happening?" asked Democrika.

"The whole bloody world is coming apart!" said Bluffasta. "You've never seen such a storm."

"Storm!" exclaimed Democrika. "'Fire and storm' is what Cassandra said. It can't be much longer now. The end is coming."

"One way or another," said Bluffasta, "I hope you're right. I can't take much more of this."

On the surface, a chastened group of ants huddled silent in the breaking light of a gray dawn. They and the world had survived the fury of the night, but they had not stomach nor thought for what they now might do. The sky was heavy with thick cloud, but still no rain would come, and a lifting in the west suggested the clouds might blow away and leave them as parched and desperate as before. It was then that Bravura, who was keeping a lookout, saw some movement down below around the hole above the bunker.

"By gosh, that's Ventura down there!" she cried, "and she's got Cassandra with her!"

In a moment, Bravura hurried down, with Pacifica and Futura close behind. The others held back, not sure what to make of this new development.

"Hello, Ventura," called Bravura. "Are we glad to see you! Thank the stars you made it through the storm!"

"Hello, everyone," Ventura said. "You had no need to worry about us. Nothing can touch a protected priestess. Cassandra just marched through all that commotion like she was on a moonlight stroll. I was as scared as hell."

Bravura looked at Cassandra. The strange creature somehow seemed more wizened and shrunken than when she had last seen her. But her eyes were alert and lively.

"Time is coming, now," Cassandra said. "Take me to Democrika."

"Okay, this way," said Bravura, heading toward the tunnel entrance. The others moved to follow.

"No!" shouted Cassandra, waving them back. "Just you," she added, pointing to Bravura.

"Must be my lucky day," said Bravura. "Come on, then, old girl, this way to the hole of hell."

Once inside, they soon reached the empty bunker. Moving quietly, they almost startled Bluffasta out of her skin. "By the force!" exclaimed the Pepper when she recognized Bravura. "Now, we've got ghosts as well as bombs and rebels. Who's this walking death?"

"Stand aside, idiot," hissed Cassandra. "There's no time left for fools."

"Cassandra!" Democrika had seen the priestess from her position just inside the bomb vault. "So you're here! Well, now's the time, then. We've had the fire and the storm. I don't know where the young ones are. But look, I've got these bombs. Am I meant to set them off?"

"Oh, zit!" Bluffasta cried. "Have we gone through all this just to be blown into the next world?"

"Shut up!" Cassandra sent a withering look at Bluffasta. Then she turned to Democrika. "The New Age comes in when the young ones take the bombs out."

"But where are the young ones?" Democrika cried.

"Yes, where the hell are they?" demanded Bluffasta.

But Cassandra did not answer. She suddenly stiffened and went into a trance.

"Oh, double zit!" Bluffasta exclaimed again. "Now she's turned into a bloody stiff! What the hell is going on?"

The answer to Bluffasta's question was unfolding on the surface. When Bravura took Cassandra down into the bunker, Pacifica returned with Futura and Ventura to where the Protectorate leaders were waiting with their followers.

"What's going on now?" asked Alexa.

"That was Cassandra who just arrived," replied Pacifica. "She's a mystic who seems to have some influence over Democrika. We hope she can convince her to come out."

"I see," said Alexa. She paused a moment, then turned to face the other leaders. "That storm last night, and what Futura said before it started, has set me thinking. Whatever happens down there today, I believe we have to destroy our stockpiles of bombs. I'll admit now when I first heard about the Salt horde, I thought I might get here first and claim them. I could have made a good, rational argument for doing it. Prevent them from getting into the wrong hands, and so on. The truth is, the bombs we've already got aren't doing us any good. I'm ready to make a motion to destroy them."

The other leaders looked solemnly at Alexa. No one agreed, but no one objected. They all stood silently, thinking. A moment later, their reverie was interrupted by an excited shout from Futura. She had climbed to a higher vantage point and was looking out across the land to the north.

"There are ants down there!" she cried. "Thousands of them coming from all directions. I can see Blacks and Whites and Yellows and Reds and Greens—all colors. What are they doing here?"

Just then, Centura, who was looking the other way along the gully to the east, cried out: "There are Sugars coming, too!" Everyone turned to see hundreds of young Sugar ants coming along the gully. The Peace Team ran to meet them and brought them in. Alexa went over to greet her young followers.

"Hello," she said, "but what are you doing here? I thought this was a secret meeting."

"We've come to raise our voices for Antale," someone replied.

"We're joining our sisters from all over the world," shouted another.

"It's 'Yes' to life and 'No' to death!" cried someone else.

"'Yes' to life and 'No' to death." They all picked it up and chanted as they went down toward the bunker with Futura leading.

"Hold it!" Centura roared. "You can't go down there! That's a restricted zone!"

A few of Centura's soldiers tried to stop the young Sugars, but to no avail. They ran on down to mingle with thousands of others who were now pouring onto the area above the bunker.

"By gosh, Pacifica," Alexa said, "I hope your Cassandra keeps that rebel under control. If she sets the bombs off now, the world will lose all of its young ants."

The same thought had certainly occurred to Pacifica. She wasn't sure what to do next herself, but she decided to go down into the midst of things. Ventura suddenly tugged her by the shoulder. "Look," she cried. "It's Electra. What's she doing here?"

Pacifica looked and saw the old scientist standing in the middle of the hole right above the bunker. She and Ventura pushed their way over to her through the chanting crowd of young ants.

"Electra!" Pacifica shouted. "Is this your idea? The bombs are right under here, you know. We've got to get these young ones back. It's too dangerous here."

"Hello, old friend," Electra shouted. "This is no time to lose our nerve. How do you get down inside?"

"You don't!" Pacifica was really worried now. "We've got sensitive negotiations going on down there. If Democrika panics, we'll all be blown sky high. We've got to clear the area."

"It can't be done," Electra shouted. "No one will listen. Just get me down inside. I can help down there."

"All right," said Pacifica, "I guess there's nothing else we can do. Follow me."

Pacifica was still new to the area herself and had some difficulty trying to find the tunnel entrance. Then she saw Bluffasta coming out.

"Bluffasta!" Pacifica cried. "Over here! What's going on down there?"

"By the force, I wish I knew," said Bluffasta. "That crazy witch has gone as stiff as a stick. Where the hell did all these ants come from?"

"Don't worry about that now," said Pacifica. "What do you mean about Cassandra? Did she talk to Democrika? What did she say?"

"Some fool thing about the New Age coming in when the young ones take the bombs out."

"That's it!" shouted Electra.

"That's what?" Bluffasta shouted back.

"We're going to take the young ants down in there and they'll each carry a bomb out."

"Are you crazy? If there's one miscalculation, we'll all be blown to the moon." Bluffasta's nerves were almost gone. "Those things are not bloody eggs, you know."

"I know what I'm doing," shouted Electra. "Pacifica, for mercy's sake, take me down into the bunker."

"All right," said Pacifica. "Bluffasta, you stay up here."

"Clear the area on the floor of the hole," said Electra. "I'm going to need it."

"Might as well be in the center of hell as on the edge," muttered Bluffasta, heading off, and more than happy not to be going down inside the bunker again.

"You come with us, too, Futura," said Electra, "and bring a few of your Peace Team. We're going to need you to get things started."

When they entered the bunker, Pacifica called out to Bravura: "Bravura, Electra's here and there's thousands of young ants up above waiting to carry out the bombs."

"Well, I'll be damned," said Bravura. "Democrika! Did you hear that?"

"Aiyee!" shouted Democrika, coming out of the bomb vault for the first time. "'When the young ones cry out with new voices!'"

Hearing this, Futura signaled to her Peace Team. "'Yes' to life and 'No' to death," she chanted.

"'Yes' to life and 'No' to death," the Peace Team picked it up, marching right up to the opening of the bomb vault.

"Aiyee! Aiyee! Do you hear?" shrieked Democrika, now beside herself. She picked up the stiff body of Cassandra and shook it. "They've come! They've come, just like you said, you beautiful witch."

"Pick up a bomb," Electra said to Futura, "and carry it out. Just don't bite too hard and you'll be all right. The rest of you follow Futura."

Bravura was staring aghast at the whole operation. Pacifica gave her a gentle shake. "Don't worry," she said, "Electra knows what she's doing. You stay here and help. I'm going on top to prepare the world up there."

When Pacifica emerged from the tunnel entrance, closely followed by Futura and the Peace Team, each one carrying a bomb, the leaders on the bluff could not believe their eyes. Pacifica waved Centura over. "We've got to open up another entrance," she said. "Each one of these young ants will carry out a bomb. You see they get in there in an orderly fashion. We don't want any accidents."

Pacifica led Futura and her team over to the site that Bluffasta had cleared. Everyone was cheering them on. "'Yes' to life and 'No' to bombs!" they shouted. The ants carrying the bombs carefully put them down on the floor of the hole above the bunker.

"What do we do now?" asked Futura.

"I don't know," said Pacifica. "We'll have to wait for Electra."

Meanwhile, Centura had managed to get a bomb line moving and soon, a steady stream of the deadly cocoons was arriving. Finally, Electra came hurrying up.

"Ah, good, good," she said, looking at the growing pile of bombs. "Bravura's got things under control down below. Now we'll destroy these things."

Bluffasta, who was standing by, leapt into the air. "What the hell do you mean, destroy them?" she cried. "By the force, are you going to blow us up?"

"No, no," said Electra. "All you have to do is slit the cocoon open. Once the chemicals inside are exposed to air and rain, they're rendered harmless."

"Air, we've got," replied Bluffasta. "But rain has been scarce of late."

"It's coming," said Electra. "Look at the clouds. We'll be lucky to get all the bombs out before it starts."

Everyone around looked up at the sky. Sure enough, the storm clouds were thickening up again.

"Come on, I'll show you how to slit the skin," said Electra, "then you can do each new one as it arrives. The trick is not to bite too hard."

She went up to the nearest bomb and carefully inserted one of her mandibles through the skin, then made a neat slit along the length of the cocoon. Everyone watching held their breath. But there was no explosion. A thick, yellow liquid trickled out.

"Be careful not to get that stuff on you," said Electra. "It will burn. Now, come on, let's do the rest of these. There's quite a job ahead of us."

For the next several hours, the bombs kept coming up out of the bunker, each one a potential catastrophe in the making, but there were no false moves and the pile of destroyed bombs grew larger and larger, until it covered the floor of the hole and spilled over onto the ground around. As each young ant finished her task, she moved out into a circle, where she stood for hours cheering her comrades on.

Finally, it was done. Bravura came up out of the tunnel and announced that every bomb was out. With her came Democrika, carrying the prone body of Cassandra. The assembled ants were cheering wildly. Pacifica, with Electra and Futura, stood in the centre. Democrika came up to them and placed Cassandra on the ground.

"I think she's gone," the old rebel said sadly. "Maybe this was all she lived for—to see the New Age for Antale. I never understood her well, but I always knew that she was right."

Electra bent over the stiff body and examined it. "Yes," she said, stepping back, "I'm afraid Cassandra's gone, but the New Age certainly has come. Now, look and feel, here's the rain coming, too. The drought's broken and the evil of these bombs will be washed away with it."

As they stood there in the circle, thousands of young ants swaying to the gentle rhythm of their chant, the clouds above grew thick and heavy and the rain came pouring down. As it did, one last participant joined the circle. The great grey hooded figure of Supreema came lumbering in to stand beside the tiny Futura.

"Thas good," she said. "No more booms, and soon there will be no more beetles, either. Dragons will see to it."

Pacifica smiled and looked up through the rain to see the four leaders of the Protectorate still standing on the bluff looking down. She waved to them to come and join her. And so they did, Alexa leading the way to stand with Pacifica and Electra and Futura and the others in the centre of the circle, while the rain poured down on the new Antale.

Pacifica closed her eyes and felt the rain drumming steadily on the grateful ground, and she listened to the quiet singing of Antale's future generation. When she opened her eyes and looked up toward the Rim, she saw a brilliant rainbow arching over all Antale from east to west. She knew then that the New Age had begun.

ISBN 141206504-6